PENGUIN BOOKS
RUMPOLE ON TRIAL

John Mortimer is a playwright, novelist and former practising bar-rister. During the war he worked with the Crown Film Unit and published a number of novels before turning to the theatre with such plays as *The Dock Brief*, *The Wrong Side of the Park* and *A Voyage Round My Father*. He has written many film scripts and radio and television plays including six plays on the life of Shake-speare, the Rumpole plays, which won him the British Academy Writer of the Year Award, and the adaptation of Evelyn Waugh's *Brideshead Revisited*. His translations of Feydeau have been per-formed at the National Theatre and are published in Penguin as *Three Boulevard Farces*.

Penguin publishes his collections of stories: *Rumpole of the Bailey*, *The Trials of Rumpole*, *Rumpole's Return*, *Rumpole for the Defence*, *Rumpole and the Golden Thread*, *Rumpole's Last Case*, *Rumpole and the Age of Miracles* and *Rumpole à la Carte*, as well as *The First Rumpole Omnibus* and *The Second Rumpole Omnibus*. Penguin also publishes two volumes of John Mortimer's plays, his acclaimed autobiography *Clinging to the Wreckage*, which won the *Yorkshire Post* Book of the Year Award, *In Character* and *Character Parts*, which contain interviews with some of the most famous men and women of our time, and his bestselling novels, *Charade*, *Like Men Betrayed*, *The Narrowing Stream*, *Paradise Postponed*, its sequel *Titmuss Regained*, *Summer's Lease* and *Dunster*. *Paradise Postponed*, *Summer's Lease*, *Titmuss Regained* and all the Rumpole books have been made into successful television series. John Mortimer lives with his wife and their two daughters in what was once his father's house in the Chilterns.

JOHN MORTIMER

RUMPOLE ON TRIAL

PENGUIN BOOKS

PENGUIN BOOKS

Published by the Penguin Group
Penguin Books Ltd, 27 Wrights Lane, London W8 5TZ, England
Penguin Books USA Inc., 375 Hudson Street, New York, New York 10014, USA
Penguin Books Australia Ltd, Ringwood, Victoria, Australia
Penguin Books Canada Ltd, 10 Alcorn Avenue, Toronto, Ontario, Canada M4V 3B2
Penguin Books (NZ) Ltd, 182–190 Wairau Road, Auckland 10, New Zealand

Penguin Books Ltd, Registered Offices: Harmondsworth, Middlesex, England

First published by Viking 1992
Published in Penguin Books 1992

10 9 8

Copyright © Advanpress Ltd, 1992
All rights reserved

The moral right of the author has been asserted

Printed in England by Clays Ltd, St Ives plc

For Richard Ingrams in memory of days in court

Contents

Rumpole and the Children
of the Devil

Sometimes, when I have nothing better to occupy my mind, when I am sitting in the bath, for instance, or in the doctor's surgery having exhausted the entertainment value of last year's *Country Life*, or when I am in the corner of Pommeroy's Wine Bar waiting for some generous spirit in Chambers, and there aren't many of them left, to come in and say, 'Care for a glass of Château Fleet Street, Rumpole?', I wonder what I would have done if I had been God. I mean, if I had been responsible for creating the world in the first place, would I have cobbled up a globe totally without the minus quantities we have grown used to, a place with no fatal diseases or traffic jams or Mr Justice Graves – and one or two others I could mention? Above all, would I have created a world entirely without evil? And, when I came to think rather further along these lines, it seems to me that a world without evil might possibly be a damned dull world – or an undamned dull world, perhaps I should say – and it would certainly be a world which would leave Rumpole without an occupation. It would also put the Old Bill and most of Her Majesty's judges, prosecutors, prison officers and screws on the breadline. So perhaps a world where everyone rushes about doing good to each other and everyone, including the aforesaid Graves, is filled with brotherly love is not such a marvellous idea after all.

Brooding a little further on this business of evil, it occurs to me that the world is fairly equally divided between those who see it everywhere because they are always looking for it and those who hardly notice it at all. Of course, the mere fact that some people recognize devilment in the most everyday matters doesn't mean that it isn't there. I have known the first indication that evil was present, in various cases that I have been concerned with, to be a missing library ticket, a car tyre punctured or the wrong overcoat taken from the cloakroom of an expensive restaurant. At other times, the signs of evil are so blatant that they are impossible to ignore, as in the dramatic start to the case which I have come to think of as concerning the Children of the Devil. They led to a serious and, at times, painful inquiry into the machinations of Satan in the Borough of Crockthorpe.

Crockthorpe is a large, sprawling, in many parts dejected, in others rather too cosy for comfort, area south of the Thames. Its inhabitants include people speaking many languages, many without jobs, many gainfully employed in legal and not so legal businesses – and the huge Timson clan, which must by now account for a sizeable chunk of the population. The Timsons, as those of you who have followed my legal career in detail will know, provide not only the bread and marge, the Vim and Brasso, but quite often the beef and butter of our life in Froxbury Mansions, Gloucester Road. A proportion of my intake of Château Thames Embankment, and my wife Hilda's gin and tonic, comes thanks to the tireless activities of the Timson family. They are such a large group, their crime rate is so high and their success rate so comparatively low, that they are perfect clients for an Old Bailey hack. They go in for theft, shopbreaking and receiving stolen property but they have never produced a Master Crook. If you are looking for sensational crimes, the Timsons won't provide them or, it would be more accurate to say, they didn't until the day that Tracy Timson apparently made a pact with the Devil.

The story began in the playground of Crockthorpe's Stafford Cripps Junior School. The building had not been much repaired since it was built in the heady days of the first post-war Labour Government, and the playground had been kicked to pieces by generations of scuffling under-twelves. It was during the mid-morning break when the children were out fighting, ganging up on each other, or unhappy because they had no one to play with – among the most active, and about to pick a fight with a far larger black boy, was Dominic Molloy, angel-faced and Irish, who will figure in this narrative – when evil appeared.

Well, as I say, it was half-way through break and the Headmistress, a certain Miss Appleyard, a woman in her early forties who would have been beautiful had not the stress of life in the Stafford Cripps Junior aged her prematurely, was walking across the playground, trying to work out how to make fifty copies of *The Little Green Reading Book* go round two hundred pupils, when she heard the sound of concerted, eerie and high-pitched screaming coming from one of the doors that led on to the playground.

Turning towards the sound of the outcry, Miss Appleyard saw a strange sight. A small posse of children, about nine of them, all girls and all screaming, came rushing out like a charge of miniature cavalry. Who they were was, at this moment, a mystery to the Headmistress for each child wore a similar mask. Above the dresses and the jeans and pullovers hung the scarlet and black, grimacing and evil faces of nine devils.

At this sight even the bravest and most unruly children in the playground were taken aback, many retreated, some of the younger ones adding to the chorus of screams. Only young Dominic Molloy, it has to be said, stood his ground and viewed the scene that followed with amusement and contempt. He saw Miss Appleyard step forward fearlessly and, when the charge halted, she plucked off the devil's mask and revealed the small, heart-shaped face of the eight-year-old Tracy, almost the youngest, and now apparently the most devilish, of the Timson family.

Events thereafter took an even more sinister turn. At first the Headmistress looked grim, confiscated the masks and ordered the children back to the classroom, but didn't speak to them again about the extraordinary demonstration. Unfortunately she laid the matter before the proper authority, which in this case was the Social Services and Welfare Department of the Crockthorpe Council. So the wheels were set in motion that would end up with young Tracy Timson being taken into what is laughingly known as care, this being the punishment meted out to children who fail to conform to a conventional and rational society.

Childhood has, I regret to say, like much else, got worse since I was a boy. We had school bullies, we had headmasters who were apparently direct descendants of Captain Bligh of the *Bounty*, we had cold baths, inedible food and long hours in chapel on Sundays, but there was one compensation. No one had invented social workers. Now British children, it seems, can expect the treatment we once thought was only meted out to the political opponents of the late unlamented Joseph Stalin. They must learn to dread the knock at the door, the tramp of the Old Bill up the stairs, and being snatched from their nearest and dearest by a member of the alleged caring professions.

The dreaded knock was to be heard at six-thirty one morning on the door of the semi in Morrison Close, where that young couple Cary and Rosemary (known as Roz) Timson lived with Tracy, their only child. There was a police car flashing its blue light outside the house and a woman police constable in uniform on the step. The knock was administered by a social worker named Mirabelle Jones, of whom we'll hear considerably more later. She was a perfectly pleasant-looking girl with well-tended hair who wore, whenever I saw her, a linen jacket and a calf-length skirt of some ethnic material. When she spoke she modulated her naturally posh tones into some semblance of a working-class accent, and she always referred to the parents of the children who came into her possession as Mum and Dad and spoke with friendliness and deep concern.

When the knock sounded, Tracy was asleep in the company of someone known as Barbie doll, which I have since discovered to be a miniature American person with a beehive hairdo and a large wardrobe. Cary Timson was pounding down the stairs in his pyjamas, unhappily convinced that the knock was in some way connected with the break-in at a shop in Gunston Avenue about which he had been repeatedly called in for questioning, although he had made it clear, on each occasion, that he knew absolutely bugger all about it.

By the time he had pulled open the door his wife, Roz, had appeared on the stairs behind him, so she was able to hear Mirabelle telling her husband, after the parties had identified each other, that she had 'come about young Tracy'. From the statements which I was able to read later it appears that the dialogue then went something like this. It began with a panic-stricken cry from Roz of 'Tracy? What about our Tracy? She's asleep upstairs. Isn't she asleep upstairs?'

'Are you Mum?' Mirabelle then asked.

'What you mean, am I Mum? Course I'm Tracy's mum. What do you want?' Roz clearly spoke with rising hysteria and Mirabelle's reply sounded, as always, reasonable. 'We want to look after your Tracy, Mum. We feel she needs rather special care. I'm sure you're both going to help us. We do rely on Mum and Dad to be *very* sensible.'

Roz was not deceived by the soothing tones and concerned smile. She got the awful message and the shock of it brought her coldly to her senses. 'You come to take Tracy away, haven't you?' And before the question was answered she shouted, 'You're not bloody taking her away!'

'We just want to do the very best for your little girl. That's all, Mum.' At which Mirabelle detached a dreaded and official-looking document from the clipboard she was carrying. 'We do have a court order. Now shall we go and wake Tracy up? Ever so gently.'

It would be unnecessarily painful to dwell on the scene that followed. Roz fought like a tigress for her young and had to be restrained, at first by her husband, who had learned, as a Juvenile, the penalty for assaulting the powers of justice, and then by the uniformed officer who was called in from the car. The Timsons were told that they would be able to argue the case in court eventually, the woman police officer helped pack a few clothes for Tracy in a small case and, as the child was removed from the house, Mirabelle took the Barbie doll from her, explaining that it was bad for children in such

5

circumstances to have too many things that reminded them of home. So young Tracy Timson was taken into custody and her parents came nearer to heartbreak than they ever had in their lives, even when Cary got a totally unexpected two years' for the theft of a clapped-out Volvo estate from Safeway's car park. Throughout it all it's fair to say that Miss Mirabelle Jones behaved with the tact and consideration which made her such a star of the Social Services and such a dangerous witness in the Juvenile Court.

Tracy Timson was removed to a gloomy Victorian villa now known as The Lilacs, Crockthorpe Council Children's Home, where she will stay for the remainder of this story, and Mirabelle set out to interview what she called Tracy's peers, by which she meant the other kids Tracy was at school with, and, in the course of her activities, she called at another house in Morrison Close, this one being occupied by the father and mother of young Dominic Molloy. Now anyone who knows anything about the world we live in, anyone who keeps his or her ear to the ground and picks up as much information as possible about family rivalry in the Crockthorpe area, will know that the Molloys and the Timsons are chalk and cheese and as deadly rivals as the Montagues and the Capulets, the Guelphs and the Ghibellines, or York and Lancaster. The Molloys are an extended family; they are also villains but of a more purposeful and efficient variety. To the Timsons' record of small-time thieving the Molloys added wounding, grievous bodily harm and an occasional murder. Now Mirabelle called on the eight-year-old Dominic Molloy and, after a preliminary consultation with him and his parents, he agreed to help her with her inquiries. This, in turn, led to a further interview in an office at the school with young Dominic which was immortalized on videotape.

I remember my first conference with Tracy's parents, because on that morning Hilda and I had a slight difference of opinion on the subject of the Scales of Justice Ball. This somewhat grizzly occasion is announced annually on a heavily embossed card which arrived, with the gas bill and various invitations to insure my life and go on Mediterranean cruises, on the Rumpole breakfast table.

I had launched this invitation towards the tidy bin to join the tea leaves and the eggshells when Hilda, whose eagle eye misses nothing, immediately retrieved it, shook various particles of food off it and challenged me with, 'And why are you throwing this away, Rumpole?'

'You don't want to go, Hilda.' I did my best to persuade her. 'Disgusting sight, Her Majesty's judges, creaking round in the fox trot at the Savoy Hotel. You wouldn't enjoy it.'

'I suppose not, Rumpole. Not in the circumstances.'

'Not in what circumstances?'

'It's too humiliating.'

'I quite agree.' I saw her point at once. 'When Mr Justice Graves breaks into the valeta I hang my head in shame.'

'It's humiliating for me, Rumpole, when other chaps in Chambers lead their wives out on to the floor.'

'Not a pretty sight, I have to agree, the waltzing Bollards, the pirouetting Erskine-Browns.'

'Why do you never lead me out on to the dance floor nowadays, Rumpole?' She asked me the question direct. 'I sometimes dream about it. We're at the Scales of Justice Ball. At the Savoy Hotel. And you lead me out on to the floor, as the first lady in Chambers.'

'You are, Hilda,' I hastened to agree with her, 'you're quite definitely the senior . . .'

'But you never lead me out, Rumpole! We have to sit there, staring at each other across the table, while all around us couples are dancing the night away.'

'Hilda' – I decided to disclose my defence – 'I have, as you know, many talents, but I'm not Nijinsky. Anyway, we don't get much practice at dancing down the Old Bailey.'

'Oh, it doesn't matter. When is the ball? Marigold Featherstone told me but I can't quite remember.' I saw, with a sort of dread, that she was checking the food-stained invitation to answer her question. 'November the 18th! It just happens to be my birthday. Well, we'll stay at home, as usual.

7

At least I won't have to sit and watch other happy people dancing together.' And now she applied the corner of a handkerchief to her eye. 'Please, Hilda,' I begged, 'not the waterworks!' At which she sniffed bravely and dismissed me from her presence. 'No, of course not. Go along now. You've got to get to work. Work's the only thing that matters to you. You'd rather defend a murderer than dance with your wife.'

'Well, yes. Perhaps,' I had to admit. 'Look, do cheer up, old thing. Please.' She gave me her last lament as I moved towards the door.

'Old, yes, I suppose. We're both too old for a party. And I'll just have to get used to the fact that I didn't marry a dancer.'

'Sorry, Hilda.'

So I left She Who Must Be Obeyed, sitting alone in the kitchen and looking, as I thought, genuinely unhappy. I had seen her miffed before. I had seen her outraged. I had seen her, all too frequently, intensely displeased at some item of Rumpole's behaviour which fell short of perfection. But I was unprepared for the sadness which seemed to have engulfed her. Had she spent her life imagining she was Ginger Rogers, and was she at last reconciled to the fact that I had neither the figure nor the top hat to play whatever his name was – Astaire? For a moment a sensation to which I am quite unused came over me. I felt inadequate. However, I pulled myself together and pointed myself in the direction of my Chambers in the Temple, where I knew I had a conference with a couple of Timsons in what I imagined would be no more than a routine case of petty thievery.

I had acted for Cary before in a little matter of lead removed from the roof of Crockthorpe Methodist Church. He was tall and thin, and usually spoke in a slow, mocking way as though he found the whole of life slightly amusing. He didn't look amused now. His wife, Roz, was a solid girl in her late twenties with broad cheek-bones and capable hands. In attendance was the faithful Mr Bernard, who, from time immemorial, has acted as the Solicitor-General to the Timson family.

'They wouldn't let Tracy take even a doll. Not one of her

Barbies. How do you think people could do that to a child?'
Roz asked me when Mr Bernard had outlined the facts of the
case. Her eyes were red and swollen and, as she sat in my
client's chair, nervously twisting her wedding ring, she looked
not much older than a child herself.

'Nicking your kid. That's what it's come to. Well, I'll allow
us Timsons may have done a fair bit of mischief in our time.
But no one in the family's ever stooped to that, Mr
Rumpole.' And Cary Timson added for greater emphasis,
'People what nick kids get boiling cocoa poured on their heads,
when they're inside like.'

'Cary worships that girl, Mr Rumpole,' Roz told me. 'No
matter what they say.'

'Take a look at these' – her husband was already pulling
out his wallet – 'and you'll see the reason why.' So the brightly
coloured snaps were laid proudly on my desk and I saw the
three of them on a Spanish beach, at a theme park or on days
out in the country. The mother and father held their child
aloft, in the manner of successful athletes with a golden prize,
triumphantly and with unmistakable delight.

'Bloody marvellous, isn't it?' Cary's gentle mocking had
turned to genuine anger. 'Eight years old and our Trace needs
a brief.'

'You'll get Tracy back for us, won't you, Mr Rumpole?' I
thought Roz must have given birth to this much-loved daughter
when she was about seventeen. 'She'll be that unhappy.'

'You seen the photos, Mr Rumpole.' And Cary asked, 'Does
she have the look of a villain?'

'I'd say not a hardened criminal,' I had to admit.

'What's her crime, Mr Rumpole? That's what Roz and I
wants to know. It's not as though she nicked things ever.'

'Well, not really –' And Roz admitted, 'She'll take a Jaffa
cake when I'm not looking, or a few sweets occasionally.'

'Our Tracy's too young for any serious nicking.' Her father
was sure of it. 'What you reckon she done, Mr Rumpole?
What they got on her charge-sheet?'

'Childhood itself seems a crime to some people.' It's a point
that has often struck me.

'We can't seem to get any sense out of that Miss Jones.' Roz looked helpless.

'Jones?'

'Officer in charge of case. Tracy's social worker.'

'One of the "caring" community.' I was sure of it.

'All she'll say is that she's making further inquiries,' Mr Bernard told me.

'I never discovered what I'd done when they banged me up in a draughty great boarding-school at the age of eight.' I looked back down the long corridor of years and began to reminisce.

'Hear that, Roz?' Cary turned to his wife. 'They banged up Mr Rumpole when he was a kid.'

'Did they, Mr Rumpole? Did they really?'

But before I could give them further and better particulars of the bird I had done at Linklaters, that downmarket public school I attended on the Norfolk coast, Mr Bernard brought us back to the fantastic facts of the case and the nature of the charges against Tracy. 'I've been talking to the solicitor for the Local Authority,' he reported, 'and their case is that the Juvenile Timson has been indulging in devil worship, hellish rituals and satanic rights.'

It might be convenient if I were to give you an account of that filmed interview with Dominic Molloy which, as I have told you, we finally saw at the trial. Before that, Mr Bernard had acquired a transcript of this dramatic scene, so we were, by bits and pieces, made aware of the bizarre charges against young Tracy, a case which began to look as though it should be transferred from Crockthorpe Juvenile Court to Seville to be decided by hooded inquisitors in the darkest days of the Spanish Inquisition.

The scene was set in the Headmistress's office in Stafford Cripps Junior. Mirabelle Jones, at her most reassuring, sat smiling on one side of the desk, while young Dominic Molloy, beaming with self-importance, played the starring role on the other.

'You remember the children wearing those horrid masks at

school, do you, Dominic?' Mirabelle kicked off the proceedings.

'They scared me!' Dominic gave a realistic shudder.

'I'm sure they did.' The social worker made a note, gave
the camera – no doubt installed in the corner of the room –
the benefit of her smile and then returned to the work in
hand.

'Did you see who was leading those children?'

'In the end I did.'

'Who was it?'

'Trace.'

'Tracy Timson?'

'Yes.'

'Your mum said you went round to Tracy Timson's a few
times. After school, was that?'

'Yes. After school like.'

'And then you said you went somewhere else. Where else,
exactly?'

'Where they put people.'

'A churchyard. Was it a churchyard?' Mirabelle gave us a
classic example of a leading question. Dominic nodded ap-
proval and she made a note. 'The one in Crockthorpe Road,
the church past the roundabout? St Elphick's?' Mirabelle suggested and Dominic nodded again. 'It was the churchyard.
Was it dark?' Dominic nodded so eagerly that his whole body
seemed to rock backwards and forwards and he was in danger
of falling off his chair.

'After school and late. A month ago? So it was dark. Did a
grown-up come with you? A man, perhaps. Did a man come
with you?'

'He said we was to play a game.' Now Dominic had resorted
to a kind of throaty whisper, guaranteed to make the flesh
creep.

'What sort of game?'

'He put something on his face.'

'A mask?'

'Red and horns on it.'

'A devil's mask.' Mirabelle was scribbling enthusiastically.

'Is that right, Dominic? He wanted you to play at devils? This man did?'

'He said he was the Devil. Yes.'

'He was to be the Devil. And what were you supposed to be?'

Dominic didn't answer that, but sat as if afraid to move.

'Perhaps you were the Devil's children?'

At this point Dominic's silence was more effective than any answer.

'What was the game you had to play?' Mirabelle tried another approach.

'Dance around.' The answer came in a whisper.

'Dance around. Now I want you to tell me, Dominic, when did you meet this man? At Tracy Timson's house? Is that where you met him?' More silence from Dominic, so Mirabelle tried again. 'Do you know who he was, Dominic?' At which Dominic nodded and looked round fearfully.

'Who was he, Dominic? You've been such a help to me so far. Can't you tell me who he was?'

'Tracy's dad.'

Everything changes and with ever-increasing rapidity. Human beings no longer sell tickets at the Temple tube station. Machines and not disillusioned waitresses dispense the so-called coffee in the Old Bailey canteen and, when I became aware that Dianne, our long-time typist and close personal friend to Henry, our clerk, had left the service, I feared and expected that she might be replaced by a robot. However, what I found behind the typewriter, when I blew into the clerk's room after a hard day's work on an actual bodily harm in Acton a few weeks after my conference with Tracy's parents, was nothing more mechanical than an unusually pretty and very young woman, wearing a skirt as short as a suspended sentence and a smile so ready that it seemed never to leave her features entirely but to be waiting around for the next opportunity to beam. Henry introduced her as Miss Clapton. 'Taken over from Dianne, Mr Rumpole, who has just got herself married. I don't know if you've heard the news.'

'Married? Henry, I'm sorry.'

'To a junior clerk in a bankruptcy set.' He spoke with considerable disgust. 'I told her she'd live to regret it.'

'Welcome to Equity Court, Miss Clapton,' I said. 'If you behave really well, you might get parole in about ten years.' She gave me the smile at full strength, but my attention was diverted by the sight of Mizz Liz Probert who had just picked up a brief from the mantelpiece and was looking at it with every sign of rapture. Liz, the daughter of Red Ron Probert, Labour leader on the Crockthorpe Council, is the most radical member of our Chambers. I greeted her with, 'Soft you now! The fair Mizz Probert! What are you fondling there, old thing?' Or words to that effect.

'What does it look like, Rumpole?'

'It looks suspiciously like a brief.'

'Got it in one!' Mizz Liz was in a perky mood that morning.

'Time marches on! My ex-pupil has begun to acquire briefs. What is it? Bad case of non-renewed dog licence?'

'A bit more serious than that. I'm for the Crockthorpe Local Authority, Rumpole.'

'I am suitably overawed.' I didn't ask whether the presence of Red Ron on the Council had anything to do with this manna from heaven, and Mizz Liz went on to tell a familiar story. 'A little girl had to be taken into care. She's in terrible danger in the home. You know what it is – the father's got a criminal record. As a matter of fact, it's a name that might be familiar to you. Timson.'

'So they took away a Timson child because the father's got form?' I asked innocently, hoping for further information.

'Not just that. Something rather awful was going on. Devil worship! The family were deeply into it. Quite seriously. It's a shocking case.'

'Is it really? Tell me, do you believe in the Devil?'

'Of course I don't, Rumpole. Don't be so ridiculous! Anyway, that's hardly the point.'

'Isn't it? It interests me, though. You see, I'm likely to be against you in the Juvenile Court.'

'You, Rumpole! On the side of the Devil?' Mizz Probert seemed genuinely shocked.

'Why not? They tell me he has the best lines.'

'Defending devil-worshippers, in a *children's* case! That's really not on, is it, Rumpole?'

'I really can't think of anyone I wouldn't defend. That's what I believe in. I was just on my way to Pommeroy's. Mizz Liz, old thing, will you join me in a stiffener?'

'I don't really think we should be seen drinking together, not now I'm appearing for the Local Authority.'

'For the Local Authority, of course!' I gave her a respectful bow on leaving. 'A great power in the land! Even if they do rather interfere with the joy of living.'

No sooner had I got to Pommeroy's Wine Bar and chalked up the first glass of Jack Pommeroy's Very Ordinary when Claude Erskine-Brown of our Chambers came into view in a state of considerable excitement about the new typist. 'An enormous asset, don't you think? Dot will bring a flood of spring sunshine into our clerk's room.'

'Dot?' I was puzzled. 'What are you babbling about?'

'Her name's Dot, Rumpole. She told me that. I said it was a beautiful name.'

I didn't need to tell the fellow he was making a complete ass of himself; this was a fact too obvious to mention.

'I've told her she must come to me if she has any problems workwise.' Claude is, of course, married to Phillida Erskine-Brown, Q.C., the attractive and highly competent Portia of our Chambers. Perhaps it's because he has to play second fiddle to this powerful advocate that Claude is for ever on the lookout for alternative company, a pursuit which brings little but embarrassment to himself and those around him. I saw nothing but trouble arising from the appearance of this Dot upon the Erskine-Brown horizon, but now the fellow completely changed the subject and said, 'You know Charlie Wisbeach?'

'I've never heard of him.'

'Wisbeach, Bottomley, Perkins & Harris.' Erskine-Brown spoke in an awe-struck whisper as though repeating a magic formula.

'Good God! Are they *all* here?'

'I rather think Claude's talking about my dad's firm.' This came from a plumpish but fairly personable young man who was in the offing, holding a bottle of champagne and a glass, which he now refilled and also gave a shower of bubbles to Erskine-Brown.

'Just the best firm in the City, Rumpole. Quality work. And Charlie here's come to the Bar. He wants a seat in Chambers.' Erskine-Brown sounded remarkably keen on the idea, no doubt hoping for work from the firm of Wisbeach, Bottomley, Perkins & Harris.

'Oh, yes?' I sniffed danger. 'And where would he like it? There might be an inch or two available in the downstairs loo. Didn't we decide we were full up at the last Chambers meeting?'

'I say, you must be old Rumpole!' Young Wisbeach was looking at me as though I were some extinct species still on show in the Natural History Museum.

'I'm afraid I've got very little choice in the matter,' I had to admit.

'You're not still practising, are you?' Charlie Wisbeach had the gall to ask.

'Not really. I suppose I've learned how to do it by now.'

'Oh, but Claude Erskine-Brown told me you'd soon be retiring.'

'Did you, Claude? Did you tell young Charlie that?' I turned upon the treacherous Erskine-Brown the searchlight eyes and spoke in the pained tones of the born cross-examiner.

'Well, no. Not exactly, Rumpole.' The man fumbled for words. 'Well, of course, I just assumed you'd be retiring some time.'

'Don't count on it, Erskine-Brown. Don't you ever count on it!'

'And Claude told me that when you retired, old chap, there might be a bit of space in your Chambers.' The usurper Wisbeach apparently found the situation amusing. 'A pretty enormous space is what I think he said. Didn't you, Claude?'

'Well no, Charlie. No ... Not *quite*.' Erskine-Brown's embarrassment proved his guilt.

'It sounds like an extremely humorous conversation.' I gave them both the look contemptuous.

'Charlie has a pretty impressive C.V., Rumpole.' Erskine-Brown tried to change the subject as his newfound friend gave him another slurp.

'See what?'

'Curriculum vitae. Eton . . .'

'Oh. Good at that as well, is he? I thought it was mainly drinkin'.'

'Claude's probably referring to the old school.' Wisbeach could not, of course, grasp the Rumpole joke.

'Oh, Eton! Well, I've no doubt you'll rise above the handicaps of a deprived childhood. In somebody else's Chambers.'

'As a matter of fact Claude showed me *your* room.' Wisbeach gave the damning evidence. 'Very attractive accommodation.'

'You did *what*, Claude?'

'Charlie and I . . . Well, we . . . called in to see you. But you were doing that long arson in Snaresbrook.'

'Historic spot, your room!' Wisbeach told me as though I'd never seen the place before. 'Fine views over the churchyard. Don't you look straight down at Dr Johnson's tomb?'

'It's Oliver Goldsmith's, as it so happens.' Eton seemed to have done little for the man's store of essential knowledge.

'No, Johnson's!' You can't tell an old Etonian anything.

'Goldsmith,' I repeated, with the last of my patience.

'Want to bet?'

'Not particularly.'

'Your old room needs a good deal of decorating, of course. And some decent furniture. But the idea is, we might share. While you're still practising, Rumpole.'

'That's not an idea. It's a bad dream.' I directed my rejection of the offer at Erskine-Brown, who started up a babble of 'Rumpole! Think of the work that Wisbeach could send us!'

'And I would like to let it be known that *I* still have work of my own to do, and I do it best alone. As a free spirit!

Wrongs are still to be righted.' Here I drained my plonk to the dregs and stood up, umbrella in hand. 'Mr Justice Graves is still putting the boot in. Chief Inspector Brush is still referring to his unreliable notebook. And an eight-year-old Timson has been banged up against her will, not in Eton College like you, Master Charlie, but in the tender care of the Crockthorpe Local Authority. The child is suspected of devil-worship. Can you believe it? An offence which I thought went out with the burning of witches.'

'Is that your case, Rumpole?' Erskine-Brown looked deeply interested.

'Indeed, yes. And I have a formidable opponent. None other than Mizz Liz Probert, with the full might of the Local Authority behind her. So, while there are such challenges to be overcome, let me tell you, Claude, and you, Charlie Whatsit, Rumpole shall never sheath the sword. Never!'

So I left the bar with my umbrella held aloft like the weapon of a crusader, and the effect of this exit was only slightly marred by my colliding with a couple of trainee solicitors who were blocking the fairway. As I apologized and lowered the umbrella I could distinctly hear the appalling Wisbeach say, 'Funny old buffer!'

In all my long experience down the Bailey and in lesser courts I have not known a villain as slithery and treacherous as Claude Erskine-Brown proved on that occasion. As soon as he could liberate himself from the cuckoo he intended to place in my nest, he dashed up to Equity Court in search of our Head of Chambers, Samuel Ballard, Q.C. Henry, who was working late on long-delayed fee notes, told him that Soapy Sam was at a service with his peer group, the Lawyers As Christians Society, in the Temple Church. Undeterred, Claude set off to disturb the holy and devoutly religious Soapy at prayer. It was, he told a mystified Henry as he departed, just the place to communicate the news he had in mind.

I am accustomed to mix with all sorts of dubious characters in pursuit of evidence and, when I bought a glass of Pommeroy's for a L.A.C. (member of the Lawyers As Christians

Society), I received an astonishing account of Claude's entry into Evensong. Pushing his way down the pew he arrived beside our Head of Chambers, who had risen to his feet to an organ accompaniment and was about to give vent to a hymn. Attending worshippers were able to hear dialogue along the following lines.

'Erskine-Brown. Have you joined us?' Ballard was surprised.

'Of course I've joined L.A.C.S. Subscription's in the post. But I had to tell you about Rumpole, as a matter of urgency.'

'Please, Erskine-Brown. This is no place to be talking about such matters as Rumpole.'

'*Devil-worshippers*. Rumpole's in with devil-worshippers,' Claude said in a voice calculated to make our leader's flesh creep.

However, at this moment, the hymn-singing began and Ballard burst out with:

> God moves in a mysterious way
> His wonders to perform;
> He plants his footsteps in the sea,
> And rides upon the storm.

Betraying a certain talent for improvisation, my informant told me that he distinctly heard Claude Erskine-Brown join in with:

> 'Rumpole in his mischievous way
> Has taken on a case
> About some devil-worshippers.
> He's had them in your place!
> Your Chambers, I mean.'

At which point Ballard apparently turned and looked at the conniving Claude with deep and horrified concern.

It was a time when everyone seemed intent on investigating the alleged satanic cult. Mirabelle Jones continued to make films for showing before the Juvenile Court and this time she interviewed Tracy Timson in a room, also equipped with a camera and recording apparatus, in the Children's Home.

Mirabelle arrived, equipped with dolls, not glamorous pin-up girls, but a somewhat drab and unsexy family consisting of a Mum and Dad, Grandpa and Grandma, who looked like solemn New England farm-workers. Tracy was ordered to play with this group, and when, without any real interest in the matter, she managed to get Grandpa lying on top of Mum, Miss Jones sucked in her breath and made a note which she underlined heavily.

Later, Tracy was shown a book in which there was a picture of a devil with a forked tail, who looked like an opera singer about to undertake Mephistopheles in *Faust*. The questioning, as recorded in the transcript, then went along these lines.

'You know who he is, don't you, Tracy?' Mirabelle was being particularly compassionate as she asked this.

'No.'

'He's the Devil. You know about devils, don't you?' And she added, still smiling, 'You put on a devil's mask at school, didn't you, Tracy?'

'I might have done.' Tracy made an admission.

'So what do you think of the Devil, then?'

'He looks funny.' Tracy was smiling, which I thought, in all the circumstances, was remarkably brave of her.

'Funny?'

'He's got a tail. The tail's funny.'

'Who first told you about the Devil, Tracy?'

'I don't know,' the child answered, but the persistent inquisitor was not to be put off so easily.

'Oh, you must know. Did you hear about the Devil at home? Was that it? Did Dad tell you about the Devil?'

Tracy shook her head. Mirabelle Jones sighed and tried again. 'Does that picture of the Devil remind you of anyone, Tracy?' Still getting no answer, Mirabelle resorted to a leading question, as was her way in these interviews. 'Do you think it looks like your dad at all?'

In search of an answer to Miss Jones's unanswered question, I summoned Cary and Roz to my presence once again. When they arrived, escorted by the faithful Bernard, I put the matter as bluntly as I knew how. At the mention of evil, Tracy's mother merely looked puzzled. 'The Devil? Tracy don't know nothing about the Devil.'

'Of course not!' Cary's denial was immediate. 'It's not as if we went to church, Mr Rumpole.'

'You've never heard of such a suggestion before?' I looked hard at Tracy's father. 'The Devil. Satan. Beelzebub. Are you saying the Timson family knows nothing of such matters?'

'Nothing at all, Mr Rumpole.'

'When they came that morning . . .'

'When they came to get our Tracy?' Roz's eyes filled with tears as she relived the moment.

'Yes. When they came for that. What did you *think* was going on exactly?' I asked Cary the question.

'I thought they come about that shop that got done over, Wedges, down Gunston Avenue. They've had me down the nick time and time again about it.'

'And it wasn't you?'

'Straight up, Mr Rumpole. Would I deceive you?'

'It has been known, but I'll believe you. Do you know who did it?' I asked Cary.

'No, Mr Rumpole. No, I won't grass. That I won't do. I've had enough trouble being accused of grassing on Gareth Molloy when he was sent down for the Tobler Road supermarket job.'

'The Timsons and the Molloys are deadly enemies. How could you know what they were up to?'

'My mate Barry Peacock was driving for them on that occasion. They thought I knew something and grassed to Chief Inspector Brush. Would I do a thing like that?'

'No, I don't suppose you would. So you thought the Old Bill were just there about ordinary, legitimate crime. You had no worries about Tracy?'

'She's a good girl, Mr Rumpole. Always has been,' Roz was quick to remind me.

'Always cheerful, isn't she, Roz?' Her husband added to the evidence of character. 'I enjoys her company.'

'So where the devil do these ideas come from? Sorry, perhaps I shouldn't've said that ... You know Dominic Molloy told the social worker you taught a lot of children satanic rituals.'

'You ever believed a Molloy, have you, Mr Rumpole, in court or out of it?' Cary Timson had a good point there, but I rather doubted if I could convince the Juvenile Court of the wisdom learned at the Old Bailey.

When our conference was over I showed my visitors out and I thought I saw, peering from a slightly open doorway at the end of the corridor, the face of Erskine-Brown, as horrified and intent as a passer-by who suddenly notices that, on the other side of the street, a witches coven is holding its annual beano. The door shut as soon as I clocked him and Claude vanished within. Twenty minutes later I received a visit from Soapy Sam Ballard, Q.C., our so-called Head of Chambers. I don't believe that these events were unconnected. As soon as he got in, Ballard sniffed the air as though detecting the scent of brimstone and said, 'You've had them in here, Rumpole?'

'Had who in here, Bollard?'

'Those who owe allegiance to the Evil One.'

'You mean the Mr Justice Graves fan club? No. They haven't been near the place.'

'Rumpole! You know perfectly well who I mean.'

'Oh, yes. Of course.' I decided to humour the fellow. 'They were all here. Lucifer, Beelzebub, Belial. All present and correct.

> High on a throne of royal state, which far
> Outshone the wealth of Ormus and of Ind,
> Or where the gorgeous East with richest hand
> Showers on her king's barbaric pearl and gold,
> Satan exalted sat, by merit raised
> To that bad eminence; and from despair
> Thus high uplifted beyond hope ...

'Grow up, Bollard! I am representing an eight-year-old child who's been torn from the bosom of her family and banged up without trial. You see here Rumpole, the protector of the innocent.'

'The protector of devil-worshippers!' Ballard said.

'Those too. If necessary.' I sat down at the desk and picked up the papers in a somewhat tedious affray.

'Rumpole. Every decent Chambers has to draw the line somewhere.'

'Does it?'

'There are certain cases, certain clients, even, which are simply, well, not acceptable.'

'Oh, I do agree.'

'Do you?'

'Oh, yes. I agree entirely.'

'Well, then. I'm glad to hear it.' Soapy Sam looked as gratified as a cleric hearing a death-bed confession from a life-long heathen.

'Didn't I catch sight of you prosecuting an accountant for unpaid V.A.T.?' I asked the puzzled Q.C. 'Some cases are simply unacceptable. Far too dull to be touched by a decent barrister with a bargepole. Don't you agree, old darling?'

'Rumpole, there's something I meant to raise with you.' The saintly Sam was growing distinctly ratty.

'Then buck up and raise it, I'm busy.' I returned to the affray.

'Young Charlie Wisbeach wants to come into these Chambers. He'd bring us a great deal of high-class, *commercial* work from his father's firm. Unfortunately we have no room for him at the moment.'

'Has he thought of a cardboard box in Middle Temple Lane?' I thought this a helpful suggestion; Bollard didn't agree.

'This is neither the time nor the place for one of your jokes, Rumpole. You have a tenancy here and tenancies can be brought to an end. Especially if the tenant in question is carrying on a practice not in the best traditions of 3 Equity Court. There is something in this room which makes me feel uneasy.'

'Oh, I do so agree. Perhaps you'll be leaving shortly.'

'I'm giving you fair warning, Rumpole. I expect you to think it over.' At which our leader made for the door and I called after him, 'Oh, before you go, Bollard, why don't you look up "exorcism" in the *Yellow Pages*? I believe there's an unfrocked Bishop in Stepney who'll quote you a very reasonable price. And if you call again, don't forget the Holy Water!'

But the man had gone and I was left alone to wonder exactly what devilment Cary Timson had been up to.

I have, or at a proper moment I will have, a confession to make. At this time I was presenting She Who Must Be Obeyed with a mystery which she no doubt found baffling, although I'm afraid a probable solution presented itself to her mind far too soon. I had reason to telephone a Miss Tatiana Fern and, not wishing to do so with Hilda's knowledge, and as the lady in question left her house early, I called when I thought She was still asleep. I now suspect Hilda was listening in on the bedroom extension, although she lay motionless and with her eyes closed when I came back to bed. Later I discovered that when Hilda went off to shop in Harrods she spotted me coming out of Knightsbridge tube station, a place far removed from the Temple and the Old Bailey, and sleuthed me to a house in Mowbray Crescent which she saw me enter when the front door was opened by the aforesaid Tatiana Fern. So it came about that She met Marigold, Mr Justice Featherstone's outspoken wife, and together they formed the opinion that Rumpole was up to no good whatsoever.

Of course, She didn't tackle me openly about this, but I could sense what was in the wind when she started up a conversation about the male libido at breakfast one morning. It followed from something she had read in her *Daily Telegraph*.

'They're doing it again, Rumpole.'

'Who are?'

'Men.'

'Ah.'

'Causing trouble in the workplace.'

'Yes. I suppose so.'

'Brushing up against their secretaries. Unnecessarily. I suppose that's something you approve of, Rumpole?'

'I haven't got a secretary, Hilda. I've got a clerk called Henry. I've never felt the slightest temptation to brush up against Henry.' And that answer you might have thought would finish the matter, but Hilda had more information from the *Telegraph* to impart. 'They put it all down to glands. Men've got too much something in their glands. That's a fine excuse, isn't it?'

'Never tried it.' But I thought it over. 'I suppose I might: "My client intends to rely on the glandular defence, my Lord."'

'It wouldn't wash.' Hilda was positive. 'When I was a child we were taught to believe in the Devil.'

'I'm sure you were.'

'He tempts people. Particularly men.'

'I thought it was Eve.'

'What?'

'I thought it was Eve he tempted first.'

'That's you all over, Rumpole.'

'Is it?'

'Blame it all on a woman! That's men all over.'

'Hilda, there's nothing I'd like more than to sit here with you all day, discussing theology. But I've got to get to work.' I was making my preparation for departure when She said darkly, 'Enjoy your lunch-hour!'

'What did you say?'

'I said, "I hope you enjoy your lunch-hour," Rumpole.'

'Well, I probably shall. It's Thursday. Steak pie day at the pub in Ludgate Circus. I shall look forward to that.'

'And a few other little treats besides, I should imagine.'

Hilda was immersed in her newspaper again when I left her. I knew then that, no matter what explanation I had given, She Who Must Be Obeyed had come to the firm conclusion that I was up to something devilish.

It's a strange fact that it was not until nearly the end of the three score years and ten allotted to me by the psalmist that I was first called upon to perform in a Juvenile Court. It was, as I was soon to discover, a place in which the law as we know and occasionally love it had very little place. It was also a soulless chamber in Crockthorpe's already chipped and crumbling, glass and concrete courthouse complex. Tracy's three judges – a large motherly-looking magistrate as Chairwoman, flanked by a small, bright-eyed Sikh Justice in a sari, and a lean and anxious headmaster – sat with their clerk, young, officious and bespectacled, to keep them in order. The defence team, Rumpole and the indispensable Bernard, together with the prosecutor, Mizz Liz Probert, and a person from the Council solicitor's office, sat at another long table opposite the Justices. Miss Mirabelle Jones, armed with a ponderous file, was comfortably ensconced in the witness chair and a large television set was playing that hit video, the interview with Dominic Molloy.

We had got to the familiar dialogue which started with Mirabelle's question: 'He wanted you to play at devils? This man did?'

'He said he was the Devil. Yes,' the picture of the boy Dominic alleged.

'He was to be the Devil. And what were you supposed to be? Perhaps you were the Devil's children?'

At which point Rumpole ruined the entertainment by rearing to his hind legs and making an objection, a process which in this court seemed as unusual and unwelcome as a guest lifting his soup plate to his mouth and slurping the contents at a state banquet at Buckingham Palace. When I said I was objecting, the clerk switched off the telly with obvious reluctance.

'That was a leading question by the social worker,' I said, although the fact would have been obvious to the most superficial reader of *Potted Rules of Evidence*. 'It and the answer are entirely inadmissable, as your clerk will no doubt tell you.' And I added, in an extremely audible whisper to Bernard, 'If he knows his business.'

'Mr Rumpole' – the Chairwoman gave me her most

motherly smile — 'Miss Mirabelle Jones is an extremely experienced social worker. We think we can rely on her to put her questions in the proper manner.'

'I was just venturing to point out that on this occasion she put her question in an entirely improper manner,' I told her, 'Madam.'

'My Bench will see the film out to the end, Mr Rumpole. You'll have a chance to make any points later.' The clerk gave his decision in a manner which caused me to whisper to Mr Bernard, 'Her Master's Voice.' I hope they all heard, but to make myself clear I said to Madam Chair, 'My point is that you shouldn't be seeing this film at all.'

'We are going to continue with it now, Mr Rumpole.' The learned clerk switched on the video again. Miss Jones appeared to ask, 'What was the game you had to play?' And Dominic answered, 'Dance around.'

'Dance around.' Mirabelle Jones's shadow repeated in case we had missed the point. 'Now I want you to tell me, Dominic, when did you meet this man? At Tracy Timson's house? Is that where you met him?'

'It's a leading question!' I said aloud, but the performance continued and Mirabelle asked, 'Do you know who he was?' And on the screen Dominic nodded politely.

'Who was he?' Mirabelle asked and Dominic replied, 'Tracy's dad.'

As the video was switched off, I was on my feet again. 'You're not going to allow that evidence?' I couldn't believe it. 'Pure hearsay! What a child who isn't called as a witness said to Miss Jones here, a child we've had no opportunity of cross-examining said, is nothing but hearsay. Absolutely worthless.'

'Madam Chairwoman.' Mizz Probert rose politely beside me.

'Yes, Miss Probert.' Liz got an even more motherly smile; she was the favourite child and Rumpole the black sheep of the family.

'Mr Rumpole is used to practising at the Old Bailey –'

'And has managed to acquire a nodding acquaintance of the law of evidence,' I added.

'And of course *this* court is not bound by strict rules of evidence. Where the welfare of a child is concerned, you're not tied down by a lot of legal quibbles about hearsay.'

'Quibbles, Mizz Probert? Did I hear you say quibbles?' My righteous indignation was only half simulated.

'You are free,' Liz told the tribunal, 'with the able assistance of Miss Mirabelle Jones, to get at the truth of this matter.'

'My learned friend was my pupil.' I was, I must confess, more than a little hurt. 'I spent months, a year of my life, in bringing her up with some rudimentary knowledge of the law. And when she says that the rule against hearsay is a legal quibble . . .'

'Mr Rumpole, I don't think my Bench wants to waste time on a legal argument.' The clerk of the court breathed heavily on his glasses and polished them briskly.

'Do they not? Indeed!' I was launched on an impassioned protest and no one was going to stop me. 'So does it come to this? Down at the Old Bailey, that backward and primitive place, no villain can be sent down to chokey as a result of a leading question, or a bit of gossip in the saloon bar, or what a child said to a social worker and wasn't even cross-examined. But little Tracy Timson, eight years old, can be banged up for an indefinite period, snatched from the family that loves her, without the protection the law affords to the most violent bank robber! Is that the proposition that Mizz Liz Probert is putting before the court? And which apparently finds favour in the so-called legal mind of the court official who keeps jumping up like a jack-in-the-box to tell you what to do?'

Even as I spoke the clerk, having shined up his spectacles to his total satisfaction, was whispering to his well-upholstered Chair. 'Mr Rumpole, My Bench would like to get on with the evidence. Speeches will come later,' the Chairwoman handed down her clerk's decision.

'They will, Madam. They most certainly will,' I promised. And then, as I sat down, profoundly discontented, Liz presumed to teach me my business. 'Let me give you a tip, Rumpole,' she whispered. 'I should keep off the law if I were you. They don't like it around here.'

While I was recovering from this lesson given to me by my ex-pupil, our Chairwoman was addressing Mirabelle as though she were a mixture of Mother Teresa and Princess Anne. 'Miss Jones,' she purred, 'we're grateful for the thoroughness with which you've gone into this difficult case on behalf of the Local Authority.'

'Oh, thank you so much, Madam Chair.'

'And we've seen the interview you carried out with Tracy on the video film. Was there anything about that interview which you thought especially significant?'

'It was when I showed her the picture of the Devil,' Mirabelle answered. 'She wasn't frightened at all. In fact she laughed. I thought . . .'

'Is there any point in my telling you that what this witness thought isn't evidence?' I sent up a cry of protest.

'Carry on, Miss Jones. If you'd be so kind.' Madam Chair decided to ignore the Rumpole interruption.

'I thought it was because it reminded her of someone she knew pretty well. Someone like Dad.' Mirabelle put in the boot with considerable delicacy.

'Someone like Dad. Yes.' Our Chair was now making a careful note, likely to be fatal to Tracy's hopes of liberty. 'Have you any questions, Mr Rumpole?'

So I rose to cross-examine. It's no easy task to attack a personable young woman from one of the caring professions, but this Mirabelle Jones was, so far as my case was concerned, a killer. I decided that there was only one way to approach her and that was to go in with all guns firing. 'Miss Jones' – I loosed the first salvo – 'you are, I take it, against cruelty to children?'

'Of course. That goes without saying.'

'Does it? Can you think of a more cruel act, to a little child, than coming at dawn with the Old Bill and snatching it away from its mother and father, without even a Barbara doll for consolation?'

'Barbie doll, Mr Rumpole,' Roz whispered urgently.

'What?'

'It's a Barbie doll, Mrs Timson says,' Mr Bernard

instructed me on what didn't seem to be the most vital point in the case.

'Very well, Barbie doll.' And I returned to the attack on Mirabelle. 'Without that, or a single toy?'

'We don't want the children to be distracted.'

'By thoughts of home?'

'Well, yes.'

'You wanted Tracy to concentrate on your dotty idea of devil-worship!' I put it bluntly.

'It wasn't a dotty idea, Mr Rumpole, and I had to act quickly. Tracy had to be removed from the presence of evil.'

'Evil? What do you mean by that exactly?' The witness hesitated, momentarily at a loss for a suitable definition in a rational age, and Mizz Liz Probert rose to the rescue. 'You ought to know, Mr Rumpole. Haven't you had plenty of experience of that down at the Old Bailey?'

'Oh, well played, Mizz Probert!' I congratulated her loudly. 'Your pupilling days are over. Now, Miss Mirabelle Jones' – I returned to my real opponent – 'let's come down, if we may, from the world of legend and hearsay and gossip and fantasy, to what we call, down at the Old Bailey, hard facts. You know that my client, Mr Cary Timson, is a small-time thief and a minor villain?'

'I have given the Bench the list of Dad's criminal convictions, yes.' Mirabelle looked obligingly into her file.

'It's not the sort of record, is it, Mr Rumpole, that you might expect a good father to have?' The Chair smiled as she invited me to agree but I declined to do so. 'Oh, I don't know,' I said. 'Are only the most law-abiding citizens meant to have children? Are we about to remove their offspring from share-pushers, insider dealers and politicians who don't tell the truth? If we did, even this tireless Local Authority would run out of Children's Homes to bang them up in.'

'Speeches come later, Mr Rumpole.' The loquacious clerk could keep silent no longer.

'They will,' I promised him. 'Cary Timson is a humble member of the Clan Timson, that vast family of South

London villains. Now, remind us of the name of that imaginative little boy you interviewed on prime-time television.'

'Dominic Molloy.' Mirabelle knew it by heart.

'Molloy, yes. And, as we've been told so often, you are an extremely experienced social worker.'

'I think so.'

'With a vast knowledge of the social life in this part of South London?'

'I get to know a good deal. Yes, of course I do.'

'Of course. So it will come as no surprise to you if I suggest that the Molloys are a large family of villains of a slightly more dangerous nature than the Timsons.'

'I didn't know that. But if you say so . . .'

'Oh, I do say so. Did you meet Dominic's mother, Mrs Peggy Molloy?'

'Oh, yes. I had a good old chat with Mum. Over a cuppa.' The Bench and Mirabelle exchanged smiles.

'And over a cuppa did she tell you that her husband, Gareth, Dominic's dad, was in Wandsworth as a result of the Tobler Road supermarket affair?'

'Mr Rumpole. My Bench is wondering if this is entirely relevant.' The clerk had been whispering to the Chair and handed the words down from on high.

'Then let your Bench keep quiet and listen,' I told him. 'It'll soon find out. So what's the answer, Miss Jones? Did you know that?'

'I didn't know that Dominic's dad was in prison.' Miss Jones adopted something of a light, insouciant tone.

'And that he suspected Tracy's dad, as you would call him, Cary Timson, of having been the police informer who put him there?'

'Did he?' The witness seemed to find all this talk of adult crime somewhat tedious.

'Oh, yes. And I shall be calling hearsay evidence to prove it. Miss Jones, are you telling this Bench that you, an experienced social worker, didn't bother to find out about the deep hatred that exists between the Molloys and the Timsons, stretching back over generations of villainy to the dark days when Crockthorpe was a village and the local villains swung at the crossroads?'

'I have nothing about that in my file,' Mirabelle told us, as though that made all such evidence completely unimportant.

'Nothing in your file. And your file hasn't considered the possibility that young Dominic Molloy might have been encouraged to put an innocent little girl of a rival family "in the frame", as we're inclined to call it down the Old Bailey?'

'It seems rather far-fetched to me.' Mirabelle gave me her most superior smile.

'Far-fetched, Miss Jones, to you who believe in devil-worship?'

'I believe in evil influences on children.' Mirabelle chose her words carefully. 'Yes.'

'Then let us just examine that. Your superstitions were first excited by the fact that a number of children appeared in the playground of Crockthorpe Junior wearing masks?'

'Devil's masks. Yes.'

'Yet the only one you took into so-called care was Tracy Timson?'

'She was the ring-leader. I discovered that Tracy had brought the masks to school in the kit-bag with her lunch and her reading books.'

'Did you ask her where she got them from?'

'I did. Of course, she wouldn't tell me.' Mirabelle smiled and I knew a possible reason for Tracy's silence. Even if Cary had been indulging in satanic rituals his daughter would never have grassed on him.

'I assumed it was from her father.' Mirabelle inserted her elegant boot once more.

'Miss Mirabelle Jones. Let's hope that at some point we'll get to a little reliable evidence, and that this case doesn't rely entirely on your assumptions.'

The lunchbreak came none too soon and Mr Bernard and I went in search of a convenient watering-hole. The Jolly Grocer was to Pommeroy's Wine Bar what the Crockthorpe Court was to the Old Bailey. It was a large, bleak pub and the lounge bar was resonant with the bleeping of computer games and the sound of muzak. Pommeroy's claret may be at the bottom end of the market, but I suspected that The Jolly Grocer's red would be pure paint stripper. I refreshed myself on a couple of bottles of Guinness and a pork pie, which was only a little better than minced rubber encased in cardboard, and then we started the short walk back to the Crockthorpe Palais de Justice.

On the way I let Bernard know my view of the proceedings so far. 'It's all very well to accuse the deeply caring Miss Mirabelle Jones of guessing,' I told him, 'but we've got to tell the old darlings on the bench, bonny Bernard, where the hell the masks came from.'

'Our client, Mr Cary Timson . . .'

'You mean "Dad"?'

'Yes. He denies all knowledge.'

'Does he?' And then, quite suddenly, I came to a halt. I found myself outside a shop called Wedges Carnival and Novelty Stores. The window was full of games, fancy-dress, hats, crackers, Hallowe'en costumes, Father Christmas costumes, masks and other equipment for parties and general merrymaking. It was while I was gazing with a wild surmise at these goods on display that I said to Mr Bernard, in the somewhat awestruck tone of a watcher of the skies when a new planet swims into his ken, 'Well, he would, wouldn't he? The honour of the Timsons.'

'What do you mean, Mr Rumpole?'

'What's the name of this street? Is it by any chance . . .?'

It was. My instructing solicitor, looking up at a street sign, said, 'Gunston Avenue.'

'Who robbed Wedges?' We had arrived back at the courthouse with ten minutes in hand and I found Cary Timson smoking a last fag on the gravel outside the main entrance. His wife was with him and I lost no time in asking the vital question.

'Mr Rumpole' – Tracy's dad looked round and lowered his voice – 'you know I can't –'

'Grass? It's the code of the Timsons, isn't it? Well, let me tell you, Cary. There's something even more important than your precious code.'

'I don't know it, then.'

'Oh, yes, you do. You know it perfectly well. Get that wallet out, why don't you? Look at the photographs you were so pleased to show me. Look at them, Cary!'

Cary took out his wallet and looked obediently at the pictures of the much-loved Tracy.

'Is she less important than honour among thieves?' I asked them both. Roz looked at her husband, her jaw set and her eyes full of determination. I knew then what the answer to my question would have to be.

The afternoon's proceedings dragged on without any new drama, and although Cary had told me what I needed to know I hadn't yet got his leave to use the information. The extended Timson family would have to be consulted. When the day's work was done I took the tube back to the Temple and, with my alcohol content having sunk to a dangerous low, I went at once to Pommeroy's for First Aid.

Then I was unfortunate enough to meet my proposed cuckoo, the old Etonian Charlie Wisbeach, who, being not entirely responsible for his actions, was administering champagne to a toothy and Sloaney girl solicitor called, if I can bring myself to remember the occasion when she instructed me in a robbery and forgot to summon the vital witness, Miss Arabella Munday. Wisbeach greeted me with a raucous cry of 'Rumpole, old man! Glass of Bolly?'

'Why? What are you celebrating?' I did my best to sound icy; all the same I possessed myself of a glass, which he filled unsteadily.

'Ballard asked me in for a chat. It seems there may be a vacancy in your Chambers, Rumpole.'

'Wherever Ballard is there's always a vacancy. What do you mean exactly?'

'Pity you blotted your copy-book.'

'My what?'

'Not very clever of you, was it? Defending devil-worshippers

33

with such a remarkably devout Head of Chambers. It seems I may soon be occupying your room, old man, looking down on the Temple Church and Oliver Goldsmith's tomb.'

I looked at the slightly swaying Wisbeach for a long time and then, as I sized up the enemy, a kind of plot began to form itself in my mind. 'Dr Johnson's,' I corrected the man again.

'You told me it was Oliver Goldsmith's.'

'No, I told you it was Dr Johnson's.'

'Goldsmith's.'

'Johnson's.'

'You want to bet?' Charlie Wisbeach's face moved uncomfortably close to mine. 'Does old roly-poly Rumpole want to put his money where his mouth is, does he?'

'Ten quid says it's Johnson.'

'I'm going to give you odds.' Charlie was clearly an experienced gambler. 'Three to one against Johnson. Olly Goldsmith evens. Twenty to one the field. Since I'm taking over the room we'll check on it tomorrow.'

'Why not now?' I challenged him.

'What?'

'Why not check on it now?' I repeated. 'Thirty quid in my pocket and I can take a taxi home.'

'Ten quid down and you'll walk. All right, then. Come on, Arabella. Bring the bottle, old girl.'

As they left Pommeroy's, I hung behind and then went to the telephone on the wall by the Gents. I had seen the light in Ballard's window when I came up from Temple station. He usually worked late, partly because he was a slow study so far as even the simplest brief was concerned and partly, I believe, because of a natural reluctance to go home to his wife, Marguerite, a trained nurse, who had once been the Old Bailey's merciless Matron. I put in a quick telephone call to Soapy Sam and advised him to look out of his window in about five minutes' time and pay particular attention to any goings on in the Temple churchyard. Then I went to view the proceedings from a safe distance.

What I saw, and what Sam Ballard saw from his grandstand view, was Charlie Wisbeach holding a bottle and a blonde. He

gave a triumphant cry of 'Oliver Goldsmith!' and then
mounted the tomb as though it were a hunter and, alternately
swigging from the bottle and kissing Miss Arabella Munday,
he laughed loudly at his triumph over Rumpole. It was a
satanic sound so far as our Head of Chambers was concerned,
and this appalling graveyard ritual convinced him that Charlie
Wisbeach, who no doubt spent his spare moments reciting
the Lord's Prayer backwards, was a quite unsuitable candidate
for a place in a Christian Chambers such as 3 Equity Court.

That night important events were also taking place in my
client's home in Morrison Close, Crockthorpe. Numerous
Timsons were assembled in the front room, assisted by minor
villains and their wives. Cary's Uncle Fred, the undisputed
head of the family, was there, as was Uncle Dennis, who should
long ago have retired from a life of crime to his holiday home
on the Costa del Sol. I have done my best to reconstruct the
debate from the account given to me by Roz. After a general
family discussion and exchange of news, Uncle Fred gave his
opinion of the Wedges job. 'Bloody joke shop. I always said it
was a bad idea, robbing a joke shop.'

'There was always money left in the till overnight. Our info
told us that. And the security was hopeless. Through the back
door, like.' Uncle Dennis explained the thinking behind the
enterprise.

'What you want to leave the stuff round my place for?'
Cary was naturally aggrieved because the booty had, it
transpired, included a box of satanic masks to which, as they
were left in her father's garage, young Tracy had easy access.
'You should have known how dangerous them things were,
what with young kids and social workers about.'

'Well, Fred's was under constant surveillance,' Uncle
Dennis explained. 'As was mine. And seeing as you and Roz
was away on Monday . . .'

'Oh, thank you very much!' Cary was sarcastic.

'And Den knowing where you kept your garage key . . .'
Uncle Fred was doing his best to protect Uncle Dennis from
charges of carelessness.

'Lucky the Bill never thought of looking there,' Cary pointed out.

'I meant to come back for the stuff some time. It was a bit of a trivial matter. It slipped my memory, quite honestly.' Uncle Dennis was notoriously forgetful, once having left his Fisherman's Diary containing his name and address at the scene of a crime.

'Well, it wasn't no trivial matter for our Tracy.'

'No, I knows, Roz. Sorry about that.'

'Look, Den,' Cary started, 'We're not asking you to put your hands up to Chief Inspector Brush . . .'

'Yes, we are, Cary.' Roz was in deadly earnest. 'That's just what we're asking. You got to do it for our Tracy.'

'Hang about a bit.' Uncle Dennis looked alarmed. 'Who says we got to?'

And then Roz told him, 'Mr Rumpole.'

So the next morning Dennis Timson gave evidence in the Juvenile Court. Although I had been careful to explain his criminal record he looked, in his comfortable tweed jacket and cavalry twill trousers, the sort of chap that might star on 'Gardeners' Question Time' and I could see that Madam Chair took quite a shine to him. After some preliminaries we got to the heart of the matter. 'I was after the money, really,' Dennis told the Bench. 'But I suppose I got a bit greedy, like. I just shoved a few of those boxes in the back of the vehicle. Then I didn't want to take them round to my place, so I left them in Cary's garage.'

'Why did you do that?' I asked.

'Well, young Cary didn't have anything to do with the Wedges job, so I thought they'd be safe enough there. Of course, I was under considerable pressure of work at that time, and it slipped my mind to tell Cary and Roz about it.'

'Did you see what was in any of those cases?'

'I had a little look-in. Seemed like a lot of carnival masks. That sort of rubbish.'

'So young Tracy getting hold of the devil's masks was just the usual Timson cock-up, was it?'

'What did you say, Mr Rumpole?' The Chairwoman wasn't quite sure she could believe her ears.

'It was a stock-up, for Christmas, Madam Chair,' I explained. 'Oh, one more thing, Mr Dennis Timson. Do you know why young Dominic Molloy has accused Tracy and her father of fiendish rituals in a churchyard?'

'Course I do.' Uncle Den had no doubt. 'Peggy Molloy told Barry Peacock's wife and Barry's wife told my Doreen down the Needle Arms last Thursday.'

'We can't possibly have this evidence!' Liz Probert rose to object. Perhaps she'd caught the habit from me.

'Oh, really, Miss Probert?' I looked at her in amazement. 'And why ever not?'

'What Barry's wife told Mrs Timson is pure hearsay.' Mizz Probert was certain of it.

'Of course it is.' And I gave her back her own argument. 'And pure hearsay is totally acceptable in the Juvenile Court. Where the interest of the child is at stake we are not bound by legal quibbles. I agree, Madam Chair, with every word which has fallen from your respected and highly learned clerk. Now then, Mr Timson, what did you hear exactly?'

'Gareth thought Cary had grassed on him over the Tobler Road supermarket job. So they got young Dominic to put the frame round Tracy and her dad.'

'So what you are telling us, Mr Timson, is that this little boy's evidence was a pure invention.' At last Madam Chair seemed to have got the message. Uncle Dennis gave her the most charming and friendliest of smiles as he said, 'Well, you can't trust the Molloys, can you, my Lady? Everyone knows they're a right family of villains.'

There comes a time in many cases when the wind changes, the tide turns and you're either blown on to the rocks or make safe harbour. Uncle Dennis's evidence changed the weather, and after it I noticed that Madam Chair no longer returned Miss Mirabelle Jones's increasingly anxious smile, Mizz Probert's final address was listened to in stony silence and I was startled to hear a distinct 'thank you' from the Bench as I sat down. After a short period of retirement the powers that were to shape young Tracy Timson's future announced that they were dissatisfied by the evidence of any satanic rituals

37

and she was, accordingly, to be released from custody forthwith. Before this judgment was over, the tears which Roz had fought to control since the dawn raid were released and, at her moment of joy, she cried helplessly.

I couldn't resist it. I got into Mr Bernard's car and followed the Timson Cortina to the Children's Home. We waited until we saw the mother and father emerge from that gaunt building, each holding one of their daughter's hands. As they came down the steps to the street they swung her in the air between them, and when they got into the car they were laughing. Miss Mirabelle Jones, who had brought the order for release, stood in the doorway of The Lilacs and watched without expression, and then Tracy's legal team drove away to do other cases with less gratifying results.

When I got home, after a conference in an obtaining credit by fraud and a modest celebration at Pommeroy's Wine Bar, Hilda was not in the best of moods. When I told her that I brought glad tidings all She said was, 'You seem full of yourself, Rumpole. Been having a good time, have you?'

'A great time! Managed to extricate young Tracy Timson from the clutches of the caring society and she's back in the bosom of her family. And I'll be getting another brief defending Dennis Timson on a charge of stealing from Wedges Carnival Novelties. Well, I expect I'll think of something.' I poured myself a glass of wine to lighten the atmosphere and Hilda said, somewhat darkly, 'You never wanted to be a judge, did you, Rumpole?'

'Judging people? Condemning them? No, that's not my line, exactly. Anyway, judges are meant to keep quiet in court.'

'And they're much more restricted, aren't they?' It may have sounded an innocent question on a matter of general interest, but her voice was full of menace.

'Restricted?' I repeated, playing for time.

'Stuck in Court all day, in the public eye and on their best behaviour. They have far less scope than you to indulge in other activities . . .'

'Activities, Hilda?'

'Oh, yes. Perhaps it's about time we really talked for once, Rumpole. Is there something that you feel you ought to tell me?'

'Well. Yes, Hilda. Yes. As a matter of fact there is.' I had in fact done something which I found it strangely embarrassing to mention.

'I suppose you've had time to think up some ridiculous defence.'

'Oh, no. I plead guilty. There are no mitigating circumstances.'

'Rumpole! How could you?' The court was clearly not going to be moved by any plea for clemency.

'Temporary insanity. But I did it at enormous expense.'

'You had to pay!' It would scarcely be an exaggeration to say that Hilda snorted.

'Well. They don't give these things away for nothing.'

'I imagine not!'

'One hundred smackers. But it *is* your birthday next week.'

'Rumpole! I can't think what my birthday's got to do with it.' At least I had managed to puzzle her a little.

'Everything, Hilda. I've just bought us two tickets for the Scales of Justice Ball. Now, what was it *you* wanted us to talk about?'

All I can say is that Hilda looked extremely confused. It was as though Mr Injustice Graves was just about to pass a stiff sentence of chokey and had received a message that, as it was the Queen's Birthday, there would be a general amnesty for all prisoners. 'Well,' she said, 'not at the moment. Perhaps some other time.' And she rescued the lamb chops from the oven with the air of a woman suddenly and unexpectedly deprived of a well-justified and satisfactory outburst of rage.

Matters were not altogether resolved when we found ourselves at a table by the dance floor in the Savoy Hotel in the company of Sam Ballard and his wife, Marguerite, who always, even in a ball gown, seemed to carry with her a slight odour of antiseptic and sensible soap. Also present were Marigold Featherstone, wife of a judge whose foot was never

far from his mouth, Claude Erskine-Brown and Liz Probert
with her partner, co-mortgagee and fellow member of 3
Equity Court, young Dave Inchcape.

'Too bad Guthrie's sitting at Newcastle!' Claude commiser-
ated with Marigold Featherstone on the absence of her
husband and told her, 'Philly's in Swansea. Prosecuting the
Leisure Centre Murder.'

'Never mind, Claude.' And Marguerite Ballard added
menacingly, 'I'll dance with you.'

'Oh, yes, Erskine-Brown' – her husband was smiling –
'you have my full permission to shake a foot with my wife.'

'Oh, well. Yes. Thank you very much. I say, I thought
Charlie Wisbeach and his girlfriend were going to join us?'
Claude seemed unreasonably disappointed.

'No, Erskine-Brown.' The Ballard lips were even more
pursed than usual. 'Young Wisbeach won't be joining us. Not
at the ball. And certainly not in Chambers.'

'Oh, really? I thought it was more or less fixed.'

'I think, Claude, it's become more or less unstuck,' I disillusioned him. In the ensuing chatter I could hear Marigold
Featherstone indulging in some whispered dialogue with my
wife which went something like this.

'Have you faced him with it yet, Hilda?'

'I was just going to do it when he told me we were coming
here. He behaved well for once.'

'They do that, occasionally. Don't let it put you off.'
Further whispers were drowned as Erskine-Brown said to
Ballard in a loud and challenging tone, 'May I ask you why
Charlie Wisbeach isn't joining us, after all?'

'Not on this otherwise happy occasion, Erskine-Brown. I
can only say . . . Practices.'

'Well, of course, he practises. In the commercial court.'
And Claude turned to me, full of suspicion. 'Do you know
anything about this, Rumpole?'

'Me? Know anything? Nothing whatever.' I certainly wasn't
prepared to incriminate myself.

'I have told Wisbeach we simply have no accommodation. I
do not regard him as a suitable candidate to share Rumpole's

room. It will be far better for everyone if we never refer to the matter again.' So our Head of Chambers disposed of the case of *Rumpole* v. *Wisbeach* and the band played an old number from the days of my youth called 'Smoke Gets in Your Eyes'.

'Now, as Head of Chambers –' Ballard claimed his alleged rights – 'I think I should lead my wife out on to the floor.'

'No. No, Ballard. With all due respect' – I rose to my feet – 'as the longest-serving Chambers wife, She that is Mrs Rumpole should be led out first. Care for a dance, Hilda?'

'Rumpole! Are you sure you can manage it?' Hilda was astonished.

'Perfectly confident, thank you.' And, without a moment's hesitation, I applied one hand to her waist, seized her hand with the other, and steered her fearlessly out on to the parquet, where, though I say it myself, I propelled my partner for life in strict time to the music. I even indulged in a little fancy footwork as we cornered in front of a table full of solicitors. 'You're chasséing, Rumpole!' She was astounded.

'Oh, yes. I do that quite a lot nowadays.'

'Wherever did you learn?'

'To be quite honest with you . . .'

'If you're capable of such a thing.' She had not been altogether won over.

'From a Miss Tatiana Fern. I looked her up in the *Yellow Pages*. One-time Southern Counties Ballroom Champion. I took a few lessons.'

'*Where* did you take lessons?'

'Place called Mowbray Crescent.'

'Somewhere off Sloane Street?'

'Hilda! You knew?'

'Oh, don't ever think you can do anything I don't know about.' At which point the Ballards passed us, not dancing in perfect harmony. 'You're really quite nippy on your feet, Rumpole. Marguerite Ballard's looking absolutely green with envy.' And then, after a long period of severity, she actually smiled at me. 'You are an old devil, Rumpole!' she said.

Rumpole and the Eternal Triangle

'Beauty is truth and truth beauty.' That's surely one of the silliest statements ever written by a great poet. I have known perfectly reliable witnesses, men and women of honour, who were certainly no oil paintings, and I have known as many unreliable ones of the sort that would make the susceptible Claude Erskine-Brown pant and tremble and come out with urgent invitations to *Das Rheingold* if they happened to be of the female persuasion. There are, of course, no certainties in the matter and a beautiful woman may yet be extremely truthful and follow all the rules laid down by John Keats, although this may not be all you need to know on earth.

I am accustomed to treat women with considerable respect, not to say caution. My wife, Hilda, known to me only as She Who Must Be Obeyed, not only rules the roost at our so-called mansion flat in the Gloucester Road, but keeps a check on my conduct in Court and on my few leisure hours in Pommeroy's Wine Bar. Mrs Phillida Erskine-Brown, Q.C., the undoubted Portia of our Chambers, is a prosecutor of deadly charm. She is held by many, perhaps most, hacks down the Old Bailey to be beautiful, but does the truth always emerge as a result of her sharp cross-examination and charming closing speeches? Mizz Liz Probert is a young radical who sees me alternately as a hero of the class war and as a contemptible puppet of the *ancien régime*, her views entirely depending on the poverty or wealth of the client I happen to be defending at the time.

These are the women in whose company I pass my days. My clients are less frequently female, as old-fashioned villains, like the Timsons, take the view that a woman's place is in the home, where she should be cooking the dinner and minding the children and not out robbing banks, which is a man's job in their opinion. It is true that certain notable women have figured in some of the trials I have conducted, and I still cannot think of Kathy Trelawny, a young person much given to ethnic clothing and dangerous substances, without a slight catch of the breath and a quickening of the pulse. During my military service with the R.A.F. groundstaff I had similar feelings about an airforcewoman of great vivacity called Bobby, but she became hitched to Pilot Officer 'Three Fingers' Dogherty and sank below my particular horizon.* But, attractive as these characters undoubtedly were, they couldn't be classed as what Sherlock Holmes called '*the* woman'. The undoubted winner of this title was Elizabeth Casterini, whose copper-coloured hair and blue eyes I will always remember as she put her hand affectionately on mine, or drew the most soulful music from her violin when at work with the Casterini Trio. There was also the fact that, from the very start of this story, she had clearly taken a considerable shine to me.

When Hilda told me that Erskine-Brown had invited us to a concert and she had accepted the engagement I was less than delighted. Young Claude had recently shown himself to be extremely treacherous in trying to prise me out of my room, and I thought it but a poor recompense to ask me to submit myself to what, for all I knew, might be seven hours of unadulterated Wagner. When we were installed in the Wigmore Hall, however, I was relieved to notice that there were only three musicians on the stage. The Casterini Trio looked to be in their thirties. The pianist was what you might expect – a thin, long-haired man who played the loud notes as though they sent an electric tremor through his body and the soft ones as though he was stroking a much-loved cat. By contrast the cello player was red-faced and burly; he sawed away at the instrument between his knees with large,

*See 'Rumpole and the Alternative Society' in *Rumpole of the Bailey*, Penguin Books, 1978.

competent hands and looked more like an amateur rugby football player than a musician. The woman of the trio was straight-backed, sitting forward on a spindly gilt chair, and I suppose I had realized she was good-looking before the music had its usual soporific effect on me and I closed my eyes.

My sleep was disturbed by what I thought was a wireless playing, but when I called out to Hilda, in that twilight state of half awakening, to turn the damn thing off, she dug me in the ribs and reminded me that we were at a concert. So my eyes opened and, sitting there as I was in the front row with nothing between us but a few potted ferns and a couple of yards of stage, I saw the violinist smiling at me. As I have said, her hair was a reddish gold, her face heart-shaped and her smile was half nervous, half amused, but generally assuming that we shared some secret. And when the music stopped and she stood up, very straight between the two men, wearing some sort of loose dress which gave her a medieval appearance, she seemed to be bowing and smiling for me alone.

After the show I discovered that chamber music leaves you with a terrible thirst, and I led my party to a pub down a side street. Many of the concert-goers had felt the same need and the place was packed. Hilda was full of gratitude to Erskine-Brown, who had, as he was at pains to tell us, only invited the Rumpoles because his wife Phillida was doing a long fraud in Swansea and her mother enjoyed only the music of Andrew Lloyd Webber. Hilda was saying she found that Schubert, who, it seemed, I had slept through, took her right out of herself. 'Can you get back inside yourself to receive a large gin and tonic?' I asked her, and then fought my way to the bar.

I think I knew, as I stood trying to catch the eye of the overworked young man with the cropped head and the earring, an enthusiast whose ambition in life seemed to be to pour a drink for everyone except Rumpole, that someone was watching me, even before I heard a soft and unexpected voice.

'I was sure it was you.' I saw that the violinist had detached herself from her fellow musicians, who were standing clutching pints further up the bar. And then, as I must have looked a trifle bewildered, she added, 'Elizabeth Casterini, now. Surely you remember?'

'Of course.' I had no recollection of ever having seen her before but I felt I couldn't offend her by admitting as much.

'I'd love to see you again,' she said, 'if you ever had time for me. Could we meet? Somewhere quieter than this.'

Could we? I had been chugging along as usual, round the Criminal Courts and Pommeroy's Wine Bar. Did I really want to be blown off-course by this siren voice?

'Does you want serving or doesn't you?' The fellow with the ear-ring gave me his attention at the most inconvenient moment. At the same time the cellist, having finished his pint, was calling, 'Come on, Elizabeth. We've got to go.'

'Please ring me.' She was smiling as she moved away. 'The number's 387–5056. I'm there most mornings.' And then she was gone.

I made my way back to Hilda with my fists full of assorted drinks, and it was clear that she hadn't noticed my encounter at the bar. When she and Claude had claimed their glasses, I pulled out a pencil and made a note on my programme.

'What are you writing, Rumpole?' She Who Must Be Obeyed misses very little.

'Oh, I wanted to remember the name of the tune they were playing. What was it again, Erskine-Brown?'

'Schubert's Piano Trio in B flat major. But it's on the programme already.'

Maybe it was, but I had written 387–5056. When I knew I had succeeded in remembering the number I said, 'Thank you, Claude. I've got it.'

It was a week later, a long dull week doing a post office fraud in Acton, that I felt driven, for the sake of adding a little colour to my life, to dial the number on my programme. Elizabeth Casterini answered at once in the soft out-of-breath voice I kept remembering. The other members of the trio were practising in the background. She said, 'I was going to ring you if you hadn't rung me.'

'Oh good. What about a spot of lunch then?'

'Of course. I'd love to.'

We fixed on Rules for the next Thursday, a day we were having off so a juryman could attend his mother-in-law's funeral. Rules in Maiden Lane is one of the few places where you can still find steak and kidney pudding and a total absence of kiwi fruit. On the morning of the assignation I called in at Alfredo's barber shop in Fetter Lane to smarten up the Rumpole appearance.

'Just a little touch off the moustache, Mr Rumpole? And the hair combed forward in the modern manner? That knocks years off your life. Will you have a little fragrancy on that now, sir?'

Alfred Crooks is a small, bird-like man who has cut my hair and trimmed my moustache since the days of the Penge Bungalow Murders. We grew old together and, as he is a Cockney from Bermondsey, I have no idea why he gave his shop its Italianate title. I was doubtful about the 'fragrancy', which would be a new departure for me (what was there in my manner that day which gave Crooks the idea that I was off to meet a thing of beauty and perhaps a joy for ever?). I asked what he was suggesting.

'Machismo for Men, Mr Rumpole,' he told me. 'Just a light, manly sort of perfume and very "you", if I may say so. Our younger customers say it does wonders for the quality of life. May I waft a little on you, sir?'

'Oh, waft away then. If you're really sure.' It was a day when all rules were to be broken.

'We have a truly distinguished head of hair now,' the man said as he wafted. 'Seems a shame to put that old hat of yours on it, sir.'

I am ashamed to say that I stopped at the Savoy Tailors on my way down the Strand and, stung by Alfred's comment, invested in a new hat. So there it was, hanging up in Rules, and there was I, clipped and perfumed, waiting in a crimson recess, under an alabaster statue of a naked goddess in a glass dome, crumbling bread and wondering if the encounter, the invitation and its acceptance, hadn't been part of a curious dream. But then she was there in front of me, smiling a breathless apology, dressed in a suede jacket, a cream silk shirt and velvet trousers and smelling of fresh fields, while I had the uneasy feeling that I was giving off the odour of a cut-price dance hall in Buenos Aires.

'Well, now.' I hoisted up a menu as soon as she had settled down. 'I don't know what you'd like. Steak and kidney, or rare beef, or Irish stew?'

'You don't eat *meat*, do you?' Elizabeth looked as amazed as she would have been if I'd confessed to robbing church poor-boxes or raping traffic wardens.

'Well, it has been known.'

'Oh. How long's that been going on?'

'Well, I suppose I must have put away a herd or two of cows over the years. A few flocks of sheep . . .'

'Mr Rumpole!' She didn't sound strict, only as though she wanted to reason with me.

'Please. Horace.'

'Horace?'

'I'm afraid so.'

'You don't believe in killing animals, do you?' She started her gentle persuasion.

'Well, animals do spend quite a lot of time killing each other.'

'Perhaps you should have more respect for them than they have for themselves.' She smiled reasonably.

'Well, of course. Naturally. Every time I pass a sheep I raise my hat. I say, "I've got an enormous amount of respect for you. Especially for your kidneys."'

'You're making a joke.' She was still smiling.

'It's a bad habit I've got into.'

I was saved from further apologies by the waiter appearing with his order pad. Meanwhile Elizabeth was surveying our fellow guests, who, in Rules at lunchtime, were largely of the masculine persuasion.

'Look at all these men around us, eating meat. Pink faces. Self-satisfied accountants, probably. You don't want to look like them, do you? So what about a selection of fresh vegetables?'

'Well, if you really think . . .' I had, after all, come to see her and not the roast pheasant.

'Perhaps some cheese afterwards?'

'Don't let's go mad.'

'Just vegetables for you, sir?' the waiter asked in the sort of voice you use when talking to the terminally ill.

'Yes. Yes, of course.' And I asked the man, 'Do you think I want to look like an accountant?'

'You look very nice,' Elizabeth told me when the waiter had left us.

'So do you.'

'In fact you look beautiful. All sort of silvery.'

'You mean, knocking on a bit?'

'Oh, I don't think age matters in the least.'

'I'm sure you're right.'

'Not when it comes to love.'

'Did you say love?' I could hardly believe my ears. But Elizabeth somewhat dashed my hopes by saying, 'In fact I can love most people, can't you, Horace? You strike me as being someone full of love.'

'Well, yes, I suppose so. I suppose I can love people – with a few exceptions. Mr Justice Oliphant, for instance, or Sam Ballard. He's the Head of my Chambers.'

'What's the matter with him, Horace? Isn't he lovable?'

'Well, I wouldn't say that being "lovable" was one of Soapy Sam's most obvious qualities.'

'Love him! That's what he probably needs most. What's your birth sign?'

So we went on to a discussion of the heavens and I was learning that Venus was moving into the path of Sagittarius, my star sign, when the waiter appeared with the wine list. I was just about to choose a better than usual claret to ginger up the vegetables, when she said, 'Meeting you's quite enough stimulation for me, Horace. Isn't it for you?'

'Well, yes. More than enough.'

'So I'm sure we don't need wine. What's their water like?'

I had to confess that I had never tasted the water in Rules, or anywhere else come to that. After the waiter had been dispatched to fetch a jug full of this unusual tipple I asked her why she'd wanted to have lunch with me.

'Does there have to be a reason?'

'There usually is.'

'You say that because you're a lawyer.' She leant forward confidentially. 'I just admired you so much when you were doing Billy's case. And then I saw you looking at me during the Schubert. I thought I'd like to get to know you better.'

'Billy's case?'

'A boy I was at college with. He was put on trial and you defended him. Brilliantly. I used to come and watch you from the public gallery every day. You must remember.'

What could I say? That Billy rang no bell with me, or I must have been too busy in court to pay the attention to the public gallery it clearly deserved? I took the line of maximum politeness and said, 'Of course, I remember.' At which point the waiter returned and asked me if I'd like to taste the water. When the joke was over and the man had withdrawn, Elizabeth pushed back her hair, looked down at the tablecloth and confessed, 'I've been so lonely lately.'

'I don't believe that. I mean, you're part of a trio.'

'We still play marvellously together', she agreed. 'But Tom can't seem to realize I *am* married to Desmond . . .'

So she began to tell me about her life with the musicians. Desmond Casterini was the pianist and her husband. Tom Randall was the hefty athlete astride the cello. He, it seemed, was terribly jealous of Desmond, and Desmond was inexcusably suspicious of Tom. The men quarrelled over Elizabeth, and their jealousy, she told me, became a sort of unlovely bond between them. In this welter of masculine emotion she felt left out, unconsidered, no more than an object they were both fighting over. And Desmond made her nervous because he had this 'wild blood' in him.

'What do you mean?'

'His father's half Italian, half Irish. Very passionate, apparently, when he was young.' And then she took me completely by surprise as she said, 'It's his father's gun.'

'His *what*?'

'An old revolver. Desmond keeps it as a sort of memento. Also he says he needs it for our protection. I suppose his father had enemies.'

'You mean it works?' I hated to think of her in such a household. 'He's got ammunition?'

She nodded and I advised her to tell him to hand it in to the police. I thought it must be an unnerving thing to have about, especially for a vegetarian.

'We're together so much, we three.' She sighed again and began to make little indented tramlines with her fork on the tablecloth. 'Sometimes I feel I want to get miles away from both of them. It would help so much if you and I could meet. Just occasionally. So I could have someone to talk to.'

'I don't see why that couldn't be arranged.'

'I get this feeling that something awful's going to happen,' she said very quietly. 'Don't ask me what exactly.'

Then I looked down and saw a strange sight. Her hand was on mine. It felt cool and comforting and as if there was no weight to it at all. She kept it there for a little while, and then I turned to the vegetables, which were no substitute for this brief contact. We talked of other things, their strange rehearsal room in an old block of studios near Warren Street station, and my triumphs in various cases. When we parted in Maiden Lane she kissed my cheek swiftly and ran off to greet a dawdling taxi. I didn't see her again until after the events which seemed to confirm all her most terrible fears.

I'm not sure how much truth there was around us legal hacks at that period, but there was certainly a good deal of beauty. I have already told you about Miss Dorothy, generally known as Dot, Clapton, who was now installed behind the typewriter in the clerk's room, getting on with her job while turning the head of Claude Erskine-Brown, a part of his body which, at the sight of any reasonably attractive young woman, spins round like a teetotum. Dot, it appeared to me, was very young, very pretty, extremely sensible and had her head screwed on firmly. Of one thing I am sure: the relationship between Claude Erskine-Brown and Dot never reached the sultry temperature which he hoped for. She treated him politely and ignored all his attempts to impress her as an important barrister or to flirt with her as a dashing young opera buff.

Now it appeared that on his way into the clerk's room one quiet afternoon, when most of the numbers of Chambers had better things to do, Claude heard, through the door which had been left open a crack, the voice of Henry, our clerk, addressing Dot in a manner most lascivious. I have since verified the words used and Henry undoubtedly referred to 'The deep pools of your eyes, the suggestion of soft breasts beneath that modest, white shirt, and the whisper your stockings make when you cross your legs'. To which Dot was heard to reply, 'You mustn't say those things. You know you mustn't', thus displaying her good taste in English prose as well as much sensible caution. At the end of it all, Henry suggested they get far away from 'the grey little people' they worked with to a place where he hoped that their bodies might mingle.

Unable to contain himself any longer, Claude burst into the clerk's room, where he saw Henry on his knees and Dot looking becomingly modest. When he asked what had been going on, Henry rose in a dignified manner and said he and our typist had been sending out fee notes 'so you and the other ladies and gentlemen in Chambers all get your creature comforts. I'm also trying to fix your civil at Romford County Court. Now, is there any other information you was requiring, sir?'

The first I heard of this remarkable scene was when I was walking back from the Old Bailey in the company of Soapy Sam Ballard, Q.C., the alleged Head of our Chambers. We had been co-defending and I had managed to get his client out as well as my own, so he was in a fairly sunny mood until Claude came panting up to him with the tale of dire deeds and desperate misconduct in the clerk's room at 3 Equity Court.

'Just the man I wanted!' Erskine-Brown addressed our Head – he didn't seem to want me particularly. 'We're in deep trouble, Ballard. I have every reason to believe there's a serious case of har*ass*ing in our midst.'

'What on earth's har*ass*ing?' Ballard was puzzled.

'Well, *ha*rassing, then. But people call it har*ass*ing nowadays. Because Americans do.'

Rumpole on Trial

'I don't understand that, Erskine-Brown. You're not American,' I told him. 'Anyway, I'm always being *ha*rassed, by solicitors who want their papers the day before yesterday and by Henry, who wants me in two places at once, and by Mr Injustice Graves, who frequently interrupts my cross-examination.'

'This is sexual har*assing*.' Claude was clearly not interested in the less sensual variety. 'Someone is trying to force their amorous advances on a defenceless and innocent young woman.'

'Did you say *sexual*?' Ballard's nose quivered slightly.

'I'm afraid so.'

'That makes a difference.'

'Indeed it does.'

'Who's the guilty party?' Ballard asked, but Claude didn't want to hand over the leading role in such a dramatic inquiry just yet. 'Someone of importance to us all' – he merely dropped a hint – 'someone we've known for a long time.'

'It can't be Rumpole?' Soapy Sam looked at me with deep suspicion.

'No, of course it can't,' Erskine-Brown reassured him. 'Look, I just thought I'd warn you of what's in the wind. I'll report further when I've got a full statement from the complainant.'

'The who?' Ballard, as usual, found events travelling a little too fast for him.

'The girl in question.' Erskine-Brown was prepared to handle her, whoever she might be. 'In my view we must get her cooperation before we move an inch further. It's the most delicate situation.'

'Oh, yes. Of course.' Ballard was persuaded. 'Clearly. Har*assing* indeed! We can't possibly have that at 3 Equity Court.'

My lunch at Rules with Elizabeth Casterini had a strange effect on me. I couldn't forget it and, at odd and inappropriate moments during the day, waiting outside Court for instance, or listening to the speeches of learned friends, I would

52

remember the look in her eyes, the faint, somehow apologetic smile, as she laid her hand on mine. I felt that there was something a little gross about my existence compared to the purity of hers. It was this thought that led me to surprise She Who Must Be Obeyed, as we sat down to dinner in the kitchen of Froxbury Mansions, by saying, 'No chops, Hilda.'

'What did you say, Rumpole?' She looked startled.

'I said, "No chops," thank you. As a matter of fact, I'm giving up meat.'

'You're *what*?'

'People who eat meat start to look like chartered accountants.'

'Well, you've eaten enough of it. You ought to be much better at sums by now. Are you feeling quite well, Rumpole?'

'I feel wonderfully well, thank you, Hilda. I'll just take a selection of vegetables.'

'Boiled potatoes and cabbage. That's the only selection we've got. Will that be quite all right for you? Rumpole! What on earth are you putting into that glass?' I was, as it so happened, filling the usual repository of Pommeroy's plonk at the tap.

'Water, Hilda. Anything wrong?'

'No, nothing wrong, I suppose. Nothing wrong with water. So far as it goes. It's just that it's, well, so unlike you, Rumpole.'

'People should be sufficiently intoxicated with each other. Why should we need artificial stimulants?' It was no doubt an indulgence to repeat Elizabeth's words, but Hilda was delighted by them.

'Why, indeed? It's very nice of you to say that, Rumpole.' And then, as she sat beside me and helped herself to chops, she gave a doubtful sniff. 'Do you notice a rather peculiar smell, Rumpole?'

'Not particularly.'

'Perhaps it's the new washing-up liquid. The Tropical Fruits detergent. I really don't know why I bought it.'

'No, Hilda, it's not the washing-up liquid. It is Machismo for Men. I acquired a bottle from Alfredo's in Fetter Lane when I popped in for a haircut.'

'A haircut? And there seems to be less of your moustache.'

'I have also got a new hat. The old one was getting a bit frayed round the edges.'

And then, I must say, she surprised me by saying, 'Rumpole! You did all this for me?'

'What did you say, Hilda?'

'Just as you learned to dance, especially for me. And came to the concert to get a bit more civilized. And gave yourself a new and powerful fragrance.'

It was, I must say, an unusual evening in the mansion flat, for as we sat opposite each other at the kitchen table I felt Hilda's hand upon mine; and she was looking into my eyes with quite unusual affection.

I should, perhaps, if I'm to make clear to you how the matter of the Chambers har*ass*ment developed, explain to you the geography of our clerk's room. It is a nondescript, fairly ill-organized and often overcrowded office space, where Henry and Dot Clapton carry on their business and where members search hopefully for briefs and consult Henry's diary in order to get their marching orders. A smaller room leads off it which houses the coffee machine and a set of All England Law Reports, which I occasionally feel called upon to consult. I was pursuing a bit of elusive law, which was relevant to a case of receiving stolen fish, when I heard Erskine-Brown accost our typist, who I knew to be reading *Hello* magazine and eating her lunchtime sandwiches. I'm not ashamed to say that I earwigged the conversation and this is roughly what I heard, starting with Erskine-Brown saying how glad he was to find Miss Clapton alone.

'Are you, Mr Erskine-Brown?' Dot sounded less than astonished.

'Would you like to' – and here Erskine-Brown gave a cautious cough – 'come into my room?'

'Well, not really, sir. You see, I'm on telephone duty. It's Henry's lunch-hour.'

Then there was a silence, broken by Erskine-Brown's, 'Dot, is there anything you'd like to tell me?'

'What would you like to know? I could tell you the time,' Dot suggested brightly. 'It's 1.25 precisely.'

'You're young, Dot' – Erskine-Brown clearly wanted to talk of more serious matters – 'and I'm sure this is very embarrassing for you. But nowadays, well, girls of your age are much more open . . . About sex and all that.'

'Do you mind if I go on with my sandwiches?' was Dot's rather discouraging reply.

'Not if it makes this easier for you. I'm sure you realize that men do get these, well, these urges that come over them, from time to time.'

'I'll take your word for it, Mr Erskine-Brown.'

'And you are, of course, desperately fanciable. I mean to say, you're an extraordinarily attractive young lady.'

'I do my best.'

'I'm sure you do. I'm absolutely sure you do. The thing is that no man is entitled to show his feelings in the work-place.'

'I agree with that, quite honestly.' Dot's answer sounded as though it came through a fair-sized bite of sandwich. 'We get a short enough lunch-hour anyway.'

'Dot' – Erskine-Brown adopted the gentle, reassuring tones of the father confessor – 'I'd like you to feel that we don't have any secrets from each other. You can trust me and I want you to succeed in Equity Court, perhaps rising from typist to junior clerk, and then, who knows? But, for your own sake, tell me what you're *really* feeling. I mean, if you don't cooper-ate, we can't do anything about it.'

There was an interruption then as I heard young Dave Inchcape come in and ask Dot to type out an urgent Statement of Claim. She agreed to do so with a vivacity and enthusiasm altogether absent from her voice when dealing with the concerned Claude. As soon as they were alone once more I heard him say, 'We really can't talk here.'

'You seem to be managing.' I heard Dot put paper into her typewriter in a business-like manner.

'I mean, we can't talk *properly*. Why don't you just come into my room for a moment?'

'And look at your etchings?' Now Miss Clapton was sounding distinctly sharp.

'No, of course not!' Claude laughed uneasily. 'Anyway, I don't have etchings. English watercolours, actually. Shall we go?'

'I don't think so, Mr Erskine-Brown, quite honestly. I must get on with Mr Inchcape's Statement of Claim. He seemed quite desperate for it, didn't he? Poor man!'

And then her typewriter started to clatter energetically and Claude must have retreated. When I emerged with the relevant volume of the All England Law Reports under my arm, Dot was alone and looking as though something had happened which she had not expected in a respectable barristers' Chambers.

While these events were unfolding in our Chambers at Equity Court a more serious and terrible drama was involving Elizabeth Casterini, whom I had come to look on as my newfound friend. The best thing I can do is to give you the facts as they emerged in the case in which I appeared.

The Casterini Trio's rehearsal room was in Butterworth Buildings, which was, as Elizabeth had said, a run-down, poorly decorated and underheated block near Warren Street station. On each floor, reached by an antique lift which the passengers had to start by pulling on a rope, there were a number of rooms from which the sound of music was constantly emerging. These could be rented by the hour, but the Casterinis had a permanent lien on theirs, which was on the fifth floor. On the floor below, a room was often rented by Peter Matheson, a horn player who had been at college with Elizabeth and was to be an important witness at the trial.

At about a quarter past six on the evening in question, Matheson was unlocking his room when Desmond Casterini came down from the floor above, using the stairs as the lift was out of order. He seemed extremely agitated and said that something had happened to Tom Randall, the cello player. At that stage Matheson noticed blood on Desmond Casterini's cuff. They went upstairs together and into the Casterini's rehearsal room. There Matheson saw Randall lying on the floor, his clothes blood-stained and his face drained of all colour. He had been shot through the heart. Matheson used the phone on the wall to make a 999 call and the police arrived on the scene at twenty-five minutes to seven. The body was removed to the mortuary and the room was searched, photographed and dusted for fingerprints. These proceedings were in the control of Detective Inspector Baker and Detective Sergeant Straw. It was D.S. Straw who found, in a space between the wall and the piano, an old Colt revolver, from which one shot had recently been fired and with two bullets left in the chamber.

So the trio was reduced to a duet. Elizabeth Casterini and her husband were playing a Brahms Sonata at the Purcell Room when the police officers appeared in the audience. During the interval D.I. Baker arrested Desmond Casterini and told him that he would be charged with the murder of Thomas Paul Randall and that anything he said would be taken down in writing and might be used in evidence at his trial.

After I had read of Casterini's arrest in *The Times* I tried to speak to Elizabeth, but there was the sound of ringing in what I imagined to be an empty room and no reply. Three weeks went by and then she rang me at Chambers. She wanted to see me urgently. She was due at a recording session in Soho, and before that she had to call at the Festival Hall. Could we meet, but not, please, in an office? Somewhere by the river, in the fresh air? She didn't want to feel she was meeting a lawyer, but seeing a friend. She needed a friend now of all times, when what she had feared for so long seemed, at last, to have happened. I had been wondering when I would see her again and I was ashamed to find myself grateful to a murder for bringing us together. I did as I was told and took a taxi across Waterloo Bridge to the Festival Hall.

I was waiting by the river, looking, on a misty morning, towards St Paul's when I heard a hoot and Elizabeth emerged from a bright-red sports car, which she left by a sign marked No Parking. She was wearing jeans and a big white sweater, looking pale as though she hadn't slept but otherwise calm. She took my arm, brushed my cheek with her lips, and asked if I'd been waiting long.

'Hardly at all. But I am in court this morning.'

And then she told me the facts of Randall's death and her husband's arrest briefly and with admirable lucidity and courage. 'It's such a nightmare,' she ended, 'and all absolute nonsense, of course, about Desmond. You will look after him, won't you? I've told him all about you, and the marvellous way you did Billy's case.'

'You mean, he wants me to defend him?'

'We both want you to.'

I told her that I'd arrange for the invaluable Mr Bernard to visit her husband in prison, and then he'd instruct me.

'I wanted to see you, anyway. Never mind about the legal business. I've felt so alone.'

'I'm sure.'

'And it's wonderful to have you on our side. Now I know Desmond's going to be all right.'

'I'll do my best.'

'It's ridiculous' – she looked at her watch – 'but I suppose life has to go on. I'm going to a music session for a commercial. "Under your arms it's always springtime" – that's what I'm playing for.'

'Not Schubert?'

'Mendelssohn. Thank God they haven't ruined Schubert for me.' And then she looked down at the river and said miserably, 'The police are always calling. They keep asking me for statements.'

'Have you given them any?'

'Don't worry. I haven't said anything that won't help Desmond. And you, of course. Shall I see you soon?'

I felt a wave of disappointment. She had made a statement and barristers aren't meant to talk to witnesses. 'Better not. I'll leave you to Bernard until the trial's over.'

'And then shall we lunch again?'

'I'd like that very much.'

So I got another kiss on the cheek, more purposeful than

the first, and then she walked quickly to her car, got in and started the engine. She didn't drive away at once, however. I saw her lift the car phone. She was still talking to it when I walked away towards the Old Bailey and a less sensational trial with no beautiful witnesses.

It was not only the ghastly case of har*ass*ment reported by Erskine-Brown that persuaded Soapy Sam Ballard that moral standards were breaking down all over the world and particularly in 3 Equity Court. Liz and her co-mortgagee managed to produce another sensational scandal. Young David Inchcape was off doing a long arson in Birmingham and Liz wanted to talk to him urgently about a divorce case in which he was for the husband and she for the wife. The matter was called *Singleton* v. *Singleton*, and Liz's client was an ex Miss Broadstairs who was dissatisfied with the pay-off of twenty thousand smackers offered to her by the filthy rich garage proprietor who she was now divorcing. So Liz put a call through to Dave in the Birmingham robing room. As they discussed the case, as barristers often do, they identified so closely with their clients that they adopted their characters as their own.

'Well, you know perfectly well I'm having a baby, Dave,' Liz was saying as Ballard entered her room in search of his missing *Archbold on Criminal Law*, which he suspected everyone in Chambers of half-inching.

Our Head of Chambers stood in amazement as Liz, ignoring him completely, continued her call. Reconstructing it as best I can from her recollection of it, it must have gone something like this:

'Of course, the baby's yours! There's not a scrap of evidence it's not yours. The Chairman of the Council? I've never even been out with the Chairman of the Council. He boasted about it in the golf club? All men boast, don't they? All right, if that's your case I'll demand a blood test and take you for every penny. Of course you can afford it. I know exactly how much you're drawing in cash out of that garage business.'

Ballard was, I have no doubt, even more shocked at the talk

of a commercial garage than he had been at the news of the expected child. He was to hear little more because Liz was nearing the end of her diatribe.

'Right, I know you've got to go. But think about it, Dave. We've got to get this settled once and for all. Of course, I miss you.' So she put down the phone and left the room, saying, 'Men! They're totally irresponsible,' as she passed our Head of Chambers. And he was so astonished that he even forgot to ask about his *Archbold*.

As he always took a long time to make up his mind on any subject, Ballard took no action on the Liz–Inchcape scandal for a while. However, when Dave got back from the Midlands and met our Head coming out as he was going into Chambers a curious conversation took place. Ballard opened with, 'Oh, Inchcape. A quick word with you of a preliminary nature. There may be more to come at a later stage, much more. But as your Head of Chambers I'm bound to advise you to get rid of your garage.'

'But we haven't got a garage in Islington.' Young Dave was totally mystified. 'We have to keep the Deux Chevaux in the street. That's why we can never get it to start on cold mornings.'

'I'm not talking of Islington, Inchcape. Forget Islington. Remember, a barrister does not engage in trade. Get rid of the business.'

'But Ballard, what business?' Inchcape asked helplessly.

'You've got to choose.' Soapy Sam was remorseless. 'I tell you that quite frankly. It's either the petrol pumps and video tapes, and bunches of flowers and all that sort of thing. Or Chambers. We'll go into the other side of it later, but at the moment forget all about garages. Do I make myself clear?'

So Ballard went about his business and Dave Inchcape was left, saying after him, 'Not in the least!'

As always Mr Bernard played his part with admirable efficiency and I soon found myself briefed and in the interview room at Brixton with Desmond Casterini, who looked, as he had done at the piano, as though he were wandering vaguely in a twilight world and would only return to ours with considerable reluctance. It was with difficulty that I persuaded him to give factual answers to simple questions, but at last I led him to deal with the message on the answering machine in the flat he shared with his wife, Elizabeth. It was from the dead man and no doubt left on the day of the murder, for the police had found it there when they took Desmond home and made a search of his premises.

'The message was from Tom Randall,' I reminded him. 'He wanted to meet you and said it was to discuss your lives since Dreams of Youth. Did you know what that meant?'

'I suppose from the time we three started together.'

'And you made a note on the pad by the machine: TOM AT THE ROOM SIX O'CLOCK. Did you think he might be going to tell you that he and your wife were lovers?'

'Dear God, Mr Rumpole! It didn't cross my mind.' Casterini shivered as though the thought chilled him to the marrow. 'I never had a single moment of doubt or suspicion about Elizabeth. Not a shadow, I can assure you.'

'Did you not? The Prosecution are going to suggest that you shot Tom Randall in a fit of jealous rage.'

'I gave you my oath, Mr Rumpole, by the great musicians I hold most dear: Mozart, Haydn, Schubert . . .' He started on a litany which I thought would strike few notes down the Old Bailey.

'Just a simple "no" will do. We might hit a judge who thinks those chaps are runners in the 3.30 at Kempton Park. This rehearsal room, did you rent it permanently?'

'We did, yes. We liked to use it whenever we pleased.'

'Wasn't that rather expensive?'

'Oh, Elizabeth has money, you know. Comfortably off. She started to make it at college. She opened a boutique to sell wonderful clothes second-hand, vintage model dresses. She was able to help Tom out when we started, so he didn't have to take so many other jobs. We're lucky in that respect. Very fortunate.'

I felt that among all this information there was a nugget of great importance. I sat in silence for a while, trying to identify it. Then I asked about something that had been on my mind for a long time. 'Apparently there was a trial when your wife was at college.'

'She told me about that,' Casterini answered without hesitation. 'They'd got to know a man called Hoffman. He'd left the college and become a musicians' agent. It seems he was also an agent for hard drugs. There was a boy in college called Billy Munn accused of being in the ring – he was a friend of Elizabeth's. Hoffman went down for ten years but Elizabeth's friend Billy was acquitted.'

'Must have had a brilliant barrister.' I didn't want to boast.

'Of course I didn't know her in those days.'

'You weren't at college together?' I don't know why that fact surprised me.

'No, I went to Guildhall. I met the other two later and we started playing together. Then we formed the Casterini Trio. Elizabeth's money helped.'

'I bet it did.' And then I turned to a more dangerous subject. 'Now. The Colt revolver. You kept it – and ammunition?'

'My old father, bless him, always slept with it loaded under his pillow. In our house in Lissmaglen.' Casterini seemed quite prepared to talk about the murder weapon. 'He was a poet by profession, but some of the bad boys were after his blood.'

'Have you any idea how that old family heirloom got behind the piano?'

'No idea in the world. I swear to you, sir, by . . .'

'Never mind about all that. You got the message around midday. Did you stay at home after you got it?'

'No, I went to lunch with my sister, Siobhan. She doesn't come over from Dublin often. We went to a film together and had tea.'

'You arrived at the building just after six?'

'The news had started on the car radio. That's exactly right.'

'What happened then?'

'Well, the lift was stuck, it's always stuck. It's a kind of prehistoric conveyance, Mr Rumpole.'

'And then?'

'I started to walk up the stairs.'

'Did you see anyone on your way up?'

'Not a solitary soul, I swear it. The place is usually empty at that time. People are away at concerts and so on.'

'When you got up to your room, was the door open?'

'It was closed. Not locked, of course.' His recollection seemed surprisingly clear.

'And then you found Mr Randall?'

'He was lying on the floor. I knelt down and felt his heart. That's how I got blood . . .'

'Yes, of course. That will be our defence.' Our defence, our whole defence and nothing but our defence. I was silent again and then I said, as I felt I had to, 'Mr Casterini, in a matter as serious as this some people might want a Q.C. to defend them.'

'A what?' The pianist was clearly a child as far as the law was concerned.

'A Q.C. Queen's Counsel. Queer Customer. I'm not saying he'd do it any better. Probably worse. But I'm sure you realize it's a difficult case.'

'I'll rely on you, Mr Rumpole.' He was quite sure about it. 'Elizabeth told me you were a wonderful man.'

'Did she really?' It was ridiculous how pleased I was. 'Did she say that?'

As we were leaving Brixton, where prisoners not yet convicted are now kept in conditions that are considerably worse than those enjoyed there a hundred years ago, when we were out in the free world, away from the stench of chamberpots and the jangle of warders' keys, I asked my instructing solicitor what I had come to think of as the thousand-dollar question. 'In all your long experience, Mr Bernard, have you ever known a villain leave his weapon at the scene of the crime?'

'Casterini might have thought he'd hidden it and he'd come back for it later. I mean, he couldn't walk out of the building with it then, could he? Seeing as he met the trumpet blower on the stairs.'

63

'What colourful lives these musicians lead!' And then I said, 'I want you to find out everything you can about the Hoffman drug case. It was on at the Old Bailey about ten years ago. Newspaper reports, everything.'

'How's all that going to help us?'

'I don't know yet. I don't honestly know at all. But we're acting for Mr Casterini. And remember, he's liable to get potted, unless we can think of some alternative explanation. So, Bonny Bernard, let us get to work!'

We set about to prepare our defence. We visited Butterworth Buildings and found the porter who, cowering behind a closed door and over a gas-fire, was unlikely to keep any check on the arrivals and departures. As apparently was often the case, the lift was stuck on the sixth floor, so we slogged up a dusty and ill-lit staircase. On the fourth floor we heard the horns of elfland faintly blowing and I assumed that Mr Peter Matheson was in residence and at work. On the fifth we went into the Casterini rehearsal room and saw only a few chairs, music stands, an upright piano, shelves for music, a table with paraphernalia to make coffee and a scrubbed patch of floor which had once been blood-stained. On the sixth floor we found the lift had stuck because the gate hadn't been shut properly. I saw a passage and a door marked FIRE EXIT. Something made me push the bar which opened it and we found a platform which led to a rusty iron fire-escape with stairs down to the street, a long way below.

Before we left Butterworth Buildings I gave Mr Bernard a further list of my requirements. 'Ask your friends in the Crown Prosecution Service to let you see the dead man's bank accounts, far back as you can go. And I'd like a copy of his birth certificate. Then, the Bill took a load of documents out of the Casterinis' flat – go through them with a fine-tooth comb.'

'What're you looking for, Mr Rumpole?' Bernard sounded resigned to my excessive demands.

'Money dealings. Telephone bills. Tell me what you find. I think particularly telephone bills.'

*

There is one thing to be said in favour of the decline of civilization as we know it: the slide into the abyss can provide some extremely comic moments. One such came when Soapy Sam Ballard called me into his presence as he had an appointment with Claude. 'I want you there as an observer, Rumpole. We are not yet ready to sit in judgment. But it's only fair that anything Erskine-Brown may have to say is said in front of witnesses.'

'You mean, taken down and used in evidence against him?' I asked hopefully.

'It may not come to that.' Ballard sounded gloomy. 'I pray to God it may not come to that.'

So I sat in Ballard's room and very soon there came a knock at the door and Erskine-Brown was with us and sprawled in Ballard's client's chair, apparently exhausted.

'The investigation into the har*ass*ment affair isn't proving all that easy. I'm getting nowhere with Dot.'

'Are you not, Erskine-Brown?' Ballard looked at him sadly. 'Well, I'm sure it's not for want of trying. She is, of course, the young lady you had in mind?'

'Oh, yes. Indeed. I'm absolutely certain she's being har*ass*ed in the workplace. But I simply can't get her to lodge a formal complaint.'

'Can you not?' Once more Ballard spoke more in sorrow than in anger. 'Well, she's made a formal complaint now. To me.'

'Has she?' Claude seemed to cheer up considerably. 'Oh, good!'

'Good? You think it's good! I don't think it's good at all. She says she's been *ha*rassed.'

'Har*ass*ed, Ballard,' Claude corrected him. 'I told you that's how they say it nowadays.'

'*Ha*rassed or har*ass*ed, it comes to exactly the same thing in the end. The fact is that Miss Clapton, who seems a perfectly respectable girl, is extremely worried.'

'I'm not at all surprised. Henry's behaviour was unforgivable,' Claude told him.

'Henry?' Ballard sounded surprised. 'She didn't say a word about *Henry*!'

'She didn't? Who's she complaining about then?'

'You!'

'What?'

'She said you pressed her to come into your room on the pretext of showing her your watercolours.' And Ballard weighed up the evidence. 'It sounds a pretty flimsy excuse to me.'

'But Ballard . . .' Erskine-Brown rose to his feet, clearly alarmed at the unexpected turn of events.

'She said you talked to her about terrible urges,' Soapy Sam went on remorselessly.

'I said I could understand them. We all have them. That's what I said.'

'Speak for yourself, Erskine-Brown,' Ballard rejected the imputation vigorously. 'And it seems you said you found her extremely "fanciable", an expression new to me, but I'm afraid I can guess its meaning. And you promised to get her promoted to a junior clerkship, no doubt for a certain consideration.'

'Ballard, this is a totally unjustified accusation!'

'You never said that?'

'Well, I may have said something *like* that. But what I meant was . . .'

'No!' Ballard held up his hand to stop further self-incrimination. 'I want to be perfectly fair to you, Erskine-Brown. I want to give you ample time to consider your defence.'

'My defence!'

'Of course.' Ballard gave his interim judgment. 'This will have to be decided, together with other rather disturbing matters, at a full Chambers meeting. Until then I hope you will have no further conversations with Miss Clapton. She, of course, will be a vital witness. I would only give you one word of advice at this time, Erskine-Brown. Make a clean breast of it to your wife!'

'Rumpole!' Erskine-Brown turned to me as the voice of sanity. 'Do you honestly believe . . .?'

'I believe nothing, Claude,' I said. 'I haven't made up my mind. I'm here purely as a witness.'

'A witness to what?'

'To your answer to the charge,' Ballard told him. 'What we

have here is moral decay,' Soapy Sam said to me after Claude had left in a state of indignation and dismay. 'You know what caused the decline and fall of the Roman Empire?'

I had to confess I wasn't entirely clear.

'Lust, Rumpole. Flagrant immorality has reared its head all over this building. Oh, yes. I will have to call on everyone to pull themselves together.'

'According to you, isn't that rather what they're doing already?'

'I really don't know what you're talking about, Rumpole.' I looked at the man. He was undoubtedly a pompous, blinkered, humourless prig who seemed to confuse the Headship of a small, mainly criminal set of Chambers with the Archbishopric of Canterbury. And yet I remembered what Elizabeth had told me I should feel about him. I tried it out.

'I love you, Ballard,' I said.

'What was that?' The poor fellow clearly couldn't believe his ears. So I repeated, 'I love you with all my heart.'

He was looking at me and his very worst suspicions seemed to be confirmed. 'Rumpole,' he asked nervously, 'do I detect a curious odour in this room?'

'Perhaps the odour of sanctity.'

'I don't think so. It's a heavy, sweet smell. Cloying. Tell me honestly. Are you perfumed, Rumpole?'

'As I was saying' – I ignored his question – 'I believe it's our duty to love everything, and because of that, well, I can only say, "I love you, Ballard."'

I had clearly gone too far and taken Elizabeth's advice too literally. The man got up, extremely alarmed. 'Another time, perhaps. I've got a case starting over the road.' And as he hurried to the door he was muttering, 'Think about it very carefully, Rumpole. Moral decay. Getting in everywhere.'

So two causes came to trial, the great harassment inquiry in Chambers and the case of *R. v. Casterini* at the Old Bailey. The second, greatly to my regret, was held before Judge Sir Oliver, or 'Ollie', Oliphant, who came, as he was never tired of reminding us, from the North of England. In fact he regarded everyone who lived south of Leeds as idle dreamers who spent their time lying in the sun, peeling grapes and strumming guitars. He was firmly of the opinion that all cases could be decided by 'good old North Country common sense', which, so far as he was concerned at least, often proved a somewhat unreliable test.

The proceedings began in a routine manner with the medical evidence and then Detective Sergeant Straw produced the revolver which he had found in the rehearsal room.

'It was not very well concealed?' I asked the officer.

'Not particularly.'

'And no fingerprints were found on the weapon?'

'That is right.'

'Did that surprise you?'

'Let's use our common sense about this, Mr Rumpole.' Mr Justice Oliphant entered the arena. 'No doubt whoever did it removed the fingerprints so as to avoid detection. Does that make sense to you, Members of the Jury? I know it does to me.'

'So is this your Lordship's theory?' I asked politely. 'My client was careful to leave his gun behind, although it could easily be traced to him, but took a lot of trouble clearing off the fingerprints.'

'Or else wore gloves,' the D.S. suggested.

'Or else wore gloves.' The Judge wrote a note. 'That's a possibility, isn't it, Members of the Jury?'

Ignoring this interruption I asked the witness, 'Mr Casterini has agreed that it was his gun. He must have been mad to leave it at the scene of the crime, mustn't he?'

'Mr Rumpole,' Ollie Oliphant answered, 'you know we have a saying up in the North where I come from: "There's nowt so queer as folks"?'

'Do you really, my Lord? Down here, in the Deep South, I suppose we're more inclined to look for some sort of logical explanation. That's what I shall invite the Jury to do.'

'And I shall be inviting them to use their common sense.' The Judge repeated his creed.

'What an excellent idea!' I bowed politely. 'I do so thoroughly agree with your Lordship.'

After this preliminary skirmish my opponent, Hilary Peek, a big beefy Q.C. with an unnervingly high voice, called Peter Matheson, the horn player. He gave the account I have outlined about seeing Desmond and finding the body but, perhaps more interestingly, he spoke of a previous conversation he had heard between Elizabeth and Tom Randall. They came down for the lift, which had chosen to be stuck, on that occasion, on the fourth floor. Matheson's door was open a little and he put down his horn long enough to hear Tom say, 'I'll have to tell him. Before everyone else knows.'

"'I'll have to tell him."' The Judge was writing it down with pleasure. 'No doubt that means, Mr Casterini, the lady's husband.'

'My Lord, there is no evidence of that,' I reminded him.

'But we can use our common sense, can't we, Mr Rumpole? Isn't this just another of those cases about the eternal triangle?'

'At the moment,' I said, 'all we know is that they were a trio.'

Not long after that I rose to cross-examine Mr Matheson, who was a nondescript, nervous young man who only came entirely to life, I imagined, when playing his horn.

'Did you hear a shot?' was my first question.

'No, I didn't.'

'And did Mr Casterini tell you, straightaway, that he had found Mr Randall dead and he had no idea who did it?'

'He told me that, yes,' Matheson agreed.

'You said you were at college with the members of the trio.'

'Just Tom and Elizabeth. Desmond Casterini met them later.'

'You said you knew Elizabeth Casterini well?'

'I suppose I was a bit in love with her. Most men were. You can understand that?'

'You mustn't ask me questions,' I told him firmly.

'But I never got to know her well. No,' Matheson conceded.

'Just help me about something. Did she start a shop, a boutique I suppose you'd call it, for the sale of model dresses?'

'Yes, she did. I think it did rather well.'

'Do you remember what the shop was called?'

'It was called Dreams of Youth, as far as I can remember.'

Mr Justice Oliphant grew restless. 'Mr Rumpole, what on earth have dreams of youth got to do with the case?'

'I'm not quite sure, my Lord. Perhaps they're just things we all like to have occasionally.' This was greeted by a stir of laughter from the Jury, who seemed easily amused, and his Lordship rebuked them.

'Members of the Jury. If we want a good laugh, we can all tune into the television set tonight. I believe they're giving us *Coronation Street*. We all thoroughly enjoy that, don't we? Shall we say ten-thirty tomorrow and then use your common sense and take this case seriously. In spite of Mr Rumpole's performance.'

'Or yours, your Lordship' was what I might have said.

Ten-thirty the next morning brought a surprise which, if I have to be honest, I had been, as I thought long and hard about the case, half expecting. My opponent announced that he was going to call Elizabeth Casterini as a witness for the Prosecution.

I went through the protests expected of me. I told him that I had been quite prepared to agree her statements, but Hilary Peek said that the Jury might like to see her in person and, as usual, Ollie agreed with the Prosecution. When she entered the witness-box the Jury can't have been disappointed. She looked as beautiful as ever and was dressed, I thought, as though for a concert, in a loose-fitting, patterned dress which again gave her the appearance of having stepped out of some medieval legend. As a concession to the time of day she was wearing boots and her hair was tied back in a way which left her pale forehead exposed. When she entered the witness-box she smiled at her husband in the dock, and he smiled back, confident, I'm sure, that she had come there to help him. But if that was her purpose the evidence she gave was, in fact, no help at all.

She stuck, in the main, to the facts in her statements. She

identified the revolver as looking like the one her husband kept in a drawer in their flat. But she told the Jury, as she had told me, that her husband seemed terribly jealous of her and Tom Randall for no earthly reason. That frightened her considerably because, of course, he had the gun. This was an answer Ollie Oliphant repeated and wrote down with considerable relish.

So I rose to talk to Elizabeth, not over a lunch table but across a crowded courtroom. And now my purpose wasn't to establish our friendship but to destroy her credibility. I spoke to her quietly, with tenderness. I had decided this was the best technique and I also found it extremely easy to do.

'When you were at college did you own a boutique called Dreams of Youth?'

'Yes, I did.'

'Mr Rumpole,' Ollie intruded into the conversation, 'are we going back to these dreams of yours?'

'Don't worry, my Lord. They may lead us to wake up to the truth.' And then I turned to the witness. 'You did well out of the shop, didn't you?'

'Yes. I sold it when I left college and invested the profits.' Elizabeth sounded unexpectedly businesslike.

'And have lived quite comfortably ever since?'

'With our fees for playing. Yes.'

'Let me just remind you of what the dead man's last message to your husband was. Here's the police note of it: I WANT TO DISCUSS OUR LIVES SINCE DREAMS OF YOUTH. Was he referring to your shop?'

'I . . . I don't think so.' She had hesitated for the first time.

'Let us suppose he was. When you were at college, a musicians' agent was tried for dealing in hard drugs. Some of your fellow students were said to be involved.'

'You know that, don't you?' She gave me a secret smile and I had to tell her, 'I may do, but the Jury don't. You attended the trial, didn't you?'

'Yes. A friend of mine was in the dock. You got him off. Brilliantly.'

'We'll take that for granted!' I got another easy stir of laughter for this and a growling 'Mr Rumpole!' from the Judge, so I went on quickly. 'During the course of the trial there were a number of references to people meeting at the Dreams of Youth boutique.'

'I can't remember all the details.' Elizabeth now looked beautifully vague.

'But you were never charged?'

'You know I wasn't.' She was still smiling. 'There was nothing I could have been charged with.'

'My Lord, if Mr Rumpole is suggesting the witness has committed some offence, she should be warned.' Hilary Peek arose in all his glory. The Judge, somewhat miffed, said, 'Thank you, Mr Peek. I do know my business,' and with exaggerated courtesy to Elizabeth, 'Mrs Casterini. I have to warn you that you needn't answer any question that might incriminate you.'

'I'm quite prepared to answer all Mr Rumpole's questions, my Lord.' And then the witness turned to me as though she trusted me entirely.

'Thank you.' And I went on. 'One of the students gave evidence for the prosecution, and he wasn't charged either. He looked a bit different then, perhaps. He had a beard and another name: Tom Cogswill. I've got a photograph of him here printed in the *News of the World* at the time. Who is that a picture of?'

She looked at the cutting the usher handed up to her and agreed, 'Tom Cogswill. So far as I can remember.'

'Later to become Tom Randall, beardless and a member of your trio. The murdered man.'

Her 'yes' to this was almost inaudible.

'He gave evidence for the Prosecution in the Hoffman trial?' I asked her.

'Yes, he did.'

'And gave no evidence implicating you in this musical drug ring?'

'Mr Rumpole, are those all the questions you have on this ancient trial?' Ollie put his oar in again. 'It seems miles away from the issue in this case.'

'For the moment, my Lord.' And then I looked at Elizabeth. 'Mrs Casterini. Your husband will say he was never jealous of you and Tom Cogswill, otherwise known as Randall.'

'You know he was, don't you, Mr Rumpole?' She smiled as though tolerant of my sudden forgetfulness.

'No. I don't.' I still did my best to sound like a kindly confidant. 'And the Jury don't know. We only know what you've told us. And perhaps we don't know whether to believe you. Let's assume for a moment that this wasn't a quarrel between two men over a beautiful woman. Now what other explanation is there for Tom Randall getting shot?'

'I have no idea. Suppose you tell me, Mr Rumpole?' Even at that point we still sounded like friends.

'Indeed I will. After a few more questions.' I picked up the bundle of bank statements we had from the Prosecution. 'Did you ever pay money to Tom Randall?'

'Money? No, I don't think so.' She was still calm and smiling.

'Just try and help us, Mrs Casterini. When the trio was formed, didn't you tell your husband you'd given Tom some of your plentiful store of money so he could turn down other work and concentrate on playing with you?'

'I said I'd helped Tom out. Yes.' Now she was hesitating.

'And did you go on paying him money from time to time?'

'What are you looking at?' She made the mistake of asking me the question.

'The dead man's bank accounts. He got a regular payment in from a certain source. Was that source you?'

'Perhaps. Sometimes. Is that what it says?'

The answer to that question was no, so I ignored it and asked another, 'Was he blackmailing you, Mrs Casterini?'

'Blackmailing? Whatever for?'

'Threatening to tell your husband, and then the police, all he knew about your part in the Hoffman drug ring if you didn't go on paying?'

'No. No, of course not.' She turned her smile on the Jury, but now, I noticed, they didn't smile back.

'You remember what Mr Matheson heard Tom Randall say

to you one day by the lift? – 'I'll have to tell him. Before everyone else knows.' Did that mean he was going to tell your husband that your nice little lump of capital came from drugs?'

'No!' Her denial was too loud, too vehement.

'What did it mean then?'

'Perhaps that he loved me. I don't really know.'

I let that answer hang in the air for a moment and then I changed the subject. 'What were you doing on the day that Tom Randall died?'

'I went out in the morning. I had a doctor's appointment. Then I went to a lunchtime concert in Portland Place. I went to buy a dress. Oh, I had to have a drink with our agent at six.'

'Before that you popped back home and saw what your husband had written on the pad by the answering machine: TOM AT THE ROOM, SIX O'CLOCK?'

'No.'

'Mrs Casterini. It didn't take you from lunchtime to six o'clock to buy a dress. Were you carrying it all the afternoon, walking about London?'

'No. I did just call at the flat, to put the dress away.'

'And you didn't look at the message pad?'

'I never saw that.' I could tell by the way the Jury was looking at her that they found it hard to believe in a woman who would come home and not bother to look at the messages.

'Did you telephone Tom Randall from your car and arrange to meet him at the rehearsal room at five-thirty, before he spoke to your husband?'

'No. No, of course I didn't.'

As she said that, I picked up another document and reminded her, 'Bills from car telephones have a nasty habit of showing the numbers called. You telephoned Tom Randall that day, didn't you?'

'No. No, I'm sure I didn't.' And then she changed it to 'I . . . I can't remember.'

'Didn't you go to the rehearsal room some time before six

o'clock, taking your husband's gun in case Tom couldn't be dissuaded?'

'No! I had to meet the agent at six at the Warren Hotel. I told you that!'

'Plenty of time to do the deed, hide the gun somewhere the police could find it, then go up the stairs, out to the fire-escape and down to the street. No doubt you arranged for the lift to be stuck at the top floor. How far from the rehearsal room to the Warren Hotel? Just around the corner?'

'Not very far away.'

'So,' I put it to her quietly, 'let's get back to the vital *question*. Who else had a motive for killing Tom Randall? Might it be someone who wanted to stop paying him blackmail and also shut his mouth?'

'Not me ... It wasn't ...' She was stumbling, but Hilary Peek rose to her rescue. 'My Lord, Mr Rumpole is putting a whole string of suppositions to this witness. He's accusing her of the very crime for which his client is on trial. How can these questions be relevant?'

'Because, my Lord, if the Jury thinks someone else *might* be guilty, my client can't be convicted.' I supplied Ollie with the answer. 'I'm fully entitled to put these suppositions to the witness. Or does your Lordship want me to argue the matter in the Court of Appeal?'

At the mention of this dreaded court Ollie looked shaken and poured a great deal of North Country oil on our troubled water. 'Let's use our common sense about this, Mr Rumpole. No need to bother the Court of Appeal, is there? They've got quite enough on their plates nowadays. You go on at your own risk. Accusing this lady may not exactly endear your client to the Jury. And remember I shall be watching you like a hawk, so "mind tha step, lad", as we say where I come from.'

So I turned to Elizabeth and asked her the single most important question. 'Why did you come here as a witness, Mrs Casterini?'

'The police asked me.'

'You know you couldn't be compelled to give evidence

against your husband – they must have told you that. So you came here of your own free will. Why?'

'To tell you the truth as I know it.'

'Or to make sure your husband gets convicted for a crime you committed?'

She didn't answer that but stood in silence for a moment. She looked suddenly older, harder and when she spoke I knew she hated me. 'Is there anything else wicked I'm supposed to have done, Mr Rumpole?'

'Oh, yes,' I told her, 'you recommended your husband to brief a barrister you hoped wouldn't attack you. I'm sorry to have disappointed you, Mrs Casterini.'

There is often a moment in a trial when you know for certain that the case is decided. *R.* v. *Casterini* was won when I had finished my cross-examination and my short, unreasonably happy and misguided friendship with Elizabeth. She left the witness-box and the court and I never saw her or spoke to her again. Three days later her husband also left the court, sad, confused but acquitted. I don't know when they met or what they said to each other. In any event their time together was short. Not long after the jury's verdict D. I. Baker and D. S. Straw called at the Butterworth Buildings rehearsal room. There they found Elizabeth playing a violin solo and charged her with the murder of Thomas Randall. In spite of her high opinion of my brilliance she didn't call upon me to defend her.

After the Casterini trial my life returned to normal, which meant another Chambers meeting. This one was to reach a final verdict on the matter of the alleged harassment of Dot Clapton. Erskine-Brown, who was, as I thought, unwisely conducting his own defence, addressed us in a plaintive fashion. 'It's totally unfair,' he submitted. 'I never intended to harass Dot. That is, Miss Clapton. I heard Henry approaching her in the most outrageous manner and I asked her to tell me about it, so we could make a proper complaint. Well, she must have misunderstood me.'

'What outrageous manner was that?' I asked.

'Well, he was going on about the swishing sound made by

her stockings and her modestly hidden breasts. Oh, and he said, "Just you and I, Annabelle. Two will become one when our bodies mingle."'

'Is that all?'

'Rumpole, just because you happen to have won in Casterini, don't feel you're entitled to take over this important inquiry.' Ballard objected to my stealing his thunder, but I was in possession of the facts.

'I have investigated the matter, Bollard,' I told him, 'as no one else seems to have bothered to do. May I just ask a simple question, with your Lordship's permission? I'm grateful to your Lordship. Erskine-Brown, is Miss Clapton's name Annabelle?'

'I . . . I don't think so,' Claude had to admit.

'It certainly isn't. Her name is Dot, short, all too short I'm afraid, for Dorothy. Have you forgotten that Henry is a thespian, a mummer, a star of the Bexleyheath Amateurs? Dot Clapton is also a native of Bexleyheath, with a taste for the stage. That ghastly dialogue was not Henry's but the product of the fevered brain of a Miss Mildred Hannay, a local author who has written a play especially for the group. What you had the misfortune to hear, Erskine-Brown, was a rehearsal. Any further questions?'

There was a silence which Mizz Probert broke by asking, 'Yes. Why are we wasting our time with this meeting?'

'It's not all a waste of time, Probert,' Ballard spoke to her severely. 'There's the matter of your baby!'

'Her *what*?' Dave asked angrily.

'And *your* garage, Inchcape.' Ballard fired off the most serious allegation. 'With all that money you're earning, how could you refuse to maintain Probert's child? Are we to have a public scandal and a paternity suit in Chambers?'

'What *have* you got into your head about me and garages?' Dave Inchcape was running out of patience.

Liz Probert started to laugh. 'I know what it was!'

'What?' Soapy Sam Ballard sounded not a little put out.

'You came into the room during my telephone call about *Singleton* v. *Singleton*,' Liz told him. 'I wasn't talking about me and Dave. We were talking about our clients. It's hilarious!'

'No, it isn't,' I corrected her. 'It's quite serious, really. You all think sex is the explanation for everything that happens, but quite often it's something else entirely.'

'Is there another chop, Hilda?' I was sitting at supper with She Who Must Be Obeyed and, having poured the remains of my bottle of Machismo for Men down the lavatory, I was reverting to my old ways.

'You've given up being a vegetarian, then?' she asked as she dropped one on my plate.

'Oh, yes. The last vegetarian I met was a murderer and a teetotaller.'

'What came over you, Rumpole, when you started to smell so exotic?'

> 'I met a lady in the meads (I explained)
> Full beautiful, a faery's child;
> Her hair was long, her foot was light,
> And her eyes were wild.'

'I suppose you're talking about that Mrs Casterini. When I think we sat and listened to her fiddling! If I'd've known what she was like I wouldn't have stayed.'

'Ah, but we didn't know, did we? *La Belle Dame Sans Merci* had us in her thrall . .'

'There are actually two chops going begging, Rumpole.' And she rewarded me with the other.

'Thank you, Hilda. Thank you very much. You were never a faery's child, were you? That's one thing to be said in your favour, old darling.'

Rumpole and the Miscarriage
of Justice

The most surprising thing about miscarriages of justice is that they should surprise everyone so much. If justice emerged as the result of an immaculate conception and miraculous birth, perfection might reasonably be expected. If judicial decisions were arrived at by some puzzled girl playing the keys of a computer I suppose they might be more reliable, although computers appear to become hysterical and absent-minded at times. The machinery of the law has to be operated by fallible human beings, some of whom, such as Mr Injustice Graves, Mr Justice 'Ollie' Oliphant, Soapy Sam Ballard, Q.C., you will have met in these pages, and you can decide whether they might – on certain rare occasions, of course – fall into error. Juries, I believe, do their best, but have to contend with the soporific effects of many summings-up and the speeches of the learned friends. The Old Bill, I am afraid, has been known to be only too anxious to achieve a quick result and hasn't always worried too much about injustice. And what of Rumpole? I suppose my job has been to prevent the huge, sometimes ill-directed legal machine totally flattening my client, so perhaps my concern has been less with legal principles than with ways of escape. For all these reasons it's dangerous to expect any trial to produce a result fit to be engraved on tablets of stone and stand unchallenged for all time. It is always as well to remember the conduct of that somewhat accident-prone old darling Mr Justice Guthrie Featherstone in the 'Pinhead' Morgan trial.

The Buttercup Meadows Estate (its rural title must have been bestowed on it as some sort of ironic joke by the town planners) occupies a desolate area to the south-east of London. Its lifts are dangerous to enter, many of its windows are broken, its concrete walkways and balconies are cracked and its walls are smeared with graffiti and worse. There is also little employment for the young men of the area, so they turn their hands to the exciting work of stealing cars, racing them at high speed round the estate and finally crashing them or setting them alight. These sporting events are usually accompanied by fights, knifings and the throwing of petrol bombs. Those elderly citizens of Buttercup Meadows who haven't resigned themselves to sleepless nights often telephone the police, who, with commendable courage, often arrive.

On one such night, when Buttercup Meadows was resounding with screaming tyres and lit with flaming Volvos and BMWs (the local youths only nicked vehicles in the upper range of the market), P. C. Yeomans, a courageous and undoubtedly straight young officer with a wife and two children, arrived on the scene to keep the peace. He left his car with a fellow copper but turned alone down a passage between two buildings, perhaps because he saw a fight or other incident taking place. There, in the shadows, he was stabbed in the throat and died almost immediately.

'Pinhead' Morgan was so unkindly called by his contemporaries because, although past twenty, he had the mental age of a child. He seemed to have come to the car racing purely as a spectator. As other officers discovered P. C. Yeomans's fallen body, Pinhead was caught running some way from the scene of the crime. He was arrested and taken into custody. The officer in charge of the case was Detective Superintendent Gannon, an apparently dependable and avuncular man, who was nearing retirement age. He was assisted in his work by Detective Inspector Farraday and Detective Sergeant Chesney Lane. Pinhead was kept in custody for three days, after applications to the magistrates. For the first two he was uncooperative and used, as an officer later testified, foul and abusive language to his interrogators. On the third day he told Detective Inspector Farraday that he was prepared to make a statement about his 'involvement'. This fact was reported to Detective Superintendent Gannon, who later wrote out a full confession, he said at Pinhead's dictation, which the young man signed.

So Pinhead was charged with murder. This clearly came as a most satisfactory outcome to the Detective Superintendent, who'd had the miserable task of waking Betty Yeomans up in the middle of the night and telling her that her husband had been murdered. All he could offer her were a few words of praise for the dead man and the promise that his killer would be convicted. With Pinhead's confession signed, it seemed that Detective Superintendent Gannon could keep his word.

The case came on before that master of indecision, Mr Justice Guthrie Featherstone. Guthrie, as regular readers of these chronicles will remember, had once been a middle-of-the-road M.P., a fairly middle-of-the-road Q.C. and the Head of our Chambers at 3 Equity Court before he was elevated (presumably they were on the lookout for middle-of-the-road judges that season). On the Bench Guthrie found it hard not to open his mouth without putting his foot in it, but the words he used when sentencing Pinhead to life imprisonment, with a recommendation that he serve at least twenty-five years, must have appeared perfectly safe at the time.

'Morgan,' he said, 'you have been convicted out of your own mouth and by your own words. Every minute this trial has lasted has made me surer and surer of your guilt.' Pinhead replied by calling the Judge a 'stupid wanker'. Whether or not the allegation was true, it had no effect on the result and he was taken down to enter the forgotten world of those who receive life sentences.

After court that day I found myself standing behind the learned Judge in a Ludgate Circus bus queue. He noticed, with apparent satisfaction, the fact that I was reading the *Evening Standard*. 'I expect you saw my face plastered all over the front page,' Guthrie said modestly. 'When one sentences a sensational murderer one does rather tend to hit the headlines.' He clearly felt that he should stop enjoying the publicity as he went on in grave, judicial tones, 'Morgan was a most serious case.'

'And you did it extraordinarily skilfully, if I may say so.'

'My dear old Rumpole. One is grateful for tributes from one of your age, and experience of course.'

'I mean, you managed to persuade the old darlings on the Jury to pot Pinhead without any real evidence to go on.'

'What do you mean, Rumpole?'

'No blood on his clothing. No evidence that the knife was his. No witness saw him anywhere near where P. C. Yeomans was found. My darling old Lordship, anyone can get a conviction on evidence. It takes a legal genius to secure one without it.'

'But Rumpole' – Guthrie played his ace of trumps – 'the accused, Morgan, had made a confession. A full and frank admission of his guilt. And he signed it!'

'Knew how to write, did he? I wasn't too sure he could read.'

The learned Judge was so intent on proving his case again that his bus had come and gone. As he watched it drive away, he naturally blamed me. 'I'll be late and Marigold's got people coming.' He stepped out into the road, waving desperately at a taxi. 'I shouldn't have stood here chattering to you, Rumpole. I must be a complete idiot.'

I don't think he heard when I asked his retreating back, 'Is that a confession that we can accept as the truth, my Lord?'

In fact Pinhead Morgan was not altogether forgotten; the questions I had asked Guthrie at the bus stop began to be taken up by others interested in detecting and denouncing miscarriages of justice. There was an article in the *Guardian*, and a dramatized reconstruction on television in which Pinhead was played by an extremely intelligent young actor who gave a moving performance as a subnormal youth. The Bishop of Worsfield, the Cardinal Archbishop of Westminster and the Chairman of the Arts Council called on Mr Timothy Bunting, the Home Secretary, to express their deep concern. And then the campaign to reopen Pinhead's case was given a final boost by a machine known as the Electro-Static Detective Apparatus, or E.S.D.A. for short. Its findings were made the more impressive as it was operated in investigations carried out by the Old Bill in person.

Chief Superintendent Belmont was the officer in charge of the section which included the Buttercup Meadows Estate. When the campaign suggesting that Pinhead had not received altogether satisfactory treatment at the hands of the law had gathered momentum, Belmont summoned Detective Inspector Farraday and Detective Sergeant Chesney Lane to a demonstration.

Belmont had found, he said, a pile of blank confession sheets in Detective Superintendent Gannon's office. When submitted to the E.S.D.A. machine this cunning device found indentations of Gannon's handwriting on the top twelve pages. The document he had been writing was that which was put before the Jury as page two of Pinhead's alleged confession. Now this page two was the only page which recorded his admission of guilt, as it contained such telling phrases as 'I came tooled up'; 'I'm sorry I cut the copper. I was all excited, what with the car racing and that'; 'I'm sorry for what I did. It's a relief now I've told you'.

Detective Superintendent Gannon said in court that he had written both pages of the confession in the interview room, in Pinhead's presence and at his dictation. Furthermore, he said that he had written it on pages which he had laid flat down on the table in front of him, with no page or paper underneath. The E.S.D.A. machine told a different story: that of page two being written by Gannon on a pile of blank sheets in his office. The clear inference was that the original page two didn't provide clear evidence against Pinhead, so Gannon had written out an alternative and incriminating page and substituted it later.

When this demonstration, apparently so clear and convincing, was over, Detective Inspector Farraday had to admit that he couldn't exactly remember what Pinhead had said at the time, but he had always assumed that it was as it appeared in the confession statement. Moreover, Mr Gannon had taken away the written pages after the accused had signed them and the two officers had no opportunity of checking their accuracy.

He seemed prepared to agree that a new and altered page two must have been written later. Detective Sergeant Chesney Lane was rather more puzzled by the demonstration, but his questions were met by Chief Superintendent Belmont saying, 'There's something that stinks to high heaven about this case of Morgan. And I'll make it my business to find out exactly what it is.' This and his subsequent actions led to high praise of Chief Superintendent Belmont in all the 'caring' newspapers as being a refreshingly honest officer who made no attempt to hide the rotten apples in his force.

There is only one other matter about this distressing scene which should be recorded. The original confession had, of course, been lodged in the court. When Belmont was conducting the demonstration he showed the two officers a photostat of page two written out in Gannon's handwriting. D. S. Chesney Lane was asked to return this document, among others, to the filing officer. Before he did so, he felt the back of the photostat. After doing so he failed, in one important respect, to carry out his orders.

For a while Guthrie dwelt in happy ignorance of this final attack on his conduct in the Buttercup Meadows case. One day, however, when he had called in at the Sheridan Club to celebrate a case that settled early with a delightful lunch among his friends and admirers, he was told by the porter that Lord Justice Parsloe, a senior judge of the Court of Appeal, was in the bar and wanted a word with him. So Guthrie mounted the stairs alight with hope that his service to the state was about to be recognized by some promotion.

I have done my best to reconstruct the conversation which in fact took place from my knowledge of the characters involved and with considerable help from a member of the Sheridan named Toby Harringay, an appalling old gossip who plays bridge with Hilda and who earwigged a great deal of the conversation. It seems that Guthrie had just ordered himself his usual modest gin and tonic at the bar when Lord

Parsloe, a small, rubicund, deceptively cheerful-looking man, came up with 'Hallo there, Guthrie. Drowning your sorrows?'

'Simon. Why? Should I have sorrows?' Guthrie was puzzled.

'Bit of a hard time for you, I'm afraid. My heart goes out to you, old fellow.' And he looked at the Judge of first instance as though he were suffering from some threatening disease. 'Keeping well, are you?'

'Apart from the usual ailments of a Trial Judge,' Guthrie replied.

'I know. Piles and sleeping sickness.' The Lord Justice still sounded sympathetic.

'And I'm looking forward to joining you Lord Justices in the peace and comfort of the Court of Appeal.' Guthrie was ever hopeful.

'Well, perhaps some day. Who knows? These things do get forgotten in time.'

'Things? Simon . . .' Panic stirred, as it so often did, in Guthrie's breast. 'What *things* are you talking about?'

'Well, let's say, things like Pinhead Morgan.'

'I sent him down with a recommendation of twenty-five years.' And the Judge sounded proud of the fact.

'I know you did, Guthrie. How many has he done now? I suppose the question we have to decide is, has he done enough?'

'*Enough*? For stabbing a police officer?'

'Ah, but can we be sure he did that?'

'I know there's been a bit of agitation by copper-hating Lefties, Simon. Professional do-gooders, members of the Howard League for Penal Reform. You're not going to take any notice of their nonsense, are you?'

'Tim Bunting referred the matter to us. I'm not sure the Home Secretary's a copper-hating Leftie, as you call it so elegantly. Look, let's go over there, where it's not quite so public.'

So Guthrie followed the Lord Justice to a couple of crumbling leather chairs in a corner of the bar, out of earshot of the gossiping Toby Harringay, and it was in that corner that the Judge realized the full seriousness of his plight as Parsloe said, with chilling gentleness, 'Guthrie, I know you'll be very brave about this. It may not be entirely nonsense. It may be just one more of these cases where the Trial Judge ends up with egg on his face, and God knows there's been enough egg lately to keep the entire Howard League for Penal Reform in omelettes for the rest of their natural lives.'

'But it was an open and shut case, Simon.' By now the Judge was sounding plaintive.

'Reopened and not yet shut, unfortunately. Oh, my dear old fellow. If only you hadn't said, "Every minute this trial has lasted has made me surer and surer of your guilt."'

'Did *I* say that?' Guthrie's memory was mercifully short.

'Oh, yes. Nailed your colours to the mast, didn't you? Silence is golden, old fellow, particularly when passing possibly dubious life sentences.'

'Possibly dubious! You mean you've made up your minds?'

'Not at all. I have no idea what conclusion I and my brother Lords Justices may come to. We might find the conviction is still safe. I just thought I should warn you. Keep your head down, Guthrie. The flak may be coming over.'

And after this dire warning Mr Justice Guthrie Featherstone had very little appetite for his lunch.

On the last day of Pinhead Morgan's appeal there was a demonstration of sorts outside the main entrance to the Law Courts by a number of M.P.s, prison reformers, television crews and Pinhead's family and friends. Some bore placards with such legends as FREE PINHEAD MORGAN, LIARS IN BLUE, DON'T LEAVE JUSTICE TO THE JUDGES, PINHEAD'S INNOCENT and THE LAW'S AN ASS. When Detective Superintendent Gannon and his Detective Inspector arrived they were roundly booed by the contingent from the Buttercup Meadows Estate.

That morning Guthrie was sitting as a judge down the Old Bailey, at the other end of Fleet Street. As he was being robed by his ancient clerk, Wilfred, he expressed considerable concern at the possible result in the Court of Appeal. 'My learned Judge,' Wilfred told me later, 'was all of a dither. To be honest I never saw anything like it in anyone who has risen to the Bench.'

'Are they giving judgment this morning? Are we sure of that, Wilfred?' Guthrie asked, as though the Jury were out and he was on trial.

'So I understand, my Lord, from Lord Justice Parsloe's clerk, Gladys,' Wilfred told him.

'It's a troublesome business, I'm afraid, Wilfred. An extremely troublesome business.'

'Pity they got rid of the rope, my Lord. Those were my very words to Gladys.' Wilfred's view of the law was as antiquated as himself.

'I was perfectly entitled to say what I did say. We had water-tight evidence.' Guthrie argued his case.

'And if that young man had been strung up, with all due respect, he'd never have come popping up in the Court of Appeal, causing us all this trouble and anxiety.'

'The point is, I've got to know the result just as soon as possible. Now, you come into my court at . . .? What time, do you think?'

'Twelve-thirty, sir. It should be all over by then, according to Gladys. And Gladys is very reliable. That's the Lord Justice's clerk, my Lord. And we have become firm friends over the years.'

'Oh, *do* stop going on about Gladys – and hanging too, come to that.' Guthrie wasn't in the best of tempers. 'Just concentrate on coming in and giving me a signal. Let's say, thumbs up if Pinhead goes back to prison and we're in the clear?'

'Otherwise thumbs down, if I may make a suggestion?'

'I'm afraid, Wilfred' – and here his Lordship sank into a deep gloom – 'there may be a terrible miscarriage of justice.'

But the miscarriage of justice, according to the Court of Appeal, was due in almost equal parts to the Detective Superintendent and Guthrie Featherstone. What follows is an extract from the judgment of the Court of Appeal, Lord

Justice Parsloe presiding. 'The officer in charge of the case,' he said, 'must bear the heavy responsibility of obtaining this worthless confession. We, as judges of the Court of Appeal, can only apologize to the public and to Mr Morgan, the unfortunate victim of this miscarriage, for the somewhat unwise remarks of the learned Trial Judge, who was reckless enough to say, and I quote, "Every minute this trial has lasted has made me surer and surer of your guilt."'

Down the road Guthrie was listening, with very little attention, to a legal argument from Claude Erskine-Brown, when the door of the court swung open and there stood Wilfred with his thumb, like that of a merciless Roman emperor, pointed towards the ground.

So Pinhead was released, to the cheers of his supporters, and the Detective Superintendent had to pay another call on Betty Yeomans to comfort her once again. I had an opportunity of meeting Mrs Yeomans later, and I found her to be a young woman of considerable spirit. I know how the conversation went, with Betty leading off on the apparently absurd result that no one had been guilty of her husband's murder. 'So Pinhead never stabbed Ted,' she said. 'Never cut him. So who did then? Would they mind telling me that?'

'I'm sorry, Betty. I know it's hard.' Gannon was as distressed as the widow.

'Or did Ted just pull out a knife and do himself? Was it all a mistake like that trial of Pinhead? Is that what they're telling us?'

'I don't know, Betty.' And Gannon told her, 'They seem to have lost interest in what Pinhead did. It's what I did, what the Judge did, where we went wrong. That's all their Lordships is concerned about.'

'Someone killed Ted, that's all I know. Someone's got to suffer!'

'The most likely person to suffer is going to be me.' Gannon looked grimly into his future.

'Not you, Roy. Not after all you've done for us. I'm not going to let that happen!' Betty Yeomans gave him her promise.

*

If the Detective Superintendent thought he was the most likely person to suffer by the change in Pinhead's fortunes he had, at least, Mr Justice Featherstone as a companion in misfortune. Of course the two never met until ... But that time was still in the future. On the night of the Appeal Judgment Guthrie was alone; his wife, the handsome but sometimes ruthless Marigold, was away on a visit to her sister in Coventry. Guthrie hoped that they would be too busy exchanging family news to watch the television, but he knew that she would learn of the public rebuke in due course, and she was unlikely to comfort him and bind up his wounds. He dined alone at the Sheridan Club; no one he knew was in that night, and those he didn't know took pains, he imagined, to ignore him.

After dinner he sat alone in the bar, drinking port and, when that occupation began to pall, he drank brandy. He was still doing this when the bar had emptied and Denver, the barman, was cleaning up and looking forward to going home to bed. Guthrie, however, seemed to be a fixture, unburdening his soul in words that Denver quite failed to keep to himself.

'Justice!' the Judge said bitterly. 'I've had no justice whatsoever.'

'I'm sorry about that, sir, truly sorry.' The Sheridan barman had a kindly heart.

'No one to represent me, Denver. No chance to put my case. Engaged in another court, as it so happened, while the Court of Appeal rubbished me. Rubbished me, Denver! "The Trial Judge was reckless enough to say ..." Reckless, Denver! You tell me, quite honestly, would you say that I was reckless?'

'No, Sir Guthrie. But you are my last gentleman, sir.'

'Your last gentleman! That's probably it. Too much of a gentleman to answer back. Not so many of us about nowadays, are there?'

'I was just about to pack up.' Denver had polished the last glass and was about to hang up his white jacket.

'Is that what you're advising me to do, Denver?' Guthrie looked more stricken than ever. 'Jack it in, hang up the scarlet dressing-gown, take to golf?'

'A very good-night to you, Sir Guthrie,' was the barman's firm reply.

So Guthrie came down the steps of the Sheridan Club unsteadily, not quite drunk but still not as sober as a judge, and in the street he bumped into someone who appeared to be leading a group of revellers and whom he recognized, after protests and apologies, as Henry, who had been his clerk when he was Head of our Chambers. 'Out on the town, are you?' And Guthrie, looking round at the clerk's friends, added, 'I say, are you all in the law? Please accept my profound sympathy.'

'Not exactly, Sir Guthrie,' Henry told him. 'Not all of us is in the law. What you see here is the cream of the Bexleyheath Thespians up in town for our annual outing.'

'And piss-up,' added a male thespian who was carrying a theatre programme.

'That was not the purpose of the evening, Sir Guthrie.' Henry maintained his dignity. 'The purpose of the evening was to witness Miss Diana Rigg performing in the living theatre.'

'I'd like to play opposite her, I honestly would,' the thespian with the programme said longingly.

'*Hedda Gabler*? Not many laughs in it, was there?' This came from Dot Clapton, who, as you will remember, was also a member of the acting group.

'Never any of those. Not in that Henry Gibson,' said another star of Bexleyheath, and Dot explained, 'So we was all off to Blokes for a bit of a bop.'

'A bit of a bop, eh?' Guthrie seemed overcome by sadness. 'There was a time when I could indulge myself in a bit of a bop. Before the pressures of life in the law became too much for me. Where is this Blokes you go to?'

'Leicester Square, just round the corner.' And Dot extended an invitation. 'Feel like a rave-up, do you?'

'Speaking for all the assembled thespians here, Sir Guthrie,' Henry told him, 'we should be honoured if you would join us, just for a drink.'

'That's very kind of you but ...' he no doubt became

aware of Dot's considerable attractions – 'that would be quite impossible.'

Like other judicial decisions, this one was almost immediately reversed and Guthrie found himself, a quarter of an hour and a couple of rum and Cokes later, standing under flashing lights and moving vaguely in time to some very loud music in what he fondly imagined to be an offhandedly seductive manner, while Dot danced expertly and appealingly around him. And even then, according to Dot's subsequent account, he was still bemoaning his lot.

'What was I meant to do, quite honestly? Go down the cells, keep a fatherly eye on Pinhead Morgan, make sure the Old Bill didn't fit him up, see he had tea and biscuits and a clever solicitor? I can't do that, you know. I simply haven't got the time. If the Judges are going to carry on, we've got to trust the police, Debby.'

'Dotty.'

'What did you call me?'

'My name's Dot, Dotty. Not Deb, Debby.'

'I'm sorry. It seems I'm always making mistakes.'

'Don't you worry, Judge. You're an excellent mover.'

The next morning, when I came into Chambers, Dot had just received a large bunch of flowers and Erskine-Brown, with his usual nose for a scandal, was reading out the inscription on the card which accompanied the tribute: FROM A JUDICIAL ADMIRER. THANKS FOR THE BOP.

'I don't read your correspondence, Mr Erskine-Brown,' Dot was entitled to say. 'So I'd be glad if you kept your eyes off mine.'

'Only taking a friendly interest, Dot. Is it serious? When's the engagement?'

'I've seen enough of married men, Mr Erskine-Brown, not to want one of my own, thank you very much.'

At which point Henry, who had been engaged on the telephone, said, 'We've been waiting for you to come in, Mr Rumpole. You've got a police officer up in your room, sir.'

'There you are, Rumpole.' Erskine-Brown was clearly delighted. 'They fingered your collar at last!'

I did, I must confess, go through a moment of extreme unease. Was it something to do with my income tax?

When I got up to my room the client's armchair was occupied by a large, comfortable, grey-haired man who looked, as I have said, less like a bent copper than everyone's favourite uncle. Also there was the indispensable Mr Bernard, who effected the introduction. 'I told Superintendent Gannon he couldn't have a better brief, Mr Rumpole. Not one with your talent for acquittals. He saw my point, didn't you, Roy?'

'Acquittals! That's what's caused all this mess, the way you lawyers let Pinhead out laughing.' His words were bitter but his voice was low and reasonable, one of the mildest-mannered men, I thought, who ever faked a confession.

'You blame the lawyers for that?' I added, in fairness to our much-abused profession, that it wasn't a lawyer who rewrote the dubious page two.

Gannon didn't answer me directly but said, 'I gave Betty Yeomans my solemn oath I'd get her a conviction. That's what's kept Betty going, my promise to her. Someone had to pay for Ted Yeomans's life.'

'Even someone who hadn't killed him?' I asked.

'Pinhead was guilty all right.'

'Beyond reasonable doubt?' I started to look at the proof of my client's evidence, prepared by Mr Bernard, while Gannon gave his views on the presumption of innocence, 'Lawyers' language!' Again the contempt was deep but the voice was gentle. 'You don't believe me, do you, Mr Rumpole? I can see that. Nobody believes a copper nowadays. The world was a whole lot better when people had faith in us. That's what I think about it.'

'All right.' I didn't argue about who had caused the loss of faith as I was anxious to get down to the facts of the matter. 'Pinhead was arrested on the night of the incident.'

'The night he killed Ted Yeomans,' Gannon insisted.

'He was someone known to the police. He'd packed a lot in. Common assault, affray, take and drive away, possession of an offensive weapon. So you thought right from the start, Pinhead Morgan was a likely suspect.'

'Seemed probable.'

'You were busy on the morning he confessed?' I asked.

'I went to see someone in hospital. When I got back to the station I was met by D. I. Farraday, who told me that Pinhead was ready to talk.'

'That's right. They'd had a short interview with him on the morning when you were away. According to Farraday's note, all Pinhead said was, "When's the guvnor back? I feel I'd now like to tell him about my involvement."'

'Something like that.'

'So what made him change his mind?'

'They need to talk, Mr Rumpole. They need to tell someone about it; they can't keep it bottled up any longer. Then the truth comes out. And you lawyers won't believe it.'

'He's said to have the mental age of a child. Did he use all the words in this confession statement?'

'As far as I'm concerned he said exactly what I wrote down.'

'You wrote on single sheets of paper. Loose sheets?'

'Yes, I'm sure I did. D. I. Farraday and D. S. Lane saw that.'

'No paper between the sheet you were writing on and the table?'

'No, I'm sure there wasn't.'

'You know the E.S.D.A. machine thinks differently?'

'You can't rely on a machine.'

I thought, well, he would say that, wouldn't he? I got up and went to the window. Then I turned back to look at the solid man filling my armchair. 'Superintendent Gannon, you do understand the case against you?'

'I wrote down what Pinhead said,' he insisted.

'You're sure you didn't improve on it later? So you could keep your promise to an unhappy woman?' I hope I made it sound as though I could understand the temptation, but he shook his head and simply answered, 'I'm sure.'

Claude Erskine-Brown had two overriding ambitions: he wanted to bring a little extra romance into his life and he wanted to become one of Her Majesty's Counsel, learned in the law. The fact that his wife Phillida could write the magic letters Q.C. after her name was, for him, a matter of continual disquiet. His efforts to achieve his two great objectives were not, at that time, wholly successful. His pursuit of young women, and his efforts to get them to accompany him to the Opera, led, as often as not, to embarrassment for all concerned. In search of the elusive silk gown he got himself elected to the Sheridan Club, where he hoped to make friends with judges and old Keith from the Lord Chancellor's office, who would further his career. So far, his membership hadn't brought him the great reward. It did, however, lead him to invite me to lunch at a time when the criminal community had apparently gone off on holiday and business was slack. I accepted with reluctance, not being greatly attracted to the sight of a lot of judges and publishers sitting together drinking Brown Windsor soup (the Sheridan was proud of its cuisine, less nursery food than old-fashioned railway dinners). However, I went along for the claret and there, in the bar before lunch, we met Guthrie Featherstone and had a conversation with him which was to add greatly to his difficulties.

'I'm so sorry, Judge,' Erskine-Brown started to commiserate with his Lordship, as I thought tactlessly, on the reverse he'd received in *R.* v. *Pinhead Morgan*. 'You must be suffering a great deal.'

'Suffering?' Guthrie smiled recklessly. 'No, I'm not suffering. I'm feeling, well, on top of the world, really.'

'You're being brave about it.' And then Claude told the Judge, even more tactlessly, 'Of course, anyone can make mistakes.'

'Mistakes?' Guthrie looked puzzled. 'What are you talking about? Who's been making mistakes? Have you heard about anyone making mistakes, Rumpole?'

'Oh, no one. Absolutely no one at all,' I tried to reassure him. 'Mistakes simply don't occur in the law.'

'I summed up in that case absolutely fairly on the evidence before me. Are you suggesting that was some kind of a mistake?'

'God forbid!' I said fervently.

'Well, anyway, you look well.' Claude was anxious to change the subject he'd introduced. 'I'm so glad you're feeling well, Guthrie.'

'Top of the world!' Guthrie smiled with boyish enthusiasm. 'There is more to life than stuffy courtrooms and summings-up, Claude. Life has better things to offer. Greater pleasures. And thank God I'm still young enough to enjoy them.'

'Of course you are!' Claude encouraged the Judge.

'At least I'm still young enough to indulge in a bit of a bop occasionally.'

'A bit of a what?' I was puzzled.

'A bop, Rumpole. That means a dance-up,' Erskine-Brown translated for me.

'A dance-*up*?'

'A modern idiom which you might be too square to understand,' Guthrie said, and Claude was unwise enough to make a joke at which he laughed prodigiously. 'Rumpole's not square. He's round!'

'Oh, I can see this is going to be a hilarious luncheon.' By this time I was feeling quite gloomy, but then Guthrie decided to make his confession.

'As a matter of fact, Marigold was away,' he began confidentially, 'and I didn't fancy spending the evening here, among a lot of dusty old lawyers, so I took a young lady out bopping.'

'Claude takes them to Wagner,' I said. 'I suppose it lasts longer.'

'A judicial bop!' Erskine-Brown thought the matter over. 'Good heavens, I'd never have imagined it.'

'What I do find interesting, to be absolutely honest with you fellows' – Guthrie seemed to be enjoying his confession – 'is how many people today . . . well, let's say young women – girls, if you like . . . how many girls rather prefer the older man as a partner, in every sense of the word.'

'Gerontophilia, is that the in-thing nowadays?' I asked, as innocently as possible.

'I mean, not really old. Not in your class, Rumpole,'

Guthrie said, as I thought unnecessarily, 'but the slightly older –'

'Judge?' I supplied the word.

'Even judges are human.' Guthrie spoke as though letting us into a closely guarded secret.

'So you mean, you actually struck lucky with your Bopee?' Erskine-Brown could hardly believe his ears.

'Oh, yes,' Guthrie answered us with some satisfaction. 'Beyond all reasonable doubt. Successful in every way, Claude. In every possible way. It was an evening to look back on with joy. When one's bopping days are over.' He looked at his watch. 'Sorry, you chaps. Lunching with a couple of the younger members.'

At that time I didn't know Toby Harringay, nor did I realize exactly who he was until he was identified as one of her partners at the Pontium Bridge School by She Who Must Be Obeyed. However, I had been conscious of him in the offing, a moist-eyed, perpetually smiling fellow with suspiciously jet-black hair and a Sheridan Club bow-tie. As soon as Guthrie had left, he showed us how much he had been enjoying the conversation by saying, 'What exotic lives judges lead nowadays, don't they?' He had quite clearly heard everything.

Erskine-Brown smiled in a noncommittal manner and led me in the general direction of the soup. As we went I quoted Robbie Burns: '"There was a chield amang us taking notes." Rather unfortunate that.'

Toby Harringay was not the sort to let a good bit of gossip waste its sweetness on the desert air. Only a few afternoons later he was seated at the green baize opposite Hilda, with another couple of senior citizens who occupied the afternoons in polishing up their bidding at the Pontium School in Sloane Street. It was while the cards were being shuffled, She told me, that Toby began to spread the story which he couldn't possibly keep to himself.

'Hanky-panky,' he said. 'And this will come as a shock to you, Mrs Rumpole, among the Judiciary. Bed-hopping! I'm afraid that's what it comes to. Like those dreadful young people that go on package holidays to Menorca. You wouldn't believe it of judges, would you? But, oh my! You should hear them talking about it in the Sheridan Club.'

'Oh, the dear old Sheridan.' Hilda as yet knew nothing of the shock in store. 'Rumpole must get round to joining it.'

Toby started to deal out the cards and the information. 'There was a judge holding forth in the bar the other day. What do you think he was on about? Points of law? Reform of the jury system? Not at all. It was all about how he'd taken some young bopper to a discothèque and how girls prefer the older man as a partner, "in every sense of the word"! Honestly, ladies. It was quite shocking to an old gentleman like me. You probably know the Judge I'm talking about, Mrs Rumpole.'

'Oh, probably,' Hilda said casually. 'Rumpole's friends with so many judges.'

'Tall chap, always looks terribly nervous. Fotheringay, no, Feather something.' Toby was now sorting out his hand.

'Not' – Hilda was almost afraid to ask – 'Featherstone?'

'That's it! Mr Justice Featherstone. Wouldn't like to be hauled up before him, would you? Not after he's spent a hard night of hanky-panky in the discothèque. Your shout, Mrs Rumpole.'

'Guthrie Featherstone! Oh, dear.' Hilda could hardly bring herself to count her points. She was already beginning to wonder if it were not her clear duty to see that Marigold knew.

The more I thought about the defence of Detective Superintendent Roy Gannon the less I gave for our prospects. Neither the Judges nor the police were having a good time that year, and they seemed to have sunk in the public estimation to the level of traffic wardens and income tax inspectors. The Electro-Static Detective Apparatus was enjoying a period of considerable success; it had proved a number of confession statements unacceptable, and a jury would be unlikely to prefer the evidence of a senior copper out to avenge the death of one of his men to that of an independent machine.

I couldn't see any way out of this impasse and didn't do so

until I met Betty Yeomans, the murder victim's widow, which I did in an unexpected way. I was setting out to do an uninteresting robbery in Acton Crown Court and, on leaving my Chambers and walking up Middle Temple Lane, I heard someone calling, 'Mr·Rumpole!' I turned and saw a youngish, dark and fairly attractive woman leaning her head out of the window of a battered motor car of indeterminate age. 'I'm Betty Yeomans,' she said as I approached her. 'I've been meaning to have a word with you, Mr Rumpole. You going anywhere?'

I told her my destination and she said, 'Jump in the minicab. I'll give you a free ride. No problems.' I thought this remarkably kind of her, and indeed she drove me to Acton very quickly and with a good deal of expertise, but our conversation was frequently interrupted as she shouted abuse at other road users. As she kept all the windows shut after we started, the only person to be affected by these outbursts was me.

'Friend of Roy Gannon's got this mini business, so he offered me a job. Part-time. Suits me. I do the hours and I can look after the kids as well.'

'Do you want to tell me something?'

'The world's full of wankers!' she shouted suddenly. 'Have a bit of bloody courage, mate!' This was directed at a car waiting to turn into the Fleet Street traffic. 'We can't all wait while you says your prayers!' And then, in more conversational tones, 'Roy's been wonderful to me and the kids, Mr Rumpole, since we lost Ted. Come on, madam! The light's gone green. Are you colour blind or something?'

'I don't think she can hear you.'

'I know, but it makes me feel better. Just like Roy made me feel better when he got our conviction.'

'But was it the right one? Isn't that the point?'

'Do you think he lied, Mr Rumpole? Just to give me the satisfaction? He's not like that, Roy isn't. Mind yourself! What're you doing, driving on your television licence? A straight copper. Roy's not the one Ted used to talk about.'

'Ted was talking about someone?' I was becoming interested.

'Oh, I know he was only a uniformed man. Ted was never that ambitious. But his friend, the one he was at school with, he's the high-flier. Went straight in the C.I.D. and got Detective Sergeant. We used to see a lot of them though, him and Doreen. Our kids was the same age.'

'Mrs Yeomans, what are you trying to tell me?'

'Why don't you go home and take driving lessons! Sorry, Mr Rumpole.'

'That's all right. I'm getting used to it.'

'It was after Mr Pertwee got convicted. There was someone else Ted's friend was worried about, but it wasn't Roy. He always said, "Superintendent Gannon's clean as a whistle, not like some others I could mention."'

'Who said that?' My interest was increasing.

'Oh, didn't I tell you? It was Chesney, of course. Oh, get a move on! What do you think this is, a funeral procession?'

Over the sound of her furious hooting I repeated, 'Chesney?'

'Yes. We all got on so well together. Haven't seen much of them though, not since Ted went. Neither him nor Doreen Lane.'

Now I remembered. Detective Sergeant Chesney Lane was one of those present when Pinhead Morgan was supposed to have signed the dubious confession. After Mrs Yeomans had vented her wrath on a taxi driver who had apparently cut her up, I asked her to tell me more.

After my exciting ride with Betty Yeomans I met the indispensable Mr Bernard in the Acton Court. During the lunch adjournment we went round the corner for a Guinness and a slice of pie. Bernard, in his line of business, had to associate fairly closely with the Old Bill; he attended their dinner dances, bumped into them at the Rotary Club evenings and was on Christian name terms with the officers of that section which included Buttercup Meadows. Relying on his fund of knowledge, I asked him what he knew about the Pertwee business.

'Oh, dear' – my instructing solicitor looked a little shifty –

'we never got instructed in that case, otherwise you'd've had the brief, Mr Rumpole. Quite definitely.'

'What was it all about?'

'A Superintendent Pertwee. Some people wanted to get rid of him. I never discovered who, or why exactly. It started with all sorts of minor persecutions. They actually did him for speeding when he was out with his family. Then he was said to be friends with a big local villain. Finally they got Jim Pertwee on a charge of perverting the course of justice, planting dope on a suspect. Although I was never sure who did the planting. Got two years and he's still at it.'

'You interest me strangely. Now, Bonny Bernard, I have work for you.'

'You usually have, Mr Rumpole.'

'Detective Sergeant Chesney Lane. Cultivate his friendship. There might be something he'd like to tell us.'

So the industrious Bernard got to know a good deal about the life and habits of Detective Sergeant Lane. His firm had, as it so happened, helped the Lanes over a mortgage and as he knew other parents at the school the Lane children attended, he called on the Lanes one Sunday afternoon to discuss a sponsored marathon to raise money for books. He was told by Mrs Lane that her husband had taken their boys to the skateboard rink in the local park. So, as the young Lanes slid and trundled around, Bernard and Chesney Lane, in their weekend uniforms of jeans and chunky patterned sweaters, with Bernard leading his elderly spaniel, discussed my encounter with Mrs Yeomans. 'Betty doesn't want Roy to go down for this,' Bernard began. 'Ted wouldn't have wanted it either. Of course, you were pretty close to Ted, weren't you, Chesney?'

'Ted was an honest policeman. Perhaps that's why he stayed in uniform.'

'Ted would have wanted justice done.'

'What's justice when it's at home?' D. S. Lane sounded bitter.

'I mean, has Pinhead got justice? Or Betty, with no one nicked after all this time? And Roy's the only one left to take the blame.'

'I know that. I've lost sleep over it.'

'You might sleep better after you've told someone,' Bernard spoke quietly.

'Doreen doesn't think so. Doreen thinks I ought to keep my head down.'

'What do *you* think?'

For a while, Bernard told me, Chesney Lane said nothing. Then he called the protesting boys away from their skateboards as it was time to go home to tea. And he extended a welcome invitation to my solicitor. 'You want to come with us? I might have something to show you.'

As events moved towards the trial of Detective Superintendent Gannon, which was also to become, in more ways than one, the trial of Mr Justice Featherstone, a further conversation took place between the Judge and Lord Justice Parsloe in the bar of the Sheridan. It started, to the surprise of my informants, by Parsloe saying, 'Well, Guthrie. Your ears should be burning. I've been having a little chat with the Lord Chief about you.'

'Nothing about dancing, was it?' The Judge was never at a loss for something to feel guilty about.

'Well, hardly. I mean, I don't suppose the Lord Chief dances much nowadays. Do you dance, Guthrie?'

'Dance? Of course not. Well, hardly at all. Well, only when I'm particularly depressed. Which, of course, is almost never!'

'Then why are we talking about it?'

'I don't know. It's probably quite irrelevant.'

'Yes, it is. Totally irrelevant. Shall we take our drinks over to the fire, away from the audience?'

I can't even give hearsay evidence of what was then discussed but I'll lay a small bet that the Appeal Judge told Guthrie that, having made an absolute pig's breakfast of the Morgan affair, he was to have a chance of redeeming himself by conducting the trial of Detective Superintendent Gannon, who had apparently misled the court and forged a confession. To this the Judge agreed enthusiastically. Of course, he said, rotten apples must be plucked out of the police barrel and destroyed. The last words of the Lord Justice, overheard by a passing member, were, 'That's settled then. And, by the way, Guthrie. I would advise you to give up dancing. You're probably far too old for it.'

In spite of this grave warning Guthrie no doubt felt cheered by this conversation and the trust the powers that be were putting in him. However, his happiness was not long-lasting. When people talk about doing things in the 'interests of justice', I have found it usually means that the act they are about to perform will be extremely unpleasant. Hilda felt that it 'would be fair' to Marigold to tell her about the ill-fated bop and the admissions of guilt attested to by the earwigger Harringay.

As I have said, Marigold, Lady Featherstone, is a handsome and stylish woman, much given to shopping in Harrods, who has very little time for the weakness of the male sex in general and her husband in particular. Hilda told me how Marigold had passed judgment on the Judge. 'Look, you're not the greatest catch in the world, Guthrie,' she told him, 'and little Miss Whatsit is perfectly welcome to you, as far as I'm concerned. But why couldn't you keep quiet about it? How do you think I felt, having Hilda Rumpole being sorry for me in the Silver Grill? Let's face it, you've got absolutely no judgement, Guthrie. That must come as something of a drawback in your profession.'

I also gather from Hilda that the Judge asked if his wife intended to leave or forgive him. To this Marigold replied, 'I'm not going to do either. Leaving would make things far too easy for you. I'm going to stay here and *not* forgive you. Now, run along and try that bent copper and please, Guthrie, do try not to make another cock-up.'

So it was not an entirely happy Mr Justice Featherstone who took his place on the Bench as the trial of Detective Superintendent Gannon started at the Old Bailey.

Miles Crudgington, Q.C., was a tall, willowy fellow with a carefully cultivated classless accent. He specialized in civil rights cases, those involving free speech, the liberty of the subject and miscarriages of justice. As a general rule he would not have been called on to appear for the Crown, but prosecuting the police was no doubt a worthy occupation for a radical lawyer. So there was the learned Miles leading for the Queen in her suit against my unfortunate Detective Superintendent. Fairly early in the proceedings my opponent was calling D.I. Farraday, a square-shouldered, square-headed officer, who answered all questions in a voice like machine-gun fire and whose face it would be hard to imagine lit up with a smile.

'So, Superintendent Gannon was the only one writing down what Morgan was saying?'

'He was.'

'Without the help of that so-called written confession, could you remember exactly what Morgan said?'

'Not exactly.'

'Thinking back to that time, are you absolutely sure he said, "I'm sorry I cut the copper"? Are you sure he said that?'

There was a silence and then the witness's answer came rattling out, 'No, sir. I'm not sure he said that at all.'

'So' – Miles Crudgington drew the ponderous deduction – 'it appears that Detective Superintendent Gannon was writing down words that Morgan didn't say, completely ignoring that young man's human rights. Is that the situation?'

'Perhaps I could remind my learned friend' – I clambered to my feet – 'that Detective Superintendents have human rights also. And one is that hostile witnesses shouldn't be asked leading questions.'

'Mr Crudgington was just drawing the obvious conclusion.' Guthrie came to the aid of the Prosecution.

'And ignoring all other possibilities. As is the way with those who talk about human rights for a carefully selected minority.'

'My Lord, I'm quite prepared to play the game by Mr Rumpole's somewhat outdated rules.' Crudgington tried to earn Brownie points.

'Not my rules. The rules of evidence. Have they gone out of fashion among radical barristers?'

'Perhaps you should rephrase your question, Mr Crudgington.'

'No, my Lord. I'm content to leave the matter to the Jury.' And the great defender of the oppressed, no doubt having forgotten what his question was, sat down, not apparently discouraged by what I thought was a particularly shrewd attack.

'Detective Inspector Farraday, you gave evidence at the trial of Pinhead Morgan?' I said, as I rose to cross-examine.

'I did, yes.'

'At the time you had no doubt that Pinhead had said what's written in the confession?'

'I couldn't recall exactly what he said but had no reason to doubt what Mr Gannon had written.' The answer came out like automatic fire.

'And you have now?'

'Since Chief Superintendent Belmont showed us the test. He proved page two had been written later.'

'Was Mr Gannon asked to attend that demonstration?' I tried to sound as though it were a matter of casual importance.

'Not so far as I know.'

'Were you and your Sergeant being asked to gang up on Mr Gannon?'

'My Lord' – the radical Q.C. rose in his wrath – 'that's an outrageous suggestion. Chief Superintendent Belmont hasn't had a chance of answering that very serious accusation.'

'You mean, Chief Superintendent Belmont has human rights, even though he's a policeman?' I asked politely.

'He has a right to answer these charges, so I shall be calling him as a witness, my Lord.' This was excellent news as I was anxious to cross-examine the top man, so I looked worried and only reluctantly agreed to Belmont being added to the list of prosecution witnesses.

When that was settled I turned back to the D.I. with, 'Just one other matter. Pinhead had refused to talk during his first three days in custody?'

'Yes.'

'Then you saw him, without Superintendent Gannon being there?'

'Detective Sergeant Lane was present on that occasion.'

'I know he was.' And then I put the questions I owed to Mr Bernard's industry, 'Did you tell him that unless he made a confession you'd hand him over to Ted Yeomans's mates and they'd do him over in a way he wasn't likely to forget.'

There was another unusual pause, but finally the answer shot out as loudly as ever, 'No, I didn't tell him that.'

'But by a remarkable coincidence the next day he talked at length to the Superintendent, and did so the minute Mr Gannon arrived at the station.'

'Yes. But I don't think it was exactly the statement that's been produced in court.'

'Not exactly the statement produced in court.' Guthrie noted down the answer carefully and then said, 'Have you any more questions, Mr Rumpole?'

'Not at the moment, my Lord.'

'Then I shall rise for a few minutes,' the Judge told us all.

'Public business, my Lord?' I asked, because that was the excuse given for all his Lordship's absences, whether caused by the need to visit the Gents, place a bet or, on one famous occasion, to help organize industrial action by the Judiciary.*

On this occasion he said, 'No, Mr Rumpole. It's an entirely private matter,' and he went off to telephone his wife and appeal to her, once more, to forgive him.

The hard-hearted Marigold later told Hilda what her answer was. 'I'm sorry, Guthrie. You've lost your appeal.' She then put down the telephone.

The operator of the E.S.D.A. machine gave evidence as to the results of the test and now the man I had been waiting for, Chief Superintendent Belmont, stood in the witness-box and answered Miles Crudgington's questions more in sorrow than in anger. He said he had always regarded Roy Gannon as a

* See 'Rumpole and the Summer of Discontent' in *Rumpole à la Carte*, Penguin Books, 1991.

competent and honest officer until the E.S.D.A. test proved otherwise. He had arranged the test because of questions that were being asked about Morgan's competence to make a confession. He had hoped that the result would exonerate his force and was deeply disappointed when it did not do so. There was no question of 'ganging up' on Mr Gannon, but he wanted to test the recollection of the other officers without any prompting from their superior. He would be pleased to stay in the box and answer any questions Mr Rumpole might care to ask.

'You took a pile of blank confession forms out of Superintendent Gannon's office for the purpose of your test. Did you do that surreptitiously?'

'I don't think he knew about it. He was on holiday.'

'And was he on holiday when you demonstrated what you assumed to be his guilt to Inspector Farraday and Sergeant Chesney Lane?'

'I don't think so.'

'But you didn't tell him what you were doing behind his back?'

'At that stage I didn't trust Mr Gannon altogether.' The deadly answer was given with a smile to the Judge, who nodded back his total understanding of the position. I pressed on, undiscouraged, 'So what did you do?'

'I made a report about the information I'd obtained. That was communicated to the Director of Public Prosecutions and then to Mr Morgan's solicitors.'

'So he was set free by the Court of Appeal?'

'Yes.'

'And Superintendent Gannon's left to face the music?'

'If he orchestrated it, yes.'

'You had another officer, didn't you, convicted for perverting the course of justice? Superintendent Pertwee?'

'You do get the occasional rotten apple, Mr Rumpole.'

'Your particular barrel seems to be unusually full of rotten apples, doesn't it, Chief Superintendent? May I suggest where the corruption starts?'

'Where?'

'At the top. With you.'

The Chief Superintendent didn't seem in the least startled.

He went on smiling politely and said, 'That's a very interesting suggestion.'

'Mr Rumpole, I'm sure you understand you're taking a great risk in making these accusations against the Chief Superintendent.' Guthrie was affecting deep concern, as though trying to save the mad old Rumpole from committing forensic suicide.

'A risk? Oh, we all have to live dangerously from time to time, don't we, my Lord?' And I continued my attack on the charming Belmont. 'I don't know what you were up to exactly,' I told him. 'I don't suppose many of the C.I.D. officers knew either, but Superintendent Pertwee rumbled you. So he had to be persecuted, accused of associating with criminals, and then have a false charge of planting dope trumped up against him.'

'Pertwee was convicted after a trial by jury.' Belmont's voice was only a little harsher, only slightly less reasonable.

'Oh, yes, Chief Superintendent. And so was Pinhead Morgan. Did my client, Mr Gannon, come to you and say he thought Pertwee might have been framed?'

'I don't remember that.'

'And was that why you had to get rid of Gannon also? And was that why you had to make it look as though he'd forged a confession?'

'So far as I was concerned, he *had* forged a confession.'

'So far as you were concerned? It may interest the Jury to know just how far that was. Just look at that document, will you?' By now the usher had reached Chief Superintendent Belmont with my trump card and prize exhibit. He glanced at it with an apparent lack of interest. 'Is that a photostat copy of page two of Morgan's confession?' I asked.

'His alleged confession.'

'We won't argue about that for the moment. The handwriting is Mr Gannon's?'

'It would seem to be.'

'Feel it with your finger, Chief Superintendent. Look at it very closely. Has someone gone over every letter with a pencil, pressing down hard?'

Belmont went through the operation half-heartedly and then, in a silent courtroom, he said, 'I can't tell.'

'Oh, yes, you can! I suggest someone did that so the impression of the letters would appear on the blank pages under it. Then it would look to the machine as if that page had been written later. You're not suggesting that Mr Gannon manufactured this evidence against himself, are you?'

At last the witness was at a loss for words, but his Lordship asked me where the document in question had come from.

'From the Chief Superintendent's office,' I was able to tell him.

I suppose I hadn't totally obliterated the once entirely confident Belmont. He hadn't fainted, or burst into tears, or begged the Judge to release my client without a stain on his character, or confessed to perverting the course of justice. But, as cross-examinations go, I felt it rated at least nine out of ten and I went down to the cells, with the attendant Bernard, expecting a word or two of gratitude. What I got was something entirely different. I might have been an uncooperative murder suspect Gannon had to interview as he greeted me with, 'What the hell are you doing, Mr Rumpole?'

'Defending you, and rather well, though I say it myself.'

'All that you put to the Chief Superintendent. What's the public going to think?'

'What's the Jury going to think? That's what interests me.'

But Roy Gannon was thinking of wider issues, and they clearly worried him. 'If that's going on at Chief Superintendent level, who're they going to trust?'

'Come on, Mr Gannon' – I tried to bring him back to the business in hand – 'you had your suspicions about Pertwee's conviction. That was why Belmont was out to get you.'

'You can't prove that.'

'We've got a witness, Roy,' Bernard told him.

'Who?'

'Chesney Lane. We weren't certain he'd come out with it in the witness-box. They've been trying to shut him up, apparently.'

'I don't blame them,' Roy Gannon nodded, understanding his enemies. 'Let young Chesney blow the whole division, the Chief Superintendent and Geoff Farraday? That's really going to take the tin lid off it!'

'I imagine he's going to tell the truth.' I had never had a less self-interested client.

'Do you think that's going to make it any better?' The Detective Superintendent looked doubtful.

'Better for you. We might even get you off.'

'I mean, better for the police?'

It was time, I realized, to make my position clear, so I gave him half a minute of the Rumpole creed. 'Listen to me, Mr Gannon. Listen. The police, the Judges, the public interest, the interests of justice – all those big words, those big ideas – they're too much for me, altogether too much. I've got a job to do. Maybe it's a small job, but to me it seems important. I'm here to see that no one gets banged up for a crime they probably didn't do. That's quite likely to happen to you, unless you help me.'

But Gannon still looked doubtful and shook his head. 'I don't want young Chesney saying all that out in public.'

'Think about it, Roy,' Mr Bernard told him. 'You've got until tomorrow to think about it.'

The next morning Miles Crudgington was in a particularly confident mood. He no doubt thought that I'd shot my bolt with Belmont and had no evidence to support the attack. So he told the Judge that Detective Sergeant Lane could corroborate D.I. Farraday's evidence. He would therefore tender him as a witness in case Mr Rumpole had any questions.

Mr Rumpole had plenty of questions but would his client let them be asked? I turned to take instructions and saw Mr Bernard standing by the dock muttering to our client.

'Have I any questions?' I asked in a resonant whisper. To my relief it seemed that good sense and Bernard had prevailed so I turned, in the friendliest manner, towards the witness.

'Detective Sergeant Lane, since you made your original statement, have you thought further about the matter?'

'Yes, I have.'

'And now?'

'Now I want to tell the truth.' The answer riveted the attention of the Jury and took the Judge by surprise. My opponent seemed about to rise and object but then thought better of it. So I ploughed on steadily.

'When you and Detective Inspector Farraday were alone with Pinhead, did Mr Farraday say something to him?'

'He said he'd get Ted Yeomans's mate to do him over.'

'Did Mr Gannon know anything about that threat?'

'Not that I know of.'

'But the next day Pinhead Morgan made a confession to the Superintendent?'

'Yes, he did. He said, "I'm sorry I cut the copper. I was all excited, what with the car racing and that." '

'You heard Pinhead say that?'

'Yes, I did.'

'Can you tell whether he said it because D. I. Farraday had threatened him or because it was true?'

'How can he possibly answer that?' My opponent could no longer keep still.

'Thank you, Mr Crudgington. I'm grateful to my learned friend for giving the answer I wanted.' Having disposed of the interruption I turned back to the witness. 'Mr Lane, is that a photostat of page two of the confession Mr Gannon wrote out?' Once again the usher took the trump card back to the witness-box.

'Yes, it is.'

'What can you tell us about it?'

Chesney Lane picked up the page and felt it with his finger, and discovered the secret of the case like a blind man reading Braille. 'Someone's gone over every letter with a pencil pressed hard down on the paper. I imagine that was done to show indentations on the sheets under it.'

'Don't let's have what he imagines!' The radical lawyer was up again.

'I quite agree. Let's only have what he knows to be true. Where did you find that document?'

And then Detective Sergeant Lane told us. 'It was in a file I brought from Chief Superintendent Belmont's office. It looked as though someone was trying to frame Roy Gannon. So I decided to keep hold of it.'

'Thank you very much, Mr Chesney Lane.' And I was, in fact, exceedingly grateful. 'Just wait there, will you? In case my learned friend can now think of something to ask you.'

After this evidence, despite Miles Crudgington's heroic efforts to discredit another copper, the Jury's verdict was a foregone conclusion. When it had been delivered, I parted with my client, who still looked saddened by the way I'd won his case, at the Old Bailey entrance. 'It's a funny thing,' he said. 'When Pinhead was found innocent, there was cameras and crowds and cheering supporters. It's very quiet now, isn't it?'

I thought, on the whole, this was how he wanted it.

In spite of my client's doubts and reservations I had had what I thought of modestly as a bit of a triumph in court, and before I got back to my Chambers in Equity Court I was able to solve another mystery. Coming up Fleet Street I saw our new secretary, Miss Dot Clapton, coming out of the Take-a-Break sandwich bar with her lunch in a paper bag. She was clearly hungry as she withdrew a sandwich, took a furtive bite and then popped it back into the bag as she heard me call, 'Dot! Just a word, if you'd be so kind. Been buying your sandwiches, have you?'

'Is that what you wanted to ask me?'

'No, not exactly. Been dancing with any more judges lately?'

'You heard about that?' Dot smiled engagingly. 'Poor old chap, he was looking that miserable. And he danced so funny! The way my dad used to.'

'So you danced. Well, I can understand that. Even judges may feel the need to dance occasionally. But Dot –' And then I tried to frame a question as difficult as any I'd had to ask in even the most delicate case. 'You'll have to help me. After the ball was over. Was there anything? Any sort of –?'

Dot was quick to come to my assistance. 'Did we knock it off? Is that what you mean?'

'Yes. Well, it probably is.'

'Do me a favour, Mr Rumpole. You have to be joking!'

'Yes. Well, yes. I probably am.' Dot Clapton was still laughing as I left her to her sandwiches. She was, if anyone ever was, a reliable witness.

I don't often play bridge, but when I heard that Hilda was going to sit down to cards with Marigold Featherstone and a woman called Josephine Tasker, who 'couldn't count her points', I decided, in the absence of any more serious crime, to join them. I partnered Hilda and, at the end of one game, She Who Must Be Obeyed and I were six down. When She accused me of overbidding in the most ridiculous manner, I had to agree. 'I was boasting,' I told them, and when Josephine Tasker left the table to order tea, I repeated, 'Boasting. Without a word of truth. Just like poor old Guthrie.'

'Guthrie?' Marigold Featherstone pricked up her ears. 'Why do you say "like poor old Guthrie"?'

'He had no points but he bid high. He'd only gone for a drink with our clerk and the amateur actors, but he boasted of some great amorous conquest. Of course, no one could ever be foolish enough to believe him.'

'You mean, nothing happened?' Marigold seemed never to have considered the possibility.

'Nothing whatsoever. When I inquired of the young lady concerned she burst into laughter at the mere idea.'

'Laughter? I really don't see that Guthrie's as funny as all that.' Lady Featherstone looked a little miffed.

'I think what so upset Marigold, Rumpole,' Hilda explained, 'was that Guthrie should have discussed it in the Sheridan Club.'

'Yes,' Marigold agreed. 'Why on earth should he do that?'

'Don't you know?' I asked them both. 'Because the poor chap was terribly unhappy.'

'Unhappy?' Marigold was incredulous. 'What on earth's Guthrie got to be unhappy about?'

'Well, he'd been pissed on from a great height.'

'Rumpole!' Hilda warned me. 'You *are* in my bridge club!'

'Sorry, Hilda. I mean, he's had a considerable amount of dirty water thrown over him by the Court of Appeal. And then the one woman he's ever really loved was far away and he was missing her dreadfully. So he tried to cheer himself up. Perhaps he danced a step out of time to the music. Nothing more.'

'But he confessed.'

'There's no evidence more unreliable than a confession. Don't imagine people tell the truth about themselves. They'll say all sorts of things because they're afraid, or vain, or want to boast about things they never did and to impress a few chaps in the Club. Guthrie's confession would never have got past the Court of Appeal.'

'Really?' Is that what you think, quite honestly?'

'Sure of it.'

'And who's this only woman he's ever really loved, in your opinion?'

'Someone not a million miles away from this table, Marigold.'

Only one other thing. Marigold had been sleeping behind a locked door in the matrimonial bedroom while Guthrie passed unhappy nights in the spare room. After our afternoon's bridge, she later told Hilda, she at last opened the door to his Lordship's tentative knock. 'You may come in now, Guthrie,' his wife told him, 'but for heaven's sake, don't boast about it in the Sheridan Club.'

Rumpole and the Family Pride

My daily round doesn't often bring me into contact with the upper crust, those who figure in Debrett and fill the gossip columns. I don't imagine they are any more law-abiding than the rest of society, but their crimes – drug abuse for the young hopefuls and city frauds for the dads – seldom come Rumpole's way as they tend to hire the most expensive, and not necessarily the best, legal hacks available. In Froxbury Mansions the blue-blooded didn't appear, nor were they much discussed until She Who Must Be Obeyed began to take in *Coronet* magazine, a glossy publication given to chronicling the goings-on in stately homes.

We were seated at breakfast one morning and I was reading the papers in a committal I was doing in Thames Magistrates Court when Hilda suddenly said, 'How extraordinary! The ffrench-Uffingtons are together again. His romance with Lady Fiona Armstead is apparently over.'

As I could make nothing of this, I gave her even more startling news from my brief. 'Walter "The Wally" Wilkinson walked into Beddoes Road nick uninvited and confessed to the Southwark triple murder. Isn't that even more extraordinary?'

Totally uninterested in this curious event, Hilda continued to read the news from her copy of *Coronet*. 'And here's Harry ffrench-Uffington enjoying a joke with his lovely wife, Myrtle, during the Save the Starving Ball at the Dorchester Hotel.'

'A sixty-year-old man of no fixed address. The Old Bill washed him down, thanked him very much and locked him up!' I interrupted her and then let her into the past life of The Wally. 'Form: drunk in charge, numerous; theft, numerous also, fraud on the social services. Pretty down-market stuff for a triple murderer.'

'Lord Luxter's put on weight', was Hilda's news. 'Don't you remember him when he was so slim and handsome on the polo field?'

'Please, Hilda. Do you *know* any of these people?'

'You can read all about them in Debby's Diary in *Coronet* magazine.'

'*You* can read all about them. I've never heard of them.'

'Well, you should, Rumpole. Then you might learn about gracious living. You might get out of the habit of blowing on your tea to cool it down.'

'I'm in a hurry!' I explained. 'What do you expect me to do, fan it with my hat?'

'Ah. There it is!' Hilda turned a page and cried triumphantly, 'That's what I was looking for! Sackbut Castle.'

'What're you going to do with it, Hilda, now you've found it?'

'Seat of the Sackbut family since the fourteenth century,' She read out. 'Romantic setting near Welldyke on the Yorkshire Moors. The 17th Baron Sackbut occupies the private wing with his young second wife, Rosemary, née Wystan. You see, Rumpole, it's *not* all about people you've never heard of.'

'You mean this Rosemary Sackbut, whatever?'

'Née W*ystan*, Rumpole!'

'It doesn't ring a bell,' I had to confess.

'Oh, really. What's my name, Rumpole?'

'She Who Must – I mean Hilda,' I corrected myself hastily.

'Hilda *what*?'

'Hilda Rumpole, of course.' During the above exchange I was darting into the hall and back to the kitchen and collecting the hat and mac while polishing off the remnants of my breakfast.

'Oh, well done!' She congratulated me ironically. 'Now, then. Hilda Rumpole, née *what*?'

'Oh, I see! Née Wystan!'

'Uncle Freddie's son was Hungerford Wystan, who went into Assorted Chemicals, and Rosemary's his youngest. She's my first cousin once removed,' Hilda explained.

'Once removed to a castle?'

'So that's why I take in *Coronet*. I knew Rosemary'd turn up in it sooner or later.'

'Section 62 committal,' I muttered as I packed the brief away in my bag. 'We'll try and get The Wally's conviction chucked out in the Magistrates Court.'

'Oh, Rumpole!' Hilda was looking at me with disapproval. 'I bet you that no one at Sackbut Castle eats breakfast with his hat on. No wonder they didn't ask us to the wedding.'

I duly arrived at Thames Magistrates Court, where I found that my opponent was Mizz Liz Probert, radical member of our Chambers, who was looking far from happy. 'You're not going to object to being sent for trial, are you?' she more or less snapped at me.

'Ask not what I am going to do, Mizz Liz. Watch me in Court. If I'm on my feet I'm probably being objectionable.'

'I shall be led by Sam Ballard at the trial,' she warned me.

'If he's prosecuting, there must be some hope for the defence.'

'Oh, please, don't try to be funny, Rumpole. Quite honestly, I just don't feel like it today.'

So I left her and went to ask a police officer if my client had arrived. I was surprised to find that he was delighted to have The Wally Wilkinson on the premises. 'You mean our triple, Mr Rumpole? We're all feeling just that little bit chuffed about having his case. It's not every day you get a triple murderer walk in with his hands up. Your solicitor's there already. Know your way down, sir, do you?'

I knew my way down and found my client and Mr Bernard in a police cell. The Wally Wilkinson was a small, chirpy man with wispy hair and an unreliable look in his eyes. Despite his age, he seemed wiry and energetic. The prison officer ushered me in, saying, 'Your brief's arrived, Walter. Got all you want, have you?' There was an unexpected note of obsequious respect in the official voice which The Wally, who was smoking a fag and holding a mug, seemed to think was no more than his due. '*This* tea?' he said. 'I wouldn't call it tea. Pour it back in the horse.'

'We're just putting on another brew. Want a couple of biscuits with that, do you, Walter?'

'I wouldn't say no.'

'I see you're all right for smokes.' The prison officer seemed relieved.

'Mr Bernard obliged,' The Wally told him. 'Oh, by the way, Perce, anything in the paper about my case, is there?'

'Just general background. The house. Victims. All that. Today's court'll be in the *Standard*.'

'Save us one, would you?'

'No probs.'

'You seem to be getting the four-star treatment,' I said when the turnkey had left us.

'Well, I'm on a triple, aren't I, Mr Rumpole?' The Wally looked modestly pleased. 'Something out of the ordinary, a very serious crime indeed. Naturally they respects you for it.'

The very serious crime occurred on the night of 12 February in a done-up Victorian house near Southwark Cathedral. It was shared by a merchant banker and his friend, who was also something in the City. The third, and younger, victim was a social worker named Gerald Vulmay, who was apparently a guest staying the night.

'That Gerald,' The Wally told us, 'he was the one who let me into the house.'

'You were on your way home' – I consulted The Wally's proof of evidence – 'and you asked him for money and told him you couldn't find a place to sleep, all the hostel beds were taken because of the cold weather.'

'Even the warm spots over the hotel kitchens. Round the Savoy and the Regent Palace. They were all booked up. So he just looked at me and said, 'All right. There's a spare bed in here. I'm sure they'll let you stay.'

'Did you meet all three of them?' I asked.

'Oh yes. They give me a meal, after they'd run a hot bath

for me. Kitted me out in a pair of pyjamas. Some sort of Greek stuff, they was eating. I had to pretend I liked it.'

'Then what happened? Can you remember?'

'That's the terrible thing, Mr Rumpole. It's like my mind went a total blank on the subject. They put words into my mouth, like, when I made the confession.'

'All right. Do you remember walking into the Beddoes Road nick?'

'Sort of.'

'What made you do that?'

'I dunno, Mr Rumpole.' The Wally looked vague.

'Did they say you could see a lawyer?'

'No, they never. And them two officers what interviewed me, they were very aggressive.'

The prison officer returned with refreshments and said, 'There you are, Walter. Bit of a better brew. And a few ginger nuts. We'll save you that *Evening Standard*.'

'Thanks, Perce. I call that very kind.' And as he drank his tea, The Wally smiled at me. 'I tell you, Mr Rumpole. This beats sleeping in a cardboard box any day of the week.'

I fought that committal for three days in the Magistrates Court and did my best to exclude the confession. I knew it was a hopeless case, and after The Wally, who didn't seem particularly disappointed, was sent for trial, I came out of court to find Liz Probert sitting on a bench in the entrance hall looking more disconsolate than ever. I tried to cheer her up by saying, 'You won the day. Next step the Old Bailey. I wonder if we can find twelve sleepers in cardboard boxes to sit on the Jury. By the way, have you seen young David Inchcape lately? We're co-defending in an affray.'

'No, I *haven't* seen "young Inchcape", as you call him. You'd better find him for yourself.'

'Mizz Probert. Liz. What on earth's the matter?'

'Absolutely nothing's the matter!'

'You don't usually burst into tears when you win cases.' I could see, with embarrassment, distinct signs of the waterworks.

'I'm not bursting into tears at all. Why should you assume

that I've burst into tears, just because I'm a woman?' she sniffed unhappily. 'It must be my contact lenses.'

'Someone in Chambers upset your contact lenses?' And then I hazarded a guess. 'Anything wrong between you and young Inchcape?'

'Isn't that you all over, Rumpole? It's just stereotypical male vanity! I'm a woman, so if I'm upset it must be about a man. Men are the only things women have got to be upset about, aren't they?' She searched in vain for a tissue in her handbag and I offered her a stereotypical male handkerchief.

'No, thanks. Oh, all right, it *is* about bloody Dave Inchcape.'

'I'm sorry. What's he done?'

'It's not what he's done. It's what he *is*! What he's been in secret all these years. And he's never had the guts to tell me about it.'

'Secretly married?' I wondered.

'I could cope with that. No. It's something ... Well, it's really unmentionable. Ugh!' she shuddered. 'Awful. He's not worth worrying about.'

Naturally I was eager to hear more, but an officer came up to tell me that my wife was on the phone and I could take it in the police room. When I heard her news, told in a voice of almost uncontainable excitement, I didn't know if I could take it. The distant cousin, Rosemary, it seemed had come through at last. We were invited for a weekend at the castle by Lord and Lady Sackbut. When I came out of the police room I saw my red and white spotted handkerchief on the bench and Liz gone. I left Thames Court and, out in the street, a press photographer snapped me just as I was blowing my nose.

Sackbut Castle, near the small town of Welldyke, was built to defend a large area of North Yorkshire. It had been besieged three times during the Wars of the Roses. Other great historical events had taken place there, but when Richard, the 17th Baron, brought home his young second wife, it was a peaceful enough place. And so it remained until shortly before the

Rumpole visit when Jonathan Sackbut, thirteen years old and on holiday from Eton, was taking Monty the family Labrador for an early run by the lake. On approaching the water the dog barked and then stood on the edge, whining. When the Hon. Jonathan joined the Labrador he saw, indeed they must have both seen, the body of an elderly woman face-down in the water. She was wearing a drenched, rabbity fur-coat and the big, plastic shopping bag she still clutched was floating like water-wings. It became clear, when she was fished out, that she was some kind of a bag lady, a female tramp. Photographs taken later showed a large, broad-cheeked face which might once have been pretty.

The boy ran home to tell his father and stepmother, for Jonathan was the son of Lord Sackbut by his first and divorced wife. In due course, the police, the ambulance, the pathologist, Dr Matthew Malkin, and Lord Sackbut himself, gathered by the lake. They were joined by Dr Hugo Swabey, the local coroner, and Mr Tonks, the coroner's officer. Swabey, as I got to know him, was a self-important and officious man in his sixties, dressed as though anxious to give the impression that he was a local squire or country landowner, although his clothes were far too new for the role. Tonks, the officer who accompanied him, was a stout and elderly ex-policeman with a Yorkshire accent and a perpetual, inappropriate smile. The coroner welcomed the pathologist, told the police he wanted the deceased's personal effects sent over to his office as soon as possible, and spoke with careful politeness to the castle owner. 'Good morning, my Lord. I thought it right to get my inquiries going as soon as possible. I must ask you, have you seen the body?'

'Yes, of course,' Richard Sackbut told him. 'My boy found it.'

'Can you help us, then. Anyone you can recognize?'

'No. No, of course not,' Lord Sackbut told him. 'No one I've ever set eyes on.' And with this he got into his Range Rover and drove back to the castle.

For our weekend visit, Hilda seemed to have packed a

wardrobe that would have seen us through a long summer holiday. Our taxi from the station dropped us outside the main entrance at the West Gate. As I staggered in with our suitcases, the attendant told us to leave our luggage with him and said, 'The rest of you've gone up. Hurry along.' So we climbed the wide stone staircase and found ourselves in a great hall with narrow windows, bare of furniture except for suits of armour and brutal-looking weapons arranged in great circles on the walls. In the distance we saw a group of people and a man in a dark suit who was signalling to us and calling out, 'Over here, my party!'

'Why does he call it "his" party, Rumpole?' Hilda was puzzled, and I let her wonder on as the man showed us the view from a window. 'From here you get a good view of the East Tower. See that narrow window up at the top there? That's what they called My Lady's Boudoir. Little room where they say the 7th Baron Sackbut locked up his lady wife on account as she'd got overly familiar with the steward. Not a very comfortable boudoir, by all accounts.'

'Is the family about?' Hilda cut him short by asking.

'Lord and Lady Sackbut are in residence,' he told her. 'Yes. They occupy the East Wing, which was built as a family mansion in the year 1792. We will now go down to the moat and the formal gardens. Come along, my party.' But Hilda had seen a door beside which a notice read PRIVATE APART-MENTS. NO ADMISSION. 'In here, Rumpole!' She gave the order as she led the way through it.

'Madam!' the tour guide said, 'that's not open to the public.'

'We are *not* the public,' Hilda said as she swept out of view. I followed murmuring an apologetic 'She Who Must . . .' to the outraged guide.

Through the magic doorway we found ourselves in a long passage which led to the open door of a drawing-room. When we reached it, we found it comfortably furnished, with chairs and sofas, a big fireplace and family pictures on the walls, a line of Sackbut faces, predominantly male. High windows opened on to the terrace of the castle. Sitting in a window-seat a pale boy was alone, reading a book. He looked up and peered through his glasses as Hilda approached.

'We are the Rumpoles. We have been invited for the weekend,' said Hilda.

The boy stared at Hilda silently.

'Is your mother . . . I mean, is Rosemary?'

'They're not back yet, I'm afraid. There's only me.'

'Oh, well. I'm Hilda Rumpole. This is my husband,' said Hilda. Jonathan put down his book carefully, having turned down the page, and advanced on Rumpole with his hand stretched out. 'Good afternoon, sir. I'm Jonathan Sackbut.'

'Horace Rumpole.' We shook hands.

'I'm Rosemary's cousin, you know.' Hilda made her position clear.

'Once removed,' I added.

'Really, Rumpole, don't let's go into all that.' At this moment, a young woman came in and called from the doorway, 'Auntie Hilda!' She had a rather solemn, sad face and floating brown hair. Her youth made her attractive; in middle age her looks might harden. She talked in a brisk manner with the brightness of youth.

'Oh, Rosemary, there you are at last!' Hilda was relieved.

'I'm sorry. Richard's driving the lorry back from Welldyke Show. I took the car. I was terrified of keeping you waiting.' And Rosemary told me, 'You must be Uncle Horace.'

'I've got no alternative.'

'Jonathan,' Rosemary spoke to the boy for the first time, 'I hope you've been entertaining the Rumpoles.'

'Not really.' He picked up his book and went out on to the terrace. Rosemary looked after him. Theirs, I thought, was not an easy relationship – stepmothers have a difficult time.

'Let's see if we can rustle up some tea.' Rosemary pushed a bell near the fireplace. 'Richard was so disappointed you couldn't come to the wedding.'

'Were we asked?' I wondered.

'Of course! Well, I'm sure you were. We sent out so many invitations . . . Perhaps you were away?'

'We're hardly ever away. Are we, Rumpole?'

'Oh, hardly ever,' I confirmed Hilda's evidence.

'You know, Rosemary dear, it was so funny when we arrived. They treated us like members of the public! Wasn't it funny, Rumpole?'

'Oh, hilarious,' I agreed.

'You *would* like a cup of tea, wouldn't you, Uncle Horace?' Rosemary was clearly trying to make up for the absence of a wedding invitation.

'Well, if you have got anything in the nature of a bottle of red. Nothing of any particular distinction. Peasants' claret would be perfectly acceptable.'

'Rumpole!' She Who Must Be Obeyed was not pleased.

'No, Auntie Hilda. Let Uncle Horace have what he wants. We're going to spoil him. Do sit down, Uncle Horace. You must be exhausted after all those absolutely splendid court cases you do.' Rosemary put her hand on my arm and guided me to a chair.

'Splendid cases?' And Hilda said, with some contempt, 'Like Walter The Wally Wilkinson!' But Rosemary continued to look at me with admiration. 'My dad,' she said, 'saw you in action in some case at the Old Bailey. He said you were absolutely super! Had the Jury eating out of your hand. I remember what he told us: "In the courtroom nobody dares say boo to Rumpole."'

'Well,' I told her modestly, 'I can be rather magnificent at times.'

'And didn't you do one hugely famous case? Oh, yonks and yonks ago. Something about a bungalow?'

'You might possibly be thinking of the Penge Bungalow Murders.'

'That's right! I say, you *must* tell us all about it. It sounds riveting. I know Richard can't wait to meet you.'

A melancholy-looking manservant did bring us tea, and I had a bottle of Château Château, but Rosemary's husband had not returned by the time we went upstairs to change. 'Of course,' Hilda had told me, 'they'll dress for dinner at the castle.' So she had brought a long ball gown, and encased in a heavy silver breastplate she looked armoured and ready to take on allcomers. I managed to button up a dinner jacket which seemed to have shrunk over the years as Hilda told me that Rosemary had said that old Lord 'Plunger' Plumstead was expected for dinner.

'Why Plunger. Does he dive?'

'He used to gamble terribly. Really, Rumpole, you ought to keep up with Debby's Diary.'

So we went down to our first castle dinner and found that all our guests and the Sackbuts had this in common – none of them were in evening-dress. The men were without ties, in sweaters, or tweed jackets worn with cord trousers. Plunger Plumstead, whose head was sunk, like that of an aged tortoise, into a collar several sizes too large for him, sported an ancient black velvet jacket and a silk scarf. The women were dressed casually, but no one commented on what now seemed our eccentric attire. Richard Sackbut had finally appeared and turned out to be a man, perhaps in his late forties, whose long chin, gingery hair and blue eyes were echoed in all the family portraits we had seen. For some reason, which I could not fathom, he seemed extremely glad to see me and kept saying it was 'jolly sporting of you to come all the way to North Yorkshire for a weekend'. This was an opinion with which I had to agree as I looked round the dinner table that night.

There was Plunger's wife, Mercia, a stately woman who looked embalmed and, so far as I can remember, never spoke. There was a young couple called the Yarrowbys, Tarquin and Helen, who talked in very loud voices about people I didn't know, and sports and pastimes of which I had no experience. Pippa and Gavin Bastion were older, I suppose in their early fifties, and more sophisticated. Gavin made cynical remarks in quiet, amused tones and Pippa, a collapsing beauty, drank a good deal and smoked between courses.

Towards the end of dinner they began to discuss Dr Hugh Swabey, the local coroner. He clearly wasn't a favourite with the upper crust. 'Of course, he's enjoying every minute of your business, Richard,' Gavin Bastion said. 'Best thing that's happened to him since he had coach lamps put round his poolside area.'

'Where's all the money come from?' Helen Yarrowby asked.

'Expensive nose jobs in Leeds, and other sorts of jobs, no doubt,' Pippa Bastion suggested.

'You've seen him out hunting, haven't you, Plunger?' Helen asked the Lord, who turned to me and said, 'Absolutely everything wrong about the chap, Rumbold. He comes out like a dog's dinner.'

'That should give him a deep understanding of foxes,' I said, but nobody laughed.

'Don't expect Swabey's ever got near enough to see a fox. He comes out with a string on his top hat!' Pippa said it as though the unfortunate coroner had committed rape on the hunting field.

'And a red coat when no one's asked him to wear such a thing,' Gavin added to the indictment.

'No, darling. That's not the point. The point is, a red coat with *flat buttons*.' And Pippa turned to Hilda for support. 'Imagine that, Mrs Rumpole!'

'Oh, dear. Of course. Flat buttons! How very extra-ordinary.' My wife did her best to sound appalled, while I asked in all innocence, 'You mean you'd prefer them *round*?'

'Flat, shiny buttons without a hunt crest on them,' Gavin explained. 'Means he just got the thing off the peg at Moss Bros.'

'Is that a serious offence?'

'I suppose it depends on what you think is serious in this world.' Plunger looked as though I were prepared to excuse any crime, however heinous.

'Oh, I'm only used to murder and robbery,' I told him. 'Suchlike trivialities. I'd never heard of the crime of *flat buttons* before.'

There was a silence then, broken by Richard Sackbut. 'We had rather a nasty accident here, Rumpole. Some old tramp woman managed to drown herself in the castle lake.'

'Is Swabey going to be a pain in the neck about it, Richard?' Gavin Bastion asked.

'Oh, you know what he is. He wants to get his name in the papers, make a sensational trial of it. He thinks he's going to discover all sorts of things that aren't there to be discovered. It's just a bore, quite honestly.'

'Well, I don't see that you're responsible for anything,' Plunger assured our host. 'Most people have got a *lake* of some sort, haven't they, Rumbold?'

'Well, we have to make do with rather a small one, in the Gloucester Road.' This was another joke which went down like a lead balloon, but Rosemary came to my rescue. 'Talking of sensational trials, darling, Uncle Horace was telling me about that one he did yonks ago. In a bungalow, wasn't it, Uncle Horace?'

Then I lent back and prepared to enjoy myself for the first time since we arrived in the castle. 'It was an extraordinary case. I was a young man then, a white wig really, and I won it alone and without a leader. It raised some most interesting questions about bruising and the time of death. I mean, it should be relatively simple to discover if a bruise were pre- or post-mortem, of course. A careless pathologist could cause bruising when removing the tongue during an autopsy. That's what happened in the Penge Bungalow Murders.' There was a somewhat embarrassed pause, and I felt that neither my jokes nor my tales from the morgue were greatly appreciated. Pippa said, 'Where is Penge, actually?'

'Isn't it somewhere near Bognor?' Tarquin Yarrowby guessed. But Richard gave a signal to his wife at the other end of the table, at which she rose, saying, 'Oh, yes. Well. Shall we leave the men to their . . .'

'Post-mortems, apparently,' Gavin finished her sentence for her gloomily.

After the ladies had left us the masculine conversation flowed like cement. Nobody told improper jokes, and, after a while, Plunger Plumstead, who had been staring at me balefully, growled, 'I say, Rumbold. Can you get your gamekeepers to eat rook?'

'Well, now you mention it. I've never really tried.'

'When I was a boy, gamekeepers pretty well lived on rook. Their wives used to make it up into pies. You won't find a woman who'll do that now.'

'Tell the truth, I don't have any gamekeepers – or rooks either, come to that.'

'Odd! I thought you said you had a place in Gloucester.'

I was saved further embarrassment as Richard moved from his place at the head of the table to sit next to me. Then, as Gavin Bastion started a long story about some local adultery, our host said, confidentially, 'Mr Rumpole, Rosemary was telling me you've had a great deal of success in your cases.'

'I suppose I have acquired a certain reputation round the Brixton cells,' I told him. 'I never knew I was famous in castles.'

'And a good many of your cases,' he went on, 'have concerned, well, dead people.'

'Dead people? Yes. I've always found, contrary to popular belief, that they can tell you a lot.'

'I wonder if you'd have time for a bit of a chat tomorrow?' he asked tentatively.

'I'm yours for the weekend.'

'You're still available for business?'

'Always. Always available.'

'Good! That's very good.' He seemed relieved and, for the first time, I saw him smile. 'Well, now. Shall we join the ladies?'

'Why not? Let's join them' – I tried a final joke – 'and make one huge, enormous lady!' Lord Sackbut was still smiling politely, but he didn't laugh. He was a man, I was later to discover, who sometimes missed the point.

As I was tearing off the stiff collar in a large and drafty bedroom, I told Hilda that I need never have gone through that blunt execution. 'I thought they were slackly dressed for a castle,' she said. 'Never mind. *We* looked smart, Rumpole.'

'We wore the wrong things, but they never referred to it. You noticed that? They never said a word.'

'It was sweet of them to ask us, wasn't it?'

'Why do you suppose they did?'

'Well, we're family, aren't we?'

'Not because we're family and not even because they never asked us to the wedding. My Lord Richard Sackbut's in trouble, Hilda. At least he's got that in common with Walter The Wally Wilkinson. He needs a good brief.'

The next morning there didn't seem to be very much to do but look around the house. At the end of the row of family portraits I saw a man who looked so like our host that he could only have been Richard's father, a long-chinned, blue-eyed, gingery-haired man in army uniform. Under the picture the legend was CAPTAIN THE LORD SACKBUT M.P., D.S.O. BORN 1912, DIED 1972. By the drawing-room fireplace Rosemary was taking Hilda through a number of volumes of family photographs leading up to an extensive record of the wedding which we had unfortunately missed. As I couldn't gasp at the length of the bride's train, or the good looks of the bridegroom, I returned down the passage to the part of the castle thrown open to the public, with whom I had decided to mingle.

I had hardly entered the Great Hall, or heard much of the guide's monologue, when a man in assertive tweeds emerged from the *hoi polloi*, and introduced himself as Dr Hugo Swabey. 'We met briefly, Mr Rumpole,' he said, 'when you came up to Leeds on that stabbing in the Old People's Home.'

'Of course. And you gave some rather novel evidence on the direction of knife wounds.'

'Well, thank you, thank you very much.' I hadn't meant it as a compliment, and, in fact, Swabey's evidence was generally ignored. 'One is sometimes able to throw a new light in dark corners, you know, given a sound medical knowledge and the sort of mind that asks the occasional awkward question. I suppose that's why they landed me with the coroner's job.'

'I hear you're enjoying it.'

'Yes, well ... Seeing the sights of North Yorkshire, are you?'

'No, as a matter of fact. We're guests of the Sackbuts.'

'You're privileged! I've never been invited on to the other side of that door, into the Holy of Holies, strange as it may seem. Though I go out with the hunt and I'm pretty well known in the neighbourhood. His Lordship invited you, did he?'

'Oh I think it was his wife.'

'It must have been his Lordship. Women don't make many decisions in the Sackbut clan. Come to think of it, it may have been rather an intelligent move with the inquest coming up.'

'I heard about that. Some poor old lady tumbled into the lake, one of the homeless.'

'Homeless? Is that what she was? Or was she looking for a home? My officer's downstairs now, taking statements. Who was she, when was she killed, how did she die? These are the questions my court will have to answer. Meanwhile, I thought I'd just wander around and soak up the castle atmosphere. All these suits of armour, for instance, maximum protection and nothing much inside them. Typical Sackbut.'

'Have you come to see my client?' I asked him.

'Oh, is his Lordship that already?' Dr Swabey seemed delighted. 'That *will* be fun. I think we'll be able to offer you a few surprises.'

'Good! I shall look forward to it,' I promised.

'I hope his Lordship will too. Just one thing you might be asking your client to explain, among others.'

'What's that?'

'I had the dead woman's possessions sent over to my office. The police like to hang on to their things, but I insisted. Well, she had a big plastic bag, full of old clothes and rotting food and a gin bottle, almost empty. But there was a sort of plastic purse, pretty well waterproof. You might be interested in its contents.'

'Might I?'

'There was a return coach ticket to Victoria, so she wasn't a local tramp, nothing like that. But more interestingly, a photograph, taken on the terrace of this castle. An old photograph. Shows a woman holding a baby and a man in uniform. No doubt who the man was. Absolutely no mistaking the family features. It was Lord Sackbut's father. Now how do you imagine a homeless old bag lady got hold of that, Mr Rumpole?' There was, I thought, a certain amount of triumph in his voice as he asked me the question.

'I really have no idea.'

'I wonder if your client has. I'm telling you all this for your assistance, of course.' As he said it, I thought that the Welldyke coroner had absolutely no intention of helping Lord Sackbut who had never invited him beyond the door marked PRIVATE.

'I'm very grateful.'

Dr Swabey was looking down to the far end of the Great Hall where the conducted tour was filing out under the command of their guide. 'I mustn't miss my chance of another look around the grounds – and the lake!'

That morning I also inspected the lake. I took a turn round the gardens and then found my host in the stables, talking to a girl in jodhpurs about the lameness of one of the horses, whose solemn faces, peering over their stable doors, put me in mind of the portraits of the Sackbut family. At my request he drove me down to the lake in his Range Rover, and took me to the spot where the drowned bag lady had been pulled out of the water. It had been a wet summer in North Yorkshire, and there were plenty of tyre marks on the grass path. Richard told me he drove past there often, on his way to a field where he had horses out.

So I looked down to the weedy, muddy water from the top of a steep, slippery bank, and at the odd branches and tree stumps on the way down. I stooped to look at a branch, freshly broken, and then I told my client that I'd met the local coroner, who didn't seem to like his Lordship very much.

'The feeling's mutual.'

It was a heavy day, with a low sky which seemed darker than the bright fields and green trees. There were insects buzzing and a party of ducks on the lake floated lethargically as though half asleep. I looked at my client and wondered what secrets he was keeping from me. 'What on earth are you worrying about?' I asked him.

'What do you mean?'

'Why call on the expert services of Rumpole of the Bailey, who has studied causes of death by cross-examining the great

Professor Andrew Ackerman, King of the Morgues. An old
bag lady slipped and drowned herself in your grounds. Sad
but hardly a threat to your peace of mind, I might have
thought.'

'We're open to the public,' he tried to explain, 'I mean,
they might say we're not safe . . .'

'Nonsense! You're not responsible for tramps in the night-
time. What's the real problem? And what's making the Grand
Inquisitor of Welldyke so excited?'

'Perhaps . . .' But if he were about to tell me something, he
changed his mind. 'It's entirely a family matter. We'd better
be getting back.'

'Tell me,' I asked him again. 'I'm used to hearing about
family matters. Murder's a family matter, nine times out of
ten.'

'Murder?' He seemed surprised. 'Who said anything about
murder?'

'Nothing yet. But dear old Dr Swabey looks as though he's
longing to come out with it.'

I didn't get any more from my client, and he drove me back to
the castle, promising a treat for the afternoon: a dog show,
bowling for a pig, a tombola and other delights in the castle
grounds. It sounded like a fête worse than death, a comment I
kept to myself.

When I entered the drawing-room, in search of She Who
Must Be Obeyed, I thought, at first, that the room was empty.
Then I heard a boy's voice, only just audible, repeating words
which were well known to me. Jonathan was alone, sitting on
his window-seat with a book, but he wasn't reading, he was
reciting, only occasionally reminding himself of the lines:

> 'So through the darkness and the cold we flew,
> And not a voice was idle; with the din,
> Meanwhile, the precipices rang aloud;
> The leafless trees and every icy crag
> Tinkled like iron; while the distant hills
> Into the tumult sent an alien sound . . .'

Jonathan continued to recite quietly, and I joined in with:

> 'Of melancholy not unnoticed, while the stars
> Eastward were sparkling clear, and in the west
> The orange sky of evening died away . . .'

The boy closed the book as soon as he heard my voice, and now he looked embarrassed.

'You like that?' I asked him.

'Well, yes. The sound of it,' he admitted reluctantly.

'So do I. I like the sound of it very much.' I went to sit at the fireside, in front of a big coffee table piled with the family photograph albums Hilda and Rosemary had been looking at. I began to turn the pages idly. 'You live here with your father in the holidays?' I asked.

'With father, yes.'

'See much of your mother, do you?'

'Not really.'

'Why's that?'

Perhaps he wouldn't have answered my question if we hadn't recited Wordsworth together, but he said, 'I went once or twice. Now it seems easier if I don't go. I didn't enjoy it much, really.'

Then there was a silence while I turned more pages of the albums. 'Fascinating,' I said at last, 'these old family photographs.' I found a page with Jonathan, aged about five, sitting on a Shetland pony. 'Is that you when you were really small and insignificant?'

He got up and stood beside me. 'That's me on Mouse.'

'Any pictures of your mother?'

'No, I don't think so.'

But perhaps there had been; there were blank spaces and small traces of paper having been torn out. 'Shall we take a dive back into history?' I found a volume dated 1940–50 and, after turning a number of pages, I found snaps of the man who looked so like Richard. 'That's your grandfather. I recognize him from his portrait.'

'Everyone says he looks just like my father,' Jonathan said. 'I don't seem to look like them at all.'

'Don't apologize. Here's Grandad on a horse, and playing tennis, and opening something and, oh, in uniform. That must have been in the last war. Is there anything like a wedding photograph?' There wasn't. What I found were the same blank spaces, the same traces of pictures torn out, the signs of a memory someone wanted to obliterate. 'Isn't that rather odd?' I asked Jonathan. 'Your grandmother doesn't seem to be here either.'

The sky remained dark, but the rain held off that afternoon. The castle walls were illuminated by a low shaft of sunlight directed from under gun-metal clouds. The stalls and tents were set out on a patch of grass under the East Tower. Hilda had gone off to buy what seemed, when I had to carry them back to London, a huge selection of jams, and I was chatting to Rosemary, who was in charge of an old clothes-stall which was being eagerly searched by the mothers and wives of the village. 'Got anything suitable for wearing in a cardboard box?' I asked her.

'You going to take up residence, Uncle Horace?' Rosemary asked.

'I've got a client who may have to go back to one. That is, if I manage to spring him from the nick. I had an interesting talk to Jonathan. He doesn't see much of his mother, does he?'

'Quite honestly, Richard thinks it best not. She made this ghastly second marriage.'

'To somebody ghastly?'

'To a chap who sold her a car. They live in Pinner or somewhere quite impossible. Can you imagine that after Richard and the castle?'

And then the loudspeakers announced that the contest for the dog who looked most like its owner was about to start. Hilda came hurrying up, saying we mustn't miss this extraordinary entertainment, and as we hurried towards the judging ring, she said, 'Just look at the castle, towering over us. Doesn't it make you feel we've been in the Middle Ages?'

'Lucky for you, we're not.'

'It must have been so romantic.'

'Not that I'd ever have locked you up in the East Tower, Hilda. I'd never have dreamt of doing anything like that, not being a Lord.'

'Oh, really, Rumpole! I hope you weren't talking that sort of nonsense to Rosemary!'

'Not quite. We were talking about Richard's first wife. Not that it could have been her, of course – she's much too young. Besides which, she's alive and wed and living in Pinner . . .' I was following a private train of thought and Hilda had stopped listening for we had arrived at the dog ring, where owners were assembling with their four-footed look-alikes. There was a fat woman with a Pekinese, a hatchet-faced man with a lurcher, and a man who had taken off his shirt and was holding his grey, long-haired Yorkshire terrier against the grey hairs on his chest. Richard stood proudly beside Monty, the Labrador, and old Plunger Plumstead was there with an ancient, watery-eyed and evil-looking bull-terrier to whom he might have been closely related. Hilda had wandered off to talk to the Yarrowbys, whom she had greeted as life-long friends, and I stood alone, watching, as Pippa Bastion, the judge, announced that the first prize went to Plunger's dog.

The prize was presented by the coroner, who stood, in another suit of brilliant checks, at the judge's table. When he had been rewarded I went up to congratulate Plunger.

'Oh, Bo'sun and I win it every year. God knows what I'm going to do when the filthy dog snuffs it. Bottle of Cherry Bounce, presented by Dr Swabey. Revolting! Can't drink the stuff.'

I told him I had spotted a beer tent where we might find something more acceptable. 'Oh, very good,' he said. 'Good idea of yours, Rumbold. You have these sort of do's in your part of Gloucester?'

When we were in the tent, coping with large plastic tumblers full of North Yorkshire bitter, I said, 'Perhaps dogs grow to look like their masters in the way that men grow up to be reproductions of their dads.'

'Reproductions? Oh, Richard certainly is. Spitting image of old Robert. Fine man, Robert. Had a bloody good war. Peace didn't treat him quite so kindly. Came back home. Found all sorts of things wrong. Lot of pheasant covers cut. Rooks out of control. Labour Government. Something seriously dicky about the roof. Things not so marvellous on the domestic front either, not too long afterward his wife bolted off.'

'Did you know Richard's mother?'

'Depends what you mean by *know*. Not in the biblical sense, old chap!' He laughed, gulped his beer and went on. 'So I was probably in a minority. But she always seemed a perfectly nice woman to me. A bit affected. I remember she always called Richard, Riccardo, with a sort of funny Italian accent. Or was it Riccardino? Of course he hated it.'

'What was her name?'

'Margaret. Maggie was what we called her.'

'And what happened to her in the end?'

'In the end? Oh, in the end she died.'

That evening we were only four at dinner but, with due formality, Hilda and Rosemary left us men to our port and I began to ask Richard about his childhood. It was then he told me something that had occurred at his prep school, a story I shall never forget. 'I suppose I was about nine,' he said. 'Just nine. And the message came: "The Headmaster wants to see you in his study after prayers." Well, you know what that meant. You got that awful sort of feeling in the pit of your stomach and sweaty hands. All the usual symptoms of terror, I suppose. Anyway, I knocked on the study door and there he was. Snowy Slocombe. A hard man. But just. Perfectly just. I've got no complaints about that. Big tall fellow with snow-white hair. And he told me to close the door and come up to the desk and then he said, "Sackbut, I know you're going to take this like a man." And then, of course, I thought I knew exactly what I was in for. But he said, "I've just had your father on the telephone, Sackbut. And he's asked me to let you know. I'm afraid your mother's dead." And do you know what I felt, Rumpole? I felt a kind of enormous relief, because he wasn't going to beat me.'

We were silent for a little, then I asked, 'Did your father tell you how she died?'

'Not really. When I came home for the holidays he said, "I suppose Slocombe gave you the message." And I told him, "Yes." I don't think we discussed it much after that.'

'Do you know how? Or where?'

'I heard vaguely. I think she left home after I'd gone back to school. She must have died soon after that, I suppose. Abroad somewhere. I've an idea it might have been Italy. France or Italy . . .'

'But didn't you make . . . any sort of inquiries?' I found it hard to believe.

'No.' He sounded quite matter of fact.

'Why not?'

'I don't think my father would have wanted me to.'

'You believed your father?'

'Of course.'

'On so little evidence?'

'I wouldn't have doubted him.'

'Do you have any idea,' I asked, 'how old she'd be now? If she'd lived, I mean.'

'I suppose late sixties.'

'It never occurred to you that she might try to get in touch with you?'

'You mean, come back from the dead?' He was smiling.

'Yes. Something like that, I suppose.'

Our new friends, the Sackbuts, invited us to the Opera, where the Bastions had taken a box. Not to be caught out a second time I arrived in a blazer and grey flannels to find the rest of the party in evening-dress. 'They're so secretive,' She complained to me in the interval. 'They never let you know what they're going to wear.' But Richard did give me some interesting information over the champagne and sandwiches. After telling me that the fellow on the stage looked a great deal too fat to be accepted into the Egyptian Army, he said, 'I say, Rumpole. I think I've got a young relative in your Chambers. David Luxter. His grandfather was Lord Chancellor and his father's my cousin.'

'You mean the present Lord Luxter?' Hilda has Debrett ever at her fingertips.

'No' – I had to disappoint Hilda – 'I'm afraid we've got no Luxter in our stable.'

'Oh, he did an odd thing,' Richard told us. 'Didn't want to rely on his family name, can't think why. So the Luxter boy went into the law under an alias. He found a name in some poem or other, Harry Luxter told me, something about a bell and a rock: "The vessel strikes with a shivering shock," I told him. "Oh Christ! it is the Inchcape Rock!" Not a great poet, Southey, but I suppose young David found him useful.'

'That's the name! Inchcape!'

'Born the son of a Lord?' And I thought I knew the reason for Mizz Probert's sorrow. I wondered if she would ever forgive him.

When the Opera was over, Hilda woke me with a sharp nudge and we set off to walk down to the Savoy, where the Sackbuts were standing us dinner. We took a short cut down the narrow street behind the Strand Palace Hotel and there men and women, young and old, were settling down for the night as near as possible to the grilles where a certain amount of hot air came streaming up from the hotel's kitchen. As our rather grand procession swept by, a voice called my name from a doorway and I turned to see a small dosser, with a bobble hat pulled down over his eyes, holding out a tattered copy of the *Evening Standard* which had formed part of his bedding. 'Mr Rumpole! I recognize you, sir.' He handed up the snap of me blowing my nose. 'I see your picture in this old paper. As you was defending Walter The Wally in the big murder case. I have got some info for you on that one, sir.' As I loitered to speak further to the man, I heard Richard say, 'What's happened to your husband?'

'I'm afraid he's met a friend,' Hilda told him, so they walked on, sure I suppose, that I'd catch them up. I didn't do so immediately as I wanted to hear the story old Arnie, as he'd introduced himself, had to tell. He would not speak of it, however, until I'd bought him a cup of tea and a couple of ham rolls in a rather affected caff, dressed up as a Parisian bar in the 1890s, in the Covent Garden Piazza. Those patrons sitting down wind of Arnie moved to other tables as he munched contentedly.

'I was with The Wally that night, Mr Rumpole,' he told me. 'We was all down under Hungerford Bridge. And he got into a bit of an argument, like, with Bronco Billington. Always a bit of a pain up the bum, Bronco, in a manner of speaking. Nick! Never seen anything like it. Well. He had Wally's drop of gin and his pie off him and a punch-up started. And a bit of manual strangulation. Wally's strong, like, when he's roused up and he left Bronco flattened. So we went off sharpish round Centrepoint, where there was still spaces. And next day we read in the papers about the triple murder. But The Wally was with me, all that night. Straight up, he was. Only thing, he reckoned he'd done in poor old Bronco, who was never in good health at the best of times. Cough his bloody guts out soon as you touch him.'

'And had he done in Bronco?'

'Bless you, no. Bronco was in the Cut, Waterloo, Thursday midnight. Singing his head off on a bottle of meths. I'd've told The Wally, only I didn't know where they got him banged up. You'll be seeing him, will you?'

'Not just yet,' I told him. 'I'm defending a Lord.'

'Oh, wonderful, Mr Rumpole. Going up in the world, are we? You couldn't spare . . .'

Of course I could. I handed him a couple of crisp tenners and told him not to waste it all on tea. Then I wondered if I could recover my outlay from the legal aid fund.

As the inquest drew near, I began to make my preparations. Cursitor & Carlill of Welldyke were the family solicitors, and I saw the prim and elderly Mr Cursitor at my Chambers on one of his visits to London. I suggested that he must have been sure that Richard's mother had died, because if she were alive she might have had some claim against the estate on his father's death.

'Not really, Mr Rumpole.' Mr Cursitor actually put the tips of his fingers together when he spoke, something he must have seen family solicitors doing in old movies. 'Richard's father had started divorce proceedings before his wife left England. She never appeared again and the case went through undefended. She was no longer married to the late Lord Sackbut, so she would have had no claim.'

'Did Richard know that?'

'I don't think we ever discussed it with him. I'm sure his father didn't.'

'And who was the man she ran off with?'

'An Italian prisoner-of-war. I believe she'd met him when he was working on one of the farms. I suppose she misconducted herself and joined him somewhere in Italy. She left no address.'

Before I parted from Mr Cursitor, I gave him a number of jobs to do and asked him to put an advertisement in the *Daily Telegraph* personal column. It was a long shot, a very long shot indeed, but then I had very little ammunition.

For someone who has had, in the course of a long life, a great deal to do with sudden and violent death, I have only rarely appeared in Coroners Courts. The proceedings are directed by the coroner, who calls for witnesses and asks the questions. The legal hack is usually limited to putting a few supplementaries. The Welldyke Court was a dark and stately Victorian affair, set in a crumbling municipal building. For the inquest on the unknown bag lady, the place was packed with friends of the Sackbuts and, I suppose, some enemies, interested members of the press and some who found an inquest a welcome addition to the pleasures of a holiday in North Yorkshire. There was a jury of local men and women, a shorthand writer and Mr Tonks, the coroner's officer, acting as the court usher. Dr Swabey sat, his face and glasses shining, thoroughly enjoying putting the grey-haired pathologist through his paces.

'Dr Malkin,' he said in his most patronizing manner, 'please use layman's language. Not all of us understand the complexities of forensic medicine.'

'Including you, old darling,' I whispered to no one in particular, but the coroner apparently heard me. 'May I remind everyone in court,' he pontificated, 'this is a solemn proceeding. Mine is the ancient office of *custos placitorum*, the Keeper of the Decisions. We have the solemn duty, you and I, Members of the Jury, to inquire into the mysteries of death. I hope we may do so without interruption.'

'Just as soon as *you* stop interrupting.' I tried another whisper which the coroner wisely ignored and asked Malkin to continue his evidence. 'She was a woman in her late sixties or early seventies, in poor general health. I came to the conclusion that death was probably caused by a blow to the head with some blunt instrument before the body entered the water. I didn't think it was a case of death by drowning because there was no water in the lungs.'

'Might death have been caused by a deliberate attack?' Swabey asked eagerly. 'A blow to the head by some assailant?'

'I thought it might.' As the pathologist said this, there was a buzz of interest in court, but I sat expressionless.

'Struck *before* the body was put into the lake?' Swabey asked.

'Yes.'

'Which would make this an unlawful killing. Or, to use a word with which the Jury might be more familiar, murder.' The coroner was delighted to say this for the first time in the proceedings.

'I couldn't rule out that possibility. No.'

'Mr Rumpole. Do you wish to apply to ask the pathologist a question?' Swabey asked with a cheerless smile in my direction.

'Yes.' I rose purposefully to my hind legs. 'A good many questions.'

'Then I shall grant your application.'

'Very generous, sir. Dr Malkin. In a case of drowning it's possible for death to occur immediately, due to a sudden cardiac arrest. Is that not so? It's happened in the case of sailors falling off ships, for instance.'

'It *has* happened.'

'And in such a case, there might be no water in the lungs.'

'There *might* not be.'

'Such deaths have often occurred with drunken sailors. They fall off the deck and alcohol produces a state of hypersensitivity to sudden and unexpected contact with water.'

'It may do so.' The pathologist was reluctant to admit it.

'Dr Malkin. You have read the great Professor Ackerman's work *The Causes of Death*, I'm sure?'

'Of course I've read it!' Dr Malkin was running out of patience before I ran out of questions.

'Professor who, Mr Rumpole?' The coroner was foolish enough to ask.

'Ackerman, sir. Required reading, I should have thought, for any Keeper of the Decisions.' After that enjoyable interruption, I returned to Dr Malkin and the business in hand. 'The Professor quotes many such cases.'

'I believe he does.'

'And we know that this old lady had an almost empty gin bottle in her possession. You found a high level of alcohol in her blood, didn't you?'

'Fairly high.'

'Fairly high. So it remains a possibility, does it not, that this unfortunate lady met her death by drowning?'

There was a long pause before Dr Malkin, with the utmost reluctance said, 'It's a possibility. Yes.'

'Dealing with the blow to the head. This was a particularly steep bit of bank, was it not?'

'It was fairly steep.'

'With a number of branches and tree stumps. On some of which traces of blood were found.'

'Yes.'

'Can you rule out the possibility that this old lady, having drunk rather more gin than was good for her, slipped and fell into the lake, striking her head on one of those tree stumps as she fell?'

'I can't rule that out altogether.' Clearly Dr Malkin hated to have to say it. Murder was a far more exciting alternative.

'Thank you, Doctor. It seems we may have reached a sensible interpretation of the facts and one that should be obvious even to those who haven't read Professor Ackerman's great work.' As I sat down I looked meaningfully at Swabey, but he was busy trying to repair the damage I had done to his witness.

'Dr Malkin,' he said, 'we gather from your evidence that this blow to the head might have been accidental, or it might have been deliberate. Is that right?'

'Quite right, sir.'

'You, of course, didn't go into the circumstances in which someone might have had a motive for causing the death of this old lady.'

'No,' Malkin started, but it was time for Rumpole to rise in, at least well-simulated, fury. 'I object to that question. How can Dr Malkin possibly answer it?'

'He can't, Mr Rumpole.' Swabey again smiled unconvincingly. 'That will be the subject of the next part of my investigation. I know you will wish to help me with it. Thank you, Dr Malkin. We would now like to ask Mr Saggers a few questions.'

Mr Saggers turned out to be the attendant at the West Gate who took charge of our luggage when we first visited the castle. He was a solid Yorkshireman, clearly reliable, and turned out to be a devastating witness. As soon as he was in the box and sworn in, Tonks, the coroner's officer, showed him the mortuary photograph of the dead bag lady, and, in particular, a close-up of her large, but possibly once pretty, face.

'Mr Saggers,' the coroner said, 'can you recognize the lady in that photograph?'

'The Lady in the Lake,' I whispered, and Swabey again made a public pronouncement. 'For those of us unused to courtroom practice, I should say that silence is kept while a witness is giving evidence.'

'Wonder who his grandmother is?' I asked Cursitor. 'And can she suck eggs?' But now Saggers was telling a story I had to listen to. 'It was the day before they found her,' he said. 'She came up to the castle entrance and wanted to go in. She wasn't with any of the groups that'd paid already, so I asked her for two pounds. She said she hadn't got it, but she wanted to see his Lordship. I told her that wouldn't be possible. I didn't think she was anyone he'd want to see. So, well, she sort of wandered off.'

'What time was that?' Swabey asked.

'Just before four, because I was going off for my tea-break. Then, as I was passing the formal gardens, you know, where the long border, the white border they call it, runs down to the statue? Well, I saw them there.'

'You saw who, Mr Saggers?'

'The old lady. And his Lordship.'

I whispered to his Lordship, urgently taking instructions, but Richard shook his head and firmly denied the suggestion. This added considerably to my worries.

'What were they doing?' Swabey asked.

'Just talking together. I saw them and then I went on for my tea.'

'Have you any questions, Mr Rumpole?' The coroner was looking more cheerful than I felt as I rose to do my best with Saggers.

'Before you went on for your tea, how long did you see these two together?'

'Perhaps half a minute. I didn't stop to look at them.'

'And how far away were they down at the end of the border? Fifty yards?'

'About that.'

'It was afternoon. Was the sun behind them?'

'I think it was. Mind you, I'd seen the woman close to, at the gate.'

'So you said. But you couldn't see Lord Sackbut's face clearly in the garden?'

'I made sure it was his Lordship.'

'How was he dressed?'

'A tweed cap, and his jersey and cord trousers. Like he does. He'd been doing something with the horses.'

'He was dressed like many other men who might have been about the garden and the statues that day, Mr Saggers. When you say you *think* it was his Lordship, will you accept the possibility that you might have been mistaken?' I did my best, as you can see, but it didn't get very far. Saggers, the reliable witness, answered, 'I know what I saw, Mr Rumpole. To be quite honest with you I got no doubt about it.'

When we were getting ready for bed in the castle, I told Hilda my worries. 'Richard's going to tell a lie! He spoke to the old lady and now he's going to deny it.'

'Oh, Richard wouldn't do a thing like that.' She was sure of it.

'Why not? Because he's a Lord? Because he lives in a castle? I tell you, Hilda. People have been lying here since the Wars of the Roses. Lying and locking up their wives or tearing their wives' photographs out of family albums. Behaving like that' – and, as I said it, I felt I had reached close to the heart of the case – 'because their fathers did it.'

The next day Lord Sackbut went into the witness-box at the coroner's request and Dr Swabey examined him in the manner of one who'd never been invited into the private apartments and wasn't going to let his Lordship forget it. To the thousand-dollar question Richard answered, 'The first time I saw the old lady was when her body was found in our lake. I had never set eyes on her before that.'

'My Lord. I remember you told me that at the time, and no doubt others heard you. But you have heard Mr Saggers's evidence. Is he lying?'

'I'm not saying that. I'm saying Mr Saggers is mistaken. I didn't speak to the old lady that afternoon.'

'Very well, the Jury will have to make up their minds who's telling the truth.' Swabey gave the Jury a trusting look and then turned to another subject. 'Lord Sackbut, when you were a boy, your mother left your father.'

'I fail to see what that's got to do with this case.'

'Bear with me, my Lord. I think it may have a great deal to do with it. At that time, did your father tell you that your mother was dead?'

'She was dead, yes.'

'But how did you know that?'

'Because my father said so.' Richard was clearly keeping his temper with difficulty. 'He told my school.'

'And you believed him?'

'Of course.'

'Did it ever occur to you that your father was so angry with your mother that he pretended she had died. He didn't want you to try to see her again?'

'It never occurred to me that my father would tell a lie, Dr Swabey. To me or anyone.'

'Do you not know that there have been many rumours, in your family and in the town, that your mother didn't die as your father said but was alive many years later and living in Italy?'

'I never heard such rumours. Anyway, they would have been untrue.'

'This is becoming intolerable.' I gave another exhibition of the Rumpole wrath. 'Lord Sackbut's here to give evidence, not to deal with tittle-tattle.'

'Please, Mr Rumpole, don't excite yourself. You have reached an age when that might be injurious to your health. Mr Tonks, the photograph, please. Now, I pass to another matter.' Tonks was handing the photograph of Richard's father in uniform, sitting on the castle terrace with a woman and a baby. As Richard looked at it, Swabey went purring on, 'We have heard evidence that that photograph was found in the old lady's possession. Let's look at it, shall we? Is that the terrace of Sackbut Castle?'

'Yes.'

'And is the man in it your father, as he was at the end of the last war?'

'It is my father, yes.'

'Oh, I am so very much obliged. Now there is also a woman with a baby. Is that woman your mother?'

'I . . . really can't say,' Richard hesitated.

'You mean you can't remember what your own mother looked like?' Swabey spoke more in sorrow than in anger, but the Jury looked at Richard with distinct disapproval.

'Not altogether clearly.'

'I suggest to you that it is a family group. Your father, your mother and yourself as a very young child.'

'I suppose that's a possibility,' the witness had to admit.

'Or a probability? Now. Can you tell the Jury why this old lady had that photograph in her possession when she came visiting Sackbut Castle?'

'How on earth can my client know that?' I was up and fuming again.

'Then let me suggest an answer to assist Lord Sackbut.' And Swabey made a suggestion which was no help at all to Richard. 'Could it be because she *was* the lady your father, in a fit of wounded pride, had given out as dead?'

'I object to that!' I fumed on. 'Is this an inquest or a lesson in writing pulp fiction? There is not a scrap of evidence . . .'

'Oh, yes, there is, Mr Rumpole. There is a photograph. Now, you shall have your opportunity to ask questions later. Let me just put this final point to you, my Lord.' So I sat down reluctantly and the coroner concluded. 'If this old lady was the Dowager Lady Sackbut, fallen on evil days, she'd hardly be a welcome visitor at the castle, would she? After all that time she'd come, no doubt, with a claim for money. Didn't it occur to you, my Lord, that she might be better dead, as your father had wished, so many, many years ago?'

His Lordship rejected the suggestion entirely and I took him through it all again and he denied it again. But during the rest of the day I had the strong feeling that the Jury didn't like Lord Sackbut, the man who couldn't remember what his mother looked like. In the middle of the afternoon, however, Mr Cursitor, who had been out of court, came back and whispered in my ear. He had a piece of news that gave us a hope of restoring the Sackbut name, and putting Dr Swabey in his place for ever. As soon as I heard it, I asked Swabey to adjourn the case until the next morning. He was about to make some trouble over this, until I reminded him that there was a writ of *mandamus* almost as old as Coroners Courts, by which I could haul him up to the Lord Chief Justice. I might even have been right about the law; anyway we took an early bath and returned the next morning to further good news from Mr Cursitor. I thought it right to keep the latest developments from the Sackbut family and, when we were back in court, I passed a note of my further application up to the coroner.

'Mr Rumpole,' he said in his most official voice, 'you've asked me to take the evidence of this witness. Mrs . . .'

'Petronelli, sir.'

'Mrs Petronelli. And I have no idea what light she can throw on this dark subject.'

'Then let me help you out. She's here now, sir. Let her come in and be sworn.'

The door of the courtroom opened and Mr Cursitor appeared. Standing aside, he let in a woman, dressed in black. She must have been almost seventy but she was still elegant, smiling, with fair hair touched with grey. Mr Tonks led her to the witness-box, where she took the oath quietly. I started my questions before the coroner quite understood what was happening.

'What was your name, Madam?' I asked, 'before you married Signor Petronelli?'

'It was Lady Sackbut.'

'And your son is?'

She looked at my client for the first time and said, 'Richard.' He had lowered his eyes and sat with his arms folded.

'Mr Rumpole, do I understand that this lady is your client's . . .?'

'His mother, sir.'

'I still don't know what evidence she can give.'

'Then perhaps it would be better if I carried on. I think the story will become quite clear to everyone.'

'Very well, Mr Rumpole. Carry on for the moment. If you please.' The coroner was suffering from a sudden lack of energy as he saw his carefully built-up case of doubt and suspicion collapsing.

'It's many years since you saw your son?' I asked the witness.

'I'm afraid it's a great many years.'

'When Signor Petronelli was alive, I think you lived in Como?'

'Yes. My husband had a hotel there. When he died I decided to sell it and come back to England.'

'To where in England?'

'To London. I live in Southwark.' Then I summoned Tonks, who took the witness the photograph of the dead bag lady.

'Look at that photograph, will you? Since you have lived there, have you become interested in a charity dealing with homeless people?'

'There seem to be so many sleeping in the street in London. We give them meals. Try to find them beds. Even invite them home sometimes.' She looked at the photograph of the dead woman. 'That's Bertha.'

'Bertha?'

'When I first met her she was sleeping at the back of Waterloo station. I let her stay with me one night, when we couldn't find her a bed anywhere else. We began to talk. She told me about her husband, who'd been a builder and gone bankrupt and been sent to prison for some reason. And, I don't know why, I told her about Sackbut Castle and my son. I never talked much about it to anyone else. But with Bertha it seemed it wouldn't matter.'

'So she stayed the night in your house. Did she leave the next morning?'

'Yes. I never saw her again.'

'Was anything missing when she left?'

'Well, yes. A photograph I'd shown her when we were talking. I kept it in a desk. Not on display or anything. And when Bertha went, that went with her. I was very angry with her for stealing it.'

Tonks handed the witness another photograph, the group on the castle terrace.

'Is that the photograph you lost?'

'Yes, it is.'

'Who are the people in that group?'

'My first husband, myself and Richard when he was a baby.'

'One final question. Did your son Richard ever hit you over the head with a blunt instrument and push you into a lake?'

'No. No, he never did that to me. Even if he thought I deserved it.' And now the witness was looking at her son, half smiling. He looked up at her.

After that, even Dr Swabey, for all his ingenuity, couldn't think of much to ask Signora Petronelli. The inquest was virtually over and the verdict inevitable. As soon as it was given, the court rose, the room emptied and Lord Sackbut

was left alone in it with the woman who had been dead to him
so long. I knew we should get away early and we had packed
our bags and taken them to the court. Mr Cursitor's clerk
found us a taxi and we drove straight to the station.

'"The Jury in the Sackbut Castle Inquest returned a verdict
of accidental death", blah, blah.' We were at breakfast again
in the kitchen at home and I was reading *The Times* and
Hilda had her *Daily Telegraph*.

'Rumpole,' she sounded worried, 'you said Richard was
lying in Court.'

'Oh, yes. Bertha waylaid him in the garden. Told him she
had some news for him. Probably asked for money. He sent
her away and wouldn't listen. She hung around Welldyke
until the evening and then went back to the castle, full of gin
and unsteady on her pins. It really was an accident. I don't
know, Hilda. Perhaps he had a secret fear that Bertha *was* his
mother. He hadn't seen the real one for thirty years. But
recognizing his mother would mean his father was a liar, the
father who could do no wrong. So he pretended that he didn't
have the faintest idea who she was.'

'That wasn't very nice of him.'

'People aren't always nice, especially if they're Lords. Luckily his real mother reads the *Daily Telegraph*.'

'Why luckily?'

'Oh, didn't I tell you? I got old Mr Dry-as-Dust Cursitor
to put an advertisement in the personal column: RICCARDINO
WANTS TO SEE HIS MOTHER. VERY URGENT. PHONE THE
SOLICITORS. And the Sackbuts read *The Times*.'

The phone on the wall was ringing. I went to answer it as
Hilda was saying, 'Poor woman. Poor, poor woman.'

The call was from Mizz Liz Probert. She was off to court
early and wanted to let me know that the Prosecution was
offering no evidence against Walter The Wally Wilkinson.
The man who really did it, apparently, was the social worker's
lover and he had made a confession and there was enough
forensic evidence to make it stick. Apparently they were all in
a rather complicated emotional situation. That seemed a

considerable understatement to me. Before she rang off I offered to buy Mizz Liz a drink in Pommeroy's that evening.

When I returned to my cooling tea and toast, I told Hilda another tale of social distinctions. 'You know why The Wally confessed to that triple murder?' I said. 'Snobbery, Hilda. Pure snobbery. He thought he'd done in an old dosser called Bronco Billington but he didn't want to be potted for anything so down-market. So he put his hands up to a smart triple murder. That way he'd join the upper crust in chokey and be treated like a Lord by all the screws.'

'Rumpole,' She said thoughtfully, 'I don't think we'll go to Sackbut Castle again.'

'I don't think we'll be asked,' I told her.

That evening, at a corner table in Pommeroy's, and over a couple of glasses of Château Fleet Street, I broached a delicate subject with Mizz Probert. 'Liz, I wanted to tell you that I know all about the Honourable David Luxter, otherwise known as Inchcape.'

'The Hon. David!' Liz spat out the title. 'It's disgusting.'

'Instead of a decent upbringing in a one-parent family in Camden, he was cursed with ex-Lord Chancellor Luxter as a grandad. He was a deprived child.'

'A *what*?' Liz sounded puzzled.

'They all are, Mizz Liz. The lot of them. The Lords and Ladies and Marquises of whatnot that figure in Debby's Diary in *Coronet* magazine. They turn their sons out of the home at a tender age. They put them into the care of some sort of young offenders' secure home like Eton. They lie to them and tell them that their mothers are dead. The dice are loaded against the young of the upper crust.'

Then we drank in silence. When she had thought it over, Liz said, 'I suppose they are.'

'What Dave needs is counselling. He needs a supportive figure in a secure one-on-one situation. He needs the confidence-building skills that you alone can bring him.'

'Does he? I suppose he has been discriminated against, really . . .'

'One of society's outcasts, I'd say.'

'I shouldn't have withdrawn my support.'

'Replace it, Liz! Prop the poor fellow up.'

She took another gulp of the Ordinary red and came to a sensible conclusion. 'It's a bloody unjust world, Rumpole,' she said.

'You've been all these years in the law, Liz. And you've only just found that out?'

Rumpole and the Soothsayer

However forward-looking we may all pretend to be, humanity is far more interested in its past than the future. Tell a man like Claude Erskine-Brown that the planet earth will be burnt to a cinder around a hundred years after his death and his eyes will glaze over and he'll change the subject to his past triumphs in motoring cases at Acton. Tell him that Mizz Liz Probert, our young radical lawyer, was seen in Pommeroy's Wine Bar a month ago holding hands with someone other than Dave Inchcape, her regular co-habitee, and the fellow will prick up his ears, his nostrils will flare and he will show an endless appetite for further and better particulars. Down at the Bailey we spend days and weeks delving into the past, trying to discover exactly who it was who was seen loitering outside the Eldorado Building Society in Surbiton on the day the Molloys did it over, or what precise form of words Tony Timson used in the police car to indicate he was prepared to accept responsibility for the Streatham Video Centre break-in. But when it comes to the future it's usually dismissed in a brief sentence like, 'You will go to prison for five years.' By and large, as I say, the future is a closed book which few people care to open. The exception to this rule was a client of mine, a somewhat odd bird called Roderick Arengo-Smythe, whose eyes were firmly fixed on the time ahead. The future was a subject on which he claimed to have a good deal of inside information, derived from his acquaintances among dead people.

Arengo-Smythe didn't burst into my life in the way some clients do, as the result of a robbery or sudden death. His approach was more circumspect, as, I suppose, might be expected of a man who spent such a lot of time whispering to the defunct. I got my first whiff of Arengo-Smythe in an oblique manner when I went into the clerk's room and discovered Soapy Sam Ballard, Q.C., the man who, by the workings of blind fate, became the Head of our Chambers, cancelling the arrangements for some much-needed repairs and refurbishments to our downstairs loo set for 14 December of that year.

'We've had all this trouble arranging the builders, sir. Why does it have to be put off?' Henry, our clerk, protested.

Considering the downstairs loo now resembles nothing so much as the black hole of Calcutta in a poor state of repair, I supported Henry's objection, 'Why not get on with it?'

'Not' – Soapy Sam Ballard was adamant – 'on the 14th of December. I can't take the responsibility for that.'

'What on earth's wrong with the 14th of December? Is it the Ides of March or something?'

'Many a true word, Rumpole, is spoken in jest.'

'Please, Ballard. Don't babble. Just give us some idea of what you're talking about.'

'No time to explain. I've got a V.A.T. fraud starting before Mr Justice Graves. 'And,' he added darkly as he departed, 'Why don't you ask your wife?'

After the fleeting thought, by no means new, that our Head of Chambers no longer had control of his marbles, I forgot our strange conversation. That evening Hilda and I sat on either side of the glowing gas-fire in Gloucester Road. I was defending Ronnie 'Rabbits' Timson at the time (so called because of his vegetarian diet and his addiction to green salad) on matters arising out of the affray in the Needle Arms, Stockwell. We were half-way through the trial; I had got a number of witnesses to contradict themselves on the question of identity and earned a few good laughs at the expense of the police officers' notebooks. Should I rest my case, or should I put Rabbits into the witness-box the next day to deny the charges?

'What's the matter, Rumpole? Wool-gathering?' She Who Must Be Obeyed demanded my attention.

'No. No, of course not. The problem is, if I call Rabbits Timson to give evidence tomorrow he'll probably convict himself out of his own mouth, and if I don't the Jury'll think he's guilty anyway.'

'Don't you know what sort of a witness the Rabbits person is going to make?'

'Not exactly. I can't see into the future.'

'Well then, you should ring Marguerite Ballard.'

'Mrs Soapy Sam' – the Head of our Chambers has taken it into his head to marry the ex-Matron down at the Bailey – 'has she got some sort of crystal ball?'

'Not that. She's got a little man who can tell her about the future.' She said it as though Mrs Ballard had rather a clever dressmaker round the corner. 'He's a fellow called Arengo-Smythe. It seems she goes to him for readings.'

'The works of Dickens?'

'No. The future. And she's taken Sam to him once or twice.'

'Why? Is Ballard particularly interested in the future?'

'Of course. Since old Tubby Mathias dropped off the twig' – Hilda always called Her Majesty's judges by their more or less affectionate nicknames – 'Sam's been hoping for a job on the High Court Bench.'

'So he's been going to a soothsayer to discover if the Lord Chancellor's going to reward his complete lack of forensic skill with a scarlet and ermine dressing-gown?'

'Something like that.' Hilda looked disapproving, as well she might.

'And does Arengo-Smythe tell him when he's going to get his bottom on the High Court Bench?'

'Marguerite didn't tell me that. But she did tell me that Sam was terribly worried about something else he said.'

'What was that?'

'That there was a great black cloud over the 14th of December.'

And, as she said that, a small part of the future jigsaw fell into place.

*

One of the best-known facts about the world is that it is exceedingly small. So it came as no particular surprise to me to be told by Henry that my old friend Mr Bernard, the faithful solicitor who goes out into the highways and byways and brings me back criminal work to enrich our lives in Gloucester Road, was coming with a new client, a certain Roderick Arengo-Smythe, who was about to face trial at the Old Bailey. So I was to be privileged to meet Sam Ballard's soothsayer.

Arengo-Smythe turned out to be a large man, but his bulk, as he sat in my client's chair, was curiously ill-defined and he seemed blurred at the edges. He looked ageless and his plump features were drained of colour, as if he had already, as Hilda would say, dropped off the twig. His hands were large, damp and looked soft, as though his fingers were made of putty. He spoke in a high, piercing North Country accent, as though he were playing the Dame in a principal pantomime, standing with his hands clasped over his stomach and calling, 'Where's that naughty boy Aladdin now?' This was the customer to whom it was my clear duty to put the indictment. When he had heard the charge against him, his voice rose to a raucous protest.

'Fraud and false deception, Mr Rumpole. Do you honestly think my spirit people would descend to that?'

'Well. Some of them might, I suppose. I mean, they're not all saints, are they? There must be quite a few villains among dead people. Con men, forgers, three-card tricksters. There's no reason to suppose that they're not all kicking about the other side, as you call it.'

'They may be there, Mr Rumpole. But White Owl would spot them a mile away. He can separate the wheat from the chaff can White Owl. He would never allow three-card tricksters in my front room.'

'Even dead ones?'

'Particularly dead ones.'

'Just remind me . . .' I searched through the open brief on my desk. 'Who is White Owl?'

'An ancient chief of the Sioux Indians, Mr Rumpole.' Mr

Bernard, my instructing solicitor, was used to repeating impossible defences in a dead-pan manner. 'He copped it, apparently, at the battle of Little Big Horn.'

'Not copped it, Mr Bernard, if you don't mind. The spirit people do not cop it. They pass over.'

'What is alleged is a perfectly simple con trick.' I brought the meeting back to reality. 'You charged your customers no less than £50 a session.'

'Summoning up the spirit people can be very draining.'

'You persuaded the punters that they were hearing the voice of this fellow White Fowl.'

'White Owl, please, Mr Rumpole. The Sioux people are extremely sensitive.'

'I beg his pardon. White Owl, you said, could foretell the future?'

'All the spirit people can, Mr Rumpole. You'll be able to as well, when you've passed over.'

'Really? I can't wait. It's further suggested' – I refreshed my memory from the Prosecution statements – 'that Woman Police Constable Battley, who attended a seance, pretending to be a member of the public . . .'

'I could tell her sort at once, Mr Rumpole. Blood red, that was the colour of her aura.'

'All the same you took her fifty quid and allowed her a punt at the passed over. White Owl apparently came through, after a good deal of delay.'

'White Owl can be a naughty boy on occasions, Mr Rumpole. He doesn't always want to come when he's sent for.'

'Later she left the room under the protest of needing the lavatory.'

'Lying bitch! You'll trip her up on that one, won't you? When it comes to my day in court?'

'She went into the door of the next room and discovered your sister Harriet crouched over a microphone.'

'Harriet's hobby is electricity, Mr Rumpole. It always has been, ever since we were nippers together.'

'The W.P.C. immediately summoned the help of Detective

Sergeant Webster, who was waiting outside the front door, armed with a search-warrant. On entering your flat he found the microphone connected to a small and unobtrusive speaker taped under the table where your seance was going on.'

'Are they suggesting that my sister and I were cheating, Mr Rumpole? Be quiet now, White Owl.' He said this to some unseen presence, apparently hovering near his left shoulder, and flapped at it with a large, white hand in the manner of a man trying to deter a mosquito. 'Don't interrupt when I'm trying to talk to Mr Rumpole. White Owl is getting a bit aerated, sir. He feels this case is a personal insult to him, quite honestly.'

'Don't worry about White Owl. He's safely outside the jurisdiction. It's you, Mr Arengo-Smith, they might put in the slammer.'

'Arengo-*Smythe*.' My client looked pained.

'Whichever. Was your sister Harriet connected to your living-room?'

'Yes, of course. She rigged that up so we could chat when we were working in different rooms. We're working on a history of the occult. We carry on a great tradition, Mr Rumpole, which goes back to Merlin, and he was By Appointment at the Court of King Arthur.'

'A fellow who ended up entangled in a thorn bush, from what I can remember. Well now, what's your defence, Mr Arengo-Smythe?'

Understandably my client was at a loss for an answer. Then he said, 'You know Mr Samuel Ballard, don't you? He will vouch for me.'

'That may not, of itself, be enough to establish your innocence.' And then I looked at him, filled with curiosity. 'What exactly did you tell my not-so-learned Head of Chambers?'

'I told him what White Owl had seen when he came for a sitting with his wife.'

'And what was that?'

'A terrible black cloud hanging over the 14th of December.

A day of extraordinary danger. What will you be doing on that precise date yourself, Mr Rumpole?'

'Defending you down the Old Bailey!' I tried to say it as cheerfully as possible. 'By the way, when you're next chatting to White Owl, ask him to have a few words with the late Sir Edward Marshall-Hall. It will need a brilliant stroke of advocacy to save you, old darling.'

As I walked down Fleet Street to Ludgate Circus to start, with no especial enthusiasm or hope of success, the case of *R. v. Arengo-Smythe*, I happened to catch up with Soapy Sam on his way to one of the lengthy tax prosecutions in which he is used to lulling the Jury to sleep. I hailed the man and told him I was defending his soothsayer.

'I know you are, Rumpole. I recommended you to him. By the way, I was very impressed by Arengo-Smythe and so was Marguerite. He seemed to have an uncanny power of seeing into the future. You'll get him off, won't you?'

'Perhaps. If the Judge and the Jury have all passed over. He gets on extremely well with the dead.'

Ballard digested this and then asked what I thought was a somewhat naïve question.

'He's not bent, is he?'

'Of course not. Straight as a corkscrew. Oh, I forgot. He no doubt brought you tidings of great joy about your future as Mr Justice Ballard, the terror of the Queen's Bench.'

'He told me something in confidence, Rumpole. That was why I didn't think it would be proper to act for him myself. I told him that, for some reason, you had a remarkable record in securing acquittals.'

'Didn't he also tell you to beware the 14th of December?'

'He did say he saw a black cloud hanging over that date, yes. That's why I thought it unwise to get the workmen into Chambers.'

'Particularly as we've got a remarkably superstitious downstairs loo.'

When I was robed and wigged and ready for the fray, I glanced at the date on the Old Bailey notice-board announcing our case as that day's attraction. It was 13 December and it was set down for two days.

Our Trial Judge was Mr Justice Teasdale: a small, highly opinionated and usually bumptious person who was unmarried, lived in Surbiton with a Persian cat, and had once achieved the considerable feat of standing as a Conservative candidate for Weston-super-Mare North and losing. The trial, turning as it did on matters arcane and communication with the dead, seemed to affect his nerves. He looked jumpy and seemed anxious to find a simple, scientific explanation for Arengo-Smythe's alleged gift of second-sight.

His Lordship was therefore greatly relieved at the police evidence, and the description of the wire which stretched from a microphone in one room to the little speaker taped under the table next door. Sister Harriet, who was found with this device, had conveniently taken refuge in a complete nervous breakdown before the trial and a doctor had certified that she was quite unfit to give evidence for either the defence or the prosecution. However, the W.P.C. told us what she had seen and Detective Sergeant Webster produced the mechanism, a microphone and a speaker connected by yards of discreet, darkly coated wire.

'Did you take this electrical equipment from my client's flat straight to the police station?' I asked the Detective Sergeant, more to kill time than because I had hit upon any brilliant line of defence.

'Yes, sir, I did.'

'And has anyone made any alteration or adjustments to it since you took it?'

'I'm sure they haven't, sir.'

'Just let me look at it, will you?' The usher came round with the exhibit in a plastic bag. I took the microphone out and looked at it, trying to seem knowledgeable on the subject of sound systems. I undid the long coil of flex and started to follow it to its connection with the small speaker. And then I saw something which seemed to offer Arengo-Smythe an unexpected, and perhaps undeserved, escape from his troubles.

The wire divided at the speaker. It looked old and rusted and one of the small screws had dropped out and only one strand was connected. With no talent for science even I knew that this was a serious fault. When the contraption was handed round the Jury, a collection of amateur electricians and Do It Yourself enthusiasts, it was clear that on the night of the visit of W.P.C. Battley, the date of the charge against my client, the hotline to Harriet Arengo-Smythe couldn't possibly have been working.

'The device was out of order. Well, of course, I knew that. It hadn't worked for years.' Arengo-Smythe was in the witness-box answering my questions.

'Did your sister know it too?'

'Oh, no. I let her carry on. She thought she was helping the spirits come through, you see. She'd done that since we started our work with the occult. That was before we charged for sittings, of course.' He was familiar enough with worldly matters to add the last sentence, calculated to save him from the charge of attempted fraud.

'So when the Woman Police Constable came to your seance, there was no voice coming down the wire?'

'Certainly not.'

'Then where was it coming from?' the Judge asked with considerable trepidation.

My client, his large head turned as he looked over his shoulder, carried on an inaudible conversation with someone unseen.

'Mr Arengo-Smythe!' The Judge was becoming testy. 'Who on earth do you think you're talking to?'

'No one on earth, my Lord. It's White Owl. He always wants to have his say. There's no keeping him quiet.'

'Who is this White Owl?' The Judge glared accusingly at me from behind his rimless spectacles. 'Do *you* know, Mr Rumpole?'

'Oh, yes, my Lord. White Owl is a Sioux Indian who, unhappily, lost his life at the battle of Little Big Horn.'

'Well, tell your client to get rid of him at once. I'm not

having him here. This is a court of law, Mr Rumpole. Not a darkened sitting-room in Earl's Court. Now, then. What's your case? Where do you say the voice came from?'

Ever ready with a familiar quotation, I was able to intone: 'There are more things in heaven and earth than are dreamed of in your philosophy.' This thought made his Lordship extremely uneasy.

'Members of the Jury, the question you have to answer is: did Mr Arengo-Smythe have the intention to deceive? It's clear now that the Prosecution case of deception has broken down like that old and useless line between the two rooms. My client has told you that he knew it was broken. But the voice of the deceased White Owl was coming from somewhere. From where, Members of the Jury? That is the question you have to ask yourselves. Is it just possible that the restless and talkative Sioux had entered that little sitting-room? Or is it possible that my client genuinely believed that he had? Either way, Members of the Jury, the Prosecution wouldn't have proved its case and Mr Arengo-Smythe would be entitled to be acquitted.'

I made the best speech possible in the circumstances and the Judge summed up nervously, as though half expecting an outraged and uncontrollable interruption from White Owl. Someone, he pointed out, had spoken in the darkened sitting-room. If it was not the microphone, as now seemed certain, was it the defendant disguising his voice or performing some act of ventriloquism? If it were his voice, did he honestly believe that he was possessed by some spirit who had died many years ago in Montana Territory? Or was it possible that some sort of paranormal manifestation had indeed taken place? The Jury must remember that even Mr Rumpole had not suggested that any of White Owl's predictions had proved correct. His Lordship then left the matter in their hands, with some relief, and popped out of court for a cup of tea and a breath of fresh air.

Whether the credit should go to me or White Owl, our day was crowned with success. After a long retirement, the Jury, having tussled with the mystery, were not convinced of my client's guilt and he was accordingly sprung by Mr Justice Teasdale, who seemed delighted to be shot of the whole business.

When we parted in the Old Bailey entrance, Arengo-Smythe came close to me and spoke unusually quietly. 'I never used White Owl's voice, Mr Rumpole,' he said. 'I swear I never.'

'But you knew that the wire was disconnected?'

'No, Mr Rumpole. I'm sorry to say I did not.'

'Don't tell me any more.' I wanted to get rid of the man as quickly as possible, but he went on. 'But I must tell you. I thought White Owl was Harriet, honestly I did. Where was he coming from?'

He looked at me, clearly frightened, but I had no comfort for him.

'The other side, as you would call it, if you're now telling the truth.' He was adding a new terror to death. Apparently you have to hang around for all eternity, waiting to be summoned to some busy seance in Earl's Court.

'It must be. Oh, Mr Rumpole. It must be so. I don't know how I'm going to cope with it, sir. I feel scared. Honestly, I do.'

'Tell me' – I couldn't spare much sympathy for the man, but there was a question that had to be answered – 'I suppose that wire must have been broken when Mr and Mrs Ballard came to you for their glimpse into the future?'

'Must have been, Mr Rumpole. That was only a day or two before we had the visit from the police.'

'And today,' I remembered, 'is the 14th of December.'

'There was a black cloud over it, White Owl said. Some disaster's sure to happen. Oh, do warn Mr Ballard, please. Do give him a serious warning.'

And then Mr Arengo-Smythe, looking extremely fearful and scrubbing his sweaty hands with a handkerchief, walked out of my life. In fact he walked out of life full stop. That afternoon, as I read in my evening paper, he stumbled and fell from the platform of the Bank tube station in front of an advancing train. White Owl had been quite correct about the black cloud hanging over that day, although Soapy Sam Ballard was unaffected by it. He remains Head of our Chambers and the downstairs loo has, at last, been dragged into the twentieth century.

Rumpole and the Reform of Joby Jonson

'Rumpole. *Rumpole!*' She Who Must Be Obeyed woke me with a sharp dig in the ribs from her side of the matrimonial bed. 'Can you hear something?'

'Yes.'

'What?'

'I can hear you.'

She was mercifully silent for a moment, listening intently, and then She renewed the attack.

'Rumpole.'

'What is it now?'

'Someone's in the flat.'

'*We're* in the flat. We usually are at night.'

'Shush!'

'Don't tell me to "shush". I'm not the one who started this conversation.'

'Can't you hear?'

'Hear what?'

'Sounds.'

'Yes, of course I can.'

'There you are. I told you!'

Thoroughly awake by now, and unable to hear anything except the usual complaining clicks, groans and rattles which the central-heating system in our ageing mansion flat gives off during the night, I thought I would calm my wife's nerves with a little poetry. 'Be not afeard, Hilda,' I told her. 'The flat is full of noises,

> Sounds, and sweet airs, that give delight, and
> hurt not.

> Sometimes a thousand twangling instruments
> Will hum about thine ears; and sometime
>   voices
> That, if I then had waked after long sleep,
> Will make me sleep again . . .

Let's hope.'

Hilda was silenced by Shakespeare, but a few seconds later She was at it again. 'You know who it is, don't you?'

'How would I know who it is?'

'So you admit it's someone.' A great cross-examiner was lost when Hilda didn't take to the Bar. 'No doubt it's one of your business associates.'

'What on earth do you mean?'

'It's some burglar or other.'

I tried to reason with her. I asked her why any half-way intelligent burglar would break into our flat for the sake of a few bottles of Pommeroy's plonk, a rented television set and her old friend Dodo Mackintosh's watercolour of a rainy afternoon in Lamorna Cove.

'I don't know, Rumpole.' Hilda thought the matter over. 'Why don't you go and see?'

The bed was warm, I'd had a hard day in front of the Recorder at the Bailey and was due for a harder one in the morning. I opted for the line of least resistance and said, unwisely, 'No need to make trouble for the fellow.'

'So you admit it's someone.' She spotted the weakness of my defence. 'Are you afraid to find out who it is?'

'Don't be ridiculous!'

'But are you?'

'I'm well known as an entirely fearless advocate. I don't mind what I say to judges.'

'I don't believe it's a judge in there, Rumpole, poking about among our things. The point is, are you afraid of burglars?'

'It's not a burglar, Hilda.' I shut my eyes and yawned as positively as I could. 'It's a figment of your imagination.'

'All right, then, prove it.'

'I can't, I'm asleep.'

'Or is that another job you'd rather leave to a woman?'

If it hadn't been dark I would have seen, I'm sure, that Hilda's glance was withering. She climbed out of bed and went off to battle.

Well, there are limits even to the Rumpole reluctance to interrupt burglars about their business. I was shamed into putting on a dressing-gown and, when I entered our sitting-room, I found Hilda, armed with an umbrella, prepared to repel invaders. The room seemed to be burglar-free, the television set was still with us and Dodo's view of Lamorna Cove had found no takers. However, the window was open and the night air was stirring the curtain above the table where I had left a brief.

'You see, Rumpole, the window's open.' She thought it proved her case.

'Didn't we leave it open?'

'I'm not sure.'

'We'd make the most terrible witnesses. But this is rather odd.' I was looking at my brief in the case of the Queen against Joby Jonson, accused of the robbery with violence of a seventy-five-year-old lady in the Euston area. Working on the papers before we went to bed I had left them, as I usually do, scattered over the table and in no particular order. Now they had been put together and neatly tied up. I undid the pink tape and started to check. Meanwhile, Hilda was going through the drawers in the bureau. 'Money. Cheque-book. Mrs O'Thingummy's wages still in her envelope,' She said. 'Nothing's missing.'

'Something is.'

'What?'

'The proof of evidence of Joby Jonson, the sixteen-year-old robber of old-age pensioners. His defence, such as it is, has melted into air, into thin air.'

'So somebody *was* here.' Hilda was triumphant. She was also right. She usually is.

*

At that period, when the rising wave of crime finally engulfed Froxbury Mansions, Claude Erskine-Brown was waiting, poised unhappily between elation and despair, to discover whether the Lord Chancellor had awarded him a silk gown and permitted him to write the letters Q.C. ('Queer Customer' is what I always say they stand for) after his name. If you want to become of Her Majesty's Counsel learned in the law you have to apply, with the support of a few judges, and await the outcome with bated breath.

So on the morning after our burglary, the Erskine-Browns were at breakfast in their tarted-up Islington house. As Phillida, the Portia of our Chambers, was reading *The Times* the conversation, I should guess from my knowledge of subsequent events, went something like this.

'Any sort of news in the paper today, Philly?' Claude would have asked as he poured skimmed milk on his muesli.

'Some sort of news, yes,' his wife told him. 'Danger of war in Bulgaria. Earthquakes in South America. Renewed threat of global warming.'

'No, I mean important news. The list of the new Q.C.s, for instance.'

'Look for yourself.' Phillida offered him *The Times*, but sudden fear overcame him. 'No, Philly, I'm not brave enough to look for myself. I don't think I could put up with another disappointment.' The truth of the matter is that the unfortunate Claude had applied for Silk five years running, and his name had not yet appeared on the magic list. Now Phillida read out some slightly more relevant news. 'The list of Queen's Counsel will be announced by the Lord Chancellor next month. It's expected to include Tabitha Merryweather, the brilliant Ghanaian woman civil-rights lawyer from Miles Crudgington's radical Chambers in the Edgware Road.'

'Nothing to say I'll get it?' Claude was downcast.

'Nothing to say you won't. I mean, you've asked often enough. They'll probably give it to you for persistence.'

'We all know you got it first time.' His tone may have become somewhat bitter.

'Rather a fluke, actually.'

'It wasn't a fluke.' Claude gave voice to a long-held grievance. 'It was because you're a woman. I mean, I know I'm not a woman, but it's a bit hard being discriminated against all the time for reasons of sex. I know what the Lord Chancellor thinks: just because I'm a man I go about with my head in the clouds dreaming. But I'm perfectly capable of coming to firm decisions. Now then, what do you think I'd like best? The organic apple juice or the mixed-berry health drink?'

'I can't help you there, Claude.' Phillida could be merciless. 'You make up your mind on that one, old chap.'

When he arrived at the Old Bailey for his day's work Claude's hopes received a severe setback. He went for a cup of coffee in the canteen and there saw Soapy Sam Ballard, the alleged Head of our Chambers, relaxing over a cup of tea and the Yorkie bar he indulged in when his wife, the ex-Old Bailey Matron, was not in view. Claude took a seat beside him and his attention was riveted when Ballard told him that his name 'cropped up when I was talking to old Keith from the Lord Chancellor's office'.

'Did it, Ballard? Did it really?'

'He naturally wanted to hear my views, as Head of Chambers, on your application for Silk.'

'Oh, Ballard, was he really interested?' Claude must have been overcome with emotion. 'I mean, they're taking my application seriously?'

'Naturally they're taking it seriously. Keith was saying it has become a sort of annual event, like Christmas.'

'You mean they look forward to it?'

'Let's say they give it serious consideration. I was able to let Keith have my views, fairly fully.'

'Oh, thank you, Ballard. Thank you very much.'

'I said we'd worked closely together over the years.'

'Yes, we have, haven't we, Ballard? Worked extremely closely.'

'And that, on the whole, you'd matured considerably.'

'Well, none of us is getting any younger.'

'I meant,' Ballard was unkind enough to explain, 'that I didn't think there would be any repetition of the incidents in which you'd been involved in the past.'

'Incidents?' Claude felt outraged and innocent. 'What incidents?'

'Incidents such as the complaint I had to deal with lodged by our new typist, Miss Clapham.'

'Clapton.'

'Yes, of course. Dorothy Clapton.'

'Dot.'

'Is that what you call her?' Ballard looked suspiciously at the ever-hopeful Claude. 'That's what you call her, do you?'

'You told Keith from the Lord Chancellor's department about Dot?' Claude was deeply shocked.

'I felt it was my duty. It was some evidence, which the Lord Chancellor would have to consider, of your lack of *gravitas*.'

'My lack of what?'

'Bottom,' Ballard explained. 'It might be some indication that you are not fundamentally sound.'

'Thank you, Ballard! That was extremely kind of you!' The Erskine-Brown heavy sarcasm was quite lost on Soapy Sam.

'I also pointed out that your elevation would mean we had three Silks in Chambers. In my opinion, too many cowboys and not enough Indians.'

'Indians!' Now Claude was losing whatever coolness he had possessed. 'I'm not an Indian, Ballard, unfortunately. If only I were an Indian, and a woman, I'd get Silk at the drop of a hat.'

'And there wouldn't be enough really important work for three leaders. You are far better off in the second eleven, Claude. One of the backroom boys we can always rely on.'

'You said that to Keith from the Lord Chancellor's office?'

'I did so in your own best interests.'

'You pompous prick!' In my opinion Claude put the matter extremely well, and with unusual brevity. It was a phrase Bollard would long remember, particularly as a party consisting of two or three solicitors, a client and an elderly lady barrister at the next table looked up with interest.

'I don't think I heard that, Erskine-Brown.' Ballard did his best to appear unmoved, but the charge was repeated. 'I said you are a pompous prick. And if you don't know what that means, I suggest you ask Dot Clapton. It's a view of your character quite commonly held in 3 Equity Court!'

So Claude left Ballard to what was left of his Yorkie bar and went off to suffer in a long post-office fraud, seeing his silk gown still eluding him.

Sixteen-year-old Joby Jonson was in custody. He was on remand, awaiting trial, a person still presumed to be innocent, and he was banged up with adult offenders in a place which, through no particular fault of the prison staff, had become a university of crime. It's overcrowded, unsanitary and prisoners on remand enjoy worse conditions than they did in the last century. As we sat in the interview room awaiting his arrival, a well-fed screw on the point of retirement told Mr Bernard and me that Joby wasn't exactly a happy boy. It seemed he was in a cell with a couple of lads only a little older than him; there had been some disagreement and a burning fag end had been stubbed out under Joby's eye. 'What can we do about it, Mr Rumpole? We've got no time, quite honestly. I'd like to give those lads a bit of G. and S., if time allowed.'

'Gin and soda?' I wasn't following the man's drift.

'Gilbert and Sullivan, sir. We did a great *Mikado* years ago when I was in the Canterbury nick.'

'Get Joby into a kimono and that'd be the answer to all his problems?'

'Absolutely certain of it, Mr Rumpole. G. and S. worked wonders for all of us when we had the time for it. I was the possessor of a reasonable bass baritone when the prisons was still a bit civilized. I can't do it now.' All the same, he went off with a gentle rendering of the one about making the punishment fit the crime, having ushered in a sullen and scarred Joby Jonson. Our client was a short, stubby, ginger-haired youth who sat with his arms crossed and an unfriendly expression on his face. When he spoke he pointed a stubby finger in my direction and called me 'yo', a word I was eventually to translate as 'you'.

The events which led up to our meeting can be summarized

as follows. One morning in the previous October a Mrs Louisa Parsons, aged seventy-five, living at 1 Pondicherry Avenue, somewhere behind Euston Station, answered a ring at her front door on the morning of 19th October. The youth who was there said, 'You still living here, Mrs Parsons?' and ran off. Later that day a person she identified as the same youth, although his face was partially covered, again rang her doorbell and, when she answered it, forced his way in, attacked her, punched her in the face and stomach, tied her up with some cloths from the kitchen, kicked her and, having broken up most of the crockery and some of the furniture in the house, left with Mrs Parsons's post-office savings book, in which there was a balance of £5.79. She later identified Joby at an identification parade in the Euston nick. 'First time I ever see the old bat,' my client told me when I had outlined the case against him, 'was at the I.D. parade.'

'It might be as well, when you come to give your evidence, if you could resist the temptation to call the victim an "old bat".' I gave him a word of warning. 'It might not endear you to the Jury.' And then I asked the attendant Bernard for a copy of our client's statement, the document which had mysteriously walked out of Froxbury Mansions in the middle of the night. Our defence, if you could call it that, was an alibi. The statement started, in a fairly unpromising way, with, 'So far as I can remember, at the time Mrs Parsons was attacked I was hanging out near the Superloo in Euston Station with three girls down from Manchester I found singing and dancing a bit. I think one of their names might have been Tina. I am unable to supply the full names and addresses of any of these persons.'

'Not exactly what I'd call a cast-iron alibi.' I had to be honest about it.

'Mr Bernard says as yo was a brilliant brief like. Can't yo get me off on that?'

'I may well be a brilliant brief, Joby, but I can't perform miracles. I am unable to walk on water or turn base metal into gold. And I can't make much use of a so-called alibi which fails to explain the most important piece of evidence in this case.'

'What's that meant to be then?'

'Your palm print,' I had to tell him. 'On the inside of Mrs Parsons's front door. How did that get there?'

'How would I know?'

'Think about it,' I advised him. 'It's a question you'll have to answer some time. By the way, what happened to your face? Looks as though you've been using it as an ashtray.'

'Something like that.'

'Shall we help you complain to the Governor?'

'Leave it out, Mr Rumpole. Yo want to get me killed?'

'No. As a matter of fact I want to get you off. So think about that palm print, why don't you?'

'Yo think about it.'

'Mr Rumpole's going to do his very best for you.' Mr Bernard was always reassuring, although I had clearly not impressed our client as a legal wizard. 'You just listen to him, Joby.'

'And yo listen to me.' Joby's finger stabbed the air in my direction. 'I'm not putting my hands up in Court. I don't care what anyone says. Yo get that into your heads. Both of yo!'

As we were waiting to be sprung from the prison gates, Mr Bernard, who rarely expresses an opinion on a client, went so far as to say that he hadn't found our latest customer a particularly likeable lad. It was, I thought, the understatement of the year. The characters of young offenders have clearly deteriorated since the good old days. Where have all the Artful Dodgers, the cheerful Cockney pickpockets sticking their thumbs in their waistcoat pockets and saying 'Watcher me old cock sparrer' gone? It was a sad day for England when John Dawkins turned into Joby Jonson.

And then one event occurred which took our Chambers at Equity Court completely by surprise and caused as much consternation as rights of audience in the higher courts being given to lay preachers and disc jockeys, or the abolition of the wig and judges listening to arguments from Counsel in T-shirts and jeans. It was something neither their legal training, nor their admittedly limited knowledge of the world about them, had equipped the learned friends to deal with. Miss Dot Clapton appeared at work with a diamond in her nose.

Her appearance wasn't entirely oriental. Otherwise she was dressed as usual in black tights, an abbreviated black skirt and some sort of reasonable jacket. I dare say the diamond had never seen Amsterdam, no doubt it was a serviceable imitation, but, fixed in some way which the members of Chambers preferred not to think about, it flashed and glittered in Miss Clapton's delicately moulded nostril like a rich jewel in an Ethiop's ear and its presence could not be disregarded. Two issues of fundamental importance and great difficulty were immediately raised by this ornament. The first was whether it is proper or professional for a barristers' Chambers to employ persons who bedeck their noses in this particular way, and the second was how the matter was to be put delicately to Miss Clapton. I happened to be loitering around the clerk's room when the diamond made its first impact and Henry tried, with no particular success, an indirect approach to the subject.

'A senior clerk couldn't want for more efficient staff than you, Dot,' he started off with some embarrassment, 'or more pleasant. I have done my very best to make you feel at home here, I'm sure. But a barristers' Chambers is, well, a barristers' Chambers.'

'You got some criticism of my typing, Henry?' Dot Clapton was giving him no sort of encouragement.

'Quite frankly, Dot, your typing has been little short of perfection,' Henry had to admit.

'Or the speed at which I gets the fee notes out?'

'You get the fee notes out, Dot, at the speed of light. But what I wanted to say is ... Well, some of our barristers are what I suppose you'd call old-fashioned.'

'Old-fashioned? I'd call them museum pieces, still in Y-fronts and braces, if anyone cared to look. Now why don't you be a good boy and let me get on with my work?' At this Dot clattered away on her typewriter and only spoke again when Claude came in, looked for a brief, failed to find one, had his eye caught by the sparkle in our typist's nose and gave a convincing imitation of a bottle of fizzy lemonade exploding on a school picnic. 'Something amusing you, Mr Erskine-Brown?' Dot asked coldly.

'No, certainly not. Nothing in particular.' And Claude did his best to explain. 'It's just that I haven't had much to laugh at lately.' Happily for him this speech was cut short by the arrival of Mizz Liz Probert, who took one look at Dot and congratulated her. 'It's what Chambers needs,' she told us. 'Someone who's not afraid to make a statement! We're not male clones, are we, Dot? We're not imitation men in pin-stripes. We're the great sisterhood of free spirits.'

During this stirring political address, Miss Clapton's fingers were dancing on the typewriter, and my attention was diverted by Henry telling me, with his hand over the telephone receiver, that he had the Home Office on the line and the Under-Secretary would greatly appreciate it if I managed to drop in for a brief chat. It's not often that I'm called in to discuss affairs of state, and we were arranging a convenient time when young David Inchcape blew in, went straight up to Dot and asked her to type out his particulars of negligence. Although she turned her face up to him, smiled and gave him a full view of its landscape, he seemed to notice nothing unusual at all.

The same could not be said for the Head of our Chambers. When Soapy Sam Ballard came in he stood transfixed, as though he had caught us lounging around smoking hookahs and watching the semi-finals of the Inns of Court belly-dancing contest. He stared at Dot and then did his best to say, in calm and confidential tones, to our clerk, 'I shall have to call a Chambers meeting on the serious situation which has just arisen, Henry. I sincerely hope all members will make it their business to attend, as a matter of urgency. I shall rely on you, Rumpole,' he avoided another glance at Dot and noticed my existence, 'as a senior member to see everyone gets the message.'

'Oh, don't rely on me,' I had to warn him. 'I'm rather overworked at the moment. Government business.'

*

I had never been inside the Home Office before. I knew it only as a threatening institution which had managed, whether by ill-luck or bad judgement, to turn prisons into slums and raise us to the proud position of number one of the European league for incarcerating our fellow citizens. I discovered a daunting concrete erection near St James's Park tube station. Inside this Lubyanka I was courteously met by a young lady civil servant and sat on a sofa in an anteroom with several back numbers of the *Illustrated London News* and the *Police Gazette*.

After a prolonged study of these publications, I was admitted into a large room, full of sunlight and abstract paintings, and into the presence of a plump, pinkish, aggressively healthy-looking person who introduced himself as 'Tom Mottram, Under-Secretary for Home Affairs, with special responsibility for prisons. I'm the fellow who tries to keep your clients in.'

'Horace Rumpole,' I told him. 'I'm the fellow who tries to keep them out.'

'Oh, good. Very good!' Mr Mottram seemed to be easily amused and he called on a pale, neat little man with outsized spectacles to join in the fun. 'Isn't that good, Gladwyn? This is Gladwyn Dodds, Parliamentary Private Secretary. I say, Rumpole, sit yourself down. You may have wondered why I asked you to drop in.' I was shown to another sofa and Tom Mottram plumped himself down beside me. 'It's about a young man called . . .' He paused as though to search his memory for the name and then came out with 'Joby Jonson'.

'Really?'

'I'm a constituency M.P. I hope a good one,' Tom Mottram told me. 'You can be more use on your own patch than in some great unwieldy place like the Home Office. Well, I've had Joby Jonson's mother round at my surgery, week in, week out, poor woman. She's really quite distracted.'

'I expect she is.'

'I told the old girl I'd make sure he was properly defended. Of course, I was delighted to hear you were appearing for him. So I can tell my constituent he's being looked after?'

'He's having the time of his young life. Banged up twenty-three hours a day in a seven-foot cell with a couple of sworn enemies and their chamber pots. They pass the time by stubbing cigarettes out in his face. And he's entirely innocent.'

'Innocent?' The Under-Secretary looked startled. 'Is that your view of the matter?'

'Innocent as we all are,' I reminded him, 'until twelve fellow citizens come back into court and find us guilty.'

'Oh. You're giving us your courtroom performance.' Mottram smiled. 'It's very good, isn't it, Gladwyn?'

'Very good indeed.' The little man behind the desk was less than enthusiastic.

'I was just trying to point out the condition of prisoners on remand.'

'Worse than they were a hundred years ago! We know that, don't we, Gladwyn?' Mottram agreed with an unexpected enthusiasm.

'Only too well, I'm afraid, Mr Rumpole. And our Minister would be the first to agree with you,' Gladwyn chimed in.

'So why doesn't your Minister do something about it?' I made so bold as to ask.

'The great British voter.' The Under-Secretary sounded weary. 'Terribly keen on seeing people banged up and terribly against them being let out. You know our prisons are bursting at the seams. You know they don't do anyone the slightest good. Halve the prison population and you might halve crime. Gladwyn and I know it. Our Minister knows it. Unfortunately we live in a democracy and we have to obey the instructions of our masters with votes. So we find it better to leave these things to the private sector. People like you, of course, and Seb Pilgrim.'

'And who?' The name meant nothing to me.

'You don't know Seb? He runs Y.E.R.T.'

'I beg your pardon?'

'Youth Enterprise Reform Trust,' Gladwyn explained. 'You must have heard of Sir Sebastian Pilgrim!'

'An absolutely splendid, super chap!' Tom Mottram was almost breathless with admiration. 'He carried his bat for

England and does wonderful things for hopeless cases like Joby Jonson. He teaches young lads cricket, gives them a bit of pride in themselves, reforms their characters. You two should get together.'

'Do you really think so?' I was doubtful. 'I never carried my bat for anywhere.'

'Never you mind, Mr Rumpole. You and Seb Pilgrim have your hearts in the right place.' Then the telephone rang on Gladwyn's desk and he said the Minister would like a word with his Under-Secretary.

'Excuse us, won't you?' Tom Mottram moved to the instrument. 'Our Master's Voice. Many thanks for dropping in. I'm sure you'll see young Jonson doesn't do anything stupid in court.'

'Stupid?' I asked as I heaved myself up from the sofa.

'Make things even worse for himself putting up some sort of idiotic defence. I've told his poor old mother you've got enormous experience in these sorts of cases. And please, keep hammering on about our ghastly prisons.'

'While you keep up your masterly inactivity?' I asked, but the Under-Secretary was now murmuring respectfully down the telephone and the audience was over.

When I opened the front door of the mansion flat that night, after only half a bottle, at the most, of Pommeroy's 9 per cent Château Thames Embankment, I suffered a severe nervous shock. The air was torn by a terrible banshee wailing, such a sound as I haven't heard since the nights of the Blitz when the Germans were overhead. I was thinking of bolting down to the cellar, or anywhere away from the bombardment, when Hilda appeared, pressed a number of buttons on some device fixed in our hallway and we had the All Clear. 'If that's going off every night,' I told her, 'I'll get a camp-bed put up in Chambers.'

'Don't be so ridiculous, Rumpole! It's a perfectly simple burglar alarm, an absolutely essential precaution since the night of the crime. You just press seven, six, nine, oh, two, three, one, eight and the yellow button twice. Then it'll be quiet immediately.'

'What else have you installed, Hilda? Death rays? Man traps? Are you going to sit up all night in the kitchen with a loaded shotgun? Come on, old girl, we've got to give the criminal classes a decent chance to earn a living.'

In fact we had even greater protection, for a member of the Old Bill emerged from the sitting room at that moment and introduced himself as Detective Sergeant Appleby of the Kensington force. He had been called in by She Who Must Be Obeyed in the great brief burglary case. 'A very thorough investigator, your good lady,' D. S. Appleby didn't need to tell me. 'Seems to know my job better than I do, tells me we must look for fingerprints. What's the matter, Mr Rumpole? Have the villains turned against you? You been losing their cases lately?'

Still recovering from the shock of the alarm, I was in no mood for a jokey D.S. 'I don't imagine you'll find any prints,' I told him, rather sharply. 'He must have been a pro, probably wore gloves.'

'And he didn't take anything of value, as I understand it, sir. Just some papers out of one of your cases? Now, I wonder who can have been interested in that?'

'Yes, Sergeant, I've been wondering that too.'

The case of Joby Jonson was attracting wide attention, from the criminals to the corridors of power. A couple of evenings later I got a telephone call from none other than that absolutely super chap, Sir Sebastian Pilgrim. He would simply love me to come down to the club and see the sort of work he was doing for lost sheep like young Joby, and, if I'd be good enough to agree, he'd send his driver for me.

A few evenings later a sedate Rolls appeared in the Gloucester Road and I was driven in an easterly direction by a chunky crop-headed man who introduced himself as Fred Bry, Sir Sebastian's driver. As we travelled along the Marylebone Road towards Euston Station, it was clear he was proud of his position, and he spoke of his employer as a great gentleman with a true understanding of delinquent lads. 'Never talks down to them, if you know what I mean. Always

speaks to them on their own level, and they appreciates that of
course. I've seen lads come to our club what you wouldn't
think fit for anywhere but an old-fashioned Borstal and
they've ended up, not saints I'm not saying that exactly, but
reasonable human beings, and pretty useful opening bats.'
Fred wore no chauffeur's uniform but was dressed like a PT
instructor, in a high-necked sweater and trainers. There was
a heart and a set of initials tattooed on the back on his hand.

'The Youth Enterprise Reform Trust' or Y.E.R.T., as the
Under-Secretary at the Home Office had called it, occupied a
delapidated building in Eversholt Street, near to the station. I
was led down a stone staircase and then into a space like a
huge, echoing gymnasium. There was a coffee bar on our side
of the room and a pool table, and ping-pong, and, at the far
end, a net had been fixed up and a line of boys were bowling
at a tall, good-looking man with dark hair touched with grey,
who plied his cricket bat with what I assumed to be considerable skill.

'Seb's what we all call him. No side to him, you see, absolutely no side at all,' Fred the driver assured me, and as we
approached the net a ball came bouncing in my direction. By
some mischance I put out my hand and caught it, something
I couldn't have believed myself capable of doing, and Seb
came out to greet me with his bat under his arm, applauding,
so far as I could see, without mockery.

'Well done, Mr Rumpole. You want to have a go in the net?'

'Not in the least,' I assured him. 'I'm allergic to any form of
sport.'

'Except teasing Her Majesty's Judges? You're a famous
man to all my lads, you know. Now, you're not allergic to a
drink, I hope.'

'I thought you'd never ask.'

Seb handed his bat to a delinquent lad and we went over to
the bar, where another delinquent was serving his fellows. My
hopes were dashed when my host uttered the dread words:
'Tea, coffee, hot soup, Seven-Up or Froo-Jucella?'

'I thought you were offering me a drink.' I'm afraid I
showed my disappointment.

'So I was.'

'Froo-Jucella might seriously damage my health, as my alcohol level has sunk to a dangerous low. Now, if you have a glass of humble claret? Château Boys Brigade, if it's available.'

'I'm afraid it isn't.' He was still smiling and made no apology.

'Or you might send over to the station for a bottle of British Rail Rouge?'

'I'll get you a coffee. And let's find ourselves a table.'

So, as you may imagine, I wasn't in the cheeriest of moods as I sat and looked round the gym. Fred the driver was now seated in the middle of a circle of delinquents, to whom he seemed to be giving some sort of pep-talk or seminar. All the youths in the room, I noticed, were wearing dark sweaters, jeans and trainers, so they looked as though they were in a kind of uniformed group. I was about to seek the company of a small cigar, and had the packet open when Seb came back with two plastic cups and told me that the lads had voted the place a Smoke-Free Zone.

I said goodbye to the small cigar. 'What're you running here, a monastery?'

'Delightful wit!' Seb seemed to be out to flatter me. 'That's what old Tom Mottram told me about you. No, I don't make the rules, the boys do. Self-discipline, that's the name of the game.'

'I thought it was cricket.' This was clearly not up to the standard of Rumpole repartee and Seb ignored it. 'No alcohol,' he told me. 'No smoking. And, of course, if we catch one of their number dropping an "E" ...'

'A what?'

'Ecstasy. Anyone indulging in any sort of a drug gets a hard time from the other fellows, a very hard time indeed.'

'So you rely on these young men to police each other?' I looked round at the uniformed squad.

'Too right we do! Well, it's the only way. No good imposing rules on them from above; they wouldn't take a blind bit of notice. How's the coffee?'

'Is it coffee?' I had been genuinely puzzling over the brew. 'I beg its pardon. I thought it was the soup.'

'I'm afraid we're not quite up to your gastronomic standards, Mr Rumpole. We've got more important things to think about.'

'Joby Jonson, for instance.' I brought him to the subject which was in so many minds.

'Well, yes. To be quite honest with you I'm worried about Joby. What we find here is that the first step to reform is to admit your guilt. If only to your mates.'

'Plead guilty?' I was doubtful. 'That's often as dangerous as Froo-Jucella.'

'Well, at least admit it to yourself. Look over there, in what we call our quiet corner.' The circle round Fred had grown even more attentive and he was addressing them with frowning sincerity. 'What is it? A prayer meeting?' I asked. 'Something like that.' Seb was still smiling. 'The young lads there are coming out with all their crimes and villainies. They talk them through. And then Fred Bry tells them where that sort of conduct leads to.'

'Your driver tells them?'

'Fred should know. He'd just come out of six years for robbery when I found a job for him.'

So I looked again at the group. One of the youths was talking, pouring his heart out, and Fred was listening patiently, his head on one side, nodding encouragement from time to time. 'You think confession's good for the soul?' I asked Seb.

'Don't you?'

'Perhaps, but it's not particularly good for keeping you out of the nick.'

'Oh come on, Mr Rumpole. You can't believe Joby's innocent. Is he going to try and put up some sort of defence, I mean apart from that alibi?'

'Which alibi, exactly?' Seb, it seemed, followed the case histories of all his delinquents.

'Three strange girls from Manchester at the railway station dancing and singing songs outside the lavatory.'

'You know that's his story?'

'Of course, the lads all talk about each other's cases. But it's not highly probable, is it?'

'One thing I have learned, after almost half a century down the Old Bailey, is that the improbable is perfectly likely to happen.'

'Perhaps your view of life is coloured by rather too much Château whatever it is?'

'Better than seeing it through a glass of Froo-Jucella, or soup, otherwise known as coffee.'

'I'm sure you want to help Joby.' Now Seb had become more serious, so I gave him a serious answer. 'It's my job to help him, not to decide his case. I might even manage to get him off.' But Seb's ideas of helping clients were a little different from mine. 'If you could get him to admit what he's done, even to himself, if you could get him to face up to it and not tell silly lies, that would really help him on his way back to reality.'

'And to about six years in the nick.' I had to point out the downside of the confessional.

'He came here often over the last two years. He had sessions in the quiet corner with Fred and the other lands. I'm not about to write him off as one of my failures. I'm sure we both want to do our best for him. Tell me how I can help.'

'I suppose I could call you as a character witness,' I told him. 'That might be more impressive than a shrink, or the local vicar. "I call Sir Sebastian Pilgrim, who carried his bat for England!"'

'Count on me, Mr Rumpole!' He seemed delighted to offer his services. 'You can count on me.'

'Thank you very much. Now, if you'll forgive me, I've got an urgent appointment with a bottle of claret.'

So Fred Bry was asked to break off his healing session and the Rolls was pointed in the direction of Froxbury Mansions and a much-needed bottle of Château Thames Embankment. 'That Joby Jonson's been a terrible disappointment to all of us,' the driver said as we were passing the Albert Memorial. 'I knew he was going wrong when I heard he was hanging round the station.'

'He wasn't train-spotting?'

'Hardly, Mr Rumpole. It's where they pick up the drugs what kids brings down from the North. It leads them to do terrible, inhuman things. We did our best with Joby, Seb and I. We both tried hard. It's over to you now, Mr Rumpole. Get the lad to face up to what he's done, it's the only way.'

It was, as you will have gathered, a time when confessions were much in fashion. I suppose the learned friends in Chambers would have liked Dot Clapton to confess that the jewel in her nose was a terrible error of judgement and throw herself on the mercy of Equity Court, promising to keep her nose out of trouble in the future. However, no one was quite sure of how to bring about this desirable result, so the matter was brought up for discussion at a Chambers meeting presided over by that pillar of respectability, Soapy Sam Ballard, Q.C. Also present were my good self, Claude Erskine-Brown, Liz Probert and Dave Inchape, who was once her partner but whom she now called her 'significant other', although I don't know if the title meant any further degree of intimacy. There were other assorted barristers and barristerettes, and Phillida Erskine-Brown, Q.C., the wife who had achieved that place on the front bench which her husband so longed for, had also made a point of attending. Claude had told her about Ballard's unhelpful attitude to his application for Silk and the fact that he had called our Head of Chambers a 'pompous prick', a verdict to which our Portia assented and had nothing to add. Had I known this at the time I shouldn't have been so surprised by the curious manner in which she treated Sam Ballard at our Chambers meeting.

'Certain basic standards of civilization have to be maintained at Equity Court.' Ballard was completing his peroration. 'I mean, we couldn't have people turning up here in war-paint.'

'No, we couldn't, Sam. You're utterly right as always.' Phillida was gazing at him with something not far off admiration. I've said her attitude to our soapy leader was distinctly curious. He thanked her and looked suitably gratified until I said, 'I don't know why they shouldn't turn up in war-paint.'

'Really, Rumpole!'

'I'm in favour of anything likely to add a touch of drama to the surroundings,' I told the meeting. 'Now, if only you'd show up in the clerk's room in war-paint, Ballard, maybe waving an assegai, on your way to a particularly bloodthirsty summons under the Rent Acts.'

'Rumpole,' said Ballard, 'we are at something of a crisis in the history of Equity Court. If this sort of thing goes unchecked we may be down a slippery slope towards . . .'

'What exactly?'

'They tell me there are men in Miles Crudgington's set who go into Chambers wearing suede shoes,' Hoskins, the greyish father of four daughters, put in gloomily.

'There you are.' Ballard was triumphant. 'You see what this sort of thing leads to?'

'I agree with you, Ballard, 100 per cent. Dot was making an unacceptable statement of female submission.' Mizz Liz Probert seemed to have changed her tune since she congratulated our typist on her nostril, but when I saw her looking warningly at her significant other I thought I could guess why she had done so. 'It was nothing more than a harem signal to any would-be Sheikh foolish enough to take her up on her offer,' Liz passed judgement. 'Dot's nostril is, not to put too fine a point on it, politically incorrect.'

'So then we're all agreed the ornament is totally unacceptable.' Ballard was delighted. 'Do you have a view on this matter, Erskine-Brown?'

'Oh, I don't suppose I've got enough *gravitas* to express an opinion.' Claude spoke with some bitterness.

'Enough what?' I was puzzled.

'*Gravitas*. Ballard doesn't think I've got enough of it.'

'Really? I thought you had it for breakfast every morning with a little skimmed milk and sugar substitute.' Having said this I pulled out my watch and hinted that I had better things to do than spend the day discussing our typist's jewellery. Before I went, the flattering Phillida suggested we leave all further action in the 'capable and tactful hands of our Head of Chambers. I'm sure,' she added, giving Ballard her smile at full beam, 'he can be trusted to have an appropriate word in the right quarter.' At this point Soapy Sam seemed quite overcome and thanked our Portia for her 'wonderful loyalty and support'. As I should have known, he was already hooked and all she had to do was wind him in.

There was one curious thing about that meeting. Dave 'the significant other' Inchcape had said nothing about the controversial diamond. When I asked him about it afterwards he told me that, quite frankly, he hadn't noticed the thing and had no views about it one way or the other.

When I was in the clerk's room a day or so later and found myself alone with Dot, I thought this much-debated subject was about to be reopened when she said that she wanted to ask my advice. 'Please don't,' I told her. 'I have absolutely no objection to it. As a matter of fact I think it adds a touch of colour to Chambers.'

'What adds a touch of colour?'

'Oh, nothing.' I had no wish to pursue the matter and Dot had other worries. 'It's about my dad. He lives not far from here, actually.'

'Does he really? I thought you and Henry hailed from Bexleyheath.'

'That's where my mum lives. Her and Dad split up when I was about seven.'

'I'm sorry to hear that.'

'Don't worry, it wasn't a great tragedy. My dad's an awkward sort of customer, call him bloody-minded and you'd be paying him a compliment. The thing is, they wants to do some new building down his street, but he won't sell his house. He says he's too old to move now anyway, and tells them to sod off, if you'll pardon my French. What he wants to know is, is there any way they can get him out, legally, I mean?'

I had to confess that property law wasn't exactly my forte, but I'd make inquiries and let her know. Then I asked her exactly where Mr Clapton lived. 'MacGlinky Terrace,' she said. 'Off Eversholt Street, behind Euston Station. Do you know the area?' I did and I had a feeling that what Dot had just told me added something to my knowledge.

When I got home I found Hilda reading the *Daily Telegraph* by the gas-fire and she was delighted to tell me that there was a long profile in it of 'my friend'.

'Really. Which friend is that?'

'Well, not one of the criminal classes certainly, not one of your beloved cat-burglars who enter by way of the fire-escape to rob us. Someone you ought to be proud of. You might invite him round to dinner so I could meet him.'

'Invite who round to dinner, Hilda?'

'Sir Sebastian Pilgrim, one-time all-rounder for England. He spends his time trying to reform young criminals. You don't spend much time trying to reform them, do you, Rumpole? That wouldn't be your sort of thing at all.'

'Neither is cricket,' I assured her.

'Exactly! And it seems that Seb – everyone calls him Seb – is a brilliant businessman as well. Chairman of something called Maiden Over Holdings. I don't know why you're not Chairman of anything, Rumpole.'

'Maiden Over? What's that, exactly?'

'Some sort of property company. He started it with Tom Mottram, M.P. Of course, now Mottram's a member of the Government he's had to resign from all his directorships.'

'Go on, Hilda,' I encouraged her. 'I'm finding your *Daily Telegraph* unusually fascinating this evening.'

'It says here that Seb believes in Britain.'

'Is that unusual? I mean, do some people think Britain's just a figment of our fevered imaginations?'

'"I have every faith in the financial future of this country, Seb told a shareholders' meeting recently,"' Hilda read out from the profile, '"which is why we're building a multi-storey hotel and shopping-mall in the area of –"' But the rest of this rousing speech was obliterated by the hysterical wail of the siren fixed to our front door as it called us to action stations. When the device had been quietened She admitted D. S. Appleby, who had at last found time to come and dust our sitting room with fingerprint powder. It wasn't until after he had done the job, been given a cup of tea and sent on his way that I was able to pick up the newspaper and discover where Sir Sebastian's faith in our country was going to find expression. It was just behind Euston Station.

Some time after the Chambers meeting when she had so shamelessly soft-soaped Sam Ballard, Phillida persuaded him to invite her to lunch, not to the place of his choice, which was a vegetarian Nut 'n' Crunch bar in Fetter Lane, but to a highly priced blow-out at the Savoy Grill. These facts may be taken as proved to the satisfaction of the jury. There is also no doubt as to the outcome of their shared smoked salmon and cutlets. It can also be assumed that Mrs Erskine-Brown used the trump card of her undoubted physical attractions (even Mr Injustice Ollie Oliphant is inclined to look misty-eyed and drool a little at the sight of our Portia in snow-white bands and a stiff collar) in a way which Mizz Liz Probert had denounced in the case of Dot Clapton.

How exactly she played her hand must remain a matter of speculation, and, although I have had to invent their dialogue (and I don't admit that my skill as a criminal defender also requires a talent for fiction), I have no doubt that the game was played along the following lines.

'You know,' Phillida probably led off as soon as their order had been placed, 'I've been longing to have someone to talk to about Claude. To be perfectly honest with you, he's not all that easy to live with these days.'

'Of course, I know nothing of that,' Ballard assured her. 'I mean, I've never actually lived with your husband.'

'No, you haven't, have you? Well, it's been pretty tough-going recently. Quite honestly, he seems to resent me being a woman. Do you think that's reasonable, Sam?'

'Well, no. Hardly,' Ballard admitted.

'Hardly! I can't help being a woman, can I? I've got no choice in the matter. You don't blame me for being a woman, do you, Sam?' This was accompanied by a slight inclination towards her lunch companion and a melting look.

'Oh. Not at all, Phillida, not in the least. I find your being a woman perfectly acceptable.'

'Somehow I thought you might say that. Claude seems to think that being a woman gives me an unfair advantage. You don't think that, do you?'

'Well, I noticed that the waiter did smile at you when he was showing us to the table.'

'Oh, Sam, I can tell you've had lots of practice chatting up women over lunch! The real trouble is that Claude believes that if he were a woman he might do better with the Lord Chancellor. What do you think of that?'

'I think that's very silly.' Ballard had no doubt about it.

'So do I.'

'Erskine-Brown couldn't possibly be a woman, could he?'

'I think he'd find it extremely difficult.' Phillida agreed.

'So he might as well give up the idea and settle down to being himself.'

'I think that's what he's afraid of.' And then she came to the real object of the exercise. 'He said you had a little chat about his application for Silk with dear old Keith from the Lord Chancellor's office.' Champagne, which she had assumed Sam Ballard would have ordered if he'd managed to think about it, was no doubt being poured as they faced up to an embarrassing moment.

'Erskine-Brown didn't seem too pleased about that. He used an expression which I certainly couldn't repeat in a public place.'

'You mean he called you a "pompous prick"?'

'Phillida! *Pas devant le* waiter! Is this champagne?'

'Of course it is.'

'Did I order it?'

'You know you did, Sam. I think you wanted to celebrate the fact that we're going out together at long last.'

'It causes rather a curious sensation in the nose.'

'You've got to forgive Claude; he had a deprived childhood. That's the sort of language chaps pick up at Winchester.' And then she gave her victim the honest and wide-eyed look which has had such a devastating effect on juries, and asked him directly, 'Don't you think Claude *ought* to get Silk?'

'In his own interests, I thought not.'

'You're fibbing, Sam.' She smiled beguilingly. 'You were thinking entirely of me.'

'Was I?' Poor old Ballard was puzzled.

'Admit it. You thought I'd get fewer leading briefs with Claude competing. Well, I want to be entirely honest with you, Sam, now that we've become real friends.'

'Do you?'

'Of course I do. I want you to be the first to know I shan't be looking for leading briefs in the future.'

'You won't?'

'I'm leaving the Bar.' This bombshell produced a distressed yelp of 'Phillida!' from Ballard. 'I've made up my mind. Don't look so sad, Sam. We'll still be able to meet for lunch. I'm not leaving the country or anything. And you know, it might make it easier for *us* if Claude were really busy and away in, let's say for instance, Hong Kong, doing leading briefs for long periods of time. We could have lunch together often. You'd like that, wouldn't you?'

'Well, as a matter of fact, Phillida, I believe I would.' This, for Ballard, was a positive statement.

'Then just lift the telephone to dear old Keith in the Lord Chancellor's office. Tell him that there could be no possible objection to Claude being entirely wrapped in silk, even though he is a man through absolutely no fault of his own.'

'And that would help you and Erskine-Brown?'

'It would help you and me, Sam. Considerably. Here's to both of us!'

This, or something very like it, was the lunchtime duet which led to agreement and the final clink of glasses. It has to be said, however, that Phillida had not yet told the whole truth to Soapy Sam Ballard.

I had a harder struggle ahead than the war of Dot Clapton's nose or the Erskine-Brown struggle for Silk. Joby Jonson's future was in my hands, and from what Mr Bernard told me the Queen was bringing all her big guns to bear at this juvenile target. A red judge had been put in charge of the case, and no less a tactician than Phillida Erskine-Brown, Q.C., who could wrap our Head of Chambers round her little finger, was in charge of the prosecution. Mugging was the flavour of that particular month and Joby Jonson, attacker of grandmothers and robber of old-age pensioners, came to stand for all that was most repulsive in British youth.

Black as the prospects seemed, I didn't despair. I gave Mr Bernard his battle orders. He was to get in touch with a Mr Clapton of MacGlinky Terrace, hard by Euston Station, and discover if that address might be anywhere near Pondicherry Avenue, home of the assaulted grannie. I also required as much information as possible on the business of Maiden Over Holdings plc and about any estate agents they might employ. 'And when we're on the subject of Dawkins –'

'Who's he, a possible witness?' The faithful Bernard wrote the name down carefully.

'Not really. I mean John Dawkins, otherwise known as the Artful Dodger. We should remember that he was only part of a wider organization run from Fagin's kitchen.'

'I don't know if you've had any experience of Mr Justice Graves?'

'As a matter of fact I've never been before him.'

'Then, Portia, you must have led a charmed life.'

We were standing side by side, Mrs Erskine-Brown and I, as the old Gravestone swept on to the bench like an icy draft. As we bowed to each other I gave my opponent a whispered character sketch. 'This judge,' I told her, 'is an absolute four-letter man. He's humourless, tedious, unimaginative and unjust. In a word, he's a judicial pain in the behind.'

Having bowed, Graves was still standing and made a pronouncement, in my direction.

'Mr Rumpole, it may come as a surprise to you to know that the acoustics in this Court are absolutely perfect and my hearing is exceptionally keen. I can hear every word that is spoken on Counsel's benches.'

At this I could do no more than bow low and mutter to Phillida, I rather hope audibly, 'See what I mean?'

We hadn't got off, I must admit, to a particularly good

start. However, we then went through the opening formalities
without any further disaster; twelve honest citizens were
sworn to try Joby Jonson according to the evidence and Phillida Erskine-Brown was opening the Prosecution case.
'Members of the Jury,' she spoke to them in her most beguil-
ing tones, 'we say that Jonson paid two visits to Number 1
Pondicherry Avenue that day. He came in the morning, to
scout out the territory, and asked Mrs Parsons if she were still
living there. When he found out she was, he returned that
afternoon, having made some attempts at covering his face.
He viciously attacked this lady, old enough to be his grandmother, and robbed her of what were no doubt her small
lifetime's savings.'

'Five pounds, 79 pence,' I murmured from my seat.

'Did you say something, Mr Rumpole?' There was an icy
interjection from the Judge.

'I was just reminding my learned friend that the sum
involved in this case was exactly £5.79,' I rose to say politely,
but Graves could quote Scripture to discomfort the defence.
'Mr Rumpole,' he told me with great satisfaction, 'the widow's
mite was, on a famous occasion, considered of great
importance to the widow.'

'I don't know if your Lordship could remind the Jury of
the present value of a mite, taking account of inflation,' I
asked innocently. 'It might come to rather more than £5.79.'

'Mr Rumpole, I have no doubt we shall be hearing from
you later. Now I think we might let Mrs Erskine-Brown open
her case without any more frivolous interruptions. Yes, Mrs
Erskine-Brown?'

For a moment, his Lordship was unable to get Phillida's
attention. She was staring in fascinated horror at the door of
the court, through which Ballard, no doubt encouraged by
events at the Savoy Grill, had entered. He raised a hand in a
mini-salute, and twisted his lips in a way which I can only
describe as a leer. After a few seconds of this lamentable
behaviour he withdrew, no doubt in search of other criminal
business, and Phillida was able to return to work.

'It remains to be seen, Members of the Jury,' she went on,

only a little shaken, 'what sort of defence, if any, will be put forward for Jonson. We have been given notice of an alibi which may be typical of the unfortunate levity with which this very serious case is being taken, both by the accused youth and his learned Counsel, Mr Rumpole. It is alleged that while this appalling attack was taking place, Jonson was, "dancing with some girls from Manchester outside the Superloo at Euston Station".'

'Did you say "dancing", Mrs Erskine-Brown?' The Judge couldn't believe his ears.

'My Lord, I'm afraid so.' Phillida was being deeply serious.

'And perhaps you can help me. What is a "Superloo", exactly?'

'It is, I believe, my Lord, a kind of superior lavatory.'

'A kind of superior lavatory.' The Judge made an extremely careful note.

Opening speeches from the Prosecution don't usually demand my full attention, unless a particularly lengthy evening at Pommeroy's has kept me from reading my brief and I have to discover from them what the case is all about. I knew the basic facts of the Queen's quarrel with Joby Jonson and, as Phillida held the floor, I was checking, once again, in the London *A–Z* and making sure that MacGlinky Terrace did, in fact, lead off Eversholt Street and into Pondicherry Avenue. The proceedings demanded my full attention only when the victim of the attack, Mrs Louisa Parsons, a bright-eyed, pink-cheeked and game old lady who would no doubt be a considerable hit with the Jury, entered the witness-box. At the end of her evidence in chief she was asked about the identification parade, on which occasion, she told us, the police had been very kind to her and saw she got a cup of tea and some very nice biscuits.

'Did you then identify the youth who visited you twice on the 19th and attacked you on the second occasion?' Phillida asked. At this the old lady, showing an unexpected sense of drama, pointed to the dock and said, 'There he stands!' No prosecutor could have asked for more and I rose to cross-examine, knowing that any attempt to rattle Mrs Louisa Parsons would sink me with the Jury for ever.

I started as though addressing my own grandmother. 'Mrs Parsons, this £5.79 in the post office didn't represent your entire worldly wealth, did it?'

'She never told us it did, Mr Rumpole.' Graves rushed in before he was needed. I ignored the interruption.

'Do you own your little house in Pondicherry Avenue?'

'My husband saved for it. Worked all his life as booking-clerk at the station. He had the mortgage paid up by the time he died.'

'Have you not been offered a considerable sum of money for that little house?'

'I wasn't going to move no matter how often they asked me. It wasn't the money, you see. That was the home Mr Parsons meant me to have for my life. I wasn't moving.' She looked at the Jury then, and they nodded back their admiration.

'Although they asked you very often?'

'I'm sick and tired of them always ringing me up,' she agreed, 'and sending letters marked "Personal to Mrs Parsons. We are most interested in the purchase of your property." Well, I said I'm not interested in selling. Not to you. Not to anybody.'

Bonny Bernard had called on Dot's father and made copies of a number of letters he'd received. I picked up this small bundle and asked Mrs Parsons, 'Did the requests to sell come from a firm of estate agents called Jebber & Jonas?'

'They may have done. I never kept the letters.'

'What did you do with them?'

'Dustbinned them. They went out with the other rubbish.'

At this point I received a blast of cold air from the bench. 'Mr Rumpole, what on earth has this fascinating information got to do with the charges against your client of robbery with violence?'

'That is something you may discover, my Lord, if I am allowed to pursue my cross-examination without interruption.' Having dealt with that I gave my full attention to the witness. 'You say that young Joby Jonson called in the morning and said, "You still living here, Mrs Parsons?"'

'Yes, he did.'

'Did you think that question might have had some connection with the repeated requests to you to sell the house?' Having thought it over, Mrs Parsons said, 'Not at the time, no.'

'Mr Rumpole, are you seriously suggesting that your client, accused of the robbery of £5.79, was working for a firm of reputable estate agents?' There is nothing so unquiet as the Graves. I told him, 'I will demonstrate that they are both working for the same organization.' And then I asked Louisa Parsons, 'Do you think now that there might have been some connection?'

'My Lord, this witness can't be invited to speculate.' Phillida rose in glorious indignation. 'We should leave such flights of fancy to my learned friend.' His Lordship, of course, agreed with this entirely and asked me to move on to the next matter, whereupon I muttered congratulations to my opponent on having got the old death's head eating out of her hand.

'Mr Rumpole, I didn't hear that,' Graves warned me in a detached sort of way.

'Did you not, my Lord? It must be the acoustics.' After which interruption I took up my conversation with the witness again. 'Later that day you say a young man rang at the door and when you opened it he attacked and robbed you.'

'I heard the bell. I thought, he's back again, I'll give him a piece of my mind.'

'You weren't frightened of him when you went to the door?'

'Not then, no. I was when I saw him, though.'

'Why?'

'Well, he had this, what they calls it? Ballycarver?'

'Balaclava, yes. He'd pulled it down, had he? You say in your statement that his face was hidden the second time he called.'

'It was hidden a bit, yes,' she had to admit.

'Mrs Parsons, can you be sure it was the same boy?'

I was rewarded by a silence, and then she said, 'I think it was the same.'

'You *think* so?'

'He had the same clothes – a dark jersey, like, and jeans, training shoes – whatever they call them – plimsolls, that's what we knew them as.'

'The uniform of thousands and thousands of young men all over London. But you didn't see his face?'

'Just his eyes. That was enough for me.'

'His eyes may have been enough for you, Mrs Parsons. They may not be enough for a jury to convict this young man on a serious charge of robbery with violence.' At which point I gave the twelve honest citizens a long and searching look and sat down, not altogether displeased with my performance.

I have often said that life at the bar would be a great deal more pleasant if we could do without clients. Clients get in the way, they fuss, they tell you things you'd rather not know, and then they prance into the witness-box and destroy the defence you have carefully built up by a moment of unnecessary candour. Some clients are, of course, more bearable than others, and as a general rule I have found that the more serious the crime the politer the client. Murderers are always grateful, those who contest parking fines, never. An exception to this rule was young Joby Jonson; the crime he was accused of was as appalling as his manners. All the same, I forced myself to pay him a visit in the cells under the Old Bailey after the first day's work was done.

'The time has come for you to tell the truth, Joby. Confession is good for the soul. Now I want you to admit that someone told you to go round to the old lady's house and ask her if she was still living there, then scarper. That was in the morning. What were you doing in the afternoon?'

'I told yo.' Joby was in his usual laconic mood. 'Did'n' I?'

'Yes, and for once I believe you. You were dropping an Ecstasy pill you'd bought off some girls down from Manchester – an activity which led to an unseemly bout of folk-dancing outside the Superloo in Euston Station, and probably a horrible reaction of shivering and thirst, plus a certain loss of memory.'

'How comes yo know so much about doing an "E", Mr Rumpole?' He made it sound like an accusation. 'How come I know so much about everything? I know you went to the house in the morning because your palm print was on the door and Mrs Parsons saw you. That was why she picked you out at the I.D. parade. I know you didn't go in the afternoon because the group you work for were so desperate to discover our defence. They're dead scared you'll say another of their lads came after you and did the serious business. Well, you'll have to tell the truth, Joby, before this case is over.' I sat down opposite him then and saw him stare at his feet. He didn't lift his eyes to ask, 'What's this group yo's on about then?'

'Don't play games with me, sunshine.' I spoke to Joby in the language he understood, that of the copper and criminal. 'You know damn well who I'm talking about. You can start telling us the truth tomorrow.' Then we left our client with a certain amount of relief and Mr Bernard went off to arrange the attendance of a witness on whom I placed our few remaining hopes.

The next morning I asked the Judge if I might call a character witness, a particularly busy man, to give his evidence before my client Jonson went into the witness-box. The old Gravestone gave his usual icy disapproval to this suggestion until he heard that Joby's character was to be vouched for by none other than Sir Sebastian Pilgrim, bat carrier, philanthropist and believer in Britain. 'Of course,' he purred. 'Sir Sebastian's time is of the greatest value, both to himself and to his country. No doubt it's only his sense of public duty which brings him to this rather sordid case. We'll certainly meet his convenience, provided you have no objection, Mrs Erskine-Brown?'

Phillida bowed in graceful agreement and Seb entered the witness-box, a handsome and imposing figure, perfectly at ease and prepared, even in his advancing years, to hit the bowling to the boundary to tumultuous applause from the

Jury. When he admitted he was Sir Sebastian Pilgrim, Graves gave him one of his spectral smiles and went off down Memory Lane. 'You need no introduction, I'm sure, to those of us who remember that century against Pakistan in your Final Test.' Seb looked charmingly modest and I got on with the business in hand. 'And do you run an organization called the Youth Enterprise Reform Trust, allegedly to help boys who have fallen into criminal ways?'

'Once again, Sir Sebastian, your wonderful work with Y.E.R.T. is well known to many of us.' Graves continued to butter up the witness, who wasn't entirely delighted with the form of my question.

'I do run that organization to help deliquent boys,' he said. 'I don't know why Mr Rumpole used the word "allegedly".'

'No doubt a slip of the tongue, wasn't it, Mr Rumpole?' the Judge suggested.

'Not exactly, my Lord. Perhaps if I go on a little my meaning may become clear.' And I asked Seb, 'Are you also Chairman of Maiden Over Holdings, which is planning a development near Euston Station that includes building a large hotel and a tourist shopping-centre?'

'I am.'

'We are most grateful to businessmen such as yourself, Sir Sebastian, who have so much faith in Britain's future,' Graves chimed in, and I wondered if we were going to have these varied versions of 'Oh, well played, sir' after every ball.

'And aren't you having trouble with certain householders who refuse to sell their homes to make way for this magnificent and palatial development?'

'No, I don't think so. Not particularly.' Now, I thought, Seb was playing for safety.

'Are you not? Do you not employ, among others, estate agents called Jebber & Jonas?' There was a pause as the witness seemed to be searching his memory. Then he said, as casually as possible, 'The name seems familiar.'

'Please answer the question. Do you employ them or not?'

'From time to time.' Seb's smile to the Jury seemed to be saying, 'It couldn't matter less,' but I asked the usher to hand him one of the estate agent's letters obtained by courtesy of

Dot. 'Is this a letter from that firm to a Mr Peter Clapton of MacGlinky Terrace, asking him to sell his house to make room for a new hotel development?'

'That would seem to be so.' Seb had just glanced at it.

'Is it *your* hotel development?'

'Well, I can't think of anyone else with similar plans.'

'Perhaps no one else is so anxious to invest in the future of this great city, Mr Rumpole.' I ignored Graves's support for the great cricketer and went on. 'And isn't Mrs Parsons of 1 Pondicherry Avenue also a householder who won't sell to your company?'

'You mean Mrs Louisa Parsons, the victim in this case?' The Judge was no longer smiling.

'Oh yes, my Lord. What's the answer, Sir Sebastian?'

'She might be.' The athlete's shoulders in the business suiting gave us a small shrug. Had I been Portia I would have interrupted long before this, for I was breaking all the rules by treating my own character witness with increasing hostility. When she did rise, to the obvious satisfaction of the learned Judge, I knew it was useless to argue and accepted her criticism with a good grace. 'Of course,' I surprised her, 'my learned friend is perfectly right. This is a character witness and I will come at once to my client's character. Sir Sebastian, do you take the view that young delinquents should admit what they've done and tell the truth about it?'

'Yes, I believe that's the start of reform.' Seb looked safely back on his home ground.

'Admirable sentiments in my view.' The Judge, of course, agreed.

'I thought your Lordship would feel that. Sir Sebastian, do you really want Joby Jonson to tell the truth about this case?'

'Yes, indeed.'

'He came to your club having been in trouble over a few minor matters. No violence in his record?'

'I think that it was only some quite trivial thieving.'

'And you hoped to reform him?'

'I always hope, and I thought there was some good in the lad. He turned up regularly at the club. I felt I might make quite a useful spin bowler out of him.'

'Not as useful as you, Sir Sebastian, if we remember the Australian wickets in 1975. They went down like ninepins, members of the Jury.' I looked at the honest twelve and thought they were becoming just a little bored with his Lordship's cricket reminiscences, so I hammered away at the case, and at Seb. 'Did you also hope to turn him into quite a useful young thug to terrorize Mrs Parsons into selling her house to your company? That's the sort of job you give your enterprising young lads, isn't it?'

'My Lord, that's the most outrageous suggestion! Mr Rumpole is cross-examining his own witness.' Phillida was up on her hind legs again and, surprise, surprise, his Lordship was on her side. 'Mrs Erskine-Brown, I am in complete agreement. That is a question that should never have been asked, as you must know perfectly well, Mr Rumpole.'

'My Lord, may I say something?' Seb looked like an honest outsider, anxious to put an end to the lawyers' bickering. 'I think it only fair that I should be allowed to answer Mr Rumpole's accusation. There is no truth in it at all.'

'No truth in it at all.' Graves dictated the words to himself and wrote them down carefully. 'Spoken, if I may say so, like a great sportsman. Mr Rumpole, you will confine yourself to questions about your client's character.'

'Delighted, my Lord. Always anxious to oblige. Sir Sebastian, despite your talents as a bowler, did you come to the conclusion that young Joby Jonson was not an entirely trustworthy criminal? Good enough to send with a final warning before lunch perhaps, but the afternoon terrorist attack had to be done by another of your protégés, shrouded in a balaclava helmet.'

'Mr Rumpole!' I had now lit the blue touch paper and Mr Justice Graves went off like a rocket. 'This is quite intolerable! I stopped you when you pursued this line before and you have totally disregarded my ruling. You persist in attempting to involve this most distinguished gentleman in the terrible crime of which your client stands accused. That is not the way in which we "play the game" in these courts, as you should know perfectly well.'

'I'm extremely sorry, my Lord.' I managed my most charming smile. 'I've never entirely understood the rules of cricket.'

Loitering outside the Court after a midday Guinness and slice of pie, I saw Ballard accost Prosecuting Counsel and tell her, with a look of triumph in his eye, that he had 'done it'.

'Oh, congratulations,' Phillida sounded unimpressed. 'Done what exactly?'

'Seen old Keith from the Lord Chancellor's office. I said that I'd been quite wrong about Claude, and that recently he's been showing a good deal of *gravitas*.'

'How about bottom?'

'Yes. Quite a lot of that too.'

'I'm glad you put that right.'

'So what about lunch? Honestly, it really is very nice in the health-food bar, and I wouldn't have to send a taxi back to Chambers, like last time, for an extra sub out of the petty cash.'

'Sorry, Ballard, I think I'm going to be rather too busy for lunches out in the foreseeable future.'

Soapy Sam looked disappointed, but our Portia had won her case. I wasn't so sure that I was going to win mine. My cross-examination of the great sportsman had been the high point. Then I had to call Joby and, although he told the truth as I had put it to Sir Sebastian, he wasn't the sort of witness the Jury could ever fall in love with and Phillida used her considerable skill to bring out his many unattractive qualities.

As always I felt a considerable relief when my client had left the dangerous prominence of the witness-box and been returned to the silence of the dock. Now it was up to me, and I've never had any doubt, since I won the Penge Bungalow Murders by my two hours of brilliant deduction and emotional appeal, of my talent for a final speech. In a notable passage I summarized the position. 'Members of the Jury.' I leant forward and spoke to them as though we were alone together and Mr Justice Graves had melted away like an icicle on a hot afternoon. 'Perhaps now young, Joby Jonson has taken the first step on the road to reform by telling you the truth. Until he went into that witness-box he was protecting his boss, his gang leader, that well-known cricketer whose performance in the Test Matches so delighted his Lordship. But the much-loved Seb Pilgrim had no intention of protecting him. He used Joby for a minor but disagreeable role in a plan to terrorize an innocent old lady into selling her house. And then he was content to see him locked up for years in a penal dustbin for the crime *he* planned.

'If that's cricket, Members of the Jury, you might think we'd all be a great deal better off playing tiddlywinks.'

When the speech was over I sat down and felt a great weight lift from my shoulders. I had done my job as well as I could, and now it was up to the honest twelve to make a decision. His Lordship, during his summing up, inserted a pointed and carefully polished boot into the defence at every possible opportunity and made it clear what he would like that decision to be. After a couple of hours in their room the Jury lost their collective bottle and agreed with him. In passing sentence Graves referred with disgust to an unwarranted attack on a great British sportsman and a public figure. 'Sir Sebastian,' he said, 'has devoted his life to the reform of youths such as you, Jonson. Unhappily you have proved quite unreformable. You will go to prison for five years.' During which time, I thought, if there were anything Joby did not know now about the life of crime, he would certainly have learned it. So he was taken down to the cells to continue his education. You can't, I suppose, win them all, but in Joby's case, it seemed to me, we had been bowled out by the umpire.

It was in a somewhat doleful mood that I went back to Chambers and, finding Dot once again alone in the clerk's room, I thanked her for the help she and her father had given us, and said he should keep a careful lookout for young men in balaclava helmets. I also thought the time had come to tell her, as both Ballard and Henry had not yet dared to do, that we'd had a Chambers meeting to discuss the exotic ornament in her nose.

'You never?' The idea of the solemn conclave entertained us both.

'Nothing much was decided,' I said, 'except young David Inchcape told me . . .'

'Yes, Mr Rumpole,' Dot Clapton sounded unusually breathless, 'what did he tell you?'

'Only that quite honestly he hadn't noticed whether you had a diamond in your nose or not.'

I left to the sound of Dot attacking her typewriter with unusual ferocity. The next day, and on all the days after, her nose was unadorned.

In the end most questions are resolved in the clerk's room. We were assembled there on the hunt for briefs one morning when Claude Erskine-Brown came bounding in, having at last had the courage to buy *The Times*, which he had opened on an inner page where the list of those privileged to be crowned in silk was printed.

'Hallo there. Hallo, you chaps. Hallo, Liz. Good morning, Dot. Hi there, Henry,' he chortled in his joy. 'You've all seen *The Times*, of course. Great news isn't it, and totally unexpected? Seen it, have you, Rumpole? I shall be leading you, my dear old fellow. I shall be sitting in front of you, doing your next murder for you.'

'Don't bother,' I begged him. 'You'll probably be too occupied with royal divorces.'

'Do you honestly think so? Well, you've seen the list, haven't you, Ballard? It seems that *gravitas* is no longer called for.'

'Congratulations,' Ballard had the grace to say. 'It's wonderful news about your wife.'

'Philly?' Claude looked unaccountably surprised. 'What about Philly?'

'Haven't you looked at the front page of that newspaper, Erskine-Brown?' Ballard was astonished. 'And the photograph.'

It seemed the poor nerve-wracked fellow had crept out of the house early, bought the paper at the Temple tube station and turned, with trembling fingers, immediately to the Silk list. Our Portia plays her cards pretty close to her chest and she had not told the rest of us, and certainly not her husband, that she was about to be wrapped not in mere silk, but in scarlet and ermine. Mrs Justice Erskine-Brown was now about to take her place on the High Court bench and, as her photograph made clear, she was going to be a good deal easier on the eye than Mr Justice Graves.

'Bless thee, Portia, thou art translated!' I said as I looked at it.

'She never even told her clerk!' Henry complained, and somewhere inside Ballard the penny finally dropped. 'So that's what she meant,' he told us, 'when she said she was leaving the Bar.'

When Erskine-Brown first stood up in Court decked out in the full glory of his new-found Silk, he found himself bowing low and saying, 'if your Ladyship pleases', and, 'with very great respect', to his promoted wife. And I had to pay a similar tribute to Hilda when D. S. Appleby telephoned to tell me the result of the long-delayed quest for fingerprints She Who Must Be Obeyed had ordered. 'They found one,' I reported to her as we sat on either side of the gas-fire in our once-violated sitting-room, 'on the window frame over there. It was the thumb print of an old con who was sent down for robbery with violence for a good many years. He now acts as father confessor and driver to that great British cricketer and reformer of the young, Sir Sebastian Pilgrim. Fred Bry it was who entered our premises by night. You know what that means, Hilda? It means that the case of Joby Jonson is not entirely over.'

'Then I'm very glad I got the burglar alarm fitted. That's all I can say.'

'It's not all I can say, old thing. I'd like to say thank you for insisting on the fingerprint evidence. It shows how important it is to have a woman on the case.'

Rumpole on Trial

I have often wondered how my career as an Old Bailey hack would terminate. Would I drop dead at the triumphant end of my most moving final speech? 'Ladies and gentlemen of the Jury, my task is done. I have said my say. This trial has been but a few days out of your life, but for me it is the *whole* of my life. And that life I leave, with the utmost confidence, in your hands,' and then keel over and out. 'Rumpole snuffs it in court'; the news would run like wild fire round the Inns of Court and I would challenge any jury to dare to convict after that forensic trick had been played upon them. Or will I die in an apoplexy after a particularly heated disagreement with Mr Injustice Graves, or Sir Oliver Oliphant? One thing I'm sure of, I shall not drift into retirement and spend my days hanging around Froxbury Mansions in a dressing-gown, nor shall I ever repair to the Golden Gate retirement home, Weston-super-Mare, and sit in the sun lounge retelling the extraordinary case of the Judge's Elbow, or the Miracle in the Ecclesiastical Court which saved a vicar from an unfrocking. No, my conclusion had better come swiftly, and Rumpole's career should end with a bang rather than a whimper. When thinking of the alternatives available, I never expected I would finish by being kicked out of the Bar, dismissed for unprofessional conduct and drummed out of the monstrous regiment of learned friends. And yet this conclusion became a distinct possibility on that dreadful day when, apparently, even I went too far and brought that weighty edifice, the legal establishment, crashing down upon my head.

The day dawned grey and wet after I had been kept awake most of the night by a raging toothache. I rang my dentist,

Mr Lionel Leering, a practitioner whose company I manage to shun until the pain becomes unbearable, and he agreed to meet me at his Harley Street rooms at nine o'clock, so giving me time to get to the Old Bailey, where I was engaged in a particularly tricky case. So picture me at the start of what was undoubtedly the worst in a long career of difficult days, stretched out on the chair of pain and terror beside the bubbling spittoon. Mr Leering, the smooth, grey-haired master of the drill, who seemed perpetually tanned from a trip to his holiday home in Ibiza, was fiddling about inside my mouth while subliminal baroque music tinkled on the cassette player and the blonde nurse looked on with well-simulated concern.

'Busy day ahead of you, Mr Rumpole?' Mr Leering was keeping up the bright chatter. 'Open just a little wider for me, will you? What sort of terrible crime are you on today then?'

'Ans . . . lorter,' I did my best to tell him.

'My daughter?' Leering purred with satisfaction. 'How kind of you to remember. Well, Jessica's just done her A-levels and she's off to Florence doing the History of Art. You should hear her on the Quattrocento. Knows a great deal more than I ever did. And of course, being blonde, the Italians are mad about her.'

'I said . . . Ans . . . lorter. Down the Ole . . . Ailey,' I tried to explain before he started the drill.

'My old lady? Oh, you mean Yolande. I'm not sure she'd be too keen on being called that. She's better now. Gone in for acupuncture. What were you saying?'

'An . . . cord . . . Tong . . .'

'Your tongue? Not hurting you, am I?'

'An . . . supposed . . . Illed is ife.'

'Something she did to her back,' Leering explained patiently. 'Playing golf. Golf covers a multitude of sins. Particularly for the women of Hampstead Garden Suburb.'

'Ell on the ender . . .'

The drill had stopped now, and he pulled the cotton wool rolls away from my gums. My effort to tell him about my life and work had obviously gone for nothing because he asked politely, 'Send her what? Your love? Yolande'll be tickled to death. Of course, she's never met you. But she'll still be tickled to death. Rinse now, will you? Now what were we talking about?'

'Manslaughter,' I told him once again as I spat out pink and chemicated fluid.

'Oh, no. Not really? Yolande can be extremely irritating at times. What woman can't? But I'm not actually tempted to bash her across the head.'

'No' – I was showing remarkable patience with this slow-witted dentist – 'I said I'm doing a case at the Old Bailey. My client's a man called Tong. Accused of manslaughter. Killed his wife, Mrs Tong. She fell down and her head hit the fender.'

'Oh, really? How fascinating.' Now he knew what I was talking about, Mr Leering had lost all interest in my case. I've just done a temporary stopping. That should see you through the day. But ring me up if you're in any trouble.'

'I think it's going to take a great deal more than a temporary stopping to see me through today,' I said as I got out of the chair and struggled into the well-worn black jacket. 'I'm before Mr Justice "Ollie" Oliphant.'

As I was walking towards the Old Bailey I felt a familiar stab of pain, warning me that the stopping might be extremely temporary. As I was going through the revolving doors, Mizz Liz Probert came flying in behind me, sent the door spinning, collided into my back, then went dashing up the stairs, calling, 'Sorry, Rumpole!' and vanished.

'Sorry, Rumpole!' I grumbled to myself. Mizz Probert cannons into you, nearly sends your brief flying and all she does is call out 'Sorry, Rumpole!' on the trot. Everyone, it seemed to me, said 'Sorry, Rumpole!' and didn't mean a word of it. They were sorry for sending my clients to chokey, sorry for not showing me all the Prosecution statements, sorry for standing on my foot in the Underground, and now, no doubt, sorry for stealing my bands. For I had reached the robing room and, while climbing into the fancy dress, searched for the little white hanging tabs that ornament a legal hack's neck and, lo and behold, these precious bands had been nicked. I looked down the robing room in desperation and saw young Dave Inchcape, Mizz Liz Probert's lover and co-mortgagee, carefully tie a snow-white pair of crisp linen bands around his winged collar. I approached him in a hostile manner.

'Inchcape' – I lost no time in coming to the point – 'have you pinched my bands?'

'Sorry, Rumpole?' He pretended to know nothing of the matter.

'You have!' I regarded the case as proved. 'Honestly, Inchcape. Nowadays the barristers' robing room is little better than a den of thieves!'

'These are my bands, Rumpole. There are some bands over there on the table. Slightly soiled. They're probably yours.'

'Slightly soiled? Sorry, Rumpole! Sorry whoever they belonged to,' and I put them on. 'The bloody man's presumably got mine, anyway.'

When I got down, correctly if sordidly decorated about the throat, to Ollie Oliphant's Court One I found Claude Erskine-Brown all tricked out as an artificial Silk and his junior, Mizz She Who Cannons Into You Probert.

'I want to ask you, Rumpole,' Claude said in his newly acquired Q.C.'s voice, 'about calling your client.'

'Mr Tong.'

'Yes. Are you calling him?'

'I call him Mr Tong because that's his name.'

'I mean,' he said with exaggerated patience, as though explaining the law to a white wig, 'are you going to put him in the witness-box? You don't have to, you know. You see, I've been asked to do a murder in Lewes. One does have so many demands on one's time in Silk. So if you're not going to call Mr Tong, I thought, well, perhaps we might finish today.'

While he was drooling on, I was looking closely at the man's neck. Then I came out with the accusation direct. 'Are those my bands you're wearing?' I took hold of the suspect tabs, lifted them and examined them closely. 'They look like my bands. They *are* my bands! What's that written on them?'

'C.E.B. stands for Claude Erskine-Brown.' This was apparently his defence.

'When did you write that?'

'Oh really, Rumpole! We don't even share the same robing room now I'm in Silk. How could I have got at your bands? Just tell me, are you calling your client?'

I wasn't satisfied with his explanation, but the usher was hurrying us in as the Judge was straining at the leash. I pushed my way into court, telling Erskine-Brown nothing of my plans.

I knew what I'd like to call my client. I'd like to call him a grade A, hundred-per-cent pain in the neck. In any team chosen to bore for England he would have been first in to bat. He was a retired civil servant and his hair, face, business suit and spectacles were of a uniform grey. When he spoke, he did so in a dreary monotone and never used one word when twenty would suffice. The only unexpected thing about him was that he ever got involved in the colourful crime of manslaughter. I had considered a long time before deciding to call Mr Tong as a witness in his own defence. I knew he would bore the Jury to distraction and no doubt drive that North Country comedian Mr Justice Oliphant into an apoplexy. However, Mrs Tong had been found dead from a head wound in the sitting-room of their semi-detached house in Rickmansworth, and I felt her husband was called upon to provide some sort of an explanation.

You will have gathered that things hadn't gone well from the start of that day for Rumpole, and matters didn't improve when my client Tong stepped into the witness-box, raised the Testament on high and gave us what appeared to be a shortened version of the oath. 'I swear by,' he said, carefully omitting any reference to the Deity, 'that the evidence I shall give shall be the truth, the whole truth and nothing but the truth.'

'Mr Rumpole. Your client has left something out of the oath.' Mr Justice Oliphant may not have been a great lawyer but at least he knew the oath by heart.

'So I noticed, my Lord.'

'Well, see to it, Mr Rumpole. Use your common sense.'

'Mr Tong,' I asked the witness, 'who is it you swear by?'

'One I wouldn't drag down to the level of this place, my Lord.'

'What's he mean, Mr Rumpole? Drag down to the level of this court? What's he mean by that?' The Judge's common sense was giving way to uncommon anger.

'I suppose he means that the Almighty might not wish to be seen in Court Number One at the Old Bailey,' I suggested.

'Not wish to be seen? I never heard of such a thing!'

'Mr Tong has some rather original ideas about theology, my Lord.' I did my best to deter further conversation on the subject. 'I'm sure he would go into the matter at considerable length if your Lordship were interested.'

'I'm not, Mr Rumpole, not interested in the least.' And here his Lordship turned on the witness with, 'Are you saying, Mr . . . What's your name again?'

'Tong, my Lord. Henry Sebastian Tong.'

'Are you saying my court isn't good enough for God? Is that what you're saying?'

'I am saying that this court, my Lord, is a place of sin and worldliness and we should not involve a Certain Being in these proceedings. May I remind you of the Book of Ezekiel: "And it shall be unto them a false divination, to them that have sworn oaths."'

'Don't let's worry about the Book of Ezekiel.' This work clearly wasn't Ollie Oliphant's bedtime reading. 'Mr Rumpole, can't you control your client?'

'Unfortunately not, my Lord.'

'When I was a young lad, the first thing we learned at the Bar was to control our clients.' The Judge was back on more familiar territory. 'It's a great pity you weren't brought up in a good old commonsensical Chambers in Leeds, Mr Rumpole.'

'I suppose I might have acquired some of your Lordship's charm and polish.' I said respectfully.

'Let's use our common sense about this, shall we? Mr Tong, do you understand what it is to tell the truth?'

'I have always told the truth. During my thirty years in the Ministry.'

'Ministry?' The Judge turned to me in some alarm. 'Is your client a man of the cloth, Mr Rumpole?'

'I think he's referring to the Ministry of Agriculture and Fisheries, where he was a clerk for many years.'

'Are you going to tell the truth?' The Judge addressed my client in a common-sense shout.

'Yes.' Mr Tong even managed to make a monosyllable sound boring.

'There you are, Mr Rumpole!' The Judge was triumphant. 'That's the way to do it. Now, let's get on with it, shall we?'

'I assure your Lordship, I can't wait. Ouch!' The tooth Mr Leering had said would see me through the day disagreed with a sharp stab of pain. I put a hand to my cheek and muttered to my instructing solicitor, the faithful Mr Bernard, 'It's the temporary stopping.'

'Stopping? Why are you stopping, Mr Rumpole?' The Judge was deeply suspicious.

Now I knew what hell was, examining a prize bore before Ollie Oliphant with a raging toothache. All the same, I soldiered on and asked Tong, 'Were you married to the late Sarah Tong?'

'We had met in the Min of Ag and Fish, where Sarah Pennington, as she then was, held a post in the typing pool. We were adjacent, as I well remember, on one occasion for the hot meal in the canteen.'

'I don't want to hurry you.'

'You hurry him, Mr Rumpole.'

'Let's come to your marriage,' I begged the witness.

'The 13th of March 1950, at the Church of St Joseph and All Angels, in what was then the village of Pinner.' Mr Tong supplied all the details. 'The weather, as I remember it, was particularly inclement. Dark skies and a late snow flurry.'

'Don't let's worry about the weather.' Ollie was using his common sense and longing to get on with it.

'I took it as a portent, my Lord, of storms to come.'

'Could you just describe your married life to the Jury?' I tried a short cut.

'I can only, with the greatest respect and due deference,

adopt the words of the psalmist. No doubt they are well known to his Lordship?'

'I shouldn't bet on it, Mr Tong,' I warned him, and, ignoring Ollie's apparent displeasure, added, 'Perhaps you could just remind us what the Good Book says?'

'"It is better to dwell on the corner of a housetop than with a brawling woman in a wide house",' Mr Tong recited. '"It is better to dwell in the wilderness than with a contentious and angry woman."'

So my client's evidence wound on, accompanied by toothache and an angry judge, and I felt that I had finally fallen out of love with the art of advocacy. I didn't want to have to worry about Mr Tong or the precise circumstances in which Mrs Tong had been released from this world. I wanted to sit down, to shut up and to close my eyes in peace. She Who Must Be Obeyed had something of the same idea. She wanted me to become a judge. Without taking me into her confidence, she met Marigold Featherstone, the Judge's wife, for coffee in Harrods for the purpose of furthering her plan. 'Rumpole gets so terribly tired at night,' Hilda said in the Silver Grill, and Marigold, with a heavy sigh, agreed. 'So does Guthrie. At night he's as flat as a pancake. Is Rumpole flat as a pancake too?'

'Well, not exactly.' Hilda told me she wasn't sure of the exact meaning of this phrase. 'But he's so irritable these days. So edgy, and then he's had this trouble with his teeth. If only he could have a job *sitting down*.'

'You mean, like a clerk or something?'

'Something like a judge.'

'Really?' Marigold was astonished at the idea.

'Oh, I don't mean a red judge,' Hilda explained. 'Not a really posh judge like Guthrie. But an ordinary sort of circus judge. And Guthrie does know such important people. You said he's always calling in at the Lord Chancellor's office.'

'Only when he's in trouble,' Marigold said grimly. 'But I suppose I might ask if he could put in a word about your Horace.'

'Oh, Marigold. Would you?'

'Why not?' I'll wake the old fellow up and tell him.'

As it happened, my possible escape from the agonies of the Bar was not by such an honourable way out as that sought by Hilda in the Silver Grill. The route began to appear as Mr Tong staggered slowly towards the high point of his evidence. We had enjoyed numerous quotations from the Old Testament. We had been treated to a blow-by-blow account of a quarrel between him and his wife during a holiday in Clacton-on-Sea and many other such incidents. We had learned a great deal more about the Ministry of Agriculture and Fisheries than we ever needed to know. And then Ollie, driven beyond endurance, said, 'For God's sake –'

'My Lord?' Mr Tong looked deeply pained.

'All right, for all our sakes. When are we going to come to the facts of this manslaughter?'

So I asked the witness, 'Now, Mr Tong, on the night this *accident* took place.'

'Accident! That's a matter for the Jury to decide!' Ollie exploded. 'Why do you call it an accident?'

'Why did your Lordship call it manslaughter? Isn't that a matter for the Jury to decide?'

'Did I say that?' the Judge asked. 'Did I say that, Mr Erskine-Brown?'

'Yes, you did,' I told him before Claude could stagger to his feet. 'I wondered if your Lordship had joined the Prosecution team, or was it a single-handed effort to prejudice the Jury?'

There was a terrible silence and I suppose I should never have said it. Mr Bernard hid his head in shame, Erskine-Brown looked disapproving and Liz appeared deeply worried. The Judge controlled himself with difficulty and then spoke in quiet but dangerous tones. 'Mr Rumpole, that was a quite intolerable thing to say.'

'My Lord. That was a quite intolerable thing to do.' I was determined to fight on.

'I may have had a momentary slip of the tongue.' It seemed that the Judge was about to retreat, but I had no intention of allowing him to do so gracefully. 'Or,' I said, 'your Lordship's well-known common sense may have deserted you.'

There was another sharp intake of breath from the attendant legal hacks and then the Judge kindly let me know what was in his mind. 'Mr Rumpole. I think you should be warned. One of these days you may go too far and behaviour such as yours can have certain consequences. Now, can we get on?'

'Certainly. I didn't wish to interrupt the flow of your Lordship's rebuke.' So I started my uphill task with the witness again. 'Mr Tong, on the night in question, did you and Mrs Tong quarrel?'

'As per usual, my Lord.'

'What was the subject of the quarrel?'

'She accused me of being overly familiar with a near neighbour. This was a certain Mrs Grabowitz, my Lord, a lady of Polish extraction, whose deceased husband had, by a curious coincidence, been a colleague of mine – it's a small world, isn't it? – in the Min of Ag and Fish.'

'Mr Tong, ignore the neighbour's deceased husband, if you'd be so kind. What did your wife do?'

'She ran at me, my Lord, with her nails poised, as though to scratch me across the face, as it was often her habit so to do. However, as ill-luck would have it, the runner in front of the gas-fire slipped beneath her feet on the highly polished flooring and she fell. As she did so, the back of her head made contact with the raised tiling in front of our hearth, my Lord, and she received the injuries which ultimately caused her to pass over.'

'Mr Rumpole, is that the explanation of this lady's death you wish to leave to the Jury?' The Judge asked with some contempt.

'Certainly, my Lord. Does your Lordship wish to prejudge the issue and are we about to hear a little premature adjudication?'

'Mr Rumpole! I have warned you twice, I shall not warn you again. I'm looking at the clock.'

'So I'd noticed.'

'We'll break off now. Back at ten past two, Members of the

Jury.' And then Ollie turned to my client and gave him the solemn warning which might help me into retirement. 'I understand you're on bail, Mr Tong, and you're in the middle of giving your evidence. It's vitally important that you speak to no one about your case during the lunchtime adjournment. And no one must speak to you, particularly your legal advisers. Is that thoroughly understood, Mr Rumpole?'

'Naturally, my Lord,' I assured him. 'I do know the rules.'

'I hope you do, Mr Rumpole. I sincerely hope you do.'

The events of that lunch-hour achieved a historic importance. After a modest meal of bean-shoot sandwiches in the Nuthouse vegetarian restaurant down by the Bank (Claude was on a regime calculated to make him more sylph-like and sexually desirable), he returned to the Old Bailey and was walking up to the Silks' robing room when he saw, through an archway, the defendant Tong seated and silent. Approaching nearer, he heard the following words (Claude was good enough to make a careful note of them at the time) shouted by Rumpole in a voice of extreme irritation.

'Listen to me,' my speech, which Claude knew to be legal advice to the client, began. 'Is this damn thing going to last for ever? Well, for God's sake, get on with it! You're driving me mad. Talk. That's all you do, you boring old fart. Just get on with it. I've got enough trouble with the Judge without you causing me all this agony. Get it out. That's all. Short and snappy. Put us out of our misery. Get it out and then shut up!'

As I say, Claude took a careful note of these words but said nothing to me about them when I emerged from behind the archway. When we got back to Court I asked my client a few more questions, which he answered with astounding brevity.

'Mr Tong. Did you ever intend to do your wife the slightest harm?'

'No.'

'Did you strike her?'

'No.'

'Or assault her in any way?'

'No.'

'Just wait there, will you?' – I sat down with considerable relief – 'in case Mr Erskine-Brown can think of anything to ask you.' Claude did have something to ask, and his first question came as something of a surprise to me. 'You've become very monosyllabic since lunch, haven't you, Mr Tong?'

'Perhaps it's something he ate,' I murmured to my confidant, Bernard.

'No' – Erskine-Brown wouldn't have this – 'it's nothing you ate, is it? as your learned counsel suggests. It's something Mr Rumpole said to you.'

'*Said* to him?' Ollie Oliphant registered profound shock. 'When are you suggesting Mr Rumpole spoke to him?'

'Oh, during the luncheon adjournment, my Lord.' Claude dropped the bombshell casually.

'Mr Rumpole!' Ollie gasped with horror. 'Mr Erskine-Brown, did I not give a solemn warning that no one was to speak to Mr Tong and he was to speak to no one during the adjournment?'

'You did, my Lord,' Claude confirmed it. 'That was why I was so surprised when I heard Mr Rumpole doing it.'

'You heard Mr Rumpole speaking to the defendant Tong?'

'I'm afraid so, my Lord.'

Again Bernard winced in agony, and there were varying reactions of shock and disgust all round. I didn't improve the situation by muttering loudly, 'Oh, come off it, Claude.'

'And what did Mr Rumpole say?' The Judge wanted all the gory details.

'He told Mr Tong he did nothing but talk. And he was to get on with it and he was to get it out and make it snappy. Oh, yes, he said he was a boring old fart.'

'A boring old what, Mr Erskine-Brown?'

'Fart, my Lord.'

'And he's not the only one around here either,' I informed Mr Bernard.

If the Judge heard this he ignored it. He went on in tones of the deepest disapproval to ask Claude, 'And, since that conversation, you say that the defendant Tong has been monosyllabic. In other words, he is obeying Mr Rumpole's quite improperly given instructions?'

'Precisely what I am suggesting, my Lord.' Claude was delighted to agree.

'Well, now, Mr Rumpole.' The Judge stared balefully at me. 'What've you got to say to Mr Erskine-Brown's accusation?'

Suddenly a great weariness came over me. For once in my long life I couldn't be bothered to argue and this legal storm in a lunch-hour bored me as much as my client's evidence. I was tired of Tong, tired of judges, tired of learned friends, tired of toothache, tired of life. I rose wearily to my feet and said, 'Nothing, my Lord.'

'Nothing?' Mr Justice Oliphant couldn't believe it.

'Absolutely nothing.'

'So you don't deny that all Mr Erskine-Brown has told the court is true?'

'I neither accept it nor deny it. It's a contemptible suggestion, made by an advocate incapable of conducting a proper cross-examination. Further than that I don't feel called upon to comment. So far as I know I am not on trial.'

'Not at the moment,' said the Judge. 'I cannot answer for the Bar Council.'

'Then I suggest we concentrate on the trial of Mr Tong and forget mine, my Lord.' That was my final word on the matter.

When we did concentrate on the trial it went extremely speedily. Mr Tong remained monosyllabic, our speeches were brief, the Judge, all passion spent by the drama of the lunch-hour, summed up briefly and by half past five the Jury were back with an acquittal. Shortly after that many of the characters important to this story had assembled in Pommeroy's Wine Bar.

Although he was buying her a drink, Liz Probert made no attempt to disguise her disapproval of the conduct of her learned leader, as she told me after these events had taken place. 'Why did you have to do that, Claude?' she asked in a severe manner. 'Why did you have to put that lunchtime conversation to Tong?'

'Rather brilliant, I thought,' he answered with some self-satisfaction and offered to split a half-bottle of his favourite Pouilly Fumé with her. 'It got the Judge on my side immediately.'

'And got the Jury on Rumpole's side. His client was acquitted, I don't know if you remember.'

'Well, win a few, lose a few,' Claude said airily. 'That's par for the course, if you're a busy Silk.'

'I mean, why did you do that to Rumpole?'

'Well, that was fair, wasn't it? He shouldn't have talked to his client when he was still in the box. It's just not on!'

'Are you sure he did?' Liz asked.

'I heard him with my own ears. You don't think I'd lie, do you?'

'Well, it has been known. Didn't you lie to your wife, about taking me to the Opera?'* Liz had no compunction about opening old wounds.

'That was love. Everyone lies when they're in love.'

'Don't ever tell me you're in love with me again. I shan't believe a single word of it. Did you really mean to get Rumpole disbarred?'

'Rumpole disbarred?' Even Claude sounded shaken by the idea. 'It's not possible.'

'Of course it's possible. Didn't you hear Ollie Oliphant?'

'That was just North Country bluff. I mean, they couldn't do a thing like that, could they? Not to Rumpole.'

'If you ask me, that's what they've been longing to do to Rumpole for years,' Liz told him. 'Now you've given them just the excuse they need.'

'Who needs?'

'The establishment, Claude! They'll use you, you know, then they'll throw you out on the scrap heap. That's what they do to spies.'

'My God!' Erskine-Brown was looking at her with considerable admiration. 'You're beautiful when you're angry!'

---

*See 'Rumpole and the Summer of Discontent' in *Rumpole à la Carte*, Penguin Books, 1991.

At which point Mizz Probert left him, having seen me alone, staring gloomily into a large brandy. Claude was surrounded with thirsty barristers, eager for news of the great Rumpole–Oliphant battle.

Before I got into conversation with Liz, who sat herself down at my table with a look of maddening pity on her face, I have to confess that I had been watching our clerk Henry at a distant table. He had bought a strange-looking white concoction for Dot Clapton, and was now sitting gazing at her in a way which made me feel that this was no longer a rehearsal for the Bexleyheath Thespians but a real-life drama which might lead to embarrassing and even disastrous results. I didn't manage to earwig all the dialogue, but I learned enough to enable me to fill in the gaps later.

'You can't imagine what it was like, Dot, when my wife was Mayor.' Henry was complaining, as he so often did, about his spouse's civic duties.

'Bet you were proud of her.' Dot seemed to be missing the point.

'Proud of her! What happened to my self-respect in those days when I was constantly referred to as the Lady Mayoress?'

'Poor old Henry!' Dot couldn't help laughing.

'Poor old Henry, yes. At council meetings I had to sit in the gallery known as the hen pen. I was sat there with the wives.'

'Things a bit better now, are they?' Dot was still hugely entertained.

'Now Eileen's reverted to Alderperson? Very minimally, Dot. She's on this slimming regime now. What shall I go back to? Lettuce salad and cottage cheese – you know, that white stuff. Tastes of soap. No drink, of course. Nothing alcoholic. You reckon you could go another Snowball?'

'I'm all right, thanks.' I saw Dot cover her glass with her hand.

'I know you are, Dot,' Henry agreed enthusiastically. 'You most certainly are all right. The trouble is, Eileen and I haven't exactly got a relationship. Not like *we've* got a relationship.'

'Well, she doesn't work with you, does she? Not on the fee notes,' Dot asked, reasonably enough.

'She doesn't work with me at all and, well, I don't feel close to her. Not as I feel close to you, Dot.'

'Well, don't get that close,' Dot warned him. 'I saw Mr Erskine-Brown give a glance in this direction.'

'Mr Erskine-Brown? He's always chasing after young girls. Makes himself ridiculous.' Henry's voice was full of contempt.

'I *had* noticed.'

'I'm not like that, Dot. I like to talk, you know, one on one. Have a relationship. May I ask you a very personal question?'

'No harm in asking.' She sounded less than fascinated.

'Do you like me, Dot? I mean, do you like me for myself?'

'Well, I don't like you for anyone else.' Dot laughed again. 'You're a very nice sort of person. Speak as you find.'

And then Henry asked anxiously, 'Am I a big part of your life?'

'Course you are!' She was still amused.

'Thank you, Dot! Thank you very much. That's all I need to know.' Henry stood up, grateful and excited. 'That deserves another Snowball!'

I saw him set out for the bar in a determined fashion, so now Dot was speaking to his back, trying to explain herself, 'I mean, you're my boss, aren't you? That's a big part of my life.'

Things had reached this somewhat tricky stage in the Dot–Henry relationship by the time Liz came and sat with me and demanded my full attention with a call to arms. 'Rumpole,' she said, 'you've got to fight it. Every inch of the way!'

'Fight what?'

'Your case. It's the establishment against Rumpole.'

'My dear Mizz Liz, there isn't any case.'

'It's a question of free speech.'

'Is it?'

'Your freedom to speak to your client during the lunch-hour. You're an issue of civil rights now, Rumpole.'

'Oh, am I? I don't think I want to be that.'

And then she looked at my glass and said, as though it were a sad sign of decline, 'You're drinking brandy!'

'Dutch courage,' I explained.

'Oh, Rumpole, that's not like you. You've never been afraid of judges.'

'Judges? Oh, no, as I always taught you, Mizz Liz, fearlessness is the first essential in an advocate. I can cope with judges. It's the other chaps that give me the jim-jams.'

'Which other chaps, Rumpole?'

'Dentists!' I took a large swig of brandy and shivered.

Time cures many things and in quite a short time old smoothy-chops Leering had the nagging tooth out of my head and I felt slightly better-tempered. Time, however, merely encouraged the growth of the great dispute and brought me nearer to an event that I'd never imagined possible, the trial of Rumpole.

You must understand that we legal hacks are divided into Inns, known as Inns of Court. These Inns are ruled by the benchers, judges and senior barristers, who elect each other to the office rather in the manner of the Council which ruled Venice during the Middle Ages. The benchers of my Inn, known as the Outer Temple, do themselves extremely proud and, once elected, pay very little for lunch in the Outer Temple Hall, and enjoy a good many ceremonial dinners, Grand Nights, Guest Nights and other such occasions, when they climb into a white tie and tails, enter the dining hall with bishops and generals on their arms, and then retire to the Parliament Room for fruit, nuts, port, brandy, Muscat de Beaumes de Venise and Romeo y Julieta cigars. There they discuss the hardships of judicial life and the sad decline in public morality and, occasionally, swap such jokes as might deprave and corrupt those likely to hear them.

On this particular Guest Night Mr Justice Graves, as Treasurer of the Inn, was presiding over the festivities. Ollie Oliphant was also present, as was a tall, handsome, only slightly overweight Q.C. called Montague Varian, who was later to act as my prosecutor. Sam Ballard, the alleged Head of our Chambers and recently elected bencher, was there, delighted and somewhat overawed by his new honour. It was Ballard who told me the drift of the after-dinner conversation in the Parliament Room, an account which I have filled up with invention founded on a hard-won knowledge of the characters concerned. Among the guests present were a Lady Mendip, a sensible grey-haired headmistress, and the Bishop of Bayswater. It was to this cleric that Graves explained one of the quainter customs of the Outer Temple dining process.

'My dear Bishop, you may have heard a porter ringing a handbell before dinner. That's a custom we've kept up since the Middle Ages. The purpose is to summon in such of our students as may be fishing in the Fleet River.'

'Oh, I like that. I like that *very* much.' The Bishop was full of enthusiasm for the Middle Ages. 'We regard it as rather a charming eccentricity.' Graves was smiling but his words immediately brought out the worst in Oliphant. 'I've had enough of eccentricity lately,' he said. 'And I don't regard it as a bit charming.'

'Ah, Oliver, I heard you'd been having a bit of trouble with Rumpole.' Graves turned the conversation to the scandal of the moment.

'You've got to admit, Rumpole's a genuine eccentric!' Montague Varian seemed to find me amusing.

'Genuine?' Oliphant cracked a nut mercilessly. 'Where I come from we know what genuine is. There's nothing more genuine than a good old Yorkshire Pudding that's risen in the oven, all fluffy and crisp outside.'

At which a voice piped up from the end of the table singing a Northern folk song with incomprehensible words 'On Ilkley Moor Ba Tat!' This was Arthur Nottley, the junior bencher, a thin, rather elegant fellow whose weary manner marked a deep and genuine cynicism. He often said he only stayed on at the Bar to keep his basset hound in the way to which it had become accustomed. Now he had not only insulted the Great Yorkshire bore, but had broken one of the rules of the Inn, so Graves rebuked him.

'Master Junior, we don't sing on Guest Nights in this Inn. Only on the Night of Grand Revelry.'

'I'm sorry, Master Treasurer.' Nottley did his best to sound apologetic.

'Please remember that. Yes, Oliver? You were saying?'

'It's all theatrical,' Oliphant grumbled. 'Those old clothes to make himself look poor and down-at-heel, put on to get a sympathy vote from the Jury. That terrible old bit of waistcoat with cigar ash and gravy stains.'

'It's no more than a façade of a waistcoat,' Varian agreed. 'A sort of dickie!'

'The old Lord Chief would never hear argument from a man he suspected of wearing a backless waistcoat.' Oliphant quoted a precedent. 'Do you remember him telling Freddy Ringwood, "It gives me little pleasure to listen to an argument from a gentleman in light trousers"? You could say the same for Rumpole's waistcoat. When he waves his arms about you can see his shirt.'

'You're telling me, Oliver!' Graves added to the horror, 'Unfortunately I've seen more than that.'

'Of course, we do have Rumpole in Chambers.' Ballard, I'm sure, felt he had to apologize for me. 'Unfortunately. I inherited him.'

'Come with the furniture, did he?' Varian laughed.

'Oh, *I'd* never have let him in,' the loyal Ballard assured them. 'And I must tell you, I've tried to raise the matter of his waistcoat on many occasions, but I can't get him to listen.'

'Well, there you go, you see.' And Graves apologized to the cleric, 'But we're boring the Bishop.'

'Not at all. It's fascinating.' The Bishop of Bayswater was enjoying the fun. 'This Rumpole you've been talking about. I gather he's a bit of a character.'

'You could say he's definitely got form.' Varian made a legal joke.

'Previous convictions that means, Bishop,' Graves explained for the benefit of the cloth.

'We get them in our business,' the Bishop told them. 'Priests who try to be characters. They've usually come to it late in life. Preach eccentric sermons, mention Saddam Hussein in their prayers, pay undue attention to the poor of

North Bayswater and never bother to drop in for a cup of tea with the perfectly decent old ladies in the South. Blame the Government for all the sins of mankind in the faint hope of getting their mugs on television. "Oh, please God," that's my nightly prayer, "save me from characters."'

Varian passed him the madeira and when he had refilled his glass the Bishop continued: 'Give me a plain, undistinguished parish priest, a chap who can marry them, bury them and still do a decent Armistice Day service for the Veterans Association.'

'Or a chap who'll put his case, keep a civil tongue in his head and not complain when you pot his client,' Oliphant agreed.

'By the way,' Graves asked, 'what did Freddy Ringwood *do* in the end? Was it that business with his girl pupil? The one who tried to slit her wrists in the women's robing room at the Old Bailey?'

'No, I don't think that was it. Didn't he cash a rubber cheque in the circuit mess?' Arthur Nottley remembered.

'That was cleared. No' – Varian put them right – 'old Freddy's trouble was that he spoke his client while he was in the middle of giving evidence.'

'It sounds familiar!' Ollie Oliphant said with relish, 'and in Rumpole's case there was also the matter of the abusive language he used to me on the Bench. Not that I mind for myself. I can use my common sense about that, I hope. But when you're sitting representing Her Majesty the Queen it amounts to *lèse majesté*.'

'High treason, Oliver?' suggested Graves languidly. 'There's a strong rumour going round the Sheridan Club that Rumpole called you a boring old fart.'

At which Arthur Nottley whispered to our leader, 'Probably the only true words spoken in the case!' and Ballard did his best to look disapproving at such impertinence.

'I know what he said.' Oliphant was overcome with terrible common sense. 'It was the clearest contempt of court. That's why I felt it was my public duty to report the matter to the Bar Council.'

'And they're also saying' – Varian was always marvellously well informed – 'that Rumpole's case has been put over to a Disciplinary Tribunal.'

'And may the Lord have mercy on his soul,' Graves intoned. 'Rumpole on trial! You must admit, it's rather an amusing idea.'

The news was bad and it had better be broken to She Who Must Be Obeyed as soon as possible. I had every reason to believe that when she heard it, the consequent eruption of just wrath against the tactless, bloody-mindedness of Rumpole would register on the Richter Scale as far away as Aldgate East and West Hampstead. So it was in the tentative and somewhat nervous way that a parent on Guy Fawkes night lights the blue touch paper and stands well back that I said to Hilda one evening when we were seated in front of the gas-fire, 'Old thing, I've got something to tell you.'

'And I've got something to tell *you*, Rumpole.' She was drinking coffee and toying with the *Telegraph* crossword and seemed in an unexpectedly good mood. All the same, I had to confess, 'I think I've about finished with this game.'

'What game is that, Rumpole?'

'Standing up and bowing, saying, "If your Lordship pleases, In my very humble submission, With the very greatest respect, my Lord" to some old fool no one has any respect for at all.'

'That's the point, Rumpole! You shouldn't have to stand up any more, or bow to anyone.'

'Those days are over, Hilda. Definitely over!'

'I *quite* agree.' I was delighted to find her so easily persuaded. 'I shall let them go through their absurd rigmarole and then they can do their worst.'

'And you'll spend the rest of your days sitting,' Hilda said. I thought that was rather an odd way of putting it, but I was glad of her support and explained my present position in greater detail. 'So be it!' I told her. 'If that's all they have to say to me after a lifetime of trying to see that some sort of justice is done to a long line of errant human beings, good luck to them. If that's my only reward for trying to open their

223

eyes and understand that there are a great many people in this world who weren't at Winchester with them, and have no desire to take port with the benchers of the Outer Temple, let them get on with it. "From this time forth I never will speak word!"'

'I'm sure that's best, Rumpole, except for your summings-up.'

'My what?' I no longer followed her drift.

'Your summings-up to the Jury, Rumpole. You can do those sitting down, can't you?'

'Hilda,' I asked patiently, 'what *are* you talking about?'

'I know what *you're* talking about. I had a word with Marigold Featherstone, in Harrods.'

'Does *she* know already?' News of Rumpole's disgrace had, of course, spread like wild-fire.

'Well, not everything. But she was going to see Guthrie did something about it.'

'Nothing he can do.' I had to shatter her hopes. 'Nothing anyone can do, now.'

'You mean, they told you?' She looked more delighted than ever.

'Told me what?'

'You're going to be a judge?'

'No, my dear old thing. I'm not going to be a judge. I'm not even going to be a barrister. I'm up before the Disciplinary Tribunal, Hilda. They're going to kick me out.'

She looked at me in silence and I steeled myself for the big bang, but to my amazement she asked, quite quietly, 'Rumpole, what is it? You've got yourself into some sort of trouble?'

'That's the understatement of the year.'

'Is it another woman?' Hilda's mind dwelt continually on sex.

'Not really. It's another man. A North Country comedian who gave me more of his down-to-earth common sense than I could put up with.'

'Sir Oliver Oliphant?' She knew her way round the Judiciary. 'You weren't rude to him, were you, Rumpole?'

'In all the circumstances, I think I behaved with remarkable courtesy,' I assured her.

'That means you were rude to him.' She was not born yesterday. 'I once poured him a cup of tea at the Outer Temple garden party.'

'What made you forget the arsenic?'

'He's probably not so bad when you get to know him.'

'When you get to know him,' I assured her, 'he's much, much worse.'

'What else have you done, Rumpole? You may as well tell me now.'

'They say I spoke to my client at lunchtime. I am alleged to have told him not to bore us all to death.'

'Was it a woman client?' She looked, for a moment, prepared to explode, but I reassured her. 'Decidedly not! It was a retired civil servant called Henry Sebastian Tong.'

'And when is this tribunal?' She was starting to sound determined, as though war had broken out and she was prepared to fight to the finish.

'Shortly. I shall treat it with the contempt it deserves,' I told her, 'and when it's all over I shall rest:

> For the sword outwears its sheath,
>   And the soul wears out the breast,
> And the heart must pause to breathe,
>   And love itself have rest.'

The sound of the words brought me some comfort, although I wasn't sure they were entirely appropriate. And then she brought back my worst fears by saying, 'I shall stand by you, Rumpole, at whatever cost. I shall stand by you, through thick and thin.'

Perhaps I should explain the obscure legal process that has to be gone through in the unfrocking, or should I say unwigging, of a barrister. The Bar Council may be said to be the guardian of our morality, there to see we don't indulge in serious crimes or conduct unbecoming to a legal hack, such as assaulting the officer in charge of the case, dealing in dangerous substances round the corridors of the Old Bailey or speaking to our clients in the lunch-hour. Mr Justice Ollie Oliphant had made a complaint to that body and a committee had decided to send me for trial before a High Court Judge, three practising barristers and a lay assessor, one of the great and the good who could be relied upon to uphold the traditions of the Bar and not ask awkward questions or give any trouble to the presiding Judge. It was the prospect of She Who Must Be Obeyed pleading my cause as a character witness before this august tribunal which made my blood run cold.

There was another offer of support which I thought was far more likely to do me harm than good. I was, a few weeks later, alone in Pommeroy's Wine Bar, contemplating the tail end of a bottle of Château Fleet Street and putting off the moment when I would have to return home to Hilda's sighs of sympathy and the often-repeated, unanswerable question, 'How *could* you have done such a thing, Rumpole? After all your years of experience', to which would no doubt be added the information that her Daddy would never have spoken to a client in the lunch-hour, or at any other time come to that, when I heard a familiar voice calling my name and I looked up to see my old friend Fred Timson, head of the great South London family of villains from which a large part of my income is derived. Naturally I asked him to pull up a chair, pour out a glass and was he in some sort of trouble?

'Not me. I heard you was, Mr Rumpole. I want you to regard me as your legal adviser.'

When I explained that the indispensable Mr Bernard was already filling that post at my trial he said, 'Bernard has put me entirely in the picture, he having called on my cousin Kevin's secondhand car lot as he was interested in a black Rover, only fifty thousand on the clock and the property of a late undertaker. We chewed the fat to a considerable extent over your case, Mr Rumpole, and I have to inform you, my own view is that you'll walk it. We'll get you out, sir, without a stain on your character.'

'Oh, really, Fred' – I already felt some foreboding – 'and how will you manage that?'

'It so happened' – he started on a long story – 'that Cary and Chas Timson, being interested spectators in the trial of Chas's brother-in-law Benny Panton on the Crockthorpe post-office job, was in the Old Bailey on that very day! And they kept your client Tongue – or whatever his name was –'

'Tong.'

'Yes, they kept Mr Tong in view throughout the lunch-hour, both of them remaining in the precincts as, owing to a family celebration the night before, they didn't fancy their dinner. And they can say, with the utmost certainty, Mr Rumpole, that you did not speak one word to your client throughout the lunchtime adjournment! So the good news is, two cast-iron alibi witnesses. I have informed Mr Bernard accordingly, and you are bound to walk!'

I don't know what Fred expected but all I could do was to look at him in silent wonder and, at last, say, 'Very interesting.'

'We thought you'd be glad to know about it.' He seemed surprised at my not hugging him with delight.

'How did they recognize Mr Tong?'

'Oh, they asked who you was defending, being interested in your movements as the regular family brief. And the usher pointed this Tong out to the witnesses.'

'Really? And who was the Judge in the robbery trial they were attending?'

'They told me that! Old Penal Parsloe, I'm sure that was him.'

'Mr Justice Parsloe is now Lord Justice Parsloe, sitting in the Court of Appeal,' I had to break the bad news to him. 'He hasn't been down the Bailey for at least two years. I'm afraid your ingenious defence wouldn't work, Fred, even if I intended to deny the charges.'

'Well, what judge was it, then, Mr Rumpole?'

'Never mind, Fred.' I had to discourage his talent for invention. 'It's the thought that counts.'

When I left Pommeroy's a good deal later, bound for Temple tube station, I had an even stranger encounter and a promise of further embarrassment at my trial. As I came down Middle Temple Lane on to the Embankment and turned right towards the station, I saw the figure of Claude Erskine-Brown approaching with his robe bag slung over his shoulder, no doubt whistling the big number from *Götterdämmerung*, perhaps kept late by some jury unable to make up its mind. Claude had been the cause of all my troubles and I had no desire to bandy words with the fellow, so I turned back and started to retrace my steps in an easterly direction. Who should I see then but Ollie Oliphant issuing from Middle Temple Lane, smoking a cigar and looking like a man who has been enjoying a good dinner. Quick as a shot I dived into such traffic as there was and crossed the road to the Embankment, where I stood, close to the wall, looking down into the inky water of the Thames, with my back well turned to the two points of danger behind me.

I hadn't been standing there very long, sniffing the night air and hoping I had got shot of my two opponents, when an unwelcome hand grasped my arm and I heard a panic-stricken voice say, 'Don't do it, Rumpole!'

'Do what?'

'Take the easy way out.'

'Bollard!' I said, for it was our Head of Chambers behaving in this extraordinary fashion. 'Let go of me, will you?'

At this, Ballard did relax his grip and stood looking at me with deep and intolerable compassion as he intoned, 'However serious the crime, all sinners may be forgiven. And remember, there are those that are standing by you, your devoted wife – and me! I have taken up the burden of your defence.'

'Well, put it down, Bollard! I have nothing whatever to say to those ridiculous charges.'

'I mean, I am acting for you, at your trial.' I then felt a genuine, if momentary, desire to hurl myself into the river, but he was preaching on. 'I think I can save you, Rumpole, if you truly repent.'

'What *is* this?' I couldn't believe my ears. 'A legal conference or a prayer meeting?'

'Good question, Rumpole! The two are never far apart. You may achieve salvation, if you will say, after me, you have erred and strayed like a lost sheep.'

'*Me?* Say that to Ollie Oliphant?' Had Bollard taken complete leave of his few remaining senses?

'Repentance, Rumpole. It's the only way.'

'Never!'

'I don't ask it for myself, Rumpole, even though I'm standing by you.'

'Well, stop standing by me, will you? I'm on my way to the Underground.' And I started to move away from the man at a fairly brisk pace.

'I ask it for that fine woman who has devoted her life to you. A somewhat unworthy cause, perhaps. But she is devoted. Rumpole, I ask it for Hilda!'

What I didn't know at that point was that Hilda was being more active in my defence than I was. She had called at our Chambers and, while I was fulfilling a previous engagement in Snaresbrook Crown Court, she had burst into Ballard's room unannounced, rousing him from some solitary religious observance or an afternoon sleep brought on by over-indulgence in bean-shoot sandwiches at the vegetarian snack bar, and told him that I was in a little difficulty. Ballard's view, when he had recovered consciousness, was that I was in fact in deep trouble and he had prayed long and earnestly about the matter.

'I hope you're going to do something a little more practical than pray!' Hilda, as you may have noticed, can be quite sharp on occasions. She went on to tell Soapy Sam that she had called at the Bar Council, indeed there was no door she wouldn't open in my cause, and had been told that what Rumpole needed was a Q.C. to defend him, and if he did his own case in the way he carried on down the Bailey 'he'd be sunk'.

'That seems to be sound advice, Mrs Rumpole.'

'I said there was no difficulty in getting a Q.C. of standing and that Rumpole's Head of Chambers would be delighted to act for him.'

'You mean' – there was, I'm sure, a note of fear in Ballard's voice – 'you want me to take on Rumpole as a *client*?'

'I want you to stand by him, Sam, as I am doing, and as any decent Head of Chambers would for a tenant in trouble.'

'But he's got to apologize to Mr Justice Oliphant, fully and sincerely. How on earth am I going to persuade Rumpole to do that?' Ballard no doubt felt like someone called upon to cleanse the Augean stables, knowing perfectly well that he'd never be a Hercules.

'Leave that to me. I'll do the persuading. You just think of how you'd put it nice and politely to the Judge.' Hilda was giving the instructions to counsel, but Ballard was still daunted. 'Rumpole as a client,' he muttered. 'God give me strength!'

'Don't worry, Sam. If God won't, I certainly will.'

After this encounter Ballard dined in his new-found splendour as a bencher and after dinner he found himself sitting next to none other than the complaining Judge Ollie Oliphant, who was in no hurry to return to his bachelor flat in Temple Gardens. Seeking to avoid a great deal of hard and thankless work before the Disciplinary Tribunal, Soapy Sam started to soften up his Lordship, who seemed astonished to hear that he was defending Rumpole.

'I am acting in the great tradition of the Bar, Judge,' Soapy Sam excused himself by saying. 'Of course we are bound to represent the most hopeless client, in the most disagreeable case.'

'Hopeless. I'm glad you see that. Shows you've got a bit of common sense.'

'Might you take' – Ballard was at his most obsequious – 'in your great wisdom and humanity, which is a byword at the Old Bailey; you are known, I believe, as the Quality of Mercy down there – a merciful view if there were to be a contrite apology?'

'Rumpole'd rather be disbarred than apologize to me.' Oliphant was probably right.

'But if he would?'

'If he would, it'd cause him more genuine pain and grief than anything else in the world.' And then the Judge, thinking it over, was heard to make some sort of gurgling noise that might have passed for a chuckle. 'I'd enjoy seeing that, I really would. I'd love to see Horace Rumpole grovel. That might be punishment enough. It would be up to the Tribunal, of course.'

'Of course. But your attitude, Judge, would have such an influence, given the great respect you're held in at the Bar. Well, thank you. Thank you very much.'

It was after that bit of crawling over the dessert that I spotted Oliphant coming out of Middle Temple Lane and Ballard imagined he'd saved me from ending my legal career in the cold and inhospitable waters of the Thames.

It soon became clear to me that my supporters expected me to appear as a penitent before Mr Justice Oliphant. This was the requirement of She Who Must Be Obeyed, who pointed out the awful consequences of my refusal to bow the knee. 'How could I bear it, Rumpole?' she said one evening when the nine o'clock news had failed to entertain us. 'I remember Daddy at the Bar and how everyone respected him. How could I bear to be the wife of a disbarred barrister? How could I meet any of the fellows in Chambers and hear them say, as I turned away, "Of course, you remember old Rumpole. Kicked out for unprofessional conduct."'

Of course I saw her point. I sighed heavily and asked her what she wanted me to do.

'Take Sam Ballard's advice. We've all told you, apologize to Sir Oliver Oliphant.'

'All right, Hilda, you win.' I hope I said it convincingly, but down towards the carpet, beside the arm of my chair, I had my fingers crossed.

Hilda and I were not the only couple whose views were not entirely at one in that uneasy period before my trial. During a quiet moment in the clerk's room, Henry came out with some startling news for Dot.

'Well, I told Eileen last night. It was an evening when she wasn't out at the Drainage Inquiry and I told my wife quite frankly what we decided.'

'What did we decide?' Dot asked nervously.

'Like, what you told me. I'm a big part of your life.'

'Did I say that?'

'You know you did. We can't hide it, can we, Dot? We're going to make a future together.'

'You told your wife that?' Dot was now seriously worried.

'She understood what I was on about. Eileen understands I got to have this one chance of happiness, while I'm still young enough to enjoy it.'

'Did you say "young enough", Henry?'

'So, we're beginning a new life together. That all right, Dot?'

Before she could answer him, the telephone rang and the clerk's room began to fill with solicitors and learned friends in search of briefs. Henry seemed to regard the matter as closed and Dot didn't dare to reopen it, at least until after my trial was over and a historic meeting took place.

During the day time, when the nuts and fruit and madeira were put away and the tables were arranged in a more threatening and judicial manner, my trial began in the Outer Temple Parliament Room. It was all, I'm sure, intended to be pleasant and informal: I wasn't guarded in a dock but sat in a comfortable chair beside my legal advisers, Sam Ballard, Q.C., Liz Probert, his junior, and Mr Bernard, my instructing solicitor. However, all friendly feelings were banished by the look on the face of the presiding Judge; I had drawn the short straw in the shape of Mr Justice Graves – or Gravestone, as I preferred to call him – who looked as though he was sick to the stomach at the thought of a barrister accused of such appalling crimes, but if someone had to be he was relieved, on the whole, that it was only Horace Rumpole.

Claude gave evidence in a highly embarrassed way of what he'd heard and I instructed Ballard not to ask him any questions. This came as a relief to him as he couldn't think of any questions to ask. And then Ollie Oliphant came puffing in, bald as an egg without his wig, wearing a dark suit and the artificial flower of some charity in his buttonhole. He was excused from taking the oath by Graves, who acted on the well-known theory that judges are incapable of fibbing, and he gave his account of all my sins and omissions to Montague Varian, Q.C., for the Prosecution. As he did so, I examined the faces of my judges. Graves might have been carved out of yellowish marble; the lay assessor was Lady Mendip, the headmistress, and she looked as though she were hearing an account of disgusting words found chalked up on a blackboard. Of the three practising barristers sent to try me only Arthur Nottley smiled faintly, but then I had seen him smile through the most horrendous murder cases.

When Varian had finished, Ballard rose, with the greatest respect, to cross-examine. 'It's extremely courteous of you to agree to attend here in person, Judge.'

'And absolutely charming of you to lodge a complaint against me,' I murmured politely.

'Now my client wants you to know that he was suffering from a severe toothache on the day in question.' Ballard was wrong; I didn't particularly want the Judge to know that. At any rate, Graves didn't think much of my temporary stopping as a defence. 'Mr Ballard,' he said, 'is toothache an excuse for speaking to a client during the luncheon-time adjournment? I should have thought Mr Rumpole would have been anxious to rest his mouth.'

'My Lord, I'm not dealing with the question of rudeness to the learned Judge.'

'The boring old fart evidence,' I thought I heard Nottley whisper to his neighbouring barrister.

And then Ballard pulled a trick on me which I hadn't expected. 'I understand my client wishes to apologize to the learned Judge in his own words,' he told the tribunal. No doubt he expected that, overcome by the solemnity of the occasion, I would run up the white flag and beg for mercy. He sat down and I did indeed rise to my feet and address Mr Justice Oliphant along these lines. 'My Lord,' I started formally, 'if it please your Lordship, I do realize there are certain things which should not be said or done in court, things that are utterly inexcusable and no doubt amount to contempt.'

As I said this, Graves leant forward and I saw, as I had

never in Court seen before, a faint smile on those gaunt features. 'Mr Rumpole, the tribunal is, I believe I can speak for us all, both surprised and gratified by this unusually apologetic attitude.' Here the quartet beside him nodded in agreement. 'I take it you're about to withdraw the inexcusable phrases.'

'Inexcusable, certainly,' I agreed. 'I was just about to put to Mr Justice Oliphant the inexcusable manner in which he sighs and rolls his eyes to heaven when he sums up the defence case.' And here I embarked on a mild imitation of Ollie Oliphant: "Of course you can believe that if you like, Members of the Jury, but use your common sense, why don't you?" And what about describing my client's conduct as manslaughter during the evidence, which was the very fact the Jury had to decide? If he's prepared to say sorry for that, then I'll apologize for pointing out his undoubted prejudice.'

Oliphant, who had slowly been coming to the boil, exploded at this point. 'Am I expected to sit here and endure a repetition of the quite intolerable . . .'

'No, no, my Lord!' Ballard fluttered to his feet. 'Of course not. Please, Mr Rumpole. If it please your Lordship, may I take instructions?' And when Graves said, 'I think you'd better', my defender turned to me with, 'You said you'd apologize.'

'I'm prepared to *swap* apologies,' I whispered back.

'I heard that, Mr Ballard.' Graves was triumphant. 'As I think your client knows perfectly well, my hearing is exceptionally keen. I wonder what Mr Rumpole's excuse is for his extraordinary behaviour today. He isn't suffering from toothache now, is he?'

'My Lord, I will take further instructions.' This time he whispered, 'Rumpole! Hadn't you better have toothache?'

'No, I had it out.'

'I'm afraid, my Lord' – Ballard turned to Graves, disappointed – 'the answer is no. He had it out during the trial.'

'So, on this occasion, Mr Ballard, you can't even plead toothache as a defence?'

'I'm afraid not, my Lord.'

'Had it out ... during the trial.' Graves was making a careful note, then he screwed the top back on his pen with the greatest care and said, 'We shall continue with this unhappy case tomorrow morning.'

'My Lord' – I rose to my feet again – 'may I make an application?'

'What is it, Mr Rumpole?' Graves asked warily, as well he might.

'I'm getting tired of Mr Ballard's attempts to get me to apologize, unilaterally. Would you ask *him* not to speak to his client over the adjournment?'

Graves had made a note of the historic fact that I had had my tooth out during the trial, and Liz had noted it down also. As she wrote she started to speculate, as I had taught her to do in the distant days when she was my pupil. As soon as the tribunal packed up business for the day she went back to Chambers and persuaded Claude Erskine-Brown to take her down to the Old Bailey and show her the *locus in quo*, the scene where the ghastly crime of chattering to a client had been committed.

Bewildered, but no doubt filled with guilt at his treacherous behaviour to a fellow hack, Claude led her to the archway through which he had seen the tedious Tong listening to Rumpole's harangue.

'And where did you see Rumpole?'

'Well, he came out through the arch after he'd finished talking to his client.'

'But *while* he was speaking to his client.'

'Well, actually,' Claude had to admit, 'I didn't see him then, at all. I mean, I suppose he was hidden from my view, Liz.'

'I suppose he was.' At which she strode purposefully through the arch and saw what, perhaps, she had expected to find, a row of telephones on the wall, in a position which would also have been invisible to the earwigging Claude. They were half covered, it's true, with plastic hoods, but a man who didn't wish to crouch under these contrivances might

235

stand freely with the connection pulled out to its full extent and speak to whoever he had chosen to abuse.

'So Rumpole might have been standing *here* when you were listening?' Liz had taken up her position by one of the phones.

'I suppose so.'

'And you heard him say words like, "Just get on with it. I've got enough trouble without you causing me all this agony. Get it out!"?'

'I told the tribunal that, don't you remember?' The true meaning of the words hadn't yet sunk into that vague repository of Wagnerian snatches and romantic longings, the Erskine-Brown mind. Liz, however, saw the truth in all its simplicity as she lifted a telephone, brushed it with her credit card in a way I could never manage, and was, in an instant, speaking to She Who Must Be Obeyed. Miss Probert had two simple requests: could Hilda come down to the Temple tomorrow and what, please, was the name of Horace's dentist?

When the tribunal met next morning, my not so learned counsel announced that my case was to be placed in more competent hands. 'My learned junior Miss Probert,' Sam Ballard said, 'will call our next witness, but first she wishes to recall Mr Erskine-Brown.'

No one objected to this and Claude returned to the witness's chair to explain the position of the archway and the telephones, and the fact that he hadn't, indeed, seen me speaking to Tong. Montague Varian had no questions and my judges were left wondering what significance, if any, to attach to this new evidence. I was sure that it would make no difference to the result, but then Liz Probert uttered the dread words, 'I will now call Mr Lionel Leering.'

I had been at a crossroads; one way led on through a countryside too well known to me. I could journey on for ever round the courts, arguing cases, winning some, losing more and more perhaps in my few remaining years. The other road was the way of escape, and once Mr Leering gave his evidence that, I know, would be closed to me. 'Don't do it,' I whispered my instructions to Miss Probert. 'I'm not fighting this case.'

'Oh, Rumpole!' She turned and leant down to my level, her face shining with enthusiasm. 'I'm going to win! It's what you taught me to do. Don't spoil it for me now.'

I thought then of all the bloody-minded clients who had wrecked the cases in which I was about to chalk up a victory. It was her big moment and who was I to snatch it from her? I was tired, too tired to win, but also too tired to lose, so I gave her her head. 'Go on, then,' I told her, 'if you *have* to.'

With her nostrils dilated and the light of battle in her eyes, Mizz Liz Probert turned on her dental witness and proceeded to demolish the prosecution case.

'Do you carry on your practice in Harley Street, in London?'

'That is so. And may I say, I have a most important bridge to insert this morning. The patient is very much in the public eye.'

'Then I'll try and make this as painless as possible,' Liz assured him. 'Did you treat Mr Rumpole on the morning of May the 16th?'

'I did. He came early because he told me he was in the middle of a case at the Old Bailey. I think he was defending in a manslaughter. I gave him a temporary stopping, which I thought would keep him going.'

'Did it?'

'Apparently not. He rang me around lunchtime. He told me that his tooth was causing him pain and he was extremely angry. He raised his voice at me.'

'Can you remember what he said?'

'So far as I can recall he said something like, "I've got enough trouble with the Judge without you causing me all this agony. Get it out!" and, "Put us out of our misery!"'

'What do you think he meant?'

'He wanted his tooth extracted.'

'Did you do it for him?'

'Yes, I stayed on late especially. I saw him at seven-thirty that evening. He was more cheerful then, but a little unsteady on his feet. I believe he'd been drinking brandy to give himself Dutch courage.'

'I think that may well have been so,' Liz agreed.

Now the members of the tribunal were whispering together. Then the whispering stopped and Mr Justice Gravestone turned an ancient and fish-like eye on my prosecutor. 'If this evidence is correct, Mr Varian, and we remember the admission made by Mr Claude Erskine-Brown and the position of the telephones, and the fact that he never saw Mr Rumpole, then this allegation about speaking to his client falls to the ground, does it not?'

'I must concede that, my Lord.'

'Then all that remains is the offensive remarks to Mr Justice Oliphant.'

'Yes, my Lord.'

'Yes, well, I'm much obliged.' The fishy beam was turned on to the Defence. 'This case now turns solely on whether your client is prepared to make a proper, unilateral apology to my brother Oliphant.'

'Indeed, my Lord.'

'Then we'll consider that matter, after a short adjournment.'

So we all did a good deal of bowing to each other and as I came out of the Parliament Room, who should I see but She Who Must Be Obeyed, who, for a reason then unknown to me, made a most surprising U-turn. 'Rumpole,' she said, 'I've been thinking things over and I think Oliphant treated you abominably. My view of the matter is that you shouldn't apologize at all!'

'Is that your view, Hilda?'

'Of course it is. I'm sure nothing will make you stop work, unless you're disbarred, and think how wonderful that will be for our marriage.'

'What *do* you mean?' But I'd already guessed, with a sort of dread, what she was driving at.

'If you can't consort with all those criminals, I'll have you at home all day! There's so many little jobs for you to do. Re-paper the kitchen, get the parquet in the hallway polished. You'd be able to help me with the shopping every day. And we'd have my friends round to tea; Dodo Mackintosh complains she sees nothing of you.' There was considerably more in this vein, but Hilda had already said enough to make up my mind. When my judges were back, refreshed with coffee, biscuits and, in certain cases, a quick drag on a Silk Cut, Sam Ballard announced that I wished to make a statement, the dye was cast and I tottered to my feet and spoke to the following effect. 'If your Lordship, and the members of the Tribunal, please. I have, I hope, some knowledge of the human race in general and the judicial race in particular. I do realize that some of those elevated to the Bench are more vulnerable, more easily offended than others. Over my years at the Old Bailey, before your Lordship and his brother judges, I have had to grow a skin like a rhinoceros. Mr Justice Oliphant, I acknowledge, is a more retiring, shy and sensitive plant, and if anything I have said may have wounded him, I do most humbly, most sincerely apologize.' At this I bowed and whispered to Mizz Liz Probert, 'Will that do?'

What went on behind closed doors between my judges I can't say. Were some of them, was even the sea-green incorruptible Graves, a little tired of Ollie's down-to-earth North Country common sense; had they been sufficiently bored by him over port and walnuts to wish to deflate, just a little, that great self-satisfied balloon? Or did they stop short of depriving the Old Bailey monument of its few moments of worthwhile drama? Would they really have wanted to take all the fun out of the criminal law? I don't know the answer to these questions but in one rather athletic bound Rumpole was free, still to be audible in the Ludgate Circus *palais de justice*.

The next events of importance occurred at an ambitious Chambers party held as a delayed celebration of the fact that Mrs Phillida Erskine-Brown, our Portia, was now elegantly perched on the High Court Bench and her husband, Claude, had received the lesser honour of being swathed in silk. This beano took place in Ballard's room and all the characters in Equity Court were there, together with their partners, as Mizz Liz would call them, and I had taken the opportunity of issuing a few further invitations on my own account.

One of the most dramatic events on this occasion was an encounter, by a table loaded with bottles and various delicacies, between Dot and a pleasant-looking woman in her forties who, between rapid inroads into a plate of tuna-fish sandwiches, said that she was Henry's wife, Eileen, and wasn't Dot the new typist, because 'Henry's been telling me all about you'?

'I don't know why he does that. He has no call, really.' Dot was confused and embarrassed. 'Look, I'm sorry about what he told you.'

'Oh, don't be,' Eileen reassured her. 'It's a great relief to me. I was on this horrible slimming diet because I thought that's how Henry liked me, but now he says you want to make your life together. So, could you just whirl those cocktail sausages in my direction?'

'We're not going to make a life together and I don't know where he got the idea from at all. I mean, I like Henry. I think he's very sweet and serious, but in a boyfriend, I'd prefer something more muscular. Know what I mean?'

'You're not going to take him on?' Henry's wife sounded disappointed.

'I couldn't entertain the idea, with all due respect to your husband.'

'He'll have to stay where he is then.' Eileen lifted another small sausage on its toothpick. 'But I'm not going back on that horrible cottage cheese. Not for him, not for anyone.'

By now the party was starting to fill up and among the first to come was old Gravestone, to whom, I thought, I owed a very small debt of gratitude. I heard him tell Ballard how surprised he was that I'd invited him and he congratulated my so-called defender (and not my wife, who deserved all the credit) on having got me to apologize. Ballard lied outrageously and said, 'As Head of these Chambers, of course, I do have a little influence on Rumpole.'

Shortly after this, another of my invitees came puffing up the stairs and Ballard, apparently in a state of shock, stammered, 'Judge! You're here!' to Mr Justice Oliphant.

'Of course I'm here,' Ollie rebuked him. 'Use your common

sense. Made Rumpole squirm, having to apologize, did it? Good, very good. That was all I needed.' Later Mr Justice Featherstone arrived with Marigold and among all these judicial stars Eileen, the ex-Mayor, had the briefest of heart to hearts with her husband. 'She doesn't want you, Henry,' she told him.

'Please!' Our clerk looked nervously round for earwiggers. 'How on earth can you say that?'

'Oh, she told me. No doubt about it. She goes for something more muscular, and I know exactly what she means.'

Oblivious of this domestic drama, the party surged on around them. Ballard told Mr Justice Featherstone that it had been a most worrying case and Guthrie said things might be even more worrying now that I'd won, and Claude asked me why I hadn't told him that I was talking to my dentist.

'Your suggestion was beneath contempt, Erskine-Brown. Besides which I rather fancied being disbarred at the time.'

'Rumpole!' The man was shocked. 'Why ever should you want that?'

'"For the sword outwears its sheath,"' I explained, '"And the soul wears out the breast, And the heart must pause to breathe." – But not yet, Claude. Not quite yet.'

At last Henry managed to corner Dot, while Claude set off in a bee-line for the personable Eileen. The first thing Henry did was to apologize. 'I never wanted her to come, Dot, but she insisted. It must have been terribly embarrassing for you.'

'She's ever so nice, isn't she? You're a very lucky bloke, Henry.'

'Having you, you mean?' He still nursed a flicker of hope.

'No' – she blew out the flame – 'having a wife who's prepared to eat cottage cheese for you.'

Marigold said to Hilda, 'I hear Rumpole's not sitting as a judge. In fact I heard he was nearly made to sit at home permanently.' Marguerite Ballard, ex-Matron down at the Old Bailey, told Mr Justice Oliphant that 'his naughty tummy was rather running away with him'. I told Liz that she had

been utterly ruthless in pursuit of victory and she asked if I
had forgiven her for saving my legal life.

'I think so. But who fed Hilda that line about having me at
home all day?'

'What are you talking about, Rumpole?' She Who Must
joined us.

'Oh, I was just saying to Liz, of course it'd be very nice if
we could spend all day together, Hilda. I mean, *that* wasn't
what led me to apologize.'

'That's the trouble with barristers.' She gave me one of her
piercing looks. 'You can't believe a word they say.'

Before I could think of any convincing defence to Hilda's
indictment, the last of my personally invited guests arrived.
This was Fred Timson, wearing a dark suit with a striped tie
and looking more than ever like a senior member of the old
Serious Crimes Squad. I found him a drink, put it into his
hand and told him how glad I was he could find time for us.

'What a do, eh?' He looked round appreciatively. 'Judges
and sparkling wine! Here's to your very good health, Mr
Rumpole.'

'No, Fred,' I told him, 'I'm going to drink to yours.' Whereupon I banged a glass against the table, called for silence and
proposed a toast. 'Listen, everybody. I want to introduce you
to Fred Timson, head of a noted family of South London
villains, minor thieves and receivers of stolen property. No
violence in his record. That right, Fred?'

'Quite right, Mr Rumpole.' Fred confirmed the absence of
violence and then I made public what had long been my
secret thoughts on the relationship between the Timsons and
the law. 'This should appeal to you, my lords, ladies and
gentlemen. Fred lives his life on strict monetarist principles.
He doesn't believe in the closed shop; he thinks that shops
should be open all night, preferably by jemmy. He believes
firmly in the marketplace, because that's where you can
dispose of articles that dropped off the back of a lorry. But
without Fred and his like, we should all be out of work. There
would be no judges, none of Her Majesty's Counsel, learned
in the law, no coppers and no humble Old Bailey hacks. So

charge your glasses, fill us up, Henry, and I would ask you to drink to Fred Timson and the criminals of England!'

I raised my glass but the faces around me registered varying degrees of disapproval and concern. Ballard bleated, 'Rumpole!', Hilda gave out a censorious, 'Really, Rumpole!', Featherstone J. said, 'He's off again,' and Mr Justice Oliphant decided that if this wasn't unprofessional conduct he didn't know what was. Only Liz, flushed with her success in Court and a few quick glasses of the *mèthode champenoise*, raised a fist and called out, 'Up the workers!'

'Oh, really!' Graves turned wearily to our Head of Chambers. 'Will Rumpole never learn?'

'I'm afraid never,' Ballard told him.

I was back at work again and life would continue much as ever at 3 Equity Court.

Discover more about our forthcoming books through Penguin's FREE newspaper...

It's packed with:

- exciting features
- author interviews
- previews & reviews
- books from your favourite films & TV series
- exclusive competitions & much, much more...

READ MORE IN PENGUIN

In every corner of the world, on every subject under the sun, Penguin represents quality and variety – the very best in publishing today.

For complete information about books available from Penguin – including Puffins, Penguin Classics and Arkana – and how to order them, write to us at the appropriate address below. Please note that for copyright reasons the selection of books varies from country to country.

In the United Kingdom: Please write to *Dept. JC, Penguin Books Ltd, FREEPOST, West Drayton, Middlesex UB7 0BR*

If you have any difficulty in obtaining a title, please send your order with the correct money, plus ten per cent for postage and packaging, to *PO Box No. 11, West Drayton, Middlesex UB7 0BR*

In the United States: Please write to *Penguin USA Inc., 375 Hudson Street, New York, NY 10014*

In Canada: Please write to *Penguin Books Canada Ltd, 10 Alcorn Avenue, Suite 300, Toronto, Ontario M4V 3B2*

In Australia: Please write to *Penguin Books Australia Ltd, 487 Maroondah Highway, Ringwood, Victoria 3134*

In New Zealand: Please write to *Penguin Books (NZ) Ltd, 182–190 Wairau Road, Private Bag, Takapuna, Auckland 9*

In India: Please write to *Penguin Books India Pvt Ltd, 706 Eros Apartments, 56 Nehru Place, New Delhi 110 019*

In the Netherlands: Please write to *Penguin Books Netherlands B.V., Keizersgracht 231 NL–1016 DV Amsterdam*

In Germany: Please write to *Penguin Books Deutschland GmbH, Friedrichstrasse 10–12, W–6000 Frankfurt/Main 1*

In Spain: Please write to *Penguin Books S. A., C. San Bernardo 117–6° E–28015 Madrid*

In Italy: Please write to *Penguin Italia s.r.l., Via Felice Casati 20, I–20124 Milano*

In France: Please write to *Penguin France S. A., 17 rue Lejeune, F–31000 Toulouse*

In Japan: Please write to *Penguin Books Japan, Ishikiribashi Building, 2–5–4, Suido, Tokyo 112*

In Greece: Please write to *Penguin Hellas Ltd, Dimocritou 3, GR–106 71 Athens*

In South Africa: Please write to *Longman Penguin Southern Africa (Pty) Ltd, Private Bag X08, Bertsham 2013*

BY THE SAME AUTHOR

The Rumpole Books

'One of the great comic creations of modern times' – Christopher Matthew in the *Evening Standard*

Rumpole of the Bailey	**Rumpole's Last Case**
The Trials of Rumpole	**Rumpole and the Age of Miracles**
Rumpole's Return	**Rumpole à la Carte**
Rumpole for the Defence	**The First Rumpole Omnibus**
Rumpole and the Golden Thread	**The Second Rumpole**
The Best of Rumpole	

Plays

A Voyage Round My Father and Other Plays

Interviews

In Character
Character Parts

Autobiography

Clinging to the Wreckage

Fiction

Paradise Postponed
'Hilarious and thoroughly recommended' – *Daily Telegraph*

Titmuss Regained
'Beautifully written, witty and often very, very funny' — *Spectator*

The Narrowing Stream
'Energy, wit and sheer professionalism – *Guardian*

Charade
'Wonderful comedy ... an almost Firbankian melancholy ... John Mortimer's hero is helplessly English' – *Punch*

and

Like Men Betrayed	**Dunster**
Summer's Lease	